Pra...

'Magical, fun and romantic, this feel-good read is guaran-
teed to lift your mood.' *Closer*

'This book is something special; it's real, funny and magical,
taking you on a whirlwind adventure through India . . . It
would make the perfect holiday read at any time of the
year.' *Onemorepage.co.uk*

'The type of fun fiction we can't resist' *Stylist*

'A new Alexandra Potter book is always something to celebrate. She's one of the only chick lit authors who puts a
magical spin on her novels, and she's always successful at
it . . . a great read' *Chicklitreviewsandnews.com*

'Funny, light and a great summer read – whether you're
lying on a sunlounger or sitting on the train to work. A fab
modern-day love story with a touch of magic.' *Fabulous*

'Yet again Alexandra Potter has written an upbeat, quirky
piece of chick lit that can't help but bring a smile to your
face' *Novelicious.com*

'Always perceptive, often funny, never dull' *Heat*

'Feel-good fiction full of unexpected twists and turns' *OK!*

'A touching, funny love story' *Company*

'Fantastically funny' *Elle*

About the author

Alexandra Potter is an award-winning author who previously worked as a features writer and sub-editor for women's glossies in both the UK and Australia. In 2007 she won the prize for Best New Fiction at the Jane Austen Regency World Awards for her bestselling novel, *Me and Mr Darcy*. Her novels have been translated into seventeen languages and *You're the One That I Don't Want* is being adapted into a film. She now lives between London and Los Angeles and writes full-time.

You can find out more at www.alexandrapotter.com, on Facebook at www.facebook.com/Alexandra.Potter.Author or follow her on Twitter @AlexPotterBooks.

Also by Alexandra Potter

The Love Detective
Don't You Forget About Me
You're the One That I Don't Want
Who's That Girl?
Me and Mr Darcy
Be Careful What You Wish For
Do You Come Here Often?
Calling Romeo
What's New, Pussycat?
Going La La

Alexandra Potter

Love From Paris

HODDER

First published in Great Britain in 2015 by Hodder & Stoughton
An Hachette UK company

1

Copyright © Alexandra Potter 2015

A CIP catalogue record for this title is available from the British Library

Paperback ISBN 978 1 444 71217 9
Ebook ISBN 978 1 444 71218 6

Typeset in Plantin Light by Hewer Text UK Ltd, Edinburgh

Printed and bound by Clays Ltd, St Ives plc

Hodder & Stoughton policy is to use papers that are natural, renewable
and recyclable products and made from wood grown in sustainable
forests. The logging and manufacturing processes are expected to
conform to the environmental regulations of the country of origin.

Hodder & Stoughton Ltd
Carmelite House
50 Victoria Embankment
London EC4Y 0DZ

www.hodder.co.uk

Dedicated to AC

For always being my glass half-full

I

OK, calm down, it's got to be here somewhere.

Rushing around my bedroom, I grab hold of my make-up bag and start rifling through it. Which of course is completely futile. I mean, is it just me, or does *anyone* ever put a lip gloss in their make-up bag? It's always stuffed in a coat pocket gathering fluff. Or lost in a random handbag. Or stuck down the back of the sofa, top off, smearing pink gloop everywhere . . .

Bollocks, where is it?

Having spewed the contents all over my dressing table, I sweep my eyes across my bedroom. It's a tip. There's stuff chucked everywhere. Normally I'm pretty tidy, but after my frantic trying-on earlier my wardrobe seems to have emptied itself all over my bed. My lovely duvet from the White Company is now hidden under a mountain of jumble. Discarded outfits are flung across the backs of chairs, hanging on doorknobs and lassoed round the ends of my curtain pole.

What the—? Glancing upwards I spy a skirt dangling mid-air and give the hem a good tug. But it's stuck fast. *Damn.* I yank harder. The curtain pole creaks ominously. Oh sod it. Just leave it. I don't have time to tidy up. I've got to finish getting ready.

I hastily pick my way over the carpet of coat hangers (have you ever *stood* on a coat hanger with bare feet? Forget standing on a plug, this is about a million times worse) and dive into the bathroom. OK, so I know a lost lip gloss doesn't seem like much of a reason to panic. Even if it is one of those super-plumping ones that are supposed to make your lips all bee-stung and Mick Jagger-esque.

Seriously, it's hardly going to make the national headlines, now is it? In the grand scheme of things it's not exactly up there with global recession, political unrest or natural disasters.

MISSING LIP GLOSS FEARED THROWN AWAY:
COUNTRY ON LOCKDOWN AS VERY BERRY
LUSCIOUS LIPS DISAPPEARS WITHOUT TRACE.
FRANTIC OWNER RUBY MILLER SAYS SHE CAN'T
REMEMBER WHERE SHE SAW IT LAST.

But today's different. Today it's super important.

Opening and closing bathroom cabinets like a woman possessed, I rummage through endless jars of creams and potions. There's everything in here. I'm a total Boots junkie. I can never resist the lure of a new product or their three-for-two offers and my cupboards are bulging. I spy a tub of Vaseline and hesitate – usually I'd just slick a bit of that on and be done with it – but that's not going to cut it today. *Today I need that bloody lip gloss!*

Snapping closed a cupboard, I catch sight of my reflection in the mirrored door. Summer is almost upon us and I'm wearing the new blouse that I just splurged on last week from one of those little boutiquey shops where you have to surreptitiously check the price tag on everything under the watchful eye of a snooty assistant.

It was a first for me. I don't normally go in those kind of shops as I find them a bit, well, intimidating would be one word, *terrifying* would be another. As my little sister Amy will tell you, I don't *do* fashion. Or, to put it another way, fashion doesn't do me. Not that I haven't tried. I've bought magazines, read about what's 'on trend', attempted to accessorise (I end up looking like a badly decorated Christmas tree), but it's always a disaster. Trust me, it's safer for everyone if I stick to my faithful wardrobe of leggings and T-shirts.

But like I said, today's different. I fiddle with my collar. It's made of this lovely silk chiffon-y material and has this really pretty neckline, but I've undone a few of the mother-of-pearl buttons to sex it up a bit. Plus, I've also added my push-up bra for a bit of extra oomph. It's sort of innocent meets guilty.

Well, that was the idea. In theory.

Feeling a flutter of nerves, I do a final make-up check. I've gone for the 'natural look'. Which, of course, is completely *un*natural. Because, of course, I got this flawless, rosy glow from sitting on my bum all day at my desk, drinking coffee and eating biscuits. *Obviously.*

And then there's the hair. I frown. It's like a soufflé that's gone all flat and deflated. Fluffing it up a bit more, I grab a can of hairspray and give my roots an extra squirt. I'm aiming for that sexy, tousled just-got-out-of-bed look they always talk about in magazines.

Which of course is total rubbish. Honestly, who are they kidding? Everyone knows a real bedhead is matted and frizzed with a fringe that sticks out at right angles, don't they?

Don't they?

I'm suddenly hit with a flicker of doubt.

Or is that just me?

Coughing as I swallow a mouthful of hairspray, I stop squirting and glance at my watch. Oh crap, look! It's nearly time!

I charge into the living room, tripping over Heathcliff, my sausage dog, who's hovering around me, like my dad used to when I was expecting a date. He gives a little disgruntled yelp.

'Oops, hey buddy, what are you doing?' Scooping him up, I give him a little tickle under his chin.

I know exactly what he's doing. He's being all protective and jealous. Not much has changed since I was a teenager. Only now it's not my dad standing guard, it's my dog.

'Go on, play outside.' I motion to the garden. The French windows are flung open wide. It's a beautiful day at the beginning of June. One of those late spring days in London that you can't ever imagine when you're stuck fast in the never-ending gloom of winter, bitching and moaning about why anyone in their right mind would choose to live in this godforsaken hellhole.

But when a warm sunny day does finally appear, all corn-flower blue skies, sun-dappled parks and bustling pavement cafés, you immediately fall madly in love with the city all over again and lose all memory of ever feeling any other way.

'Go on,' I shoo, and as Heathcliff skulks off outside, I quickly sit down at my desk and open my laptop.

Now, before anyone gets the wrong idea, this is not how I usually look when I'm at my desk. Being a writer and working from home it's normally a case of no make-up, hair in a scrunchie, tatty old towelling dressing gown and my sheep-skin slippers. I call it my scare-the-postman look. Or my care-in-the-community look.

I cannot, by any stretch of the imagination, call it my sexy, flirty, fabulous girlfriend look.

Nerves jangle in the pit of my stomach. Which is ridiculous. It's not like this is a first date or anything, it's just—

Oh my god, it's there! My lip gloss! In my pen-holder! Grabbing it, I start slicking it on at exactly the same time as Skype starts ringing.

Argh, quick, *quick*!

A face flashes up on the screen. Dark hair, lots of stubble and the most gorgeous hazel eyes you've ever seen.

Jack.

'Hey babe,' he smiles, flashing his perfect white American grin.

My heart skips a beat. It's been three months since we first got together, yet whenever he smiles at me like that it feels like the first time.

'You look cute.'

I feel a flash of pleasure.

'Do I?' I say, trying to sound all surprised, like I haven't just been rushing around my flat like a mad thing for the last hour.

'Did you do something with your hair?'

'My hair?' I raise a hand to my rock-solid fringe and pat it gingerly. 'Oh, no, it was just like this when I woke up this morning . . .' I say nonchalantly, crossing my fingers under my desk. 'I've just been sitting here in my scruffs all day writing, I haven't even looked in the mirror . . .'

I know, I'm a terrible, *terrible* liar, but do you blame me? It's one thing letting your boyfriend see you in the 'Before' stage when you've been together for ages and see each other every day, but it's quite another when you're in a long-distance relationship and it's all still quite new.

It feels like both yesterday and for ever since we first kissed on that snowy pavement in London. Sometimes when I think about it I almost have to pinch myself. I still can't quite believe how we managed to find each other, and not just once but twice. Meeting each other on the train in India was a chance in a million, but bumping into each other again in London was more than just a lucky chance. It was like Fate, or destiny, *or magic*.

But then love is a kind of magic, isn't it?

For a moment my memory flicks back. It's hard to imagine that for a while there I lost my belief in love. My heart had been so badly bruised I no longer thought it existed. That it was just the stuff of fantasy and fiction. But India and Jack proved me wrong. Together they had me falling in love with love all over again.

And once we did find each other, Jack and I were determined not to lose each other again. After that kiss he spent the night at my flat and didn't leave until two weeks later. Fortunately he could do a lot of work remotely via Skype and email, but still, there came a time when he had to fly back to the States. I went with him to the airport, trying not to cry buckets as I waved him off in Departures.

'Seriously, you look gorgeous,' he says approvingly now, and I snap back to attention. 'Is that a new dress?'

My modesty tries to stifle my smile, but it's impossible. 'No, just a blouse,' I grin.

'Just a blouse?' He raises his eyebrows.

'Hey!' I discipline, flirtily.

'C'mon, what else you got on there, Miller?' he demands with mock seriousness.

'Jack!' I admonish him, but secretly I feel a thrill. Well, let's be honest, ten weeks is a very long time.

'Let's have a look.'

Suddenly, in the middle of flirting, I feel a clunk of horror.

'Don't tell me you've gone all shy.' His eyes flash wickedly.

No, more like mortified. You see the thing is I didn't bother with the bottom half. I didn't think it would be on camera. A bit like newsreaders who you see all smartly dressed in a suit, but you can imagine that if the cameraman makes a faux pas and you get a flash underneath the desk, it will be revealed on national TV that they're sitting there in their underpants.

'Um yes . . . just a little,' I reply, trying to continue the flirtation, but now my voice comes out a bit strangled.

'I don't believe you,' he teases.

'No, really,' I protest.

In my case it's worse than underpants. I'm in my pyjama bottoms. Which sounds innocent enough. Cute, almost. Except they're not just any old pyjama bottoms.

They're novelty pyjama bottoms.

'I think I need to see,' he says firmly, arching one eyebrow.

Oh fuck. Mum bought them for me one Christmas and they're made of bright red fleece and covered in lots of Rudolph the Red-nosed Reindeers and Christmas puddings. Which is bad enough by itself, considering it's six months after Christmas, but teamed with a sexy chiffon blouse and a pair of giant furry sheepskin slippers, they make me look like a crazy person.

'Er . . . you do?'

Oh god. How embarrassing. How am I going to get out of this?

'Totally.' He nods.

'Well . . . um . . . you'll have to wait,' I stall.

Jack pulls a face. 'Holy moly, c'mon, don't tease.'

'Nope.' I shake my head firmly, as I'm suddenly hit by an idea. Of course! Why didn't I think of this before? I'll pretend I'm being all treat 'em mean, keep 'em keen.

'Are you playing hard to get?'

'Well, they do say the best things in life are worth waiting for,' I reply flirtily.

God, the irony. If he could see my fleecy pyjama bottoms and slippers. There is no way anyone could describe that combo as one of 'the best things in life'.

'You can say that again.' He smiles.

My heart does that thing again. And to think my drama teacher, Miss Shrimpton, wrote on my school report, 'Ruby will never make the stage. She is unable to play any role convincingly.'

'I've really missed you, you know.' Jack's face falls serious and as his eyes meet mine, he fixes me with his gaze.

'Me too,' I say quietly. I feel that familiar tug in the bottom of my stomach. It's true what they say. Love *bloody* hurts. Ever since Jack disappeared behind that sliding glass door at Security, I've been missing him like crazy, but until now it's been impossible to meet up because of his work commitments. One thing I've learned about Jack is that he's completely passionate about his work. In fact, to be honest, he's a bit of a workaholic. Still, finally we're going to get to be together again.

'Not long now, less than forty-eight hours.'

'Forty-three,' I correct him quickly, then blush.

'Are you counting?' he teases.

'No, sorry, when is it you're arriving again?' I frown, as if trying to remember. 'Is it next week? Or the week after?'

He laughs loudly. 'The day after tomorrow and I'm counting too. You think I'd miss your birthday?'

'Good, glad to hear it.' I grin.

'And miss a chance to stay in that fancy hotel?' he goes on. 'Oi!'

He winks and I start laughing. It's my birthday next weekend and we've arranged to go away and stay in one of those swanky country hotels. You know, the ones you always seem to read about in magazines when you're single and feel utterly depressed at the photos of couples snuggling up in front of a cosy log fire or enjoying the luxury spa.

But now, I *am* part of a couple! I have a gorgeous American boyfriend and he's flying over soon to whisk me away! And we're going to lounge around in waffle bathrobes and raid the minibar and sleep in a four-poster bed and—

'Hey, you know I'm only joking,' he says, and I snap back from my fantasies. 'We're gonna have so much fun celebrating your birthday.'

'I know.' I nod, feeling a prickle of excitement. God, it's been so long since . . . Well, put it this way, Skype sex only gets you so far.

At the memory I feel a flush of embarrassment. Yes we have tried it. And no, I wasn't very good at it. It's not that I'm a prude. On the contrary I was the one who jumped on Jack the first night we spent together (not that he put up much of a fight, I might add). But for someone who doesn't even like having their picture taken, seeing myself on screen while I'm—

Well, let's just say I was camera-shy and leave it at that.

We're interrupted by the sound of a phone ringing in the background. Jack picks up his iPhone and glances at the screen. He frowns. 'Sorry babe, I need to get this, it's work.'

'But it's Sunday . . . '

He pulls an apologetic face. Disappointment clunks. We've only spoken for a few minutes.

'OK, never mind.' I nod. 'I'll speak to you later.'

'In person,' he grins and gives me a look that sends a shiver down my spine. 'Oh, and Ruby—'

'Yes?'

'You sure I can't get one little look at that gorgeous ass of yours before I go? Just to remind me what I'm missing?'

Oh crap! I feel a beat of panic. 'Um – no – er . . . the best things in life are worth waiting for, remember?' I gabble, forcing a flirty smile.

'You're a hard woman, Ruby Miller.' He shakes his head, grinning, and with that, the window with his face disappears.

As the screen goes blank I collapse with relief back into my chair. *Phew*, that was a close thing! Nobody ever told me this long-distance relationship stuff could be so stressful.

Still, it's not going to be long-distance for much longer, is it? I remind myself. Two more sleeps and Jack will be here. After all this time, waiting and missing each other, we're going to get up close and personal.

I feel a rush of excitement, swiftly followed by a clutch of anxiety. In the last three months the only male to see me naked has been Heathcliff.

But there's no need to worry, I tell myself firmly. Jack loves me for who I am. He won't care about the bit of cellulite on the backs of my legs. Or the little roll above my jeans that refuses to budge. If you love someone you don't care about that stuff. Love is blind, right? He won't even notice if I haven't exfoliated, or waxed my bikini line, or bleached that little moustache I sometimes get on my top lip—

I catch myself. Oh my god, what am I thinking? Love isn't *that* blind!

And that's not all. I sweep my eyes around my flat, suddenly seeing it afresh. Forget potential love nest. There's not a vase of flowers or a scented candle in sight. Just dozens of empty coffee cups and mounds of discarded clothes. There's not going to be a whole lot of loving going on in here if we can't find the bed. Or even the floor!

Anxiously I glance at the clock on the wall. I've got exactly forty-two hours and fifty-five minutes to get ready for love.

I jump up from my chair.

And the countdown starts now.

LOVE LIST

OK, so I've made a sort of checklist.

1. Scented candles ✓

Though to be honest, I have no idea what the big deal is about scented candles. OK, they're nice and smelly and all that, but have you *seen* the price of them? Plus why do magazines always suggest scented candles to 'relax and get you in the mood'?

Personally they do the opposite as I'm always terrified I'll forget to blow them out and burn the house down. In fact I was having sex with a boyfriend once and I had to make him stop so I could check on the ones in the living room.

The only mood was the right one he got in afterwards.

But then that's probably my mum's fault. Like all good parents, she taught me as a child to stay away from danger – only the problem is my mum sees danger everywhere. You see a lovely vanilla-scented candle; Mum sees a house fire. You see a gorgeous swimming pool to dive into on holiday; Mum sees a broken neck. And it's the same with:

2. Champagne ✓

I have a confession that's going to make me sound weird. Whereas a normal person sees a bottle of lovely, cold fizzy stuff, all I see is a cork that's going to blind me. There's going to be Jack tearing off the tinfoil all seductively, and there's going to be me shrieking and diving for cover round the back of the sofa.

Thankfully there's nothing scary about:

3. Massage oil ✓

For his'n'hers massages. After all, who doesn't love a massage? Though the last time we gave each other massages, Jack went first and got to enjoy a lovely hour-long one. When it came to my turn it lasted less than five minutes. This time I'll have to explain that a massage is like Christmas: it's all in the giving.

4. Chocolate ✓

I Googled 'Top Ten Aphrodisiac Foods' and it turns out pure chocolate is the king of aphrodisiacs. Apparently it's packed with PEA, 'the love chemical' that peaks during orgasm. Though, quite frankly who needs an excuse to buy chocolate?

5. ~~Oysters~~

Actually, scrap that. I was going to buy half a dozen as they're supposed to increase the libido. But I've never had them before and what if I'm allergic and go into anaphylactic shock? (Thanks Mum.)

6. Asparagus ✓

Much safer. Though considering that it makes your wee smell funny, I'm not sure how it can be much of an aphrodisiac.

Unlike:

7. Flowers ?

Everyone loves flowers, right? Unless . . . what if he suffers from hayfever like my little sister Amy? On second thoughts, maybe I should get a house plant instead.

8. Music ?

This one's a bit trickier. Jack listens to all these cool and trendy bands I've never even heard of. When he saw the music on my iPod he fell about laughing. Which was a bit mean. What's so wrong with Abba and Taylor Swift? They're great to dance around my bedroom to when I'm getting ready.

Which of course is something I can *never ever* let him witness.

9. Floss ✓

He's American. Enough said.

10. Jam & peanut butter ✓

Ditto.

11. Game of Thrones DVD ✓

Love is all about sharing each other's passions. Unfortunately for me, this is one of his.

12. Me **!!!**

Well, if I'm getting ready for love, I need more than scented candles and a few vases of flowers; I need to get *myself* ready for love. And, as any woman knows, it takes quite a bit of effort to go from normal pop-to-the-shops ready and hot-sex ready.

13. Exfoliate ✓

No one wants to cuddle a crocodile, do they? So, I bought one of those spa-type salt scrubs in a jar *and* a loofah and spent last night scrubbing in the shower. According to the instructions my skin was supposed to be left 'soft and glowing' but I think I overdid it a bit as I ended up lobster-red and rubbed raw.

Saying that, it probably wouldn't have been so bad if it hadn't been for:

14. Moisturise ✓

Normally I'm strictly a Nivea girl, but I read this magazine article about how olive oil is supposed to be the best moisturiser, so after exfoliating I smothered myself in extra virgin. Only I didn't look at the label and used one of those fancy flavoured oils instead. It was only when it started tingling in all the wrong places I realised it was 'chilli-infused'.

Please note: This is *not* what I had in mind by trying to get hot-sex ready.

15. Fake tan ✓

I hate fake tan. It smells funny. And it gets all over your sheets. But I have such pale freckly skin, I want to be all bronzed limbs and sun-kissed for when Jack sees me again.

I did not, repeat, *not* want to be pumpkin orange. Still, maybe it will fade by the time I meet him at the airport. *It has to.*

16. Bleach top lip ✓

I mean, *hello*? Do I really want to look like my old maths teacher? Next I'll start wearing American tan tights and having hairy legs. Which leads me to:

17. Wax everything ✓

What. Was. I. Thinking.

Normally I'm simply a short back and sides girl, but yesterday my friend Milly in LA convinced me to go Hollywood and take it all off. 'He's American, he'll love it!' she'd enthused in her email, which is why I made an appointment at Splitz.

In hindsight, I should have been worried by the name of the salon, but it wasn't until I met the Russian woman who was doing my bikini wax that I got scared. 'You Do Yoga!' she'd barked, grabbing my legs and yanking them into positions only an Olympic gymnast should have their legs yanked into, while pouring boiling oil on my nether regions.

Seriously, hundreds of years into the future, women will read about Hollywood bikini waxes like we read about medieval torture museums today, while gasping in disbelief that we could do this to ourselves. *And pay for it!*

Did I mention that this getting-ready-for-love business also costs an absolute fortune? Seriously, I'm not sure I can afford to have sex! Because then of course there's the:

18. Lingerie ✓

Usually I'm strictly an M&S girl: good value, comfy, machine washable. None of which can be said for my newly purchased scraps of frothy lace wrapped in blush pink tissue paper. But they're not meant for wearing, they're meant for taking off.

By Jack. Tomorrow.

Oh god, I can't believe he's going to arrive tomorrow! Finally. After all this missing and waiting and *effort*. It's all going to be so worth it.

19. Set alarm clock ✓

One more sleep and he's here!

2

Beep beep be—

The alarm doesn't even get to its third beep before my arm shoots out from underneath the duvet to turn it off. As it falls silent I jump – nay, *leap* – out of bed.

This, quite frankly, is akin to the kind of miracles you read about in newspapers. Actually, finding Jesus's face in a slice of toast, or someone rising from the dead, is nothing compared to me rising from underneath my duvet without hitting the snooze button about a million times.

But today you couldn't keep me in bed. Finally, after all this time, today's the day Jack arrives!

Pulling on my dressing gown, I dash excitedly into the living room. It's unrecognisable. Last night, I stayed up into the early hours getting everything prepared for Jack's arrival and my little flat has been completely transformed. Seriously, I feel as if I've stepped into one of those house makeover shows.

Hurrying into my gleaming kitchen I fill my espresso pot, pop it on the stove, then go to wake Heathcliff, who's still fast asleep in his basket. 'Morning buddy,' I coo, squatting down to stroke his little silky body, curled up tight like a croissant. Reluctantly he raises one sleepy eyelid and looks at me as if to say 'What on earth are you doing up at this ungodly hour?'

'Jack's coming!' I announce, as if in answer to his question. 'Isn't that exciting? You'll see Jack today!'

At the mention of Jack's name, he jumps out of his basket and starts wagging his tail excitedly. Normally Heathcliff can be very grumpy around men – it's the classic male competition complex – but for some reason he loves Jack. Like his owner, I think happily. Scooping him up, I bury my nose in his fur and we do a sort of celebratory dance around the kitchen. The coffee pot bubbles on the hob, mirroring the excitement bubbling inside me, and I twirl Heathcliff around, grinning from ear to ear as he barks delightedly.

I haven't been this excited for ages. I feel like a kid at Christmas. Last night I barely slept for thinking about today. I've been playing out the scene of meeting Jack at the airport over and over. Of coming back here to the flat with him. Talking, smiling, kissing . . . My stomach flips over as I imagine running my fingers through his messy shock of dark hair, inhaling his familiar scent, falling asleep with him curled up next to me, my face buried in that small dip in the middle of his chest.

Putting Heathcliff down before we both get dizzy, I feed him his breakfast then pour myself a coffee and, flinging open the French windows, gaze up into the expanse of freshly laundered blue sky. Just think, Jack's up there somewhere. Right at this moment, he's in a metal bird winging his way towards me. I try to imagine what he's doing. He's probably snoozing in his seat, or watching the end of a bad movie, or maybe he's looking out of the window, at the patchwork of English countryside below.

Actually no, he won't be over England yet, I realise, glancing at my watch. There's still a couple of hours until he lands. At least I think so, unless of course his flight's been delayed. Feeling a prickle of doubt, I pad over to my desk and open my laptop. I'd better check the status of his flight, just to make sure everything's OK.

I quickly type in the web address, but instead of the American Airlines page popping up, I get a grey screen and the message:

You are not connected to the Internet.

This page could not be displayed as you are currently offline.

I frown. How can that be? I check the Wi-Fi symbol at the top of my screen, only instead of the comforting four bars there's a scary little exclamation mark telling me there is no Wi-Fi.

Damn.

Dropping to my knees, I begin scrambling around under my desk among the jumble of cables and wires. What a day for my Internet to go on the blink. I find the modem and turn it off and on again. It's been acting up lately. Something to do with updating broadband speeds or something—

I wait expectantly for the flashing lights to turn green.

Nothing. *Bollocks.*

Of course, the simplest solution to all this would be to ring the airport and check it on my shiny new iPhone instead. After being nagged relentlessly by Jack I'd recently given up my ancient Nokia and entered the twenty-first century. So now I'm never without email or the Internet. There's just one tiny problem.

Grabbing the phone from my desk, I march into my tiny garden in my pyjamas. That's one of the downsides of living in a basement flat. Absolutely no phone reception whatsoever.

'You all right there, sweetheart?'

In the middle of futilely waving my phone around I glance over the garden fence to see my neighbour, Mrs Flannegan. She's standing at her back door with her walking stick, smoking a cigarette.

'Oh hi, I didn't see you there.' I smile.

'Doing your exercises?' She raises an eyebrow.

'Er no.' I blush slightly. 'I'm trying to get reception on my iPhone.' I waggle it as evidence to show I haven't completely lost the plot.

'Oooh, don't be showing me that newfangled nonsense.' She clicks her tongue and puffs heartily on her cigarette. 'I like the old-fashioned ones you plug into the wall. You can borrow it if you need to make a phone call.'

'No, thanks, I was just trying to get online—'

'You youngsters and the interweb,' she tuts, shaking her head. 'My granddaughter's forever telling me to get on it so I can "surf".' She pulls a face.

'You should.'

'What do I want to be surfing for at my age?' she protests indignantly. 'Never mind that, I can't even swim!'

I stifle a smile and decide against explaining.

'I shall tell her that as well, when I see her,' she continues, shaking her head.

'Is she still coming to visit?' Her granddaughter, Linda, lives in New Zealand after her mother, Mrs Flannegan's daughter, emigrated there with her husband some years ago. So she was thrilled when her Linda announced she was taking a gap year and her first stop was London.

'Yes, she's due to fly in today.' She smiles, her face flushing with excitement.

'Wow, that's great.' I beam. 'So's Jack.'

Mrs Flannegan clamps one of her bony hands to her chest, '*GI Jack*?' she swoons girlishly. That's her nickname for him. Apparently he reminded her of the Americans who came over during the war and used to give her chewing gum. 'You're lucky I'm not ten years younger, otherwise you'd have trouble on your hands!' She laughs her hacking smoker's laugh.

I laugh too. I don't doubt it. Mrs Flannegan's a widow and must be in her mid-eighties if she's a day, but she'd flirted around Jack as if she was a young girl again.

'You must be looking forward to seeing him, eh?'

'Yes, very much,' I nod, feeling a familiar ache as I think about the last ten weeks.

'When my Bert went away for National Service, I missed him like you wouldn't believe. I remember the day he came home like yesterday, I was so excited . . .' She trails off, suddenly going all misty-eyed. 'Sometimes I still look out of that window and I can see him, walking up the path, all smart in his uniform . . .'

'You must miss him,' I say softly.

'Aye, I do. But I'm not getting any younger, so I'll see him soon enough,' she laughs and I smile at her characteristic candour.

'What time's Jack arriving?' she goes on.

'His plane is due to land at one. I'm going to Heathrow to meet him.'

'That's the same time as my granddaughter,' she replies. 'If you see her, give a wave for me. Her name's Linda Gledhill, maybe you can hold up one of those signs.'

'You're not going to meet her?'

'I wanted to, but I can't really manage it.' Her smile slips and she gestures to her walking stick. 'I might feel twenty-one sometimes but my hips have got other ideas.'

I hesitate. I was planning on getting ready and jumping on the tube. I glance at my watch. And it's already getting late. I should really hurry.

And yet—

I look at Mrs Flannegan. I know how much she'd love to meet her granddaughter at the airport, how much she's missed her. It really wouldn't hurt, would it?

'Why don't you come with me?' I suggest, before I can change my mind.

For a moment she seems thrilled by the possibility, before seeming to remember herself and shaking her head. 'Don't be silly, you don't want an old thing like me slowing you down.'

'You're the one being silly,' I remonstrate. 'Go and get

ready, you can't have your granddaughter seeing you with your pinny on.'

'Well if you're sure—'

'Absolutely.' I nod. 'Now hurry up. We can't have Linda and Jack standing waiting for us at the airport.'

'Well if you put it like that . . .'

As Mrs Flannegan grinds out her cigarette under her tartan slipper, I go back inside and jump in the shower. I had all these big plans about taking a long bath, spending ages doing my hair and make-up . . . But now all that's flown out the window and I've only got time for a quick blow-dry, a slick of lip gloss and some mascara.

However, I do have time to slip into my gorgeous new lingerie. Well, I say slip, but the satin thong is a bit of a squeeze and the silk balconette bra is definitely a bit of a struggle to hoick my boobs into. But it will all be worth it later when Jack gets to take it off again . . .

Relishing that thought, I pull on a new summer dress I've bought especially for the occasion. It's from the same little boutique as my chiffon blouse and has the same eye-watering kind of price tag. But it's not every day your boyfriend flies five thousand miles to see you, so I want to look nice. I mean, I can't truck up in a pair of old leggings and a T-shirt, can I?

Giving a little twirl in the mirror to check my reflection, I team the dress with the pair of sandals I bought in India. I had a cobbler on the high street fix them so they don't fall off my feet any more. I glance down at them, feeling a burst of happiness as the sequins catch the sunlight, and for a moment I'm transported back there to the rooftop in Udaipur overlooking the lake where Jack first kissed me . . .

Savouring the moment, I dab some of my Indian perfumed oils on my wrists, then notice the time on my watch.

Immediately I snap to. It's getting late. We should get going.

Throwing the lip gloss, my phone and a pashmina in my bag, I grab my keys and dash for the door. There's some post on the mat and picking it up, I absently notice a card among the bills, with a Paris postmark. That will be from my friend Harriet, I think happily, popping it on the side to open when I get back. She never forgets my birthday, not even now she's moved to Paris, I think fondly. No doubt she's having a fabulous time there, I must ring her when I have a moment and catch up.

'Be a good boy,' I call out to Heathcliff, who's gone back to bed and is curled up in his basket. 'Next time you see me, I'll be with Jack!'

There's a sleepy wag of his tail at the mention of Jack's name.

Slamming the front door behind me, I collect Mrs Flannegan from next door and help her up the stairs to the road. Together we walk to the tube at a snail's pace. I can feel the minutes ticking away but I try to ignore my impatience. We'll all be old one day, if we're lucky, I tell myself, as I link arms to help her shuffle across the pedestrian crossing.

Finally, after what feels like for ever, we reach the station and together we glide down the escalators. Mrs Flannegan confesses she hasn't been on a tube train for over twenty years, and spends the whole time exclaiming at everything. From the touch-in, touch-out barriers, to the animated posters, to the sheer number of people, she's almost like a child on their first trip to the fair.

Fortunately the train isn't too busy and I manage to secure a seat next to Mrs Flannegan, who spends the next forty minutes regaling me with anecdotes about her granddaughter Linda. I listen, nodding and commenting, until after a while I feel myself zoning out and thinking about Jack. About how with every second that ticks by, every metre I travel, every building and tree that passes by in a blur, I'm getting closer and closer to seeing him again.

I still can't quite believe how lucky I am. After I split up with Sam I never thought I would ever feel this way about someone, not just because my belief in love was so shaken and my heart was so bruised, but because I feared I could never trust a man again. Trust is so intangible you can't see it, you can't touch it, but it's as vital to the soul as the air that you breathe.

People always say things happen for a reason, or it's for the best, but for a long time I couldn't see how that applied to finding my fiancé in bed with another woman. But now I can see just how right they were. All that heartbreak was necessary for me to learn and grow, to find myself *and love* again.

It made me do things I would never have done in my normal, everyday life. It gave me the courage, or the desperation, to get on a plane and fly to India, to meet a stranger on a train and go with him on a crazy road trip across Rajasthan. It triggered a course of events that led me to Jack. And for that, I am forever grateful.

Finally, the train pulls into the stop for Heathrow Terminal Three. I help Mrs Flannegan disembark and we make our way into the arrivals lounge. Hastily I check the board, praying I'm not late, and it's a relief to see that Jack's flight has only just landed.

'What number is Linda's flight?' Positioning myself and Mrs Flannegan near the barrier so we have a good view of the automatic doors through which the arriving passengers appear, I turn to my neighbour. But no sooner have I spoken than I hear:

'*Nan?* Is that you?' in a strong New Zealand accent.

We both turn to see a suntanned blonde wearing a giant backpack, hurtling towards us, a huge grin on her face. At the sight of her, Mrs Flannegan's face lights up.

'Linda!'

Linda flings herself at her grandmother, almost knocking

her clean over, and together they hug and laugh and cry, all the time talking over each other at a million miles an hour. Until, finally breaking away, Mrs Flannegan introduces me to her granddaughter and they say their goodbyes.

'I hope you don't have to wait too long.' She smiles.

'Me too.' I smile excitedly, waving them off, before turning back to the doors.

I'm all jittery and nervous. Every time the door opens I forget to breathe. I wait on tenterhooks, my stomach doing somersaults. God, I love airport reunions – whenever I see couples greeting each other it's always so romantic, like something out of *Love Actually*. And now I get to have my own reunion moment with Jack!

Any minute now . . . any minute now . . .

The doors open again and a swell of people surges forwards. I strain on tiptoes. And then—

Oh my god, I think I can see him, I think that's Jack, I think he's here—!

3

Honestly, I think I need glasses.

Five minutes later and I'm still waiting for Jack to arrive. That man wasn't him at all. In fact, on closer inspection, he looked nothing like him whatsoever. But it was too late. By the time I realised, I was already waving madly at him and grinning like a loon. God, it was so embarrassing. I had to pretend I was greeting someone behind him, although I'm not sure he believed me as it was a group of Japanese pensioners.

Still, I suppose it could have been worse. I could have given him a hug and been arrested for sexual assault. Just imagine! Being carted off in handcuffs just as Jack arrived!

Shuddering at the thought, I squint even harder at the doors so as not to make the same mistake again. The people coming through them seem to ebb and flow – one minute there's a stampede of passengers with their luggage, the next minute there's no one. But I keep focused. I don't want to take my eyes off the doors in case I miss him.

I wait.

Hmm, it feels like I've been here a while. Surely he should be through by now? I briefly snatch my gaze away from the doors to glance at my watch. Gosh, is it that time already? It's getting late. I *have* been here ages.

Worry pricks. Maybe he's got stuck in Immigration. Or maybe his bags haven't arrived or something. *Something* starts to escalate. That will teach me to watch *Banged Up Abroad*. Not that I'm abroad or Jack's banged up. But still.

Suddenly I feel something vibrating in my bag and remember my phone. There's been so much going on I'd forgotten all about it, what with helping Mrs Flannegan get to the airport and meeting her granddaughter and Jack arriving.

Only he hasn't arrived, has he?

Abandoning my sentry position, I rummage around in my bag for my iPhone. Damn, where is it? Squatting down on the floor, I start pulling everything out: keys, pashmina, wallet – chucking it all on the floor of the arrivals hall. It crosses my mind briefly that it would be just my luck for Jack to arrive at this precise moment, me scrambling around on the floor, my hair all over the place, my possessions strewn around me, but at this point I'm starting to feel slightly panicked.

Finally! Finding it buried at the bottom of my bag, I snatch it up and glance at the screen. And get the shock of my life. *Six missed calls, four voicemails and ten emails?* I stare at the numbers on the little icons with disbelief. For a moment I stand paralysed, not sure what to check first, then hit the email icon.

They're all from Jack.

My stomach lurches.

The first one is entitled 'CALL ME'. Or is that the last one? I can't tell; they're all in some kind of message stream. I hit the email and impatiently wait for it to open up, only instead I'm automatically redirected to a hotspot. *A hotspot?* I don't want a hotspot! I want to read my emails! I start furiously jabbing my phone to cancel and go back to my emails, but the icon is just whirring and whirring and nothing is loading. Oh for fuck's sake, come on, come on, *come—*

Your message has not been downloaded from the server.

What the—?

I stare at the blank email from Jack with frustration. I feel like screaming.

Instead I hit voicemail. I wait for it to connect. Everything feels like it's taking for ever. Finally I get through and am forced to listen to the woman telling me how many messages I have and how to retrieve them.

Like I don't know how to do that! Quit with the explaining, just hurry up. *Hurry up!* Is it just me or does she have the slowest speaking voice?

'Hey, I'm at the airport—'

Finally. As I hear Jack's soft drawl the panic that's been building to explosive proportions melts quickly away and I feel a swell of love. Aww, he's leaving me a message before he gets on the plane, probably telling me he loves me. Standing up again I focus back on the doors at the new surge of people appearing.

'—and something's come up—'

Something's come up?

My insides freeze over. Three words. But they're not the three words I was expecting.

'. . . look, I'm really sorry.'

Sorry? Sorry for what? Have I missed something?

My mind is scrambling but somewhere, deep inside me, deep in the stillness of my core, I get that awful feeling of dread. Like when you think you've lost your purse, or realise you've locked yourself out of your flat—

Or the man you're in love with has done something you don't want to hear.

'I've tried calling you but it's after midnight there, you'll be asleep, and I didn't want to tell you on email, so I hope you get this as soon as you wake up—'

What has happened?

'I'm as disappointed as you are but I know you'll understand, I'll make it up to you, I promise—'

I'm still watching the people coming through arrivals. They've slowed to a trickle. My eyes are glazed. Is he saying what I think he's saying? Does he mean what I think he means?

'Call me as soon as you get this message. I love you babe.'

He's not coming.

I feel a sickening thud of disappointment. I can't believe it. It can't be true. This must be some sort of joke. Jack likes his jokes. Jack's always been a bit of a joker.

Right? *Right?*

I start hastily trying to dial his number but I'm all fingers and thumbs. My throat is dry and I have to swallow hard. It seems to ring for ages and then finally connects.

Someone picks up.

'Hello, Jack?' I gasp.

There's a sleepy groan from the other end and I hear a groggy voice. 'Ruby . . . is that you?'

'Yes, it's me,' I say urgently. 'Where are you?'

'Um . . . hang on . . . what time is it?' His voice is thick with sleep and there's the sound of lots of shuffling around, as if he's sitting himself up in bed.

'1.45,' I say, glancing at my watch.

'That makes it 5.45 in the morning here . . .'

'Here?'

'I'm still in LA,' he says raspily, 'didn't you get any of my messages?'

It's like a boxer's jab. So it's true. He hasn't come. I'm crushed.

'I only got your voicemail just now, there wasn't any reception at my flat—'

'Where are you?'

'At Heathrow.'

He lets out a loud groan. 'Oh jeez, Ruby. Didn't you get any of my emails either?'

'What's happened?' I bat away thoughts of myself.

Something terrible must have happened for him not to get on the flight. 'You're OK, aren't you? You haven't had an accident?'

As I say the words, I feel a sudden rush of panic.

'No, no, I'm fine.'

'Is it your mum?' Recently he'd told me she wasn't very well, something about a cough. I'd dismissed it as nothing, but now—

'No, Mom's fine.' He cuts off my scary train of thought.

'So what is it?'

'It's work—'

'*Work?*' I interrupt, my voice coming out a little more hard-edged than I'd intended.

All the worries and concern suddenly vanish. He's not had some terrible accident and is lying in intensive care. None of his family is sick. He's fine.

'Yes, they called me when I was at the airport. There's been a bit of a crisis on one of our projects—'

'Crisis, what kind of crisis?' I fire back before he's finished talking.

'It's too hard to explain over the phone—'

'*Try.*'

'Ruby please, I've just woken up, I don't want to go into it. I just have to sort it out, that's all.'

'Can't someone else sort it out?' Disbelief stabs. I can't believe he's putting work first.

'No, otherwise they wouldn't have called me,' he replies a little impatiently.

I pick up on his irritation immediately. Hang on a minute, he should be apologising like crazy and instead *he's getting impatient with me?*

'Well they're just going to have to call someone else,' I snap back. Any feeling of being upset is fast being replaced with fury. 'We've had this arranged for months.'

'Ruby, you're not being reasonable,' he says, reprimanding me as if I'm a small child.

'*Reasonable!*' I gasp. 'I'm the one that's been stood up at the airport!'

Several people walking past with their suitcases glance over at me and I have a flashback to India, standing at Goa airport, waiting for Amy. What is it about me and airports and people not showing up?

'Look, I'm sorry. It's not like I wanted this to happen,' continues Jack on the other end of the line, 'but I just can't let them down.'

'But you'll let me down instead?'

There's a pause and he lets out a long sigh. 'You're being unfair, this is killing me too, you know.'

His voice is weary and he sounds as disappointed as I am. My fury disappears as quickly as it had appeared. Oh god, this is awful. Why are we arguing? All I want to do is see him. Be with him. And if he can't come here—

'Look, why don't I come out there then instead?' I suggest, suddenly hit with an idea. 'I've never been to LA and I could write while you work . . .' As the idea takes hold and grows, so does my enthusiasm: 'and we'd be able to spend the evenings together at least, I mean I know it's not perfect, and it's not a hotel in the country, but we'll still be together and that's what matters—'

'I won't be here, I've got to fly to Colombia.' Jack cuts me off.

'*Colombia?*' My imagined trip to LA screeches to a halt. '*When?*'

'I have to catch a flight this afternoon.'

I feel myself reel. 'When will you be back?'

'That I don't know,' he admits, 'the project's based in a town a couple of hundred miles or so south of Cartagena, and I'll know more when I arrive.'

I feel as if I've just stumbled into the middle of a movie and I'm frantically trying to make sense of what's going on.

'As soon as I've sorted out the issues I'll jump on a plane to London, I promise.'

'But that could be ages!' I protest. I shoot a look at the man who's been staring at me this whole time, and he finally turns away.

'Ruby, please, I'm stressed enough as it is.' His voice is impatient again. 'I don't want to argue.'

'I'm not arguing, *I'm upset!*' I cry, fighting back tears. 'Don't you get it? *It's different!*'

'And I've said I'm sorry,' he snaps, 'what more do you want? *Blood?*'

It's like a slap in the face.

For a moment I'm shocked into silence. How did we get here? How has this happened? It feels like everything has just come crashing down around me. My heart thumping, I press my phone to my ear and listen to the silence on the other end of the line. He's not speaking, but he's still there and for a moment I wonder how we can salvage the situation. How we can turn it all round and put things back to how they were just a short time ago, to when I was happy and excited to see him and everything was right with the world.

But I'm too pissed off, too upset and too bloody hurt to care any more.

'No, I wanted to spend my birthday with my boyfriend,' I reply coolly. 'Is that too much to ask?'

'You know what, maybe it is right now.'

An iciness grips me, but I keep my voice steady. 'What's that supposed to mean?'

'It means I'm not having this conversation with you right now when you're being like this.'

'Like what?'

'Like you were at the train station in Delhi when you lost it.'

I'm suddenly reminded of my outburst in India. Which, quite frankly, was perfectly understandable. I'd had all my things stolen. I'd been upset. And there'd been Jack, being totally patronising.

Exactly like he is now.

'Get lost, Jack,' I fire back, infuriated. 'Don't treat me like a child.'

'Well, stop acting like one,' he snaps.

There's a pause, insults and hurt hanging in the air. I can already feel them setting, hardening, forming an impenetrable wedge between us.

'OK, well it's nearly 6 a.m. and I have a flight to catch in four hours. I'll call you when I get to Colombia.'

'Don't bother—'

'Ruby, don't make this into something it's not.'

But it's too late. It already is something else. This argument is no longer about Jack not showing up at the airport and missing my birthday, it's about me being afraid he's going to be like all the other guys. It's about being let down. It's about being scared I'm going to get my heart broken all over again.

After Sam cheated on me, I never thought I'd be able to trust another man, but Jack changed all that. Jack wasn't going to let me down or disappoint me. He was different.

At least I thought he was.

'Look, I think we both need to take a timeout to cool off and think about things,' he says, his voice hard and flat as if he's speaking to a stranger. Not to me, Ruby, the girl he's supposed to be in love with.

'OK, fine,' I say flatly, keeping the hurt out of my voice.

Then we both hang up.

Dazed, I stare in disbelief at my phone. Tears are pricking my eyelashes and I have to brush them roughly away. I can hardly believe what just happened. In a few moments I've gone from excitedly waiting for my boyfriend, and two whole weeks of romantic fabulousness ahead of me, to no boyfriend and a bloody big row.

I sniff and wipe my nose on my pashmina. I notice the man who was staring at me is staring at me again.

'You know it's rude to stare,' I call over loudly. 'Didn't anyone ever tell you that?'

He looks shocked and turns bright red.

'Especially when someone is upset,' I continue furiously. 'How would you like it if I stared at you when you were having a row with your girlfriend, or your wife?'

'No, it's not that—' he begins, but I don't let him finish.

'I feel horrible enough, but then people like you have to just stare at me the whole time like I'm some kind of freak!' All the upset I feel about Jack is suddenly misdirected at him and comes pouring out. 'OK, so I'm crying at Heathrow airport, blubbing like a baby in a public place, but so what? Is that a crime?'

'Miss, I think you're mistaken—'

'You have no idea how I feel, it's my birthday at the weekend and my boyfriend was supposed to be arriving from America and now he's not coming!'

'It's your dress—'

'And we'd booked a lovely hotel in the country that had a spa and waffle bathrobes and everything—'

'It's come undone.'

I stop mid-sentence and glance down. Mortification rushes over me. My lovely chiffon dress has come unbuttoned at the front, revealing my bra. But even worse, I'm not wearing my comfy padded T-shirt bra. Oh no, I'm wearing my lacy peek-a-boo barely-anything-there bra.

'Oh . . . um . . . thanks,' I croak, my cheeks blazing like an inferno and my fingers fumbling as I try to quickly button myself up again.

Oh my god, how embarrassing! I'm hanging out at Heathrow airport in front of everyone! I'm practically topless!

'And I'm really sorry about your boyfriend and your birthday and everything.'

'Right, yes . . . thanks,' I manage, shooting him a mortified smile.

Mumbling my apologies, I'm scuttling off when I hear my phone buzzing again in my pocket. *It's Jack! He's phoned back!* I snatch up my phone with relief.

'I'm so sorry,' I blurt, before he can say anything, 'it was just the shock and the disappointment that's all, I don't want to argue—'

'Ruby?'

Only it's not Jack, it's my friend, Harriet, who lives in Paris.

'Darling, what's happened? Are you OK?'

It's the friendly voice that does it. Up until this moment I've been trying and succeeding in not crying, but now I suddenly burst into tears. 'Oh Hattie!' I sob, my voice breaking, 'Jack was due to fly in today for my birthday—'

'I know, that's why I'm ringing, you must be so excited,' she enthuses.

'No, I'm not excited!' I wail. 'He's not coming, he's had to cancel.'

'*Cancel?*' Her voice drops in confusion. 'But I don't understand, I thought his flight had already arrived . . .'

All my friends know every last detail about Jack's arrival; I've talked of nothing else for weeks now.

'It did arrive, but he wasn't on it and we just had the most awful row,' I sniffle, digging around in my pockets for a tissue to blow my nose. 'He said he couldn't come, something to do with having to go to Colombia for work—'

'*Colombia?*' repeats Harriet, incredulous.

'. . . I got everything ready, I was so excited—' I break off as I think about my flat: the champagne, the flowers, the food, *the effort* . . . I'm aware of my bra strap digging in and my lacy thong, which now feels as if it's cutting me in two. It makes me feel even more upset and I let out another loud sob.

'Oh Ruby, sweetie, I'm so sorry, please don't cry—'

'And it's my birthday this weekend and we were going away to the country to stay in a hotel . . .' I find a tissue and blow my nose loudly.

'Yes, I know, you emailed me a picture, the spa looked gorgeous—' She breaks off. 'Well, not *that* gorgeous,' she says quickly, backtracking, 'in fact I think jacuzzis are just a breeding ground for germs and who wants to sit in a sauna and go all red-faced and sweaty in front of your boyfriend, anyway? It sounds absolutely beastly.'

I make a snuffling noise from beneath my tissue.

'Anyway, enough about that,' she says briskly. 'More importantly, what are you going to do now?'

I think about going back to the flat and my heart sinks even further. 'I don't know,' I sniff, trying to collect my thoughts, which are flopping over themselves, each one more miserable than before.

'Well in that case, you must come to Paris,' she says, suddenly taking control. 'Celebrate your birthday here with me.'

'Oh thanks, that's a lovely idea, but I can't . . .' I know Harriet is being kind, and who doesn't want to go to Paris? But I can't even think straight right now. 'There's Heathcliff for a start, I can't leave him with Mrs Flannegan, she's got her granddaughter staying with her—'

'Not a problem,' she cuts in. 'The French love dogs. Bring him with you.'

I fall silent. I'm still trying to take everything in.

'Come on Ruby,' she cajoles, 'I haven't seen you for ages and this is the perfect opportunity. And to tell you the truth . . .' She falters slightly, her tone quietening, 'it would be good to see a friendly face.'

Immediately I pick up on her tone. 'Why, what's wrong?' I ask with a beat of concern. Harriet is always so upbeat, it's rare for her to say anything's wrong. She's the kind of person who could have her house burn down and when you asked her how she was, she'd say she was 'Super, thanks.' 'I got your card this morning,' I say, suddenly remembering, 'thank you so much, but I didn't have time to read it yet. Is everything OK?' Harriet isn't the kind of person to simply scribble a few kisses, her cards are always filled with heartfelt messages.

'Yes, fine, it's just – well, I know Paris is a wonderful city and everything, but, I'm actually really lonely,' she admits, suddenly sounding sad.

And in that moment my mind's made up. It's not about Jack any more. Or me. It's about one of my closest friends, and she needs me.

Stuffing my tissue determinedly in my pocket, I head for the exit. 'Actually, on second thoughts, it's ages since I was last in Paris. A visit is long overdue.'

'So you'll come?' She sounds delighted.

I smile. 'Try and stop me.'

4

Letting myself into my flat, I'm greeted by Heathcliff, who comes running up, tail wagging excitedly, then promptly runs past me as if looking for someone else.

'He's not here, buddy,' I say, breaking the bad news.

Standing on the path, Heathcliff turns to me and tips his head on one side as if to say, 'Er, hang on a minute, what's going on?'

'He's going to Colombia instead,' I continue, glancing at my reflection in the hallway mirror. What a difference a few hours makes. I'd left the house all bright-eyed and bushy-tailed and now I'm all puffy-faced from crying, with mascara halfway down my cheeks. And there was me thinking my days of having to buy waterproof mascara were over.

I go into the flat. Like Heathcliff, it too seems to greet me as if expecting someone else. All the cushions on the sofa are sitting up straight on their corners, as if on their best behaviour. The flowers in the vases are standing tall. The scented candle is sitting in pride of place on the mantelpiece ready to be lit. Even the freshly polished French windows, cleaned of smears on the glass where Heathcliff presses his nose, wait in spotless anticipation.

Faced with all this effort, I feel all my hurt and disappointment mutating into a fresh wave of fury towards Jack.

'Damn you,' I say out loud, bashing a defenceless cushion to get rid of some of its plumpness. '*Damn you, Jack!*'

Aware that I'm still bashing the cushion, I stop before the
feathers literally start flying. Still, no point feeling sorry for
myself, I tell myself firmly, quickly walking into my bedroom.
I need to pack – I want to catch the Eurostar this afternoon.
Well, no point hanging around here, is there? Luckily I can
take off to Paris without worrying about work as my deadline
for my new book isn't for some time.

To tell the truth, I still haven't worked out what it's going
to be about. My last novel was inspired by my trip to India
and it was so magical and romantic it's proving hard to write
a follow-up. But maybe I'll find inspiration in Paris. Though,
after what's just happened, I'm not exactly in the best frame
of mind to be writing a love story. It will need to be something quite extraordinary to inspire me.

I fling open my wardrobe and stare at my clothes. I have
no idea what to pack. My mind hasn't yet changed gear to
single-girl-in-Paris and is still stuck on loved-up-weekend-
with-boyfriend-in-the-Cotswolds.

Where, quite frankly, I wasn't planning on wearing much,
other than a waffle bathrobe and the aforementioned
lingerie.

Oh sod it. Grabbing my wheelie suitcase I randomly grab
things from their hangers and then, zipping it up, stride into
the kitchen and clear the fridge of its contents. I was going
to cook Jack a lovely romantic dinner and I spent a fortune
on all this delicious organic food; I can't see it going to
waste. Especially when I nearly had to remortgage the flat
to buy it.

Gathering together the last of my things, including
Heathcliff's pet passport and my own, I grab my wheelie and
the bag of food. There's just one last thing. Plucking the flowers from their vases, I march outside and ring next door's
doorbell. Usually this is followed by the soft shuffling of slippers, but today there's an unfamiliar bounding of footsteps

and the door is flung open by a young girl. Mrs Flannegan's granddaughter, Linda.

'I'm Ruby, I live next door, we just met at the airport—'

'Oh hi,' she says, 'do you want to speak to Nan?'

'No, don't bother her, would you just give her these?' I give her the bag of food and the flowers. 'Tell her I'm going away for a few days and taking Heathcliff.'

He's still lying on the path, face flat against his paws. One ear cocks at me reluctantly.

'Sure.' She nods. 'Anywhere nice?'

'Paris.'

'Oooh, how romantic.' She grins.

Forcing a smile, I quickly say bye, then grab the rest of the things from my flat. Pausing at the doorway, I notice Harriet's card on the side. I open it, quickly reading her birthday wishes and message which she signs off, 'Wish you were here!' and smile, despite what's happened. Then, locking up my flat, I put Heathcliff on his lead and we set off down the street together. Me and my sausage dog. Off to the City of Love.

I think that's what they call irony.

Arriving at St Pancras International, I go to the automated ticket machine to buy a ticket for the Eurostar. Despite my mood I can't help marvelling at how great it is that I can just catch a train to Paris. I mean, how wonderful is that? What an amazing feat of engineering. I just turn up at the station, buy a ticket, and in a little over two hours I'll be there. It's so easy and hassle-free and—'

How much?

I stare in disbelief at the display. Er, hang on a minute. What happened to all those cheap deals to Paris that I'm always seeing advertised? I hesitate as it briefly crosses my mind to wonder if I can get a better deal if I wait until tomorrow. Oh sod the price. I don't want to wait, I want to see

Harriet. I stick in my credit card and cross my fingers. After what's happened today, I'm in a sod-it kind of mood.

Fortunately my credit card is in the same mood, and instead of being swallowed up, spits out a ticket and I quickly make my way towards Passports and Security. Gosh, it's so busy! The departures hall is filled with all kinds of travellers, but among them I notice a large party of elderly war veterans in uniform, their decorated chests bursting with medals and ribbons. They all look to be in their eighties and nineties and many of them have canes or wheelchairs, but there's also a large number proudly walking tall as they greet each other warmly with handshakes and hugs.

Standing in line, I watch as a girl with pink hair pushes up her charge, a huge bear of a man in a wheelchair wearing a beret and so many medals you can hardly see the uniform, and joins the queue behind me.

'Please, go ahead.' I smile, making room for them both.

'Why, that's very kind of you,' says the elderly gentleman, and the young girl smiles gratefully.

Deftly she manoeuvres his chair in front of me.

'What's happening?' I ask, curiously. 'Is there some kind of ceremony?'

'It's the seventieth anniversary of the D-Day landings this weekend,' she replies, smiling. 'We're all heading out to Paris for the Queen's state visit.'

'Oh gosh, of course.' I feel a flash of embarrassment that I'd forgotten. With everything that's been going on these past few days with Jack's visit, it had completely slipped my mind. 'I've been seeing lots about it on the news.'

'Yes, it's huge,' she nods, her tiny nose-stud twinkling as it catches the light. 'There's going to be a procession down the Champs Élysées on Thursday, followed by a big international ceremony on the beach at Normandy. Even Obama's going to be there, isn't he, Granddad?'

'Aye,' he nods, then smiles. 'I won't know which hand to shake first.'

'Wow, that's amazing,'

'Granddad was a gunner in the Royal Artillery and landed on Gold Beach,' she says proudly and pauses to gaze at him with a mixture of awe and devotion. 'He's a real hero.'

'I was just doing my job,' he says simply, with the kind of breathtaking humility you don't hear very often. 'We were all just doing our job.' He gestures to the dozens of elderly veterans around him, each and every one of them heavily decorated with awards for bravery. 'There were thousands more of us, we were just the lucky ones.'

'No, we were the lucky ones,' I reply quietly, feeling a swell of admiration and gratitude for all these strangers.

His granddaughter smiles and squeezes her granddad's hand, then notices Heathcliff, who's been hidden behind my suitcase.

'Ooh, who's this?' she says with delight. She crouches down and he immediately rolls over so she can tickle his tummy.

'Heathcliff,' I smile. 'He likes playing hard to get.'

She laughs. 'Look Granddad, he's just like Sizzle! Granddad's regiment used to have a dachshund as a mascot in the war,' she explains. 'They called him Sizzle because he was like a little sausage.'

I laugh as Heathcliff plays up to his new fans and, jumping on his hind legs, licks the old man's hand.

'Next in line, please!'

We've been so busy chatting we haven't realised we've reached the front of the queue.

'Oh, that's us.' Straightening up, she quickly pushes her grandfather up to the passport window.

A few moments later I'm called forward by the official at the next window. Grabbing my suitcase and Heathcliff, I hand over my ticket and passport and wait to be waved through.

'I'm sorry, no pets are allowed on the Eurostar.'

'Excuse me?' I look at him in surprise. It had never occurred to me I couldn't take Heathcliff on the Eurostar. I mean, it's a train!

'Only guide or special assistance dogs can travel.'

Oh god, can today get any worse? Harriet's going to be so disappointed. What am I going to do now?

'If you could please step aside, there is a line of people waiting—'

'There you are!'

Hearing a voice, I twirl around to see the granddaughter with pink hair bending down and scooping up Heathcliff. 'I'm sorry, Officer, I was so busy with my granddad's wheelchair I didn't realise we'd left him behind.' Smiling cheerfully, she places him in her grandfather's lap. 'My grandfather is a diabetic. Heathcliff is his special assistance dog.'

I look at them both with astonishment, and she throws me a wink.

'Is that so?' The official remains stony-faced. I have to confess, I'm not sure I'd believe us either. Heathcliff looks nothing like a golden retriever.

'Absolutely,' nods her granddad, patting Heathcliff, who's curled up in his lap as if they've known each other for years. I can't believe it. He hates being picked up by strangers. 'I couldn't be without him.'

The officer shifts uncomfortably. 'Do you have the relevant paperwork?'

Oh shit.

The granddaughter shoots me a look. 'Actually, I think I might have dropped it—'

'Ah yes, here it is,' I say quickly, cottoning on. Opening Heathcliff's passport at the page with all his vaccinations, I pass it across. Oh god, I hope he doesn't turn to the page about the legal owner. My heart races.

'Look, can we please hurry this along? We mustn't miss the train. We have an important ceremony to attend.' The grand-daughter raises her eyebrows and motions to her grandfather and the other soldiers still waiting in the queue behind us.

'The Queen is attending,' says her grandfather, pointedly.

At which point the official surrenders and, handing back Heathcliff's passport, hurriedly waves us through.

'Thank you so much,' I whisper, once we're out of earshot and, after giving the granddaughter a hug, I go to shake her grandfather's hand. 'You're my hero, in more ways than one.'

'Well, if you can't break a few rules at my age, then when can you?' He chuckles. 'And anyway, I owed it to Sizzle. Lovely fellow he was, brave as they come.' He tickles Heathcliff, who's still lying curled up in his lap. Trust him to snooze his way through it all.

'It was a pleasure to meet you both.' I smile, scooping him up.

'You too my dear.'

'And don't forget, if you're in Paris you should try to catch the parade, it'll be quite something,' says his granddaughter, and giving both Heathcliff and me a wave, she wheels her grandfather away to join the rest of his friends and comrades.

Five minutes later, we board the train and I find my seat. The last time I was on a train other than the tube, I was in India. On that fateful train journey from Goa to Delhi where I met Jack. My mind leaps back to him. He should be awake by now. I wonder what he's doing, if he's packing for Colombia, or maybe he's already left for the airport—

Putting down my half-finished latte, I dig out the phone in my pocket. I've checked it countless times already, reading the emails he wrote earlier, which don't say much other than for me to call him, and hoping for a new text or an email from him.

But nothing. We're having a timeout, I remind myself; what did I expect?

Yet, disappointment still crushes. It's made worse by the texts I do have, from Amy and my parents. I've been so excited about Jack's visit it's all I've talked about for weeks now. So on top of feeling upset and angry, I feel like an idiot. I know it's not my fault he hasn't come, but even so I know what people will think. After all, I don't exactly have the best track record when it comes to romance, do I?

Give Jack a big hug from me & have a fab time in the country! You lucky thing! Amy xxxx

I trust Jack landed safely. Hope we meet him soon! Btw be careful travelling home on the tube, it says on the news it's rife with a new wave of pickpockets. Love Mum (and Dad) xxx

And one from my friend Rachel.

Have fun with Jack! I want a FULL report after the weekend!!! R x

I turn off my phone.

On the seat next to me, Heathcliff is curled up fast asleep. I envy him. I wish I could do the same, but I'm wide awake. We're already whizzing out of London and as I watch the high-rises and warehouse buildings give way to garden suburbs, my mind flicks back to its default setting: Jack.

We were supposed to be together right now, making up for lost time at my flat, and instead I'm hurtling towards Paris without him. This wasn't what I thought was going to happen when I woke up this morning. This wasn't part of the plan.

But then life has a funny way of going off-plan, doesn't it?

I stare out of the window, lost in my own thoughts. Everyone always says long-distance relationships never work, but I thought we were different. I thought we were special. So what if we're from two completely different sides of the world, with different backgrounds and cultures and lives? It didn't matter – we loved each other and that was enough.

But maybe I was wrong. Maybe everyone else is right and I've just been completely naive. The last three months have been like a honeymoon period, but now I feel like I've just come down to earth with a bloody great bump and I'm worried about our future.

Do we even have one?

Leaning my forehead against the coolness of the glass, I gaze out of the window, wishing I could see the answers. But all I can see is my reflection staring back at me, and before I know it we're plunged into the darkness of the tunnel.

I always thought falling in love was hard, but now I realise that was the easy bit.

It's staying in love that's the hard part.

5

I must have fallen asleep; the next time I look out of the window we're on the outskirts of Paris. My gaze passes over the ugly scrawl of graffiti plastered all over the buildings and the jumble of concrete and power lines. It's not the prettiest of places, but it's the same in nature. Like a rose surrounded by thorns, or a pearl encased by an oyster shell, the rough casing is there to protect and emphasise the jewel that lies inside:

Paris.

Disembarking at the Gare du Nord, I follow the swell of people making their way towards the exit. Heathcliff trots dutifully alongside me, sniffing the air around him curiously. Wafts of *café au lait* and freshly baked croissants, cigarette smoke and perfume swirl around us. You don't have to be able to read the signs or understand the foreign accents to know we're no longer in London. It just *smells* French.

Pulling my wheelie case behind me and holding tightly on to Heathcliff's lead, I scan the crowds for a tall, and what people often unkindly call 'well-built', brunette in baggy cords and a T-shirt. In all the time I've known Harriet, I've never seen her wear anything remotely figure-hugging, much to the horror of her French-born mother, who's not only the epitome of elegance but also the size of a sparrow. As are Harriet's five younger sisters.

Harriet, however, inherited her father's sturdy aristocratic genes. Brigadier Fortescue-Blake is a giant of a man, with big bushy eyebrows that look as if they're about to take flight and hands the size of dinner plates. Harriet is his much-adored eldest daughter. But while she often jokes that to inherit the family silver, you have to inherit the huge feet that go with it, I know how much she hates being about a foot taller than the rest of her siblings and twice the size.

While her mum and her sisters swap size zero designer outfits, Harriet insists on hiding her figure underneath baggy clothes that she always teams with a waxed jacket and old brogues that have seen better days. She looks like she should be living in a farmhouse in the country, with an Aga and several border collies; not a city girl living in a two-bedroom flat in central London and commuting on the tube to her job at Sotheby's in the heart of Mayfair.

Well, she was, until she got headhunted by a private auction house in Paris and moved across the Channel for a promotion and a better salary. Fortunately for Harriet, not only is her mother French, she also had an expensive private education and can speak the language fluently, along with several others. Unlike my own Comprehensive one where French lessons, by contrast, consisted of making fun of yet another supply teacher and learning swear words.

Nope, can't see her. *Merde!*

See, I still remember them.

'Ruby!'

Suddenly, above the noise and chatter of the station, I hear someone calling my name. I twirl round, glancing back and forth. That can't be Harriet; she would never have spotted me – she's a bit vague and short-sighted even with the super-strong prescription glasses she wears.

'*Yoo-hoo*, over here!'

Then again, it has to be – who else would be calling me? And who else, quite frankly, says 'yoo-hoo' unless they're about ninety and your maiden aunt? The only thing is, I can hear her voice, but she's nowhere to be seen.

And then I spot her. At least, it must be her, as it's a girl waving madly at me. Except she's unrecognisable as the Harriet I said goodbye to in London. Gone is the brown-haired girl in shapeless cords, ancient brogues and wire-framed spectacles. Instead I see a statuesque blonde in a classic black dress and heels, eyes hidden by dark sunglasses.

I stare in astonishment as she makes her way towards me.

'*Harriet?*' I gasp. 'Is that you?'

'Of course it's me, darling!' she enthuses, flinging her arms round me and engulfing me in a cloud of unmistakably expensive perfume. 'Golly, it's so good to see you!'

After a few moments she releases me and, slightly dazed, I stand back to take another look. The transformation is incredible. Not only is she wearing a dress (!) and heels (!) that show off her figure but she just looks so *put together*. Her unruly brown hair, which could never be tamed, despite copious amounts of Frizz Ease and an ever-present scrunchie, is now a perfectly blow-dried bob with warm honey highlights. She's also wearing nail polish. And scarlet lipstick.

I stare at her in disbelief. In the whole time I have known Harriet I have never seen her wear a scrap of make-up. She's always bare-faced and rosy-cheeked as if she's been marching over the countryside in the fresh air. In fact the only thing I've ever seen her apply is lip salve.

But now here she is sporting classic red lips and – I almost do a double-take as she pushes her sunglasses on to her head – *is that liquid eyeliner?*

'Wow, I would never have recognised you! Look at your hair!'

'I discovered blow-drys,' she says, smiling, 'all the Parisian women have them, it's practically mandatory.'

'And what happened to your glasses?'

'Contact lenses. Bit fiddly at first, but I've got the hang of them now.'

'You just look . . .' I search around for the right word.

'Thinner?' she prompts.

Every time I see Harriet she demands to know if she's lost weight. Personally I don't think she's got any weight to lose; she's the right size for her height – but for as long as I've known her, she's been on a diet in her quest to drop a dress size.

'Yes, much.' I nod dutifully.

'Liar!' She grins.

'OK, then different,' I say, smiling, '*stylish*.'

'Paris does that to you,' she replies, 'watch out, you'll be next.'

'Oh, I don't know about that,' I say ruefully. I looked at my reflection in the bathroom mirror on the train earlier and tried to do something with my hair, which had gone all flat and floppy, and my blotchy face. Then gave up. It was hopeless.

'Well you do look rather terrible,' she concedes, 'but it's only to be expected under the circumstances. Which you're going to have to tell me all about—' She breaks off as she suddenly notices Heathcliff, and lets out a delighted whoop.

'Oooh, fabulous, you've brought the pooch! The perfect Parisian accessory!'

Bending down, she begins fussing over Heathcliff, but rather uncharacteristically he doesn't make a fuss back. I don't think he likes being described as an accessory.

'Oh, aren't you a cutie. We'll have to get you a little diamanté collar,' she coos.

He gives a little growl. There's nothing I can think of that Heathcliff would hate more than wearing a diamanté collar. Other than being carried in a handbag.

No sooner has the thought struck me than I spy Harriet's oversized one. Quickly I change the subject.

'It's so great to see you, and thanks so much for inviting me to come and stay—'

She cuts me off immediately. 'Nonsense darling, the pleasure's all mine. Jack's loss is my gain,' she says firmly and, reaching for the handle of my wheelie case, she sets off briskly. 'Now come along, let's get you home.'

I watch her for a moment, marvelling at how quickly she's walking in those heels, and with barely a wobble. Well OK, maybe a *slight* wobble. I wince as one of her ankles goes over rather dangerously, but she quickly grabs a railing to regain her balance.

'Shall we take a taxi?' I suggest, gesturing to the cab rank outside. 'I'll pay.'

'Don't be silly,' she says dismissively.

'No, seriously,' I protest, 'it's the least I can do.'

'We're not getting a cab.' She wobbles on ahead past the line of passengers.

'Oh OK, well I suppose the Métro is probably quicker . . .' Though I have no idea how she's going to navigate all the steps in those heels, I worry, following her dutifully.

'What on earth are you talking about?' Abruptly she stops dead and there's the sound of two loud beeps and the flash of a car's lights. 'I have wheels.'

'Wheels?' The surprises are coming thick and fast. I watch in disbelief as Harriet reaches for the door of a shiny red Citroën. 'You've got a car?'

'Yes, didn't I tell you? It was a Christmas pressie from Daddy.'

This is just one of the many differences between mine and Harriet's families. In our house we exchange jumpers and DVDs as gifts at Christmas, and maybe some cashmere gloves if you're lucky. Last year, Harriet's mum got a Rembrandt. OK, so it was 'only' an etching, but still.

'Hop in,' she says cheerfully, chucking my wheelie case in the boot.

Scooping up Heathcliff, I climb into the passenger seat

and almost before I've had time to close the door, the sunroof is down and her foot's on the accelerator.

'So you don't have a problem driving on the wrong side of the road?' I ask, clutching on to the sides of my seat as we swerve out into the traffic. Before my trip to India I was a bit of a nervous backseat driver, but getting behind the wheel and navigating the craziness that is the roads in India cured all that.

At least I'd thought so.

'No, not at all,' she says, beaming, clipping the wing mirror of a parked car as we shoot round a corner. 'It's quite easy, once you get the hang of it.'

Her confidence is admirable; alas it would appear she has absolutely no reason to be so sure of herself. It's only taken me two minutes in this car to realise she is a *terrible* driver. Harriet's about the least coordinated person I know, which, together with her tendency to get distracted easily, makes for a lethal combination behind the wheel.

Grabbing the gearstick, she shoves it into gear, which makes a horrible crunching sound that sets my teeth on edge. How on earth did she ever pass her driving test?'

'I didn't know you could drive,' I say, trying to sound nonchalant.

'Oh god, yes, I've been driving for years,' she replies gaily.

I feel reassured. Honestly, I'm such a worrier.

'Unofficially.'

'*Unofficially?*'

'Yes, on the estate.' She nods cheerfully.

That's another thing about Harriet's family. They live on an estate. And I don't mean a housing estate. I mean *an estate*. Like in *Downton Abbey*.

'But I finally got my licence last year after taking that silly test god knows how many times – I mean, honestly, there's nothing to driving, I don't know why they kept failing me—'

The back tyres go up on to the pavement and there's an ominous clunking.

'Don't worry, that's nothing important,' she says, shooting me a look, 'just the exhaust.'

'Isn't the exhaust pipe quite important?' I say nervously.

She hoots loudly. 'Oh I do love you, Ruby, you always make me laugh with your jokes!'

I'm not actually joking but despite everything that's happened today, I find myself smiling. Plus quite frankly, if I can survive a road trip in India, I can survive a car journey from the Gare du Nord. Even with Harriet driving.

'Shall I put on some music?' she trills. 'I have this great new salsa CD somewhere . . .' Taking her eyes off the road, she leans over and starts rummaging around in the glove compartment.

'No – no!' I cry hastily as I see us veering towards the oncoming traffic. 'I'd much rather talk, it's been ages.'

'Oh right, yes of course darling,' she says quickly, straightening up again and focusing back on the road.

'So how are you?' I ask, 'how's life in Paris?'

'Oh, I'll tell you all about that later,' she says, sweeping away my concerns with a hand gesture, 'let's talk about you first, that's far more important.'

It's not, but I know there's no point in trying to get Harriet to talk when she's in stiff-upper-lip mode. I'll have to try later.

'How are you feeling?' she asks.

'I've been better,' I admit truthfully.

'Have you spoken to him?'

'Not since the airport when I found out he wasn't on the flight.'

Harriet gives a sharp intake of breath. 'He stood you up at the airport?' She looks aghast.

'Well, he left me voicemails and lots of emails, but I didn't get them until it was too late.'

'Unforgiveable,' she says, shaking her head.

'Do you think so?'

'Yes, unless there's a bloody good reason.'

'He said it was work, some crisis—'

'If he's not a brain surgeon or the President of the United States, no crisis is good enough for leaving your girlfriend waiting at the airport. On her birthday.' She shoots me a thunderous look.

'Well it's not my actual birthday until Sunday.'

I realise I'm defending Jack, but I can't help it. I love him. At the thought I can feel my eyes water again and I blink rapidly before Harriet notices.

Which she does immediately. 'Oh I'm sorry darling, I don't mean to upset you, ignore me,' she backtracks hastily, 'after all, what on earth do I know about relationships?'

'Haven't you met any nice men in Paris?'

'Yes, lots, but none that are interested in me, plus they're all so *tiny*.' She pulls a face, 'I feel like a giant next to them.'

'I thought you were seeing that guy – Pierre, wasn't it?'

I feel bad that I can't remember his name, but I can never keep track of Harriet's love life. She seems to be always going on dates, yet is permanently single.

'Pascal,' she corrects me, 'but we never went on an actual date.'

I look at her in confusion. 'Call me stupid, but how can you be seeing someone and not actually see them?'

Pulling up to some lights, she slams on the brakes and turns to me. 'You've never done online dating, have you?' she asks pointedly, raising an eyebrow that I notice has been newly plucked into a perfect arch.

It's true. Call me a philistine but I've always dated the old-fashioned way.

'Trust me, finding someone is not like it used to be.'

I look at her curiously. I'm not sure I like the sound of it.

'You don't go to a bar and get chatted up,' she continues. 'No one buys you a drink or asks you out for dinner. You have to try to write something witty about yourself, post photos of yourself that you hope don't make you look crazy, or fat, or old – oh and don't get me started on the dating apps that are just about whether someone in the immediate vicinity wants to shag you . . .'

Listening to Harriet, I feel as if I've just stumbled out from under a couples rock. The only apps I have on my phone are the ones for Goodreads and eBay.

'And then if someone likes the look of you, they often just wink at you.'

'*Wink?*'

'Well, it's not a real wink, they just click a button. Or they might add you to their favourites.'

'Then what do you do?'

'If they look OK, I'll wink back and see if they email me.'

'And if they do?'

'I'll email them back. Often you just email back and forth for a few weeks,' she explains, seeing my slightly bewildered expression. 'You can also friend them on Facebook and follow them on Instagram or Twitter.'

'It doesn't sound very romantic,' I say uncertainly.

'It's not,' she says, matter-of-factly, 'but everything's online these days. Even love.'

If I felt sad earlier, now I feel even more so. But not about Jack – about love. Is that how you're supposed to find your soulmate and fall in love these days? By flirting in 140-character tweets and stalking each other's social media pages?

'Oh, it's so good to see you Rubes,' says Harriet, breaking off and heaving a sigh. Reaching out, she squeezes my hand and I can't help feeling that it's more to reassure herself than me. 'I'm so pleased you came.'

'Me too.' I smile, squeezing it back.

The lights change and we accelerate away. It's hot in the car, even with the sunroof open, and I wind down my window. A warm gust of wind blasts through my hair and, resting my head on my hand, I watch Paris fly by as we whizz along wide, tree-lined boulevards, past crowded pavement cafés and striped shop-awnings.

Until after a while I stop thinking about London, about Jack, about our row at the airport. Instead my thoughts are taken up by the gorgeous architecture and beautiful parks, the faded shutters and wrought-iron balconies out of which peek bright geraniums in terracotta plant pots, the flashes of hidden courtyards and cascading fountains . . . I feel my spirits rise higher and higher until finally we reach the banks of the Seine and I see Notre Dame rising in front of me.

Gazing up at the gothic spires reaching into a perfect, spotless blue sky, I feel a burst of exhilaration. Incredible really, considering how I felt this morning. Then I notice them. Strolling hand in hand along the Seine, taking photographs, laughing . . .

Couples.

And as we drive over one of the bridges that cross the river, I look down at them from my vantage point and my eye is caught by one particular man and woman. Arms wrapped round each other, holding out a phone, they're laughing as they kiss each other for their selfie. And as quickly as my spirits had risen they fall again, like a kite swooping and plummeting to the ground.

My heart aches. I'm here in Paris. The most romantic city in the world.

Without Jack.

It's not going to be that easy.

6

After crossing the river, we spend the next few minutes navigating a labyrinth of streets, their unfamiliar names written on little blue and white plaques on the sides of the buildings that go by so fast I can barely get to read them, let alone try to pronounce them.

I have no idea where we are, or what direction we're heading in, I'm so turned around; but soon we leave behind the wider streets with the bustling pavement cafés and fashionable shop windows and enter a quieter, more residential neighbourhood. Here the streets are so narrow they're plunged entirely into shade by the six or seven-storey nineteenth-century buildings that line either side.

Though they could be even older, I muse, gazing up at their old stone facades and floor-length windows and wondering what their history is. Maybe I should buy a guidebook tomorrow. Despite living just across the Channel I've only been to Paris twice; once on a school trip when I was ten and once when Dad bought the whole family Eurostar tickets so we could 'experience this amazing piece of engineering', which he insisted was down to the British, of course.

Neither trip holds great memories. The first time I was sick on the ferry going across and on the second, I was twenty-one and Paris was the last place I wanted to spend a weekend with my parents and little sister. Even worse, Amy was only eleven and all she wanted to do was go to Disneyland Paris. A trip to the Louvre instead resulted in a full-blown tantrum. Despite being arguably the most famous painting in the world, the *Mona Lisa* could never hope to compete with Snow White and the Seven Dwarves.

That was ten years ago and I remember promising myself that the next time I came to this city it would be with the man I loved . . .

Right, that's it, I'm definitely buying a guidebook. While Harriet is at work I'm going to be a tourist and throw myself into sightseeing; it will help take my mind off things.

We pass a couple of small two-star hotels, an *épicerie* with the grille pulled down and a dusty-looking bookshop, before finally turning in to a small cobbled side street where cars are squeezed bumper-to-bumper along one side.

We slow down.

Uh-oh. Realising Harriet is looking for a space, I feel a beat of concern.

'Maybe there's more room on the next street—' I suggest, but she shushes me.

'Nonsense, there's plenty of room here,' she says, and gestures to the tiniest of spaces.

Now usually I hate that stereotype of women not being able to park a car. Of course we can park cars! Except – this isn't just any old woman; it's Harriet. And it seems I've every reason to be concerned. Her parallel parking is even worse than her driving and I have to cover my eyes as she rocks back and forth, hitting the bumpers both in front and behind, until finally she manages to wedge the car into the space, rather like forcing a cork back into a wine bottle.

'Home sweet home!' Clambering out of the car, she walks over to a large, somewhat shabby metal door covered in peeling billposters and punches a security code into a metal box on the wall. The door releases. Taking Heathcliff's lead and dragging my wheelie case with the other hand, I follow her into a small, quiet courtyard. Shaded by the high walls of the surrounding buildings, it's much cooler than outside and the trees cast a dappled sunlight across the worn cobbles.

We walk across the courtyard and into a small passageway that leads to another door and a flight of stairs with peeling paintwork and exposed pipework.

'I'm afraid there's no lift,' she says apologetically, 'do you want me to help you with your bag?'

'No, it's fine, I packed light,' I fib, regretting my chuck-it-all-in approach earlier as I lug it behind me up the narrow, twisting staircase. Heathcliff follows, struggling slightly with his little legs. Still, hopefully there aren't too many flights to climb.

As it turns out Harriet's apartment is six storeys up and I'm seriously out of breath by the time we reach the top floor of the building and shuffle on to a dingy, narrow landing that has a distinct smell of damp. It's illuminated by a single bare light bulb that can hardly be more than about forty watts and I can only dimly make out two doors facing each other. As she puts her key in the door on the left, I try not to think about my five-star hotel room and spa that I'd booked and paid for. I'm here for Harriet, remember?

'I tidied up specially,' she grins ruefully, unlocking the door.

Harriet is very messy. Her flat in London was in a constant state of chaos; sometimes I would walk in and have to actually *hunt* for her sofa. She blamed it on growing up with a house-keeper and maids. Apparently it wasn't until she left home that she discovered if you dropped something on the floor it didn't magically hang itself up, but actually stayed there.

Something that she is very embarrassed about now, of course.

But this apartment is as unrecognisable as she is. 'Wow, it *is* tidy,' I pant, as I'm unexpectedly greeted by a charming little attic room flooded with natural light. Tucked under-neath the eaves, it has sloping beamed ceilings and a row of arched windows along one side. Painted all white, apart from the wooden beams, it has an open-plan kitchen and living area, with just enough room for a small table and two chairs, a TV and, 'Look, I can see the sofa!' I gasp, gesturing to it.

'It's actually a sofa bed,' she grins, then wrinkles her nose. 'I'm afraid there's only one bedroom, are you all right sleeping on there? You could share with me, but I don't think you'd want to after the black eye . . .'

She's referring to the last time we shared a bed. It was last summer and I'd invited Harriet over for dinner to cheer her up after yet another ill-fated fling, this time with Heinrich, a banker who'd pursued her like crazy then vanished after the second date. I'd made an attempt at spaghetti bolognese and she'd brought the wine and we'd sat up into the early hours looking for clues to his disappearance in his text messages.

It's amazing how long you can actually spend analysing just a couple of lines and it soon passed midnight. Realising it was too late for the tube and too pricey for a taxi, she'd stayed over, but in the middle of the night I was woken by a sharp kick in the shins. Which was bad enough, but it was followed by a walloping right hook that gave me a shiner for days. Apparently she'd been fast asleep and dreaming I was Heinrich. She was mortified and terribly apologetic.

That said, until she's happily married and therefore not dreaming about whacking hopeless boyfriends, I don't think I'm going to risk sharing a bed with her again.

'The sofa bed's great,' I smile, trying not to think about the four-poster bed I'd booked for me and Jack. What's the big deal about four-poster beds, anyway? A sofa bed is probably much comfier, I tell myself firmly.

Heathcliff is already busy exploring the place, his tail wagging excitedly. Putting down my bag, I walk over to the window and, without warning, have my breath taken away. I wasn't prepared for this at all. The view is incredible. It's like being on top of the world. 'Oh wow,' I gasp as I gaze across the rooftops and beyond, the whole city of Paris stretching out beneath us, as far as the eye can see. 'It's beautiful.'

'Isn't it?' Harriet nods. 'I know this apartment is as tiny as anything but that's what sold it for me,' she says, flinging open a window and taking a deep lungful of city air. 'It comes with a view of *la tour Eiffel* – the Eiffel Tower,' she adds for my benefit. Unnecessarily. I know my French is bad, but it's not *that* bad.

'Really?' I stand on my tiptoes, scanning the skyline.

'Well, sort of,' she admits. 'If you lean out far enough and sort of crick your neck . . .'

Opening a window, I do as she says, but no, it's no good, I can't . . . I crane my neck even further, tracing the river, the bridges, the roads that criss-cross the city like a spider's web, and then – oh, there it is!

'Gosh, yes,' I gasp as I finally catch a glimpse of the famous landmark. I stare at it for a few minutes, drinking it in. I've seen it in so many photographs, in so many paintings, in so many films, but there's something very special about seeing the Eiffel Tower in real life.

'Did you know that when it was first built locals hated it and demanded it was demolished?'

'Really?' I frown, trying to imagine Paris without the Eiffel Tower, and not being able to.

'It's incredible isn't it?' She shakes her head in disbelief. 'Later on tonight when it gets dark you'll be able to see the light show. It's amazing.'

'Sounds great,' I enthuse, trying not to think about how I'd like to see it with Jack. God, this is harder than I thought. I came to Paris to spend time with Harriet, but it doesn't help that the city oozes romance. 'Maybe we can drink this while we watch it,' I suggest, going over to my wheelie and pulling out the bottle of champagne I've been lugging around with me. 'It needs chilling first though.'

Harriet's eyes light up. 'Ooh, yes please,' she grins, taking it from me and putting it in the fridge. 'Like I said, Jack's loss is definitely my gain.'

'Well, it seemed a shame to let it go to waste,' I smile ruefully, 'unless of course you've got plans for tonight.'

'You mean all the handsome, eligible men lining up to take me out for dinner?' Grinning, she flops down onto the sofa beside me and is just kicking off her heels when we're interrupted by the burbling of her mobile phone. She glances at the screen. 'Hang on, it's the office,' she says, making that little signal with her finger that she won't be a minute. She picks up and starts speaking in a torrent of fluent French. I'm impressed. I mean, I knew she was fluent, but still, hearing her makes me wish I'd paid more attention to our supply teachers with their imperfect verbs.

I see her frown and even though I don't understand what she's saying, she seems to be unhappy about something. She looks at her watch, then at me, then sighs.

'*D'accord*, I'll be right there.' She puts down the phone.

'Everything OK?'

'Not really. I was booked to do a valuation at an apartment tomorrow morning, but the *avocat*, sorry, I mean the lawyer, who has the keys is now saying his diary is full for tomorrow. He wants to meet now instead. I tried to explain I'm busy and asked if he'd reschedule, but he's insisting it's his only free slot and his clients can't wait—'

'Oh, don't worry about me,' I say quickly, 'you go ahead.'

'Are you sure? I don't like leaving you on your own.' She looks doubtful.

'Don't be silly, I'll be fine,' I reassure her.

Appeased, she slips her heels back on and gets up from the sofa. 'I'll try to be as quick as I can but I might be a couple of hours, it's over in the third *arrondissement*—'

'Seriously, there's no need to rush. I'll take a shower, maybe watch some TV—'

And see if Jack's called, pipes up a voice in my head.

As she starts collecting her things, I dig my phone out of my pocket. I know he said we needed some time out, but maybe he's emailed or left a message. Earlier, we were both pretty angry; tempers were frayed and emotions were running high, but now we've both had time to calm down and think about things.

I switch it back on and as it comes alive it buzzes with text and email alerts. I feel a beat of anticipation. One must be from Jack . . . I quickly hit the little text message icon, but it's only a text from Vodafone welcoming me to France. But that's OK, Jack probably wanted to explain properly, you can't do that in a text . . .

I open my email inbox. The past few months since we've been apart he's been constantly emailing and calling. There've been no games with Jack. No playing it cool. On the contrary, he's forever sending me songs on iTunes that he thinks I might like, or links to articles that he knows I'll find funny or silly selfies he's taken. Never a day goes by without something from him appearing in my inbox.

My heart leaps. Look! I have three new emails. I quickly glance through them. One is about an item I'm watching on eBay. One is from my bank saying my credit card payment is due. And the last one is from the hotel in the Cotswolds, confirming the double room I booked and reminding me of the strict non-refundable cancellation policy.

Disappointment stabs. No email from Jack. No apology. No 'let's talk about this'.

No nothing.

'Sure you don't want to come with me?'

I look up to see Harriet watching me.

'It'll stop you sitting here checking your phone all evening . . .'

A look of understanding passes between us. After all, what girl hasn't stayed in with her phone waiting for some man to call? Or text. Or email. Or send a message through the dozens of apps installed on your smartphone. In fact, there are so many ways to get in touch these days, it's even more crushing now when they don't.

'I could tell the lawyer you're my assistant,' Harriet continues, but she can't persuade me.

'Thanks, but I'll probably only get in the way.' I once went along on a job with her and she got really excited about a chest of drawers that smelled of mothballs and looked like something my granny used to have. Apparently it was worth an absolute fortune and attracted a bidding frenzy at auction from all these buyers in Japan.

Call me a philistine, but I'd much rather have something in a nice oak veneer from Ikea. Which unfortunately I blurted out to the owner of the aforementioned mouldy chest of drawers. Suffice to say, it didn't go down too well.

'Plus I don't really want to leave Heathcliff.'

'Oh that's not a problem, you can bring him. The French bring their dogs everywhere.'

'I'm actually a little tired . . .'

'OK, well suit yourself,' she shrugs, grabbing her car keys, 'but I thought you might be interested as the apartment's got quite a mystery attached to it.'

'*Mystery?*' My ears prick up. 'What kind of mystery?'

'It was an old lady's, but she'd kept it locked up for over seventy years. No one even knew about its existence until after she died. Apparently she'd been secretly paying rent on it all these years and never told a soul.'

'But why?' I ask, intrigued.

Harriet shrugs. 'Well that's the mystery, nobody knows.'

As I absorb these few details, something unexpected catches hold inside of me. A familiar stirring of fascination, curiosity and excitement. And an absolute certainty. That there's only one reason someone would do something like that. *Love*.

'Actually, on second thoughts, I'm not as tired as I thought.' As Harriet reaches for the door handle, I jump up from the sofa. 'I think I'll come with you.'

7

We clamber back into the car, including Heathcliff who's had enough of being stuck in the footwell and this time insists on sitting perched on my knee, staring out of the window as if he's sightseeing, just like any other tourist.

'Honestly, this lawyer person is so annoying,' grumbles Harriet as we head back across the river. 'If I'd have known he wanted to meet now, we could have gone straight there from the station. Still, at least you get to see more of Paris this way.'

'Where's the apartment?' I ask above the noise of the tyres rattling over the cobbled streets.

'The Marais,' she replies, turning right without indicating.

'Is that where the Sacré-Coeur is?'

'No, that's Montmartre.'

'Oh, I see,' I blush, embarrassed by my terrible sense of geography. 'I knew it began with an M.'

'Easily done,' she grins, rather graciously. 'They're very different neighbourhoods but they're both really interesting. The Marais is a very historic district. It actually means "the marsh" and it used to be where they grew all the vegetables for the city, but then the French nobility took over the land and built these huge residences. The architecture is amazing, the buildings are like actual palaces . . .'

I listen to Harriet acting the tour guide and in spite of my mood about Jack, I feel a beat of excitement. '. . . Then the nobility started moving out and at the end of the nineteenth and the first half of the twentieth centuries it became this thriving Jewish community. Then of course, came the war . . .' She falls silent, reflective for a moment, then starts up again. 'And now it's extremely fashionable; there are some wonderful galleries I can take you to.'

'Sounds good,' I enthuse.

'Though we should also go to Montmartre,' she continues. 'It's famous for the basilica, but also for being this amazing bohemian mecca where lots of artists like Picasso, Van Gogh, Renoir and Toulouse-Lautrec used to live and work . . .'

'Is that where the Moulin Rouge was?' I ask, feeling very much the tourist.

'That's Pigalle, at the foot of Montmartre, which used to be the red light district. A short walk from there are Printemps and Galeries Lafayette, two famous department stores and the best shopping in Paris. We'll have to go, we can buy you some new clothes.'

'What's wrong with my clothes?' I look down at my new dress, which admittedly is now crumpled and covered in dog hairs.

'You're in Paris, you don't need an excuse to buy new clothes,' she says, as if that's perfectly obvious. 'That's the first lesson I learned when I moved here.'

I look at Harriet incredulously. She always used to hate clothes shopping. I once took her into Zara and she broke out in hives. But now here she is, talking like she's some kind of fashionista.

'Plus it's your birthday, you'll need something new when we go out and celebrate.'

Reminded, I feel a familiar pang. The last thing I feel like doing is celebrating. I just want to stay in with a bottle of wine and a bucket of Häagen-Dazs and pretend it's not happening. Maybe even stick my head underneath a duvet. You know, that kind of celebrating.

But judging by Harriet's phone call earlier, she could do with a night out and so instead I force a smile. 'Great,' I reply, putting on a brave face. 'I can't wait.'

After several minutes we turn off the main boulevard and begin making our way through narrower streets, lined with cafés and tourists.

'Hmm, now it's around here somewhere . . .' She takes her eyes off the road to look at her phone. 'Hang on, I've got the address—'

We swerve sharply, narrowly missing a whole row of parked cars.

'Here, let me look,' I say, trying to grab her phone, but she shoos me away.

'Don't worry, I've got it,' she says cheerfully, 'you just relax.'

Relax? I white-knuckle Heathcliff's fur.

After a couple more minutes of zigzagging around we turn into a much quieter street, on the corner of which appears to be a small, secluded park, almost hidden away, and surrounded by iron railings.

'This is it,' announces Harriet, looking triumphant.

We start looking for the number. Ahead, I notice a male figure with his back to us. Dressed in a sharply cut suit and carrying a briefcase, he's waiting outside on the pavement, smoking a cigarette. Checking his watch, he pulls out his phone.

Harriet's immediately starts ringing. It's the lawyer. He's already called wanting to know our whereabouts and she gasps infuriatedly. 'Honestly, I'm not even five minutes late!'

We both glance at the clock on the dashboard. Admittedly Harriet's not the best timekeeper, but this time she's right. It's two minutes past.

'You know, I've never met this chap but he seems like a total pain in the—' She suddenly breaks off. 'Golly, *that's the lawyer?*'

We both stare as he turns towards us. With his wavy dark hair swept off his face, cheekbones so chiselled they're like coat hangers and a large Roman nose, he looks like he's just stepped off a Paris catwalk, not out of a law office.

'*Woweee*,' whistles Harriet through her teeth.

I have to admit, since falling in love with Jack I haven't even noticed other men. It's like they're invisible. The moment we kissed on the rooftop in Udaipur, every other man ceased to exist. They don't even appear on my radar. But this man is so jaw-droppingly handsome he'd send any woman's radar into a beeping frenzy.

Quickly applying a fresh coat of scarlet lipstick, Harriet scrambles out of the car and hurries towards him, apologising profusely.

'*C'est un plaisir de vous rencontrer.*' He nods, putting out his cigarette and briskly shaking her hand.

Harriet says something else in French then, turning to me, says in English, 'This is my assistant from London. Ruby, this is Monsieur Moreau.'

'Please, call me Xavier,' he replies in the kind of heavy French accent that has been sending women weak at the knees for centuries. Fixing me with his dark, steady gaze, he flashes me a charming smile. 'Welcome to Paris.'

'Thanks,' I reply and as I go to shake his hand he seems to hold both eye contact and my fingers for just a beat longer than feels necessary.

Hang on a minute – *is he flirting with me?* But no sooner has the thought flashed through my brain than it's chased by another. Of course he's flirting with you, Ruby, he's French! All French men flirt; they're famous for it. I don't need a guide-book to know that flirtation is a national pastime in France.

'I apologise for spoiling your evening.'

'Oh, not at all, on the contrary,' interrupts Harriet quickly, then laughs nervously. 'I mean, work is work and all that . . .'

I notice a blush creeping over her neck and flustered, she accidentally drops her phone.

Xavier swoops to pick it up. 'I do hope there are no Ming vases inside, no?'

'No, indeed.' She nods gravely.

As he hands it back I catch a flicker of amusement in his eyes and have to stifle a smile. OK so he's a terrible flirt, but he's also kind of funny.

'So, if we are all ready . . .' There's a code for the large front door and he pulls out a piece of paper from his breast pocket, then gives a little tut. '*Mes lunettes*. I left them in the office . . .'

'Reading glasses,' translates Harriet at my blank look.

'Oh, do you want me to do it?' I offer and as he passes me the slip of paper I quickly read out the digits.

'Thank you.' He smiles gratefully and, punching them in, releases the door.

We follow him inside, into the elegant hallway laid with the original patterned floor tiles and lit by two ornate gilt wall lamps. Ahead of us is a small elevator. It's one of those turn-of-the-century ones, with metal lattice doors that concertina back and a small red velvet bench inside.

I scoop up Heathcliff, who grumbles and wriggles with displeasure like a recalcitrant child. He was having way too much fun sniffing all these new and exciting smells.

'Golly, it's rather a tight squeeze,' says Harriet as we all step inside. 'Perhaps if I sit down . . .'

Xavier pulls closed the metal grilles and presses the button. Slowly we start to rise upwards. It's stiflingly hot. Standing so close to each other, our bodies almost touching, I'm conscious of the scent of Xavier's aftershave and find myself staring at the nape of his neck. The elevator suddenly seems incredibly intimate.

I glance quickly down at my feet.

'So, as you know this apartment has been left untouched

for nearly three-quarters of a century,' he says to Harriet, continuing to speak in English for my benefit. Not surprisingly, his English is perfect; somehow I can't imagine anything about Xavier not being perfect. 'Which is why my clients want your expert opinion on the furniture, paintings, personal belongings and so forth. We are expecting there to be many valuable antiques.'

'Yes, of course.' Harriet nods. 'I can do a full inventory and if there is anything that requires specialist knowledge we have a team of experts at the office I can call upon.'

As the lift arrives at the right floor, we walk out of the elevator.

'My clients are eager to sort out this matter as quickly as possible; they have asked me to advise you that they would like to organise an auction for this weekend.'

'Golly, that's very soon, usually we need several weeks at least—'

'My clients are very busy people. I was told your company is one of the best in Paris, but if you cannot manage this, I'm sure we can find someone else—'

'No, no, we can manage this,' says Harriet hurriedly. 'Depending on the number of artefacts, we usually put together a detailed catalogue over a few weeks and then schedule an auction, but I'm sure we can hurry things along.'

'Excellent.' He nods. 'My clients will be happy to hear this.'

I listen to them in astonishment. Neither of them has even mentioned the story behind the apartment. Surely that's so much more interesting.

'But do you know why the woman who lived here abandoned the apartment?' I interrupt.

They both stop talking business and turn to me.

'Because of the war.' Xavier frowns as if it's obvious. 'Many Parisians left the city ahead of the German troops. The owner, Madame Dumont would have been no different.'

'But I thought France had already surrendered?' queries Harriet innocently, before catching the thunderous look on Xavier's face and blanching.

'Only in the history books. Never in our hearts,' he says firmly, his dark eyes flashing.

'And is it true she never came back?' I say quickly, trying to steer the conversation away from a heated argument about the Second World War.

'According to our records Madame Dumont left Paris sometime in 1940 for Provence, where she was later married and lived for the rest of her life. She passed away recently at the age of ninety-five, having never returned to the city again.'

'Did she leave a will?' I ask curiously.

He shakes his head. 'She left no will and the Dumonts had no children. They owned a vineyard in Provence and this, along with the rest of their estate, was inherited by Monsieur Dumont's distant relatives. These relatives are my clients. It was only when they hired my firm to look into Madame Dumont's affairs that the existence of this apartment was discovered. It was rented in her maiden name, Emmanuelle Renoir.'

Xavier is full of factual information and yet it still doesn't explain things.

'And her husband never knew about this apartment?'

'He died many years ago, but apparently not, no.' Xavier shakes his head. 'He took care of all their financial affairs, but rent and *taxe d'habitation* was paid personally by Madame Dumont in her maiden name. The couple's accountants had no knowledge of this.'

'Mummy keeps secrets from Daddy all the time,' interjects Harriet, 'she went grey twenty years ago and he has no idea. He still thinks she's a strawberry blonde.'

'But why did she lock it up for over seventy years and still keep paying the rent if she was never going to come back?' I persist.

Harriet shoots me a look. 'My assistant's always full of questions.' She laughs lightly.

'I am afraid that I cannot answer,' shrugs Xavier nonchalantly. 'I am only a lawyer.' And turning away, he strides towards a heavy panelled door with an old brass doorknob covered in patina, and puts the key into the lock. 'That is a mystery for a detective to solve.'

The lock is stiff. It takes several moments of jiggling the key for the mechanism to finally turn, and when it does the door makes a loud cracking noise as if suddenly released from its frame.

'Is this the first time anyone's been inside?' I feel a flutter of anticipation.

'A colleague of mine came yesterday, just to make sure there were no dead bodies.'

'And were there?' Harriet looks alarmed.

'*Non.*' Xavier shakes his head, somewhat amused. 'Only ghosts.'

'*Ghosts?*' I look at him sharply, trying to search his face to see if he's kidding or not. I feel unexpectedly spooked.

'Nonsense, there's no such thing,' snorts Harriet dismissively.

And now I feel faintly ridiculous. Honestly, what am I like? Of course he's joking. Harriet is right – ghosts don't exist in real life, there's no such thing.

But still, I stand back a little bit as the door opens and we peer inside.

'*Sensationnel,*' murmurs Xavier under his breath and I hear Harriet give a sharp intake of breath.

Me, I'm simply speechless.

As I step through the doorway, it's as if a spell descends upon me. Cobwebs flutter like ghostly butterflies and there's a sense of years of being left completely undisturbed, of time being allowed to stand still. And a silence. A quiet stillness that makes it hard to imagine that we are in the middle of a city, with all its noise and energy and twenty-first-century life swirling around outside us. Cocooned inside these walls, it's as if we've crossed a threshold and entered an entirely different world.

Everything is in dark shadow. The shutters are firmly closed and the only light is seeping in from the doorway behind us. And yet even while my eyes are slowly adjusting, I can clearly see the grandeur of this apartment with its high moulded ceilings and floor-length French windows. Casting my gaze around me, I'm able to make out the pale glimmer of the large marble fireplace in the centre of the room, glints of gilt-edged picture frames on the walls, the sweeping folds of heavy velvet curtains. It's hauntingly beautiful.

Wordlessly Xavier walks across the parquet floor and unfastens the shutters. Having been closed for so many years, they creak open almost reluctantly, as if yawning awake from a deep sleep, but the effect is instantaneous. Suddenly the apartment is transformed. The evening light floods in, bathing everything in a golden glow and lighting up the dust particles. Glittering and sparkling, they swirl all around us as if we were figures in a snow globe that has just been shaken up. Millions of tiny pieces of glitter.

I stand, mesmerised. It's like being in a fairy tale. As the light dances around the apartment, lighting up hidden corners and casting reflections in antique mirrors, I experience a sense of breathless excitement. Of wonder. Of anticipation. I can't believe this is real. It's as if I've travelled back into the past. And yet, it's more than just that. It feels like something else. It feels like . . .

Like magic, I suddenly realise. That's how it feels. *Like magic*.

8

'Gosh, it's like a time capsule,' says Harriet finally.

She's the first to speak. It's as if the effect of the apartment had momentarily silenced us all.

'Look at all these things.'

She gestures around her. Even with my untrained eye I can tell there are lots of valuable antiques. A pale lavender chaise longue stretches out in front of one of the French windows; a huge ornate mirror hangs over the fireplace, its glaze speckled with age; several oil paintings are displayed on the walls; a floor-to-ceiling bookcase is lined with leather-bound books . . . My heart skips a beat. It's probably filled with first editions.

'Look at all these books,' I murmur, resisting the urge to run my fingers along their spines.

Harriet shakes her head. 'It's incredible.'

'The table is set for tea,' I point out, my gaze landing on the large ornate dining table that stands proudly in the middle of the room. Surrounded by the kind of carved wooden chairs and embroidered upholstery I've only ever seen in museums, it's laid out with a china tea set and silver candelabra.

'Maybe she thought she was coming back,' suggests Harriet, walking over to the table and carefully picking up a teacup. 'Turn of the century, Limoges tea set,' she says expertly. 'This mould is sought after but very rarely found.'

'It is valuable?' asks Xavier, raising an eyebrow.

'Golly yes, absolutely.' She nods, turning it over and peering at it closely. 'Just look at the beautifully hand-painted pink roses and gold highlights, the wonderful scallop-shaped rims . . .'

Leaving them both examining the china, I turn away and walk over to the marble fireplace, still holding Heathcliff. I notice there are still ashes in the grate. I stare at them, my mind turning. Someone lit that fire and watched it burn. But they didn't have time to clean out the grate. It's as if they left suddenly, or unexpectedly . . .

In the background I can hear Harriet, '. . . no cracks, or hairline fractures, it's in flawless condition . . .'

I glance over to the armchair next to the fire. I notice a brandy glass on the side table next to it, and an ashtray, empty but for a trace of ash. Someone has been here drinking brandy and smoking cigarettes, but it doesn't seem like something a woman would do. Did Madame Dumont entertain a man in here? Was it her future husband, Monsieur Dumont?

Or was it someone else?

Questions are bubbling up in my mind. Questions, but no answers. Like Xavier said, it's a mystery for a detective to solve. *A love detective*, whispers a voice inside my head and I feel a flutter of excitement. I think of all the fascinating stories I've read about love, all the legends and superstitions, all the great acts and amazing lengths that people will go to in the name of a great love.

Glancing across at the newspaper and the brandy glass, the cushion still crumpled from where someone has leant against it, I feel more certain about that than about anything in a long time. Love has to be the key that will unlock this mystery. But with love comes a million questions—

'I'll start logging everything now, but there is so much here to go through I'm going to need more than a few hours, Monsieur Moreau.'

I turn to see Harriet, notepad and pen in her hand.

'I will provide you with a set of keys so that you can come

and go as you please, Mademoiselle Fortescue-Blake,' replies Xavier.

I'd been half hoping there might have been some flirting going on over the china, but listening to them calling each other by their surnames, that hope deflates.

'If you could, that would be very helpful. I can finish up some of the smaller pieces this evening, but there's so much, it's incredible!'

'It is like unlocking a hidden vault, no?' He raises an eyebrow as he surveys the room.

And someone's home, I can't help thinking silently to myself, someone's life. I know Harriet and Xavier are here to do their jobs – his to represent his clients; hers to catalogue and value so they can auction everything off to the highest bidder – but I can't help feeling emotional. This was Madame Dumont's home, somewhere she lived, loved, laughed and left – and perhaps one day hoped to return. This is more than just a few rooms filled with antiques and price tags; it holds emotions and memories, passions and hopes, youth and energy—

And a secret, whispers a voice in my head.

I look around me. If only these walls could talk. Gazing at the faded blue wallpaper, I gently brush my fingertips against it, my imagination taking flight as I wonder about everything they've witnessed, all the moments and memories they've absorbed.

'Would you ladies excuse me for a moment?'

I snap back and turn to see Xavier looking at us both, an eyebrow raised in question.

'I am going to smoke a cigarette outside . . .'

'Yes, of course,' says Harriet, 'we don't want any smoke near the paintings, though I've had a quick look and don't think we have any hidden masterpieces.' She pulls a face.

'That would have been too much to hope for.' Xavier shrugs and gives a small smile, before turning on his heel and leaving the apartment.

As Harriet goes back to cataloguing I glance toward the other rooms.

'Can I have a look around?'

She nods. 'But just don't touch anything,' she warns, not looking up.

With Heathcliff in my arms, I leave Harriet photographing various objects and wander through the apartment. It's grand by any standards, and made up of what appears to be three rooms. I pass into another drawing room, lined with more bookcases and an old gramophone player that sits in the corner, and into what must have been Madame Dumont's bedroom.

The shutters are closed, allowing the room to slumber in shadow, but even in the dimness I can see a wrought-iron bed in the corner, its covers thrown back almost as if someone had just climbed out of it. Next to it stands a wardrobe, its door slightly ajar. I glimpse a woman's clothes: sleeves with delicate lace edging, skirts of pale silks and lush velvets.

I resist the urge to look inside and instead I turn my gaze to a floor-length mirror, over which hangs a dress made of pale yellow silk and covered in white polka dots. With its short puff sleeves, nipped-in waist and full skirt it looks like the style I've seen girls wearing in old photographs from the 1930s and 40s. I gaze at it, trying to imagine the owner wearing it. A young girl in a polka dot dress. She must have looked beautiful.

By the window stands an ornate dressing table with a triple mirror edged in gilt. A silver candelabra sits on one side, the candles with their melted wax still in place, while on the dust-covered surface of the table lies a collection of silver combs and hairbrushes, a small mother-of-pearl jewellery box out of which hangs a string of pearls, and several old glass perfume bottles. It's as if she'd been getting ready to go somewhere . . .

Unexpectedly, I feel a connection. In a way it reminds me of my own messy dressing table back at my flat in London.

My own brushes might be cheap plastic instead of silver and my jewellery's mostly from Accessorize, but it's still the same. Nearly three-quarters of a century and a world war later and in a way nothing has changed. I even have the candles, although mine are scented and cost an absolute fortune, I muse, suddenly reminded of the one I bought for Jack's arrival and then wishing I hadn't thought of it.

In my arms Heathcliff distracts me by wriggling impatiently.

'Come on buddy,' I cajole. 'I'm the one having to carry you and even though you're little you're heavy,' I reason, but he shoots me a mournful look. I feel a stab of guilt. So far this Paris trip hasn't been much fun for Heathcliff. Apart from a brief spot of sightseeing on my lap, he's been stuck in the footwell of the car, on the Eurostar and now he's stuck inside an apartment. Even worse, he hasn't been able to stretch his little legs at all today. He usually gets taken on at least one walk a day so he can do his favourite thing of sniffing around.

'OK, but make sure you're good,' I say, giving in and putting him down. I give him a little stern waggle with my finger. 'And I mean it.'

Thrilled to be given his freedom, he promptly busies himself by sticking his long nose on the floor like a vacuum cleaner – and explodes into a sneezing fit.

'Be careful, there's a lot of dust.' I smile.

I turn my attention back to the dressing table, marvelling at everything. There's a lipstick, a jewelled compact, what looks like an ornate silver letter opener shaped like a fish—

I'm distracted by the sound of loud rustling and look up.

'Heathcliff?'

But he's disappeared. I glance quickly about the room. Where is he? Then I hear a scrambling sound under the bed. Oh fuck.

Dropping to my hands and knees, I peer under the bed. It's full of dust and steeped in shadow. My eyes take a moment to adjust, then I see that it appears to be crammed with objects: what looks like an old leather trunk, a couple of hatboxes. I peer harder; it's difficult to make out. Then I spot Heathcliff squeezed into the space.

'Hey, what are you doing under there?' I hiss, and try to grab him, but he's had enough of being held prisoner and is making the most of his new-found freedom. He wriggles further away.

'Come here,' I command bossily, but he just flatly ignores me. This is one of those times I wish I'd invested in obedience classes.

Damn.

I hesitate to glance down at the faded rug beneath my knees, trying not to think about what a good vacuum it needs, then lie down on my stomach and try to wriggle my arm underneath. Hoping to touch warm fur, I feel blindly around, my fingertips fumbling against the hard edges of the suit-cases and boxes— hang on, *what's that*? My hand brushes what feels like papers. Curiously I pull them out.

It's a bundle of letters, tied together with a faded pink ribbon. I stare at them for a moment. There must be a dozen envelopes, all the same size and pale blue colour. I try to deci-pher the handwriting on the front of the first envelope. It's in a flowing, cursive script that reminds me of the old-fashioned way my grandmother used to write, and the ink's faded, making it difficult to read. I turn it towards the window and in the fading sunlight I make out the address – it's the address of this apartment – before moving the ribbon with my fingers to reveal the name hidden underneath.

Emmanuelle Renoir.

That was Madame Dumont's name before she was married.

No sooner has the thought struck than a piece of note-paper drops out from between the letters. Unlike the rest it's not in an envelope, and instead of being blue the paper is a delicate shade of coral. Curiously, I unfold it. It's a letter.

> *Darling H,*
>
> *Please forgive me if I make any mistakes in my English, but I am writing this in haste. My father has heard word that the Germans are soon to be upon us and he is demanding we leave Paris immediately and flee to the south ahead of them.*
>
> *Oh, my darling H, I hope it is not too late. I too am so sorry we argued and I pray more than anything that you have not left the city as you threatened in your letter. As soon as you read these words, please come to me at once. I don't want to leave you or Paris, but I am so afraid.*
>
> *Finally, I have found the courage to go against my family's wishes. I will not marry Monsieur Dumont. You must know this. My heart is yours for ever. Yet there is something else I must share with you, something that makes my heart beat even faster, something that involves our future happiness. I should have told you sooner, but I was so scared. Now, after many nights of unrest, I know that I can no longer delay what it is I have to say.*
>
> *We have our own secret world but no secrets between us, except I confess I have a secret and it is one I must tell you, share with you. I dare not write this down for fear this letter may fall into the wrong hands. You must hurry here when you get this, I shall wait for you.*
>
> *Oh, there is someone hammering at the door! It is my Papa! I must hide this but after I will try to post this letter, my final letter to you, so that we are never again*

The letter stops. The sentence unfinished. The last word smudged. What had happened? There's no date. Who was H? What did she have to tell him? What was the secret? Has it something to do with the mystery of why she kept this apartment for so long?

'Ruby?'

As the questions swirl around me, I'm distracted by Harriet calling, then the sound of Xavier's voice and footsteps. Oh shit, they're coming in here!

I pause, frozen, my eyes fixed on the door, the letters still in my hand. I need to put them back.

And yet, more than anything I need to know what happened. 'There you are!'

The door swings open and in that split second before they enter I impulsively stuff the letters in my bag.

'I was just looking for Heathcliff,' I fluster, as Harriet appears, 'he slipped the lead.'

As if on cue Heathcliff appears, looking sheepish. I pick him up.

'Wow, just look at this room,' she gasps, glancing around, her eyes lighting up as they land on the dressing table. 'What a gorgeous example of a serpentine-fronted tulipwood dressing table!' she cries. 'Just look at the gorgeous floral motifs and exquisite ormulu mounts . . .'

I feel a beat of relief. Fortunately she's been too distracted by the antiques to ask me any questions.

'Valuable?' Standing at the doorway, Xavier raises an eyebrow.

'Very.' She nods. 'Your clients will be happy.'

'Good.' He nods back. 'I like happy clients.'

Hearing them talk I feel something twist up inside me.

'We should leave, it's getting late,' he continues. 'We can make further arrangements for you to finish the cataloguing.'

'Yes, absolutely.'

'Ready?'

I zone back in to see them both looking at me expectantly.

'Um, yes – ready,' I nod, and as they turn to leave I slip my hand into my bag to check the letters are still there, then follow them out of the apartment.

9

Forty minutes later we're sitting on Harriet's sofa, drinking champagne out of mugs and surrounded by pizza boxes.

'I'm so embarrassed,' Harriet is mumbling through a mouthful of margherita with extra olives, 'your first night in Paris, the world's capital of fine dining, and you're eating takeaway pizza. I'm a terrible host. I don't even own any champagne flutes.'

'Rubbish,' I refute, tipping my head back to catch the dollop of cheese stretching from my *Reine d'un Jour* pizza. 'You're a wonderful host, this is delicious.'

'Promise me you won't tell a soul,' she begs, breaking off a piece of garlic bread.

'Cross my heart with a slice of pizza,' I say solemnly, 'plus champagne tastes better this way.'

She grins and mops up the trickle of garlic butter that's dripping down her chin.

'So anyway, you still haven't told me how you've been,' I remind her, making another attempt at getting her to confide in me about how she's been feeling. 'How's Paris been treating you?'

'It's great, the city's beautiful, the job's amazing . . .'

There's a pause.

'But?' I prompt.

I know how hard it is for Harriet to open up. Her family isn't exactly known for talking about their feelings and over the years she's learned to bury them.

She fidgets uncomfortably. 'Oh nothing, I've just been really busy, what with the move and everything.' Turning her attentions back to the garlic bread, she avoids my gaze.

'You seemed pretty down on the phone when you called me,' I coax.

'Oh, golly, did I? I'm sorry,' she says, apologetically, 'I didn't mean to alarm you. I've just missed you, that's all. I've met some wonderful people, but it's not the same as being with your old friends.'

'I've missed you too.' I smile.

She smiles back, but it doesn't quite reach her eyes. 'But anyway, you're here now, so it's all better.'

Something tells me there's more to it than she's letting on, but as she reaches for her mug and drains the rest of her champagne it's obvious she's not going to say any more on the matter.

Not for now, anyway.

'So Xavier the lawyer seemed nice,' I say pointedly, changing the subject and topping up her mug with what's left of the champagne. We've made quick work of it. The bottle's almost empty.

'Oooh, do you want his number?' Shoving in the last of the garlic bread, she scrambles quickly for her phone. 'You could ask him out for a drink, take your mind off Jack—'

'Not for me, silly!' I gasp, frowning. 'I meant for you.'

'Golly no, he's not my type.' She shakes her head dismissively and takes a glug of champagne.

'Why not? He's very handsome.'

'Exactly. Too handsome.'

I look at her blankly. 'Since when can a man be *too* handsome?'

'When he's your boyfriend,' she says simply. 'It would be like owning a Ferrari. Sooner or later you know someone's going to steal it.'

Harriet, I've learned, always has a new theory about dating, many of which I'm not too sure about.

'Xavier's a ten, maybe even an eleven,' she continues, 'whereas I'm a seven, maybe an eight in good lighting and Spanx.'

'Harriet, you're gorgeous,' I protest.

'No woman can ever be gorgeous with these monstrosities,' she counters, lifting up her feet and waggling them at me menacingly. 'Just look at them!'

I look at them. Admittedly they are rather large, but still.

'Who cares about the size of your feet?' I shrug.

'Men,' she replies matter-of-factly. 'Mummy always told me no man wants a wife who has bigger feet then they do and she's right.'

I feel a stirring of protectiveness. I won't say that I don't like Harriet's mum, as she's always been very nice and polite to me, but she's just not very nice to Harriet.

'Bollocks,' I retort, taking another swig of champagne. Personally, I think it's because Harriet's mum is jealous of the close bond between her husband and his oldest daughter. Either that, or she's just a mean, skinny witch.

'No, honestly, it's true,' continues Harriet. 'When we were little our nanny used to take me and my sisters up to London to get our feet measured on those machines at Clarks.'

'Oh, I used to love those things,' I cry, remembering my own childhood visits to our local store with my mum. 'They were so much fun.'

'For you and my sisters maybe, but not for me. I used to dread it. Every time I went my feet had just grown bigger and bigger and instead of getting pretty shoes like my sisters, I used to have to get these big ugly things. Anyway this one time my foot wouldn't even fit in the machine—' Shaking her head, she takes another bite of pizza. 'And it gets even worse. I so wanted to be like my sisters, I tried to wedge my foot inside it and ended up breaking the bloody machine.'

Poor Harriet. I can just imagine her as a little girl, with the same determined expression and a mop of curly hair.

'So what happened?'

'An engineer had to come out and remove my foot because it was trapped. All my sisters were laughing and I was trying so very hard not to cry.' She takes another, even bigger bite of pizza. 'And Mummy was furious because I didn't get any new shoes and had to wear my wellington boots to the summer ball. They were the only things that would fit.'

'Well, at least you were ahead of your time.' I smile. 'Wellingtons and dresses are all the rage now at Glastonbury.'

'Tell that to my mother. I still don't think she's ever forgiven me for spoiling the annual family photo.' She grins, and something tells me Harriet actually gets some enjoyment out of that fact.

'Anyway, Xavier fancies *you*,' she adds matter-of-factly.

'Me?' I feel a stab of surprise. And something that feels curiously like flattery. 'Don't be silly,' I protest, to myself as much as Harriet.

'I saw the way he looked at you.' She waggles the last slice of pizza at me.

'Rubbish.' I feel my cheeks flush. It's the champagne, I've drunk too much. 'He's French, he was just flirting,' I say firmly. 'And anyway, I'm not interested in Xavier or any man,' I add resolutely, 'I've got a boyfriend.' Taking another swig, I relish the sensation of bubbles bursting on my tongue. 'At least I had this morning,' I add as an afterthought, feeling the bubbles slowly dissipating.

'No word from Jack, then?'

I shake my head. 'He said we needed time out,' I confess, feeling a lump in my throat as I remember. 'That we needed some time to cool off and think about things.'

'Well maybe that's a good thing,' says Harriet brightly.

'Time apart in a relationship is very healthy. I read that in one of Mummy's magazines once.'

'You did?' I feel a beat of hope. 'What did the article say?'

'Well, it was more focused on the relationship between you and the household staff and how live-ins are becoming less popular . . . but a relationship is a relationship,' she finishes confidently.

I love Harriet, I really do, but sometimes I feel like we're from different planets.

'That's the thing, I'm not sure I still have a relationship.'

'Nonsense, a break is not a break-up.'

'Are we talking about butlers now or boyfriends?'

She reddens and takes a gulp of champagne. 'I'm sure this will all blow over. He's probably still on the plane to Colombia. I'm sure as soon as he lands he'll call you.'

'Yes.' I nod, but I'm unconvinced. Harriet wasn't witness to the humdinger of a row we had at the airport and the way it was left between us.

'So what work is he doing there that's so important, anyway?'

'I have no idea,' I shake my head. 'Architect things?'

'So all a bit of a mystery then,' she ponders, picking at the pizza crusts that she'd earlier discarded, 'like Madame Dumont's apartment.'

At the mention of the apartment I'm reminded of the stolen letters in my bag. I feel a secret flutter of excitement, followed by a rush of guilt. I need to tell Harriet about them. After all, it's technically stealing.

'Actually, I've got a confession—'

'Me too.' She cuts me off.

'You do?' I stare at her in surprise. Don't tell me she took something from Madame Dumont's apartment as well. I feel a beat of anticipation. Maybe it's something that will help shed light on the mystery.

'I winked at someone.'

'You did *what*?'

'I know, I know, it's terrible,' she groans, misinterpreting my confusion as disapproval.

'So, this isn't about Madame Dumont's apartment?' I feel a blow of disappointment.

She looks at me as if I'm bonkers. 'No, of course not silly,' she frowns and, reaching for her laptop, logs in to her dating site. Up pops a profile:

WineNot, 32, M
Women are like wine and get better with age

She angles the screen to me. 'So what do you think?'

I peer at the black and white headshot. It's like one of those professionally taken photos of actors. Or the pictures you see of dodgy haircuts in the windows of barber's shops. 'Is he an actor?' I plump for the first option considering his haircut is fairly decent.

Harriet frowns. 'No, he's a wine merchant,' she replies. '*WineNot*, get it?'

'Oh, right.' I nod, registering. Like I said, I'm not used to online dating. 'Clever play on words,' I add, somewhat unconvincingly.

'I know, isn't it?' enthuses Harriet.

It's immediately obvious Harriet really likes him and it's not my opinion she wants but my confirmation.

'He's from London but works here in Paris. We've got lots in common.' She smiles. 'Plus, more importantly it says he's six foot seven, which means he's bound to have bigger feet than me.'

'Are there any more photos?' I feel like such a hypocrite even asking as I've always held firmly to the belief that it's personality that counts and not what someone looks like.

And I still do in real life. Well, *within reason*. But that's before I knew about online dating and men with black and white headshots.

'Yes, lots,' she says excitedly and starts scrolling through. There's *WineNot* on a mountain bike, *WineNot* playing tennis, *WineNot* doing something goofy on a pair of skis . . .

'Are you sure he's not too sporty for you?' I muse doubtfully. Harriet's idea of getting her heart rate up is reading old Jilly Cooper novels.

'Oh, the pictures don't mean anything,' she says dismissively.

'They don't?' I frown, then gasp as she clicks on a picture of him jumping out of a plane. 'Wow, look, in this one he's skydiving!'

'Find me a man on this website who *doesn't* have a photo of himself skydiving,' she says dismissively.

'Really?' I had no idea there was so much to learn about online dating.

'Absolutely,' she nods. 'Just like every girl has a picture of themselves swimming with dolphins.'

'How do you know?'

'Well, I had to check out the competition, obviously.'

'Do *you* have a photograph of yourself swimming with dolphins?'

'No, but I've got this.' She clicks on her profile and up pops a photo of Harriet in an ancient Barbour raincoat with the family's beloved but even more ancient King Charles spaniel, Mr Piggywinkle.

There's a pause as we both study it. As much as I adore Mr Piggywinkle, it's not quite bikinis and dolphins.

'Oh golly, I'm not much competition, am I?' she says in a small voice.

'Dolphins *schmolphins*.' I pull a face.

She smiles gratefully. 'Maybe, but he hasn't winked back,' she says after a moment.

'Yet,' I add, but she's in a downward spiral of regret and too much champagne and is not to be reassured.

'I know I shouldn't have, but I'm desperate.'

'Don't say that!' I protest loyally.

'But I am, I've got the summer ball to go to!'

Abruptly I'm silenced. Oh god, the annual summer ball. I'd forgotten all about that. Harriet's parents live in this big stately home and every year they have this ball where they invite all their friends and relatives, not to mention practically all the village. And every year Harriet goes by herself and has to put up with a barrage of questions from all her elderly relatives about when she's going to meet a nice man and settle down.

'I can't go by myself again this year, I just can't' – she's started to wail – 'not after Imogen's news.'

Harriet has five sisters and one by one they've all gone off and got married, all except her youngest sister Imogen; something she took great comfort in. Until last week, when Imogen's Swiss banker boyfriend popped the question. Which of course is lovely and wonderful and Harriet is thrilled for her.

Just not for herself, as she's now officially the spinster sister.

'My little sister's getting married too.' I attempt a note of solidarity.

'But it's different for you, you'll be going with Jack.'

'Unless he stands me up again.'

Harriet pulls a face.

'Look, I get it. No one wants to be the single big sister at their little sister's wedding. When Amy met her fiancé in India I had, well let's just say, "my reservations" about him, then once I got to know him I was really happy for them. But if I'm honest, I was even more happy that I had Jack to take with me.'

'See!' wails Harriet.

'Yes, but a lot of that was because I was going to be the big sister who'd got cheated on a week before her own wedding,' I point out, thinking about my ex-fiancé Sam and then trying not to. 'At least you don't have that embarrassment.'

'No, I have a different kind. Did you know last year Great Aunt Mildred asked me if I batted for the other team?'

'What did you say?'

'I said yes.'

There's a pause and then—

'Do you?' I ask cautiously, as suddenly I see another reason entirely for the lack of boyfriends in Harriet's life. 'Not that it would affect our friendship at all,' I add hastily, but she lets out a snort.

'Of course not, silly,' she retorts, 'I just thought it would stop her asking why I don't have a boyfriend, let alone a husband, but instead she told Mummy. I had no idea until one day she invited me for tea at the Wolseley and started telling me all about an experience she had at her Swiss finishing school with another girl called Claudette . . .' Harriet trails off and gives a little shudder. 'I think she was trying to be nice for once, but it was so embarrassing.'

'Because I want you to know our friendship would stay the same,' I continue. 'I have a lot of gay friends—'

'Ruby, I'm not gay,' she says, glugging back the rest of her mug. 'I'm single, and I've been single for ever—' She breaks off and heaves a heavy sigh. 'It's all right for you, you were with Sam, and now you're with Jack.'

'Well, I'm not too sure—' I begin, but she cuts me off.

'But you've had love in your life Ruby, you've been in love. I never have. I've never been in love and no one has ever been in love with me. Oh, I've had silly crushes and stupid flings and too many dates to even talk about, but no one has ever told me they loved me. Not one man. Not ever.'

She swallows hard and looks at me and I see her eyes brimming with tears and I know in that moment this is the real reason why she needed me to come to Paris.

'Everyone thinks I took the job in Paris because it was a promotion and a better salary, but that wasn't the real reason. I wanted to find love and where else but the city of love?' She smiles, almost with embarrassment, then falls silent.

I wait patiently for her to continue.

'And so I gave myself a makeover,' she says after a few moments, 'and I did all the things you're supposed to do. I read all the articles, I signed up online, I went on another diet. And still it eludes me . . .' She shakes her head and chews her lip, fighting back the tears that are threatening to fall.

'You'll find love Harriet, you will,' I say, reaching out and rubbing her upper arm. Hearing her say all this breaks my heart. If anyone deserves love, it's Harriet. 'I'm no expert, far from it, but I do know it never quite looks like you expect it to. Like how you've imagined. It comes along when you least expect it, and in the strangest of places. You've just got to be open to it—'

'But I am open,' she protests, 'I'm open to all of it, even the heartbreak that comes with it, because at least then you've felt love, you've experienced it . . .'

I think about Jack, about everything I've felt since the airport, and she's right. Better all of that, and whatever is yet to come, than we'd never met and none of this had happened.

'It'll happen,' I say softly, 'I promise.'

Harriet gives a little smile, but it doesn't reach her eyes. 'I think I might go to bed, it's late,' she says, putting down her mug.

'Good idea, it's been a long day.' I nod.

'Do you want me to help you make up the sofa bed?'

'No, it's fine, I can do it.'

'OK.' She gets up and stacks up the pizza boxes, then turns to me. 'Oh, I nearly forgot, so what was yours?'

'Sorry?'

'You said you had a confession.' She looks at me expectantly.

I suddenly remember the love letters. But the moment of confession has gone now. 'Oh, um . . . it was nothing,' I say, shaking my head dismissively.

'OK, well goodnight, sleep well – and thanks for listening, Ruby.'

'Any time.' I smile. 'Night Hattie.'

'Night.' And, giving a little wave, she pads a little tipsily into her bedroom.

10

It's not stealing, it's *borrowing*.

Ten minutes later and I'm tucked up on the sofa bed with Heathcliff snuggled up at my feet. OK, so it's not a four-poster, but it's not as bad as I thought. It's actually quite comfortable. Well, -ish.

Though to be honest, I'm not really thinking about my comfort levels right now, I muse, feeling a flutter of excitement as I reach for my bag and pull out the bundle of letters. Then pause. Next door I can hear Harriet's bed creaking. I wait and listen, careful not to make a noise. Until after a few moments it's followed by the sound of faint snoring.

The flat is in darkness, apart from the glow from the small table lamp, and I angle the letters to the light. Seeing the faded address once again I feel a prickle of anticipation. I'm going to put them back, I promise. Apart from that one note I read this morning, they're most likely to be all written in French anyway, so it's not as if I'll be able to understand them, apart from the odd word. Google Translate has its limits too.

But even as I'm thinking that, a part of me can't help knowing I will be able to make out what they say. That I have found these letters for a reason and that somehow they are going to unravel the mystery of the apartment. What was the secret that Emmanuelle had to tell H? Did she see him again to tell him? Why had they rowed? And, more importantly, who *was* H?

Something tells me that in order to find out I need to go back to the beginning. Right back to where this story first began.

Carefully untying the pink ribbon, I glance through the envelopes, noticing the postmarks. They were all written over a period of roughly six months, between late September 1939 and the beginning of April 1940, and are neatly arranged in date order, the earliest at the top. Picking up the first letter, I turn it over. As I expected it's already been opened, neatly, as if with a letter opener, most likely the same letter opener I had seen on Madame Dumont's dressing table. I take out its contents.

It's a folded slip of paper, the same pale blue colour as the envelope. I open it.

> *Dearest Emmanuelle,*
>   *Forgive me for writing without asking you to allow it, and in my mother tongue, but I feel I have no choice in the matter. For after our chance meeting outside Café de Flore, the image of your tumbling red hair and pale blue eyes has been imprinted on my mind, and I cannot stop thinking about you.*

Just a few lines, written over seventy years ago, but the emotion hits me right off the bat. I pause, feeling both elated that it's written in English and also an uncertainty. This is undoubtedly a love letter. I shouldn't be reading this. Even though Madame Dumont's died it somehow feels wrong, as if I'm intruding.

Yet it also feels as if I'm bringing her back to life again. And not as an old lady of ninety-five, whose belongings are to be broken up and auctioned off to the highest bidder, but as a beautiful, vibrant young woman with her whole life ahead of her.

My eyes sweep again over the author's handwriting. Curly and slightly messy, it rushes across the page as if unable to stop itself. I can feel the immediacy of the emotion; even now, after being hidden for all these years, it's still there in his words.

I read on.

Was it fate that caused our lives to collide? The universe that conspired to bring us together? Or was it just an accident and I am simply a lucky fellow? The romantic and the realist will forever disagree and I confess I am both. Yet, it matters not. All I know is that our meeting on that warm evening two days ago has brought a smile to my lips more times than I can count.

When I walked you home you asked me about my life, and I told you I was just a boy from Brooklyn, here in Paris as a writer eager to learn my craft, following in the footsteps of some of the greatest writers who have ever lived. All of this is true but what I failed to tell you is that words have eluded me of late. Nothing can be worse for a writer than to stare at a blank page, to be devoid of inspiration.

But now everything has changed. After meeting you it seems that my thoughts and ideas have come rushing back, eager to jump on the blank pages I have been for so long waiting to fill. Thank you Emmanuelle, for it is you, and you alone, who has inspired me.

I will keep this letter short, but before I go, may I ask you one more thing? I know this may seem forward but I would very much like to spend more time with you. If we are to believe these terrible rumors of war, time is a luxury we may not have and I do not want to waste a precious moment of it. That evening we walked together we talked of many things, but one was our shared love of jazz. I have tickets to see Django Reinhardt and his quintet this weekend and I would be nothing less than a fool if I did not ask you to accompany me.

I anxiously await your response.

Henry

Henry must be H, the intended recipient of the note that Emmanuelle wrote but never sent. This must be how they first met.

I finish reading, but the words on the page are now in my head, catching hold of my imagination and creating a whole new world. A world that is Paris in 1939, before war had broken out, a city enjoying the warm evenings of late summer. I can see the lively pavement cafés filled with patrons enjoying their carafes of wine and aperitifs, hear the laughter and the chatter and the distant sounds of jazz, smell the scent of cigarettes and perfume . . .

Gazing at the letter in my hand, I'm distracted by prisms of light dancing among the words, as if the faded notepaper has come alive, and looking up I glimpse the Eiffel Tower out of the window. From the angle at which I'm lying, I can see it sparkling in the darkness, illuminating the sky like a million shooting stars.

Mesmerised, I watch as it glitters and shimmers, my eyes growing heavy, my mind drifting. What happened between now and then? What story do these two people have to tell? Madame Dumont kept these letters for nearly three-quarters of a century, hidden away in a secret apartment in Paris for safe keeping. What secrets do they hold?

There are so many unanswered questions, so much more I want to know, but tiredness has finally caught up with me. With the letter still in my hand, and the bundle of letters still to read, I close my eyes. And, dreaming of Emmanuelle and Henry, I abandon myself to sleep.

II

The next morning I'm woken by bright sunshine pouring in through the arched windows. For a moment I lie there, still half-asleep, listening to the faint billing and cooing of pigeons and wondering where I am, until suddenly it registers. I'm on Harriet's sofa bed. In Paris. Without Jack.

I groan loudly and roll over, burying my face in my pillow and inadvertently squashing Heathcliff, who I'd forgotten was there.

He lets out a muffled yelp and furiously attempts to wriggle away, but he's stuck fast beneath me.

'Oops, sorry buddy!' I gasp, blinking my eyes open and quickly moving.

Freed, he looks down his long nose at me; then, turning his back on me, he shuffles grumpily to the end of the bed and curls up there.

Great. Now even my dog is mad at me.

Still, new day and all that, and climbing out of the sofa bed I walk over to the windows. Unfastening the old iron latch on one, I push it open.

Instantly the city comes rushing in. The sounds of traffic in the streets below, the rumblings of tyres across cobbles, car horns, a bicycle bell, a man's voice shouting something in French, a peal of girlish laughter, a startled flock of pigeons taking flight, the smells of freshly baked croissants, strong coffee, Gauloises . . .

Taking it all in, I close my eyes, lifting my face to the warmth of the early morning sunshine. Wow, I'm in Paris.

'You're awake!'

I twirl round to see Harriet in the doorway of her bedroom. Gone is the chic French woman in her classic navy blue and black ensemble, hair blow-dried, make-up perfectly applied; in her place is the old Harriet in mismatched stripy pyjamas, frizzy hair all over the place, sporting freckles and rosy cheeks.

I feel a rush of affection for my old friend.

Finishing cleaning the lenses of her glasses on the sleeve of her pyjama top, she shoves them up her nose and beams at me, as if seeing me for the first time.

'How was the sofa bed? Did you sleep OK?'

'Great, super comfy,' I fib, my back twinging. I take it back about the four-poster.

'Oh jolly good, that's what everyone says,' she says, looking pleased and padding into the tiny kitchenette.

And now I don't feel bad about fibbing, as obviously everyone else fibs too.

'Shall we have coffee?' She waves a silver espresso pot at me from over the small partition.

'Ooh, yes please.' I nod, thinking of my own coffee pot back home on my stove in London. I can't start the day without my morning cup of coffee. Hearing the pot bubbling on the hob has to be one of my all-time favourite sounds, and the aroma has to be one of the best in the world. In fact I've always thought someone should create a perfume, Eau d'Espresso. I mean, seriously, is there anything more delicious than inhaling strong, dark-roasted freshly brewed coffee?

'Bollocks.' There's lots of banging around coming from the kitchenette and Harriet reappears, her face flushed and frowning. 'I'm out of milk.'

Disappointment flickers but is quickly shoved to one side. 'No worries, I can drink it black.'

There's more crashing of cupboard doors. 'Buggery bollocks. I'm also out of coffee,' she tuts. 'Honestly I really am the most shocking host.' Seeing my doleful expression, she adds brightly, 'but not to worry, we can go to this fabulous little café on the corner, it does the most delicious café crème and croissants – not that I'd know about the croissants,' she adds hastily, 'I'm on a diet.'

'A pizza diet,' I tease, revealing a crust underneath the sofa bed as I fold it away.

She blushes bright red. 'A momentary lapse,' she says, then frowns. 'What's that?'

'What?' I look up from folding up the blanket and follow her gaze, to see that one of the letters has slipped out from beneath the covers and is lying on the floor. Right by her bare feet.

'It looks like a letter.'

My heart almost stops as she steps forward to pick it up, but luckily my reflexes are faster and I sweep in and scoop it up before she's had a chance.

'Oh, it's just a credit card bill,' I fluster, 'I brought it with me to pay otherwise I'd forget to do it.' I stuff it quickly back in my bag and zip it up tightly. 'So, c'mon, let me treat you to a coffee.'

'Super.' She beams. 'I just need to jump in the shower and throw on some clothes.' She disappears into the bathroom. 'I'll be ready in two ticks.'

Two ticks turns out to be nearly an hour of blow-drying, make-up applying and more outfit changes than you'd see backstage at a catwalk show. Finally she appears in a navy shift dress with tasteful accessories.

'Ready?' she says brightly, as if I've been the one barricaded in the bathroom all this time.

'As I'll ever be,' I nod, glancing at my mismatched, crumpled figure in the mirror and wishing I hadn't. Packing in a hurry isn't ideal when you're heading to the style capital of the world. Absolutely nothing I've brought goes with anything else, everything is creased beyond all hope of an iron, plus now I'm here all my clothes look a bit . . .

For once in my life I'm lost for words. In my defence I'm a writer. I know about words, not clothes. About dialogue and plot twists, not hemlines and accessories.

Though somehow I don't think that excuse is going to cut the mustard here. No one's going to mistake me for being Parisian, that's for sure.

I clip Heathcliff on to his lead and we all leave the apartment, which involves shuffling out in single file on to the narrow, dimly lit landing. It seems even smaller than yesterday and, after the brightness of the apartment, even darker. Suddenly the door opposite swings open and someone bumps into me in the shadows.

'*Mon Dieu!*' gasps a voice, followed by a loud shriek, and I hear Heathcliff yelp as he gets trodden on.

'Oh, I'm sorry,' I apologise, as the English are wont to do even when it's not their fault, quickly scooping Heathcliff up before he's trampled.

I hear a flurry of French between Harriet and this person I can't see, as my eyes are taking a moment to adjust, but who I can hear is female.

'Celeste, this is my friend Ruby,' says Harriet, switching into English. 'Ruby, this is Celeste, my neighbour.'

As she's introduced the dimness seems to dissipate and I make out an achingly stylish blonde, her skinny figure dressed all in black, but for a perfectly tied patterned scarf round her neck.

She turns to me and I brace myself for a cool response, but instead she flashes me the widest smile. 'Hi, I'm so sorry, you scared the shit out of me,' she laughs, kissing me on both cheeks, then switches her attention to Heathcliff, who she strokes on the head. 'I thought it was, how you say, a big mouse!'

She laughs again, a hearty barrel of a laugh that should belong to a man twice her size, and despite her calling Heathcliff a rodent, it's impossible not to instantly like her.

'Celeste owns a boutique,' continues Harriet, as we all start making our way down the narrow staircase, 'she's my personal stylist. I owe everything to her.'

'*Non*, this is not true,' she demurs, expertly descending the wooden treads on towering needle-thin stilettos, 'I just gave you a little help, told you a few secrets.' She taps the side of her nose. 'Every woman needs a few secrets.'

Finally reaching the bottom of the stairs, we walk outside into the courtyard. In the daylight Celeste looks even more stylish than before. With long blond hair, a perfect complexion and the kind of reed-thin body seen on store mannequins, she looks like she's just stepped out from the pages of *Vogue*.

Immediately she reaches into her quilted Chanel purse, which is slung messenger-style across her tailored jacket, in the kind of effortless way that people like me can't hope to achieve even after about half an hour faffing about in front of the mirror, and pulls out a packet of cigarettes. She lights up and blows out a chimney of smoke from her nostrils. As she does, years of 'smoking causes cancer' propaganda goes flying out of the window. She even makes that look elegant.

'What are the secrets?' I ask curiously, as we cross the courtyard to the main entrance. If I felt crumpled and mismatched before, now add lumpen-like-a-sack-of-potatoes to the mix.

Celeste's exquisite face creases up into a mischievous smile and she puts her finger over her mouth, 'Shhhh,' she whispers conspiratorially and as we step out into the street, I look around to see who could be listening. All I can see is a rather large man in a string vest unloading crates of bottles from a van.

Slipping a card out of her purse, she passes it to me. 'Come visit anytime and I will share them with you.' She winks.

Then, calling '*au revoir*' to '*Arriet*, she tosses her blonde mane of hair over her shoulder and sashays down the street.

I stare after her, in a sort of dazed wonder.

'Amazing, isn't she?' sighs Harriet wistfully, at my elbow. 'And so tiny.'

'She probably doesn't eat,' I reflect, 'just smokes cigarettes.'

'And drinks coffee,' adds Harriet, 'it's the diet most Parisian women are on.'

'Speaking of which . . .' I remind her.

'I'm afraid I don't have any.' She sighs. 'Daddy always called it a filthy habit so I never took up the habit, though perhaps I should—'

'I'm not talking about cigarettes,' I gasp, 'I'm talking about coffee!'

'Oh golly, my brain is like a sieve!' She bangs on the side of her head and shakes it a bit, 'yes of course, the café. It's right here on the corner.'

She motions towards the red awning at the end of the street, from underneath which tables and chairs are spilling out on to the pavement. Even this early, every single one is already taken with people basking in the sunshine as they sip cafés crèmes and eat croissants. 'Don't worry, Luc will find us a spot,' she reassures me as we walk the short distance to the entrance.

'Who's Luc?' I ask, but my voice is drowned out as I push open the door.

Inside it's a hive of activity. A zinc-covered counter filled with pastries greets us, along with the smell of freshly roasted coffee and the cacophony of spoons clattering against cups, milk frothing and people chattering. It's a small café, squeezed full of paper-covered tables, around which is expertly weaving a young, shaven-headed waiter, his sleeves rolled up to reveal tattooed arms on which he's balancing several cups and saucers.

As soon as he sees Harriet, his face lights up.

So this is Luc.

'*Bonjour*,' he says with a grin, proceeding to give her a hands-free kiss on both cheeks, before saying something in French and hurrying away. Only to return a few moments later minus the plates but with a small metal table, held aloft over his head. He wedges it into the tiniest space I've ever seen, then conjures up a couple of chairs like a magician.

'I'm Luc,' he grins boyishly, as he pulls out my chair for me to sit down and I hook Heathcliff's lead under its leg.

'Ruby.' I smile, completely charmed as he kisses me on both cheeks and then pulls out Harriet's chair too before deftly setting up our table with condiments, sugar and a small jam jar of wild daisies.

'Café crème?'

'Mmm, yes please,' says Harriet.

'And the same for me.' I nod.

'OK, cool.' He winks and, sliding his lean hips between the tables, he disappears back into the throng.

'I think someone likes you,' I whisper, turning back to Harriet.

She laughs good-naturedly. 'We're just good friends. I've been helping him with his English.'

'I think he wants to be more than just friends,' I say, smiling as I catch him staring across at Harriet from behind the espresso machine and he looks away, blushing.

'Don't be so ridiculous, I'm old enough to be his mother.'

'Now you're the one being ridiculous,' I reply.

'Not at all.' She shakes her head. 'If you do the maths, Luc is twenty-one, I'm thirty-two, and I was eleven when Granny Scarlet first paid a visit.'

'Granny Scarlet?'

She colours. 'That's what our matron at boarding school used to call your period. She said to tell boys that to keep them away, as no boys want to be around when their granny's visiting.'

Sometimes I wonder about Harriet and her public school education.

'Well I suppose biologically speaking I could have given birth to half of One Direction,' I concede, suddenly feeling rather old, 'but so what if there's an age difference? He's lovely—'

I break off as Luc reappears with two coffees.

'I also have croissants,' he announces, putting down a plate of delicious-looking pastries in front of us, 'your favourite.'

Harriet looks suddenly guilty and averts her gaze from mine. 'Thanks, that's so sweet of you, but I'm watching my figure.'

'Ah, nonsense!' he protests, frowning.

Harriet reddens. 'Well, that's a little rude . . .'

Now it's Luc's turn to redden. 'Rude?' he repeats, looking confused.

'Just because I have the occasional blip,' she says, offended.

'I don't understand this "*blip*,"' he says with a frown, 'but what I am saying is why does every woman want to look like a skinny boy?' and I realise he wasn't talking about her diet at all, but about society and the pressure that makes women want to diet. 'A woman should look like a woman!'

'I'll eat them, they look delicious,' I interrupt, trying to put him at ease, but the flush from his cheeks has crept all over his shaven head.

There's a pause as he looks at Harriet, but she doesn't meet his gaze.

'Well, I must go, there are lots of thirsty people. Enjoy your coffee,' he says and, casting a lingering glance at Harriet, he disappears.

We both reach for our coffees, which is when I notice the one he's given Harriet has a loveheart shaped into the foam.

I raise my eyebrows in a see-I-told-you-so way and she takes a spoon and stirs her coffee firmly.

'Guess what? WineNot emailed me this morning asking for my number,' she says.

I'm completely sold on Luc, but I try to be enthusiastic. Harriet likes WineNot and after our conversation last night, I know how much this means to her. 'That's great, did you give it to him?'

'Of course.' She beams. 'And he's already texted.'

'Texted? But I thought if you asked someone for their number it meant you were going to call them?'

Harriet rolls her eyes as if to say 'get with the programme, Ruby'.

'So, what he did say?' I ignore my reservations.

Digging her smartphone out of her bag, she passes it across the table like contraband goods. I look at the screen in anticipation.

'Want 2 meet 4 a drink?' I read out.

That's it? Six words? Actually, it's only four – two of them are numericals.

My mind flashes back to the love letter Henry wrote to Emmanuelle, asking if she'd accompany him to a dance. Handwritten on beautiful stationery and scented with his cologne; he'd gone to such an effort. The way he expressed his feelings was so beautiful and sweet and romantic. Just imagine getting a letter like that through the post, being able to read it over and over—

I glance back at the text. *Call this progress?*

'So what do you think?' Harriet looks at me expectantly, as if waiting for me to analyse this and decipher some hidden code.

'Have you replied?'

'Not yet, I wasn't sure what to put.'

'Yes?' I suggest simply.

'I thought you were the writer,' she grumbles.

'OK, well how about yes, that would be great,' I concede.

'I can't put that!' she gasps.

'Why not?'

'I need to be more strategic.' Tearing off a piece of croissant, she chews thoughtfully.

'This isn't a game of chess,' I remind her.

'No, but dating is still a game.'

'But you haven't dated him yet.'

'And I won't get to if I just put yes straight away,' she argues.

I fall silent. I want to be supportive, I know how much Harriet wants to find love, but I can't help thinking this isn't the way. But then, what do I know? I'm hardly an advert for success in love.

'What about you,' she asks, obviously unimpressed with my advice and changing the subject, 'did you hear from him?'

She doesn't mention Jack by name but there's only one person she could be referring to.

'No.' I shake my head, a leaden feeling descending on my chest as I'm reminded. It's been less than twenty-four hours since we spoke – correction, *rowed* – at the airport, but it already feels a lot longer. 'But anyway, I came to Paris to see you, not to talk about Jack.'

'Don't be silly, we're friends, we're here for each other.'

I smile gratefully and she gestures towards the plate of pastries but suddenly I'm not hungry.

'He might still be on the plane,' she suggests.

'Thanks, but I think that excuse is wearing a bit thin, don't you? It doesn't take that long to fly to Colombia. He obviously doesn't want to speak to me.'

She frowns, as if deep in thought, then her face lights up. 'I know! What if he's arrived and been kidnapped by drug lords? I've heard Colombia's super dangerous.'

'Is that supposed to make me feel better?'

'Well at least that way there would be a good reason he couldn't get in touch.'

I love Harriet, but sometimes her logic gets a little skewed.

'I'd rather he was mad at me than being chopped up into little bits and sent back to me as a ransom.'

'If anyone should be mad, it's you. Standing you up at the airport like that! I'd be so mad I'd want to kill him,' she gasps loyally, tearing off another piece of croissant as if she's tearing off one of his limbs.

'To be honest, I want to forget about it,' I say firmly, 'at least while I'm here in Paris.'

'Hear hear,' cheers Harriet, approvingly. 'That's the spirit.'

'So I've decided, I'm going to buy a guidebook and do some sightseeing. I really want to go to the Louvre, I haven't been since I was a teenager.'

'Ooh, sounds lovely.' She nods. 'I've been six times and I've barely scraped the surface. You know someone once told me that if you looked at every artwork for one minute it would take you almost four years to see everything.'

'Well, why don't you join me? We can go for lunch somewhere fancy, my treat. I might as well make the most of it while my credit card is still working,' I joke, even though I'm not really joking.

'Oh I wish,' she says wistfully, 'but I've got a bit of a mental day. I've got to finish off cataloguing the apartment we went to yesterday.'

At the mention of Madame Dumont's apartment, I feel myself stiffen and I reach under my chair to check on my bag, where I've hidden the bundle of letters. 'Oh yes, I suppose it's going to be hectic trying to prepare for the auction this weekend,' I say, trying to sound casual.

'Yes, and they could easily go to another auction house if we said no.' Harriet pulls a face. 'It's complete madness. Fortunately my company's one of the oldest in Paris so they have the connections and experience to make it happen, but still. Quite what is the rush, I don't know, but then the whole thing's a bit of a mystery isn't it?' She checks her watch. 'Anyway, orders are orders – I'd better hurry, I'm meeting my boss there.'

'Everything is OK?' Luc reappears by our table.

'Yes, great, thanks,' we both chorus.

'Excellent.' A large smile splits across his face. 'The croissants were good, no?'

I look down to see that the plate is completely empty apart from a few golden, buttery crumbs. Harriet colours. 'Goodness me, how did that happen?' she says, in an attempt at sounding shocked.

'Ah these croissants, they are always disappearing.' As he scratches his fuzzy head as if trying to figure out where they could have gone, Luc's eyes twinkle with amusement. 'It is, how you say, a puzzle.'

Harriet's face reddens a shade deeper and she busies herself by pulling out her purse and a euro bill.

'Ah no, it's on me,' he insists, pushing away her money.

'*Merci beaucoup*,' I smile, trying out my rusty French as we stand up to leave. My accent is horrible, but he smiles graciously.

'That's so very kind of you. OK, well better dash!' Quickly kissing Luc goodbye, Harriet hurriedly leads the way outside where she hands me a spare set of keys for her flat. 'Any problems, just call me,' she says, throwing her arms round me in a hug.

At the prospect of being alone for the first time in a strange city, I feel my resolve waver. 'I'll be fine, don't worry,' I reassure her as she sets off wobbling down the street.

But my face must have betrayed me as after a moment she turns and calls after me, 'Just remember what Audrey Hepburn said.'

'Why, what did she say?'

She shoots me a grin. 'Paris is always a good idea!'

12

OK, well if Audrey Hepburn said that it has to be true, doesn't it?

I mean, she breakfasted at Tiffany's, she can't be wrong.

Standing alone on the pavement, I take a deep breath and look around me. A whole day in Paris stretches ahead of me, filled with infinite possibilities. I can go anywhere or do anything I want. I don't have to ask or answer to anyone. No one even knows I'm here, I suddenly realise.

As the thought strikes, whatever doubts I might have had are replaced by an unexpected sense of liberation. Despite the circumstances that brought me here, I can't help but feel a tingle of adventure.

Plus absolutely no clue whereabouts I am.

Probably a bit silly not to have asked Harriet for a few directions, I realise, but she's already disappeared now, and I don't want to turn on data roaming on my iPhone to use Google Maps. Only last week I read another one of those newspaper articles about how someone went to Spain for a week and ran up a bill into the thousands using Facebook. 'SOME BARGAIN BREAK!' ran the headlines. According to her status update the poor woman was distraught.

So with Heathcliff trotting along beside me on his lead, I set off in no particular direction. It's not long, however, before I find a small souvenir stall selling guidebooks in all different languages. I buy one. Then, feeling like a complete tourist, I spend a good twenty minutes sitting on a bench trying to make sense of the pull-out map.

It's not easy. Round and round I turn it, making the big, fat, blue line that is the river Seine horizontal, vertical and every which way, trying to work out which way is the Louvre. Finally I give up in frustration. I'm hopeless at maps. Wrong Way Ruby was always my nickname at school and while some things have changed about my schooldays (I no longer have a perm and a crush on Mr Hodgkins, my English teacher), my sense of direction is still much the same.

I briefly think about asking someone, but several stylishly put-together women glide by and I'm too embarrassed by both my outfit and my pidgin French to try.

God, if only Jack was here, he's great at directions . . .

I catch the thought as it appears, like a cartoon bubble above my head, and firmly pop it. I'm not going to think about Jack, remember? I'm having a Jack-free day. In fact, this will be the first day in months I haven't thought about him, which isn't a bad thing. After all, it's not good to think about your boyfriend all the time. *Even if he does have the kind of smile that makes your legs turn to jelly . . .*

Damn, there I go again.

Folding up my map, I put the guidebook firmly in my pocket. I have no idea which way to head, but surely no way is the wrong way in Paris, I decide, as I set off walking. Everywhere I look is so incredibly beautiful. Just the way the sunshine streams across the elegant facades of buildings, a cobbled side street beckons invitingly or an ancient brass door knocker has been rubbed golden from all those callers over the years. Simple, everyday things are transformed into something special, making you want to whip out your camera and try to capture the magic.

Turning a corner in Paris, I soon realise, is like unwrapping a gift. Round each one is something new to be discovered and I breathe it all in. There might only be a tunnel separating us, but Paris feels a million miles away from London. Wrapped up in a language that sounds so wonderful that I keep catching myself eavesdropping on conversations, even though I have no clue what's being said, I see something gorgeous everywhere I look.

Correction: gawp. I'm not kidding. I spend half the time pinned to the spot staring at things with my mouth wide open.

No wonder this city has inspired so many love stories, I reflect, as I weave my way through cobbled backstreets and onto wide boulevards. Paris is just so seductive. Even the harshest cynic couldn't fail to be charmed by the romance coming out of every cobble, every hidden courtyard, every snippet of French and whiff of a Gauloise cigarette.

Accordion music drifts towards me and I pass a café and a musician serenading tables of nuzzling couples. I walk on, crossing a small square lit by dappled sunlight, where there's a man selling roses. Towards an exquisite marble fountain and carousels of postcards, filled with Robert Doisneau's famous black and white photograph taken outside the Hôtel de Ville of two lovers kissing.

Right, OK, that's enough.

Seriously, I know it's gorgeous and all that, but could there *be* a worse place to visit when you've had a row with your boyfriend?

Catching sight of yet another couple strolling hand in hand, I stuff my hands firmly in my pockets. Paris is for lovers. It's not for single girls who've been stood up at the airport, let down on their birthday and are on a timeout from their relationship. My shoulders slump and I feel my earlier resolve weaken. What was I doing, thinking I could come here and forget all about what's happened? I should have stayed home and eaten my own bodyweight in chocolate or drunk too much wine or read all his old emails, like normal people do. Or better still, all three.

But you didn't, did you? You came because Harriet needed you, a voice reminds me firmly. Because one of your closest friends has been having a hard time too and your first impulse was to be there for her, just like she's been there for you. And because relationships may come and go, but true friendships last a lifetime.

Plus, look on the bright side, I tell myself. At least this way I don't have a hangover and my jeans still fit.

After walking for a while, I turn a corner and stumble across the Luxembourg Gardens. I walk towards the fountain, the gravel making a satisfying sound beneath my sandals, and rest for a few moments in one of the green metal chairs. According to my guidebook, this is where the lovers Marius and Cosette meet for the first time in Victor Hugo's *Les Miserables*.

I look up from the pages and take in my surroundings. Bursting with lawns, fountains and an ornamental pond where children play with toy sailboats, it's an oasis dropped in the middle of Paris. Slightly different to the circumstances in which I met Jack, I reflect, thinking about the row we had on that train in India the first time we laid eyes on each other. How he kicked me out of my berth and I thought he was a rude, smug, annoying idiot – but in fact he turned out to be the kindest, funniest man I've ever met.

Right, OK, well enough about all that. Good or bad thoughts, it doesn't matter. Today's going to be a Jack-free zone, remember? Closing my book, I stand up and urge Heathcliff to his feet. So, moving on . . .

Eventually I reach the river and make my way towards one of the bridges. It's super busy. From a distance I can see the railings of the bridge shimmering in the sunlight and crowds of people congregating. I know Paris is busy at this time of year, but even so, it's almost gridlocked with people.

I start trying to make my way through them, excusing myself in my terrible French. What is everyone doing? And then, as I get closer, I suddenly realise. The bridge is covered in millions of padlocks.

Behind me I overhear a tour guide explaining to a group of tourists, 'There are two bridges in Paris with these love locks. A couple writes both their names on a padlock and locks it on to one of the bridges. They then throw the key into the Seine as a symbol of their undying love. But you must be very careful which bridge you put your lock on because Pont des Arts is for your committed love, while Pont de l'Archevêché is for your lover.'

Love locks.

I turn to look at them, in all their different shapes and sizes and colours. Some are carefully initialled, some engraved, some scrawled. Every tiny space is covered – surely there can't be any more room? – and yet couples are still locking them to the bridge, finding even the tiniest gap.

Because that's the power of love, I reflect, watching a couple carefully locking theirs on. It might be a silly superstition, a tourist trap, that's actually damaging the bridge with all the weight from the locks and just lining the street vendors' pockets.

But it doesn't matter. It symbolises everlasting love and from time immemorial people have proved that they will do anything for that. Be it a great act or a small one, like locking a padlock on to a bridge. Because love is such an incredible thing, once you find it you never, ever want to let it go.

And *bam*, it hits me.

All day long I've been trying not to think about Jack. To push any thoughts of him aside and play the tourist. But now they all come rushing back in with the force of a tidal wave: the way the corners of his hazel eyes crinkle up when he smiles; him dancing around my living room in just his boxer shorts, doing a stupid chicken dance to my Avril Lavigne album; insisting on buying giant ice creams when it's pouring down with rain and saying how much better they taste when you're wet. I miss everything about him; the yearning is almost palpable.

God, this is crazy. I can't forget about him, and I don't *want* to forget about him.

Impulsively, I dig out my phone and dial Jack's number. My heart racing, I wait for it to connect.

It starts ringing and I hold my breath. I feel absurdly nervous.

'Hey, this is Jack—'

It's his voicemail. I let out my breath, struck by crushing disappointment. I really want to speak to him. I *need* to speak to him. I listen to his recorded voice, the familiarity of it triggering all my old feelings.

'Hi Jack, it's me. Look, about yesterday – I'm sorry about the row. I didn't want us to argue. I didn't mean all those things I said – well I did at the time, but it was just that I was so looking forward to seeing you and when you didn't arrive it was all such a shock . . . and, well, I was so disappointed and upset as we'd made all these plans and it was my birthday, and then when you said you were going to Colombia . . .'

It all comes out in a big rush, my words falling over each other as I try to explain, to make things right. 'But anyway, it doesn't matter now, because you're not here, you're there and, well, I know we're supposed to be on a timeout, but I'm English, and I don't really know what a timeout is or how long it lasts . . .' I pause, feeling suddenly choked, then, swallowing hard, whisper into my phone: 'I love you Jack, will you please call me back?'

And as I say those words, my mind flicks back to the first time he told me he was in love with me, on that rooftop in Udaipur, as the night sky lit up with a thousand fireworks bursting over our heads. And how when he pulled me towards him and wrapped his arms round me, I never, ever wanted him to let me go.

BEEP.

I snap back. I've been cut off. That was the end of the voicemail. I must have run out of space.

'*Cadenas?*'

I turn to see a vendor holding up a large cardboard display of locks. '*Cadenas,*' he repeats, waving them at me. I hang up. It's only then I realise I forgot to tell Jack I'm in Paris.

I shake my head. '*Non merci.*'

He looks at me, then shrugs and walks by. Tears prickle, and quickly brushing them away, I look out across the Seine.

I'm not so sure Audrey Hepburn got it right after all.

13

The Louvre is on the other side of the river, just a short walk across the bridge, and as I walk through the grand archway I feel my spirits lift slightly. Even if my love life feels like it's lying in tatters, I can't fail to be wowed by this former grand palace. Standing in the courtyard, I tilt my head back and look all around me at its elegant architecture juxtaposed against the modern glass pyramid, which rises up from the centre. It really is the most incredible building. Even more incredible is the collection of art inside.

Or so my guidebook says. Not that I know much about art. Probably like most tourists, I just know this is the home of Leonardo da Vinci's *Mona Lisa*. Still, it will take my mind off things. After all, you can't be in Paris and not go to the Louvre.

Correction: *Apparently you can.*

After patiently standing in line for forever, I finally enter the glass pyramid and glide down the escalator to the ticket hall beneath, only to be told by the woman at the ticket desk that there's a problem. They don't allow dogs. Not even cute sausage ones called Heathcliff. So I have no choice but to turn right round and glide back up again.

Oh well, I've never really understood what the big fuss was about the *Mona Lisa* anyway. I mean, why is she so famous? It's not like she's particularly attractive, or anyone special. But then I suppose you could say the same about most so-called famous people these days. Maybe if the cast of

TOWIE was around in Leonardo da Vinci's day, there'd be portraits of them hanging in the Louvre too.

Back outside, I sit down on the edge of the fountain and dig out my guidebook. OK, now what? I flick through some more museums, but they all seem to operate a no-pet policy. I suppose I could always go for a walk; the Tuileries Garden looks pretty impressive, I muse, glancing out across it stretching far into the distance with its manicured lawns and classical statues. It will make a bit of a change from our usual once round the local park back home.

'OK, come on buddy.' I motion to Heathcliff, who's flaked out in the shade. 'We're going for a walk.' Zero enthusiasm. Not even a wag of his tail. Though to be honest, I don't blame him. I'm a little tired myself as we've been walking all morning. Plus, to be honest, after the incident on the bridge, I've lost my enthusiasm.

I'm also a bit hungry.

No sooner has the thought popped into my head than I notice people eating and drinking at tables underneath the arcades of the Louvre. I watch for a moment as suited waiters flit back and forth serving things on trays that, even at this distance, I know will be delicious.

My stomach growls. I didn't have any breakfast. I glance at my watch. And it's nearly lunchtime. I hesitate. I'm sure it's really expensive though, not to mention completely booked up, and they probably won't allow dogs either. Plus I'm really broke and should just buy a sandwich somewhere.

I stand up. Yes, that's a lot more sensible. That's exactly what I should do.

'Would you like me to show you to your table?'

Standing at the entrance of the restaurant, I'm beckoned by a tall, impeccably dressed maitre d' who looks like a supermodel. Slipping a menu under her arm, she motions for me to follow her.

'Thanks.' I beam, and hurry after her as she glides through the long sweep of the café's stylish outdoor terrace, with its stone arched ceilings and sumptuous decor.

Well, being sensible is just so boring isn't it? My whole life I've been sensible, and trust me, it's completely overrated. The few times I've done impulsive things, like jump on a plane to India or a train to Paris, things have been a lot more, how shall I put it, *interesting*.

Plus, how could I refuse? Especially when I found out that they allowed pets *and* I didn't need a reservation. Well, it would have been *rude* not to have lunch here.

The model-slash-maitre d' shows me to the most gorgeous table, overlooking the glass pyramid. The view is breathtaking. In fact, it's probably up there with one of the most perfect views in the world. Perfect for people-watching, which is one of my all-time favourite pastimes.

Sitting down in one of the padded cream-piped armchairs, I absorb it all like a sponge. All around me, well-heeled people are drinking wine and eating tiny amounts of food, arranged beautifully on big white plates. Waiters sweep and glide in and out, in that very attentive yet unobtrusive way that only waiters in expensive restaurants can achieve. In the background there's the hum of silver cutlery chinking on porcelain plates and the murmuring of voices, while the whiff of expensive perfume fills the air.

I feel like I did the one time I got a surprise upgrade to first class on an aeroplane. It was a total fluke; apparently the plane was full and the economy seats had been overbooked, but the first I knew of it was when I was boarding, all hot and sweaty and weighed down with carrier bags, and the stewardess took one look at my boarding card and told me to turn left.

Turn left. It's such a little, innocuous phrase, but only then did I discover what different worlds left and right inhabit. It was like walking into Narnia. Flat beds, feather duvets and proper A-list celebrities in sleepsuits on either side of me. Not only that, but suddenly I'd turned into a Madam. As in, 'Would Madam like more champagne?' 'Would Madam like her bed making up?' 'Would Madam care for another chocolate truffle?'

Of course the whole time I felt that everyone knew I was a fake and didn't really belong there, and that any minute the stewardess would whip the complimentary champagne from my hand, strip me out of my sleepsuit and march me back into economy.

A bit like now, I muse, as a smartly dressed waiter appears and asks me what I'd like to order. I've been so busy taking in the view I haven't looked at the menu. I take a quick look and try not to blanch at the prices under his watchful gaze. Saying that, everything sounds divine. Trying to appear as if this is the way I eat lunch every day, and not sitting at my desk with a bag of Kettle chips and a pot of hummus, I order a very fancy-sounding omelette. It's fine. I'll just eat cereal for a week when I get back to London.

'And to drink?'

I'm about to say just water thanks, when I stop myself. Hang on, I'm in Paris. In a super stylish café overlooking the Louvre. Water just isn't going to cut it.

'A glass of champagne, *merci*,' I say, feeling a flash of decadence.

I don't even look at the price list. Sod it. I've drunk nothing but coffee and champagne for the past twenty-four hours – why change things now? Handing back the menu, I try not to think about my credit card, which is probably taking its last gasp in my handbag.

The waiter nods and disappears.

I look across at the woman sitting at the table opposite me. She has her little dog next to her in a Louis Vuitton bag and I glance down at Heathcliff, who's curled up under the table. I contemplate it . . . No, I can't do it to him. I might be trying to get into the French swing of things, but I think that's taking matters too far. Plus, Heathcliff would hate me for ever.

Instead I put my non-designer handbag on the chair next to me and pull out the bundle of love letters from Madame Dumont's apartment. I fell asleep last night reading the letter from Henry, but now, looking at the date of the postmarks, I reach for the next one. It's the same handwriting. It must be from Henry again.

Slipping it out of the envelope, I unfold it with a sense of anticipation. I wonder what will have happened. Are his affections returned? Did she go to the jazz club with him? I know she fell in love with him – she wrote of it in her note that was never sent – but how did it all begin? How did *they* begin? Excitement flutters. Between my fingertips lies a whole other world and already I can feel myself slipping into the past, into another time, another Paris . . .

My dearest Emmanuelle,

I was so happy when you wrote me back and said yes to my invitation, so much so I confess I read your letter several times. My favorite part was when you wrote that our meeting at the café was as memorable for you as it was for me, though I find that hard to believe. I am just a lucky fellow from Brooklyn, but you . . . you are something special.

I don't think I will ever forget the image of you as we danced together, my arm around your waist, your hand on my shoulder, your gaze upon mine. You looked so beautiful in your silk dress and such a wonderful dancer too. I was the envy of all the men in that room, not that I noticed anyone else as I couldn't take my eyes off you.

I wanted the evening to last for ever, for the clocks to stop and time to stand still. I wished that the music would never stop playing and we would forever twirl together around the dancefloor.

And in my heart we always will . . .

Afterwards you broke the news to me that we cannot be seen together again. You told me if your family knew about me, they would never allow it. You spoke of society and tradition, of rules to be followed and appearances to be maintained. Yet you also spoke of your secret desire for freedom. Of being true to yourself. Of being able to follow your heart wherever it leads you.

There were so many things I wanted to say, but I could not bring myself to say them so I simply listened. But do not be mistaken, my silence was not a form of agreement. I need you to know that. Just as I need to now ask you the only question that matters.

If you were to follow your heart my dearest, should I dare hope that it leads you to me?

H

14

'Ruby?'

At first, I don't look up. They can't mean me. No one knows me here. Lost in the world of Henry and Emmanuelle, I continue reading the letter, absorbing the words. Until after a few moments I become vaguely aware of a presence next to me and I look up to see Xavier the lawyer.

'It is you!'

I jump a mile. Oh shit. Impulsively, I clamp the letter to my chest.

'I'm sorry, I didn't mean to scare you.' He smiles apologetically.

'No, not at all.' I try to sound casual as I fluster around, folding the letter and trying to tuck it in my lap underneath the table. I quickly cover it with a napkin.

'I was having a meeting.' He gestures over to a group of men in suits who are getting up from round a table and putting on their jackets. 'I looked across and I thought I am sure I know that girl.'

Wagging his finger, he screws up his eyes, forming a deep crevice in his brow, and peers at me intently.

This is obviously just his attempt at re-enactment, but I suddenly feel very self-conscious.

'Oh, yes, it's me.' I smile awkwardly. It's not just the letter; I'd forgotten how good-looking he was, and now faced with him in such close proximity I'm all jittery.

And hot.

It's like someone just turned up the temperature about twenty degrees. Snatching up a menu, I start fanning myself like my mum used to when she was having one of her hot flushes.

'Do you mind if I . . . ?' He gestures to the empty seat across from me.

Oh god, he's going to join me. My stomach shoots up and down, like a heartbeat on a monitor. A sort of panic mixed with something that feels almost like a slight thrill.

'No, of course not.'

Well, it's not every day you get to sit in a café with a handsome Frenchman, is it? It's the stuff of romantic novels. The kind I write. Only this time it's not fiction – it's actually for real.

Of course, the difference is that in my novel my heroine and the Frenchman would end up falling madly in love and into bed and— I slam on the brakes on my imagination. Well anyway, like I said, there's a *very* big difference between fiction and reality.

I watch as Xavier says his goodbyes to the suits, then sits down across from me.   Heathcliff wriggles from underneath the table and begins sniffing his ankles madly.

'I have a cat, should I be worried?' His eyes flash with amusement.

'I think you're safe.' I smile, relaxing a bit.

'Good.' He grins. 'I don't want him doing a pee-pee on me.'

'He only does that if he likes you,' I tease, then quickly catch myself. What am I doing? Am I *flirting*?

'Well then I am sure I am safe,' he nods mock-seriously. 'I am very unlikeable.'

No, of course I'm not flirting. I'm just being friendly. I'm in love with Jack.

Who stood you up at the airport, reminds a voice in my head.

The waiter arrives with my drink and I take a thirsty gulp. Bubbles fizz up to the roof of my mouth. Gosh, that tastes good.

'I don't normally drink champagne at lunchtime,' I say hurriedly, noticing Xavier watching me. Well, I don't want him thinking I'm an old soak.

'Why not?' He smiles, and despite myself, I can't help smiling back. 'The French say a day without wine is a day without sunshine. Champagne is just wine with bubbles.'

I'm beginning to really like the French way of thinking. I take another sip, enjoying the buzz of the ice-cold bubbles weaving their way down into my empty stomach.

'So have you found out any more about Madame Dumont's apartment?' I ask, emboldened by the champagne.

'What is there to find out?' He shrugs dismissively. 'So a rich old woman kept a secret residence, so what? She paid the rent, the taxes, everything was in order.'

'Yes, but don't you think it's strange that she would do that?'

'I see many strange things in my business, I know not to ask too many questions.' He pauses to look at me, his brow furrowed. 'I think it is more of a mystery why a beautiful young woman would be having lunch alone in Paris.'

I feel myself blush under his gaze.

'Harriet's working,' I explain, 'so I thought I would explore a little, do some sightseeing.' I wave my guidebook at him as evidence.

'She doesn't need your assistance today?'

Oh crap, I'd forgotten Harriet had introduced me as her assistant.

'No, um, not today, I'm sort of part-time,' I say vaguely and take a gulp of champagne.

'Excellent, well if you need a tour guide, I know the best in town.'

'You do?'

'I think I have his card somewhere . . .' He slips his wallet out of his breast pocket and pulls out a business card.

As he passes it to me I read the name. *Monsieur Xavier Moreau.*

'But that's you.' I look up in confusion.

'But of course.' He smiles.

I can't help but laugh and he observes me for a moment, before his expression turns serious.

'Now, as your tour guide I must give you the most important piece of advice,' he says gravely.

I stop laughing. 'What's that?'

'Throw away your guidebook.'

'What? I can't do that!' I protest, 'I only just bought it!'

'But you do not need it,' he says simply. 'This is not the way to see Paris. Nothing that is worth anything will be documented in the pages of your book.'

'But there are all these itineraries!' I flick open the book and thrust it at him.

Shaking his head, he takes it from me and, closing it, places it on the table between us. 'The city keeps the best bits to itself. Everything is hidden. It is up to you to discover it.' He motions for me to come closer and as I do he leans forward and places his mouth by my ear. 'Trust me,' he whispers, his warm breath on my cheek. 'Paris is full of secrets.'

'Madame, Monsieur?'

I jump back, startled, as the waiter interrupts us both with my food. I'd forgotten all about it. My appetite has vanished and I feel rather woozy. And, suddenly, extremely guilty. Here I am, in a fancy café in Paris, drinking champagne with a very handsome Frenchman. It's all completely innocent, but still—'

'I'm not *alone*, alone,' I say suddenly, feeling I should make it clear. 'I have a boyfriend.'

Xavier frowns. 'And he lets you come to Paris without him?'

'He had to work,' I say firmly, as much to convince myself as him.

'It must be very important work.'

I feel a slight niggle. Earlier on the bridge, I didn't care any more about who was wrong and who was right. In that moment it no longer mattered that Jack hadn't shown up, or that I'd been hurt and upset. I didn't even care about that stupid row. Seeing all those padlocks made me realise how much I loved Jack and how much I missed him. In that moment, that's the only thing that was important.

But now Xavier's comment touches a nerve.

'You must never put work before pleasure,' he continues, fixing me with his slate-grey eyes, then shrugs. 'But maybe this is the French way.'

'He's American,' I reply.

'Ah well, this explains it.' He observes me for a moment, then smiles. 'He is a very brave man.'

'Brave?'

'To let you come to Paris without him.'

I feel myself blush and reach for another much-needed gulp of champagne, only to realise that I've drunk it all and have touched hardly any of my food. I put my glass down and suddenly it's whisked away and another appears, along with one for Xavier.

'Like magic,' he says, at my expression.

Our eyes meet. He leans forwards and chinks my glass. 'To a day with sunshine.'

I take a sip of icy champagne. I know I shouldn't; one glass is plenty. I'm already tipsy. But it would be rude not to drink it. Plus, it's not like I'm doing anything wrong. Jack was the one who stood me up, remember. If he'd been on that flight, I wouldn't even *be* here in Paris, let alone drinking champagne with Xavier.

The shrill burble of a phone interrupts my thoughts and Xavier answers it. He speaks in rapid French, then hangs up. 'I'm sorry, demanding clients.' He smiles, slipping the phone back into his breast pocket. 'I am afraid I must leave you and return to the office.' Draining his glass, he stands up and I go to do the same, but he quickly gestures for me to remain seated. 'Stay and enjoy your food,' he says, referring to my forgotten omelette, 'and remember, if you need a tour guide . . .' He gestures to his card, which is still lying on the table.

'I will, thanks,' I smile, grateful that I didn't have to stand up. I'm feeling rather light-headed.

'It has been a pleasure,' he says, handing his credit card to the waiter.

'No please, let me—' I begin, but he waves away my protestations.

I watch as he leaves the restaurant, walking down the long terrace like a model on a catwalk. Various women at other tables stop talking and eating to watch him as he glides past, then glance over at me with a mixture of curiosity and envy. Feeling their eyes on me, I turn back to my food and reach for my napkin, which is when I remember the letter still hidden in my lap, and Henry's heartfelt plea.

Carefully slipping it back in its envelope, I pull out the next one. I need to know what happens next. Does Emmanuelle choose love over tradition? Or does her family and social standing come between them?

My darling Emmanuelle,

There are no words to describe how I felt when I opened your letter, confessing your true feelings for me. Me, a writer, lost for words.

Before I met you I believed my life here in Paris was a good one. I was content to be a spectator in life, to write about what I

*see and not what I feel. Only now do I realize I was sleepwalking
through life. I was living a life without purpose. A life without a
passion. Now I truly know what it feels like to be alive and that is
by being by your side.*

*Have I said too much? Do I frighten you with the depth of my
feelings? I know I am just a poor orphaned writer from America
and you are from one of France's finest and oldest families. We
could not be more opposite, and yet in so many ways, we could
not be more alike. Together we should be able to live the lives we
want and not those imposed on us by your family.*

*Yet, even though I protest like an angry young man, I will do
anything for you, so of course I agree to your request. It will be
hard for me to meet only in secret in your apartment. I want to
shout my feelings from the rooftops and dance with you in the
streets, but I will do anything not to endanger what we have.*

*I want only to be with you, Emmanuelle. I love watching how
you twirl your hair around your fingers when you are deep in
thought and the way your cheeks dimple when you smile. I love
listening to you talk excitedly about your beloved ballet and
singing along to my favorite jazz records even though you forget
all the words. I even love the way you tease me for my terrible
French.*

*There are so many things I could write about, so much I want
to say to you. You have captured my heart and lifted my soul.
But know only this, my darling. I may not be a wealthy man,
but if my love for you was a currency, you would be the richest
woman in the world.*

Your beloved,

H

Unexpectedly, my eyes well up with tears. To be loved like
that. A love that great. I imagine them dancing together, his
hand on her tiny waist as they spin around the dance floor.
They must have made a wonderful sight, Emmanuelle with

her long red hair and silk dress, and Henry the dashing American. At least, I imagine he was dashing – of course I have no idea what he looked like, but I'm sure his looks were as wonderful as his writing.

Because that's the magic of writing. As I read again his descriptions and emotions, they are no longer just words on a page; they are two people who have come to life from over seventy years ago. They are a poor American who loves jazz and writing and a beautiful, rich Parisian who teases him about his terrible French. They are real people, with a real love story. A love story that has to be kept secret for fear of retribution from her family. A story I want to continue.

I carefully slip the letter back into the bundle and am just reaching for the next one when I'm distracted by something buzzing under my napkin on the table. For a split second I peer at it curiously, then suddenly my heart leaps. It's my phone and it's on vibrate! It must be Jack!

I snatch up the phone. But instead it's Harriet. I feel a lurch of disappointment. Then feel immediately bad for that.

'Where are you?' she demands.

'At the Louvre.'

'Oh fabulous! Isn't it amazing?'

'Yes, stunning.' I nod, looking at the breathtaking view across the courtyard.

'I particularly love Jacques-Louis David's *The Coronation of Napoleon*. Such a magnificent painting and stunning detail, don't you agree?'

'Er, I don't think I saw that one,' I say vaguely. My bladder twinges from all that champagne. I need the loo. Abandoning my omelette, I gather up my things.

'Oh well, never mind, there's always a next time,' she encourages swiftly, 'anyway, I was calling to tell you that I completely forgot it's my company's annual summer party tonight. You're my plus one.'

'Oh, er, great.' To be honest, I'm not really in the mood for a party, but I don't want to disappoint Harriet.

'A party is just what we both need,' she steamrollers.

'Great,' I reply again, weakly. Wedging my phone under my ear, I grab Heathcliff's lead and begin making my way upstairs to the bathroom.

'Excellent! Well, see you later then – oh, and before I forget, there's a dress code.'

'There is?' My heart sinks. Oh god, I hate dress codes. I always get them wrong. I mean, what is smart casual exactly?

'Don't worry, this one's easy.'

I push open the door of the ladies' loos.

'It's Parisian Chic.'

At which point I catch sight of a girl with messy hair and baggy leggings reflected in the washbasin mirrors and realise with a sort of slow-motion horror that:

A) That's me.

B) In just a few hours I will be at a party in the fashion capital of the world.

C) Forget Parisian Chic, my dress code is Crumpled Mismatched.

'Harriet?' I yelp.

But she's already hung up.

Oh god.

15

OK, deep breaths.

Back outside, I plonk myself down on the edge of the fountain and try to concentrate on my breathing. Just like I was taught in the one yoga class I did in India that time. Which was about all I learned as I was completely hopeless at the actual poses. Though I'm not sure my yoga teacher had 'fashion crisis in Paris' in mind when he was teaching us about the importance of the ancient Sanskrit art of pranayama, or 'life breath'.

Taking a few deep inhales and exhales I take a tentative look around me. OK, so everyone knows that French women have drool-worthy style. But it can't be that hard to dress like a French woman, can it? I mean, come on. It's not rocket science.

I survey the women walking past me, and it's not hard to distinguish Parisians from tourists. Whereas the latter are stumbling around in trainers and shorts, sporting an ensemble of mismatched colours and patterns and an alarming number of clothes that neither flatter nor fit, the locals stride past looking the epitome of style. Slim, groomed and perfectly colour coordinated, they make it look so effortless.

And another thing: I might not know much about fashion, but I know a designer handbag when I see one and I have never seen so many being paraded around. In Paris, it would appear a Birkin is more common than a Tesco carrier bag.

Glancing at my own accessory of choice – a well-worn backpack that looked perfectly fine in London but here looks like a monstrosity – I feel a sinking feeling in the pit of my stomach. It's hopeless. There is no way I can compete. I just don't have what it takes. I turn to Heathcliff, who's sitting in the shade surveying the steady stream of dogs that parade past with stylish collars and matching leads. Something about the way he's peering at them and sniffing the air makes me wonder if he's feeling the same way.

Seriously, I have nothing to wear.

And not in the usual sense of, my wardrobe is bursting with lots of perfectly nice outfits but there's nothing I feel like wearing. I mean in the sense of, all I have is a holdall of screwed-up clothes, most of which are T-shirts and leggings, none of which go together, and some of which might even have stains on.

For a brief moment I think about giving up and backing out, before quickly pulling myself together. I can't and won't let Harriet down. Letting people down is Jack's forte, remember?

Plus, Harriet is right; a party will probably do us both the world of good. So, emboldened by the two glasses of champagne, I take a deep breath, put aside my fears and reservations and stand up.

I, Ruby Miller, am going clothes shopping.

I continue with this positive attitude all the way to Boulevard Haussmann, which according to my guidebook houses the famous department stores that Harriet told me about. It's not that far to walk from the Louvre, and along the way I do my affirmations. Now, just to make this clear, I'm not an affirmation type of person. I don't practise yoga, I don't own any of those inspirational quote fridge magnets and the one time I tried to meditate I woke myself up by snoring. But I read about them recently on one of those lifestyle blogs and at this point I'll try anything.

1) I am confident about solving life's problems successfully . . .
   *like for example, finding something that doesn't make my
   bum look big.*
2) The future is good, I look towards it with hope and
   happiness . . . *and a little black dress that makes me look
   fabulous and fashionable.*
3) I transcend stress of any kind, I live in peace . . . *and a
   fab pair of heels that I can actually walk in.*

Wow, this stuff actually works! In fact, by the time I reach
my destination I'm feeling really confident – until I'm greeted
by the grandest department stores I've ever seen. Momentarily
overwhelmed, for a moment I stand frozen on the pavement.
Oh crap, this takes shopping to a whole new level.

Then I remember my affirmations and pull myself
together. I'm confident about solving life's problems, remember? It will be fine. I'll just go inside and grab a few bits and
I'll be out of here in half an hour. Nothing to worry about.

And, scooping up Heathcliff, I head for the nearest one
and step bravely into the revolving door.

Easy peasy.

Inside the building is simply stunning, with amazing art
deco architecture and a beautiful stained-glass dome overhead. Everything is bright and shiny, with designer stores
and marble floors and gorgeous staircases. It's also teeming
with shoppers. Think first day of the Harrods sale then times
it by about a hundred.

Holding firmly on to Heathcliff's lead, I manage to navigate myself to the escalator and glide up to the women's floor.
It's huge. Faced with hundreds of clothes racks and different
designers, I feel slightly woozy, and it's not just the champagne. But I stay focused. I just want something very simple
and stylish. Something very French. You know, something
chic and *Gallic.*

I mean, c'mon, how hard that can be? I've written books. I have a mortgage. I have travelled alone on a train journey across India. I can totally do this.

Within moments I spot just the thing: a stripy Breton top. What could be more French than that? I pluck it quickly off the rail and team it with a classic pair of black trousers. See, these will look perfect! Thrilled by how easy it was, I can't resist a matching beret and dive confidently into the changing room. Seriously, all that business about how French women are born with this amazing sense of style that can't be learned. I mean, honestly, what a load of old rubbish!

I turn to look at myself in the mirror – and balk at my reflection. Oh my god, I don't look French, I look ridiculous! All I need is a bicycle and a string of onions.

Hurriedly tugging off the outfit, I dive back outside. OK, maybe I was being a little too adventurous to begin with, trying to run before I could walk kind of thing. Maybe I should start with the basics. I wander round the various racks of clothes, casting my eyes around and trying to appear as if I actually know what I'm looking for. A sales assistant catches my eye and says something to me in French that I'm pretty sure means 'Can I help you?' Well, it's either that or 'What on earth are you wearing?'

I go for option one.

'*Oui, merci,*' I begin, then realising that's about the extent of my vocabulary, continue in English, 'I'm looking for a dress.'

Well how more basic can you get?

'*Une robe?*' she repeats.

Oh dear, she thinks I mean a dressing gown. Jack calls it a robe too.

'*Non,* a dress,' I say, shaking my head, doing a bit of hand-gesturing to show that I mean a dress that comes to about knee-length.

She nods. '*Oui, une robe,*' and tries to lead me off in another direction.

Oh god, how embarrassing, I knew I should have paid more attention in French lessons.

'*Non,* a dress,' I repeat, shaking my head.

The assistant looks perplexed as back and forth we go a couple more times, like a game of ping pong, until finally I give up, apologising profusely, '*Pardonnez-moi,* I um – oh, look at the time! I have to go . . .' and quickly dash off into another department.

Well that's it, I'm doomed. I mean, there's nothing more basic than a dress, is there? Suddenly realising I'm surrounded by tables, upon which several sales assistants are busy folding up pieces of brightly patterned silk, I stop dead. Of course! Why didn't I think of it before: *scarves!*

What could be more simple than a scarf? Or more French?

Excited, I swoop upon the tables. Every woman in Paris seems to be sporting one; it's obviously the must-have accessory, even in summer. Expensive silk Hermès ones, patterned tie-dye ones, skinny woven ones: they come in all different colours, materials and prices, even ones to match my budget.

Eagerly I grab a handful and race into a changing room. What could be easier to wear than a scarf? It will instantly make me look chic and Gallic! Like Catherine Deneuve, or Juliette Binoche, or one of those other wonderfully stylish French women who just have that *je ne sais quoi*!

Thrilled, I take my first scarf, a delicious swathe of scarlet satin, and start draping it round my shoulders. Now, how do the French women do it, they always seem so effortless. I frown at myself in the mirror. Hmm . . . no, that doesn't look quite right, hang on, maybe if I just do this . . .

Twirling around behind the curtain, like a dervish, I take the ends and fling them around a bit more. Yes, that looks much better. Then, maybe if I tie it into a knot like this—

Actually, on second thoughts, perhaps not, that's actually a bit tight. I try to rearrange it, but for some reason the scarf seems to be getting even tighter. Hang on, I must be wrapping it the wrong way, it must be the other way. But now it's not getting looser; in fact it's getting tighter still. I feel a slight panic. I'm actually getting a bit breathless, like it's cutting off my air supply.

An assistant says something to me in French through the curtain and it's all I can do to respond with a sort of croaking, '*Oui, c'est bon.*' At least that's what I try to say but it comes out in a rasping voice, like I'm being strangled.

Which I am. By a scarf.

Suddenly I have visions of being found asphyxiated in the changing rooms like a victim of an erotic sex game gone wrong. Can you imagine? I feel a clutch of terror. Oh my god, what would my parents think? Mum would never be able to face the neighbours again. It was bad enough when Peter from next door was caught not swiping a jar of pesto through the Tesco self-scanners.

My mind flashes back. It was the talk of the village for weeks, though it wasn't the fact that he'd been caught not paying for something that had caused such a furore; it was his choice of item that got the tongues wagging. *Pesto? That fancy Italian stuff? But he's always been strictly a meat and two veg man!* I don't think Dad has got over the shock still.

And what would Jack think? At the thought, I feel quite dizzy. Actually, no, it's not the thought of Jack that's making me dizzy, I suddenly realise, it's the lack of oxygen. I start panting breathlessly and tugging frantically at the scarf. Oh fuck, this is it, I'm going to die!

I try doing my affirmations: *I transcend stress of any kind, I live in peace—*

ARGGGHHH!

Clutching at my throat, I suddenly lose my balance and

crash through the curtain, into the arms of the stylish sales assistant.

'Ayeeeee!'

That's her shrieking loudly as we go flying and land in a heap on the floor. Or maybe it's me. I don't know. All I know is that all hell breaks loose. It's chaos with lots of yelling, people rushing over, a baby screaming, Heathcliff barking – and oh god, now there's someone lunging at me with a giant pair of very scary-looking scissors . . .

Which is the bit where I pass out.

I wake up to find myself lying on the floor, surrounded by a crowd of goggling spectators. Thankfully I'm OK. Well, as OK as you can be lying flat out on the floor of an upmarket department store in Paris, while shoppers stand around you, whispering and pointing. The scarf is ruined though. The security guard had to cut it into shreds and it lies there next to me in tatters. I buy it anyway. I'm too embarrassed not to.

And that's when I find it. Tucked into my wallet, it falls out as I'm pulling out my credit card to pay. The answer to all my problems.

Twenty minutes later I arrive at a tiny boutique. The outside is painted a dark, boudoir red and the window display offers up a few tantalising items, including a black velvet jacket with exquisite beading and a gorgeous mother-of-pearl clutch that looks like something you'd see a supermodel carrying and wonder, where on earth did she get that? I glance at the vintage sign, which is hammered out of metal and hangs discreetly over the door: 'Le Secret.'

How apt. Tucked away down a tiny backstreet, away from passers-by and the steady stream of tourists, this is one of those places you'd never find unless someone let you into the secret. Like someone did for me, I muse, glancing once more at the card held tightly in my hand to double-check I've got the right place before I push open the door.

'Ruby, it is so good to see you!'

As I enter the treasure trove, a tiny blonde dressed head-to-toe in black rushes towards me.

'It's even better to see you, Celeste,' I say with a feeling of relief, as she embraces me with two scarlet kisses.

'It is good you came,' she nods, looking me up and down with a critical eye.

I'd explained everything to her on the phone, about the party, about my clothes, about why I'm in Paris, even about the scarf, which had taken a few explanations due to the language difference, but which once she'd understood had resulted in peals of laughter.

'And I thought '*Arriet* was trouble,' she says, clucking her tongue and shaking her head.

Oh dear. I hate that. It's the same noise and expression that my hairdresser makes whenever I go to see her. I seem to have that effect on people.

'No woman should be wearing these athletic clothes,' she says, wrinkling up her perfect nose at me as if there was a bad smell.

'They're not athletic clothes,' I protest, 'they're just leggings and a T-shirt.'

Celeste pulls a face, closes one eye and sort of squints at me as if it's too painful to look properly. 'Everything is so . . .' She seems to cast around in her head for a word, then gives up and finally spits, 'There is no shape, no silhouette!'

'But they're really comfy,' I mumble.

'*Com-fee?*' she repeats, a deep furrow forming down her brow. 'What is this, *com-fee?*'

'Comfortable,' I explain.

Her face floods with understanding. '*Non!* A Chanel jacket is comfortable,' she replies, wagging her finger. 'This is not comfortable, this is something that you should only wear at the gym,' she goes on sternly. 'You must never leave the house like this again, not ever!'

Celeste can actually be pretty scary when she wants to be. '*Compris?*'

'*Compris.*' I nod, dutifully.

'OK.' She nods, looking satisfied. 'So I need to teach you the rules.'

'*Rules?*' I repeat, feeling a prick of anxiety. Oh god, I knew it. Coming to Paris was a big mistake. I should never have accepted Harriet's invitation. I should have just stayed home in my slobby clothes, feeling sorry for myself and waiting for Jack to ring.

'But of course,' she says with a nod, her face solemn, 'to be stylish you have to follow certain rules, otherwise you will look . . .' She trails off and we both look at my crumpled reflection in the full-length mirror on the wall. It's quite clear to all that the only rule I have been following is 'chuck it on and hope for the best'.

'Remember, fashions change, but style never goes out of fashion,' she says, seeming to think better of trying to describe my own non-style and moving briskly along. 'Number one, never show too much skin.'

Striding over to a rack of clothes, she starts deftly pulling out items with the speed and confidence of someone who knows exactly what they're doing. As opposed to myself, I tend to approach a clothes rail like a teenage boy on a first date, all awkward fumbling and uncertainty.

Thrusting several items at me, she says authoritatively, 'As the hem goes up the heel goes down.'

'It does?'

Celeste shoots me a look that says that wasn't open to debate. 'Right, OK.' I nod hurriedly.

'Number two, stay away from colour—'

I'd ventured tentatively over towards a bright flash of

crimson I'd spotted hanging from a rail and was just reaching out to touch it. I snatch my hand back quickly like I've been burned.

'Colour is very powerful; until you have learned the basics it is better for you to wear only the classic palette,' she adds, a little more kindly. She hands me another couple of hangers with something cream and navy blue hanging on them.

I've never been a fan of navy blue – it always reminds me of my school uniform – but I take them wordlessly as she shoos me inside a tiny cubicle and swiftly pulls closed the curtain.

'OK, let's go,' she instructs, clapping her hands.

It's a complete eye-opener. Celeste has chosen items that I would have never even noticed. Dresses that look like baggy, shapeless items on the hanger are transformed with a belt. A skirt that looks unflattering on the hanger looks great on. A pair of cream culottes that I assumed would make my hips look bigger actually makes them look smaller! Until now my little sister Amy has been my go-to person for fashion advice, but Celeste is something else.

Effortlessly she puts together outfits: a blouse with a skirt with a belt with a cardigan. As she snaps her fingers, I take things on and off and she frowns and nods, tuts and smiles, shaking her head one minute, looking delighted the next. Working her magic.

'Rule number three: you must make friends with scarves.'

I balk, but she ignores me. Taking a scarf, she throws it effortlessly round my shoulders and, with a quick flick of her wrist, ties a loose knot. '*Parfait.*' She nods.

I goggle at myself in the mirror. It looks amazing. How did she do that? After my earlier debacle in the department store, I'm aghast. It's like a magic trick.

'Number four, only one sexy thing. Never more.' Taking a

pair of vintage heels in bright purple satin, she slips them on my feet. Instantly I feel amazing. '*Cindrillon*,' she quips, laughing at my astounded expression.

Well, who would have thought of trying on *purple* shoes?

Celeste, I discover, has spent her whole life in fashion, and it's her passion. 'Which is probably why I'm single,' she laughs throatily, turning back to the clothes rack.

'You? Single?' I look at her in surprise. She's so drop dead good-looking, I'd imagined she would have a harem of men.

'Yes.' She shrugs. 'I have never loved a man more than a Chanel jacket.'

I laugh. 'You can't be serious.'

'*Absolument*.' She nods firmly. 'A Chanel jacket will keep you warm, will never you let you down and will always make you feel fabulous.'

'So does true love,' I protest.

Brandishing one off a rack, she insists I try it on.

Actually, maybe she has a point, I reflect, thinking about Jack as I slip it on and give her a twirl. There are plenty of words to describe how I've been feeling since he stood me up at Heathrow and still hasn't called, and none of them are fabulous.

And then suddenly, after less than an hour, I'm standing in front of the mirror wearing a simple navy silk dress and purple heels (would you believe it, blue and purple look *great* together), a pair of 1940s drop earrings and matching choker and a gorgeous tan belt. I swear, I almost don't recognise myself.

'Finally, the last rule. Before you go out, take a look in the mirror and take one thing off,' and, walking behind me, she unhooks my necklace.

I begin to protest as it falls away from my throat, 'But I love that necklace—' then fall silent. Because she's absolutely right. 'It looks so much better without it.'

'But of course,' she says, and flashes a smile. 'Now, you go enjoy your party, and always remember the most important rule of all.'

I frown. 'What's that?'

'To look effortless requires effort. It is the same with everything in life. Nothing worth anything is easy.'

I smile. 'Thank you so much—' I begin, but Celeste waves my thanks away.

'I just told you a few secrets.' She winks.

16

After making a quick dash back to the apartment to drop off Heathcliff and give him his dinner, I jump on the Métro and head straight to meet Harriet. She's given me directions to the party, but even so it takes me a while to get there, partly because of my terrible sense of direction, but mostly because of these new heels.

Ouch! I wince as my ankle nearly goes over on the cobbles for about the millionth time, and shoot an envious glance at an impeccably dressed woman who strides past nonchalantly in a pair of needle-thin stilettos. Honestly, how on earth do these Parisian women do it?

The sun is hanging low in the sky as I finally reach the banks of the Seine. I pause. Hang on, this can't be right. I must have missed a turning. I look down at my hastily scribbled directions. No, it says Île de la Cité and that's where I am. Confused, I glance around this island in the middle of the Seine. All I can see are several barges and boats and—

It's the music I hear first. Wafting towards me. I turn towards the Latin dance tunes to see a large white boat moored further along the quay. Its wooden decks are adorned with a canopy of carnival lights and there's a stream of stylishly dressed people making their way up the gangplank.

My eyes zoom in. *The party is on a boat?*

Then suddenly I spot Harriet, standing on deck myopically scanning the crowds for me. I hurry towards her, waving. She does a double-take when she sees me.

'Wowee,' she gasps, goggling at me in disbelief as I navigate my way gingerly up the gangplank. 'What a transformation!'

'Celeste worked her magic.' I smile, proudly.

'Aha, that explains it.' She nods, her face flooding with comprehension, before adding quickly. 'Not that you don't always look amazing.'

I pull a face. Trust me, the only thing amazing about my earlier outfit is that I wasn't arrested by the *gendarmerie* for crimes against fashion.

'Just one thing – how do women in Paris walk in these heels?'

'A lifetime of practice,' says Harriet, knowledgably. 'Failing that—' She digs out a bottle of ibuprofen from her bag and rattles it at me, '—for the blisters.'

'Thanks, but I think I'll try a cocktail instead,' I reply, turning to a passing tray of brightly coloured drinks. 'Want one?'

Harriet pulls a face. 'I shouldn't really, have you any idea how many empty calories there are in alcohol?'

I reach out to take just one drink.

'Oh go on then, if you insist,' she adds hastily.

I take two and pass her one.

'There's so many people!' I comment, glancing around the busy deck.

'Don't worry, I don't know most of them either. We have a large client list and my boss likes to invite everyone, plus a few French celebrities and some journalists. That way we can guarantee column inches.'

'Wow, I never knew auctioneering was so glitzy.' And there was me thinking it was just musty old antiques and old men in corduroy jackets.

'It's not, but there's a lot of competition and we need to stay ahead of it—' She suddenly straightens up like a sentry, a large smile pinned on her face. 'Monsieur Richard, meet my friend Ruby, Ruby—'

I turn to see a grey-haired man in a blue blazer with lots of gold buttons. He looks suitably serious. 'A pleasure.' He shakes my hand, then, saying something to Harriet in rapid French, moves off to introduce himself to a large crowd of people.

'Golly, who was that? He's a bit scary.'

'My boss.' She pulls a face. 'I've been trying to impress him for months, but I'm not sure he really knows who I am. I'm hoping my work for Madame Dumont's auction will put me on his radar and up for promotion.'

At the mention of Madame Dumont I think about her letters, still tucked in my bag. I should really tell Harriet about them. I open my mouth to say something—

'Oh look, we're off.'

I turn to see the gangplank has been drawn up and we've set sail down the Seine, floating past Notre Dame and towards the Louvre. It really is quite impressive. It's been a long time since I went to a party and certainly one as fancy as this, I muse, feeling a bit intimidated. *God I miss Jack*. Out of nowhere the thought flashes across my mind and tugs at my heartstrings. I drain my drink.

'Wow, you're thirsty.'

'Um – yes.' I nod, suddenly feeling a bit unsteady as the alcohol goes straight to my head. Oh dear. Getting drunk and being on a boat are not a good combination. I feel a beat of relief as a tray of canapés comes into view, followed by a familiar face.

'Luc!' says Harriet, in surprise, 'what are you doing here?'

'Can I be tempting?' He grins, wafting dozens of small triangles of pastry, layered with all kinds of delicious-looking ingredients, under our noses.

'It's "can I tempt you",' she corrects, smiling.

He shrugs his shoulders in a Gallic way, and I have a feeling he wasn't just talking about the canapés.

'What are they?' I ask, my stomach grumbling.

'*Artichauts*—'

'Artichokes,' repeats Harriet automatically, like something from Rosetta Stone.

'Ah yes.' He nods, 'and, how you say, *champignons* . . . ?'

'Mushrooms,' she says patiently, articulating each vowel.

'Of course,' Luc says, smiling, tutting at himself and shaking his head, 'Mush-*rooooms*!' He repeats it enthusiastically, trying to copy her with almost comical pronunciation.

'Excellent.' She smiles, looking delighted.

Standing between them, I feel as if I'm intruding on a private lesson. I don't care what Harriet says about the age difference, they are very cute together.

'And I make a mousse with some of the '*erbs* I took from my garden,' he continues, wafting the tray under our noses.

'You made these?' Impressed, I pluck one from the tray and take a bite.

He nods, proudly.

'Wow, they're delicious,' I groan through a mouthful of puff pastry and the yummiest tasting filling I've ever eaten. How on earth did he make that out of just a few veggies? It's like he's added some magic ingredient.

'Mmm, yes,' says Harriet, who doesn't need much encouragement and is already on her second. She's obviously on the canapé and cocktail diet tonight, I muse, following her lead and taking another.

'I'm not just a pretty face,' he grins and flashes a look at Harriet, but at that moment her phone makes a beep and she glances down at it.

Her face lights up like the Eiffel Tower. 'It's Rupert,' she says, opening a text.

'Who's Rupert?' I mumble, through a mouthful of crumbs.

'*WineNot*,' she explains, her eyes still locked to the screen of her phone as she reads his message, 'that's his real name.'

This morning when I left her she'd heard just six words

from him, so at least this is progress of a kind. Though I'm not sure discovering that your date is called Rupert can be called progress, *exactly*. Seriously, Rupert is a cartoon bear who wears tartan trousers.

'So are you meeting him for a drink?' I cut to the chase.

'Yes, tomorrow night.' She nods excitedly, still reading his text. 'He's having dinner with friends first, so we're going to meet later.' She quickly types a response and hits send.

'How much later?' I ask, doubtfully.

I don't like the sound of dinner with friends first, it makes Harriet seem like an afterthought.

There's a pause, then a ping as a new text arrives. 'About 9.30, or maybe 10,' she says after she opens it. 'He says he'll call me.'

'That's a bit late for a first date,' I say unsurely.

Or is it a booty call?

'No, you cannot go,' interrupts a stern voice, and we both turn to see Luc, shaking his head firmly.

'Why not?' asks Harriet, though I have a feeling there was no pun intended.

'It is not respectful,' he says, protectively. 'When a man takes out a woman for the first time, it should be romantic and special, and how you say, *exceptionnel—*'

'Exception-*al*,' corrects Harriet automatically.

'Dinner in a rooftop restaurant, dancing in the park – a moonlight *Vélib'* ride around the city . . .' He trails off, his chest heaving with passion.

If I had something of a soft spot for Luc beforehand, it's now a *really big* soft spot.

'What is this "drink"?' He frowns, his expression grave. 'Pah, this is not good enough!'

Actually, make that a *bloody huge* soft spot.

'It's a drink at a nice hotel,' she says defensively.

'*An 'otel*!' Luc looks even more shocked. Which is kind of

amusing, considering he's reacting the way you'd imagine an elderly, conservative old man to react, not a twenty-something with a shaved head and tattoos of bloody daggers up his forearm.

'I'm a big girl,' Harriet retorts, a little snippily. 'I can look after myself.'

'I will go with you,' he says, authoritatively.

She looks aghast. 'You can't go with me!' she gasps. 'It's a first date!'

Luc's face crumples and he looks momentarily crushed. '*J'ai reçu ton message*,' he replies tightly.

'I get the message,' she translates for me, equally tightly.

I fidget uncomfortably. Now, instead of feeling like I'm intruding on a private lesson, it feels like I'm in the middle of a lovers' tiff.

'I think I'll go get myself a drink,' I say hastily.

'But you haven't even finished that one,' says Harriet, and we both glance at the cocktail I'm holding in my hand.

I down it in one. 'Raging thirst,' I splutter, almost choking on the alcohol fumes, 'I'll be back in a jiffy.'

I quickly dash off before Harriet can protest further and Luc can ask me for the translation of 'jiffy' and accidentally find myself on the busy dance floor. A shirtless DJ is bent low over the decks, headphones clutched to one ear, spinning tracks for the achingly hip crowd. There are lots of tall, skinny girls in leather jackets and men with elaborate facial hair.

For several excruciating moments I get caught in the middle of a couple twerking, until finally I manage to escape. Freed, I try to find somewhere quiet. Which is nearly impossible as, as well as the music, there's the chatter and laughter of the other passengers. Eventually I stumble across a quieter spot at the back of the deck where there aren't so many people and, leaning against the handrail, I watch as Paris floats by.

Which is when I suddenly become aware of the faint burbling of my phone.

How long has that been ringing? I dig it out. It's a number I don't recognise. I pick up.

'Hello?'

'Ruby, it's me.'

The line is terrible, but his voice is unmistakable. *Jack*. My legs wobble and I cling to the handrail of the boat to avoid losing my balance.

'Hello me,' I say, trying to keep my voice level. I've tried to block him out, pretend like I don't care, but adrenalin floods through my body, melting my insides and sending my heart racing. It's incredible the effect he has on me, even from thousands of miles away.

'I got your message, I'm sorry I haven't been in touch.'

'It's OK,' I reply automatically, my self-preservation suddenly kicking in like some primal security blanket.

'There's been a bad storm out here and my connecting flight was delayed,' he continues. 'It's been chaos, a lot of the power lines are down and there's no cell reception or wireless. I'm calling from a hotel in the main town—'

'Honestly, it's fine,' I protest, talking over him before he can finish. 'You don't need to explain.'

He falls silent and there's one of those awkward pauses where no one says anything out loud but there's a million thoughts happening.

'How are you?' he asks, after a moment.

Upset, confused, missing you, I think, my heart aching, but instead I reply stiffly, 'Fine.'

'That's two fines in less than two minutes.'

'So?' My tone is defensive.

'So, I know you well enough to know you're not a "fine" kind of person,' he says evenly, 'you're an angry, ecstatic, upset, crazy, passionate, pig-headed kind of person.'

That's the annoying thing about Jack; he makes it impossible for me to stay angry with him.

'You're my kind of person.'

Hearing him say those words, I feel myself melt.

'I thought you wanted a timeout,' I retort.

But that doesn't mean I'm not still angry about what happened. He let me down and really hurt me. And now he thinks he can just call up like this, expecting everything to be normal again.

'I just thought we both needed some time to calm down, we were both pretty upset.'

Listening to his voice, I look up at the night sky. He feels so near and yet so far away. I think of our voices beaming up into the sky and bouncing off a satellite. Two people, two dots, connected over this vast galaxy.

'And do you blame me?' I ask, pressing the phone harder to my ear. God, I hate this distance between us.

'Look, I realise I may have handled it badly, and I promise I was all set to come and see you in London, spend your birthday with you, but at the last minute I had this emergency work situation—'

And you put work first, a voice in my head reminds me. I don't care what he says, there's no reason good enough for him to choose work over our plans to see each other. Nothing can be that important.

'—normally I would have said no way, but it's for a charity.'

Except that one.

'A charity?' I repeat, not sure I heard him right.

'Yeah, I do a lot of pro bono for Give the World a Home, a homeless charity that works in developing countries. They needed an architect to help with the building of new housing and when they approached me I was more than happy to help. Mostly, I've been doing it remotely from the States, but there's been a major structural problem and there's no one else on the ground they could ask. I needed to come out here and be on site . . .'

As he's speaking any anger I had been feeling has trickled away and I'm hit with a double-edged sword of emotions: immense pride in Jack and incredible shame at myself. How could I have doubted him like this? How could I have jumped to such conclusions? I have a flashback to my meltdown at the airport.

'—and it's actually worse than I thought. There's loads to do and it's all volunteers, so I need to roll up my sleeves and get dirty—'

Oh god, and now I feel terrible. To think I made such a fuss about my birthday when all the time he was flying thousands of miles to help those less fortunate.

'Anyway, I'll stop talking about me, what about you? What have you been doing?'

Having lunch with handsome Frenchmen in Paris, drinking champagne, feeling sorry for myself. I feel a stab of guilt. Suddenly the tables have turned. And they've turned so fast I feel all in a spin.

'Umm, not much . . .' I say vaguely.

'Where are you now? At your apartment?'

Still, I have to tell him. It's not as if I've done anything wrong by coming here. And it was still pretty crappy what happened. Charity or no charity.

'Actually—'

'Don't tell me. It's late, you're curled up on the couch watching TV with Heathcliff, the lucky guy.' He sighs deeply at the other end of the line. 'Seriously Ruby, there's nowhere I'd like to be more right now, than curled up with you.'

I feel a pang of longing. 'Me too,' I reply. On second thoughts I'll tell him later. Now's not the right time.

A passing boat goes by and gives a loud toot.

'What was that?' asks Jack.

Oh fuck. 'The TV,' I fluster, playing along. 'I'm watching a movie—'

'Which movie?'

His voice is drowned out as our boat suddenly gives another loud foghorn toot back.

'Um, *Titanic*,' I blurt, my mind scrambling.

'For about the hundredth time, right?' He laughs good-naturedly.

'Ha, ha yes, something like that,' I reply awkwardly. Oh god, what am I doing? Relationships are built on trust. It's the bedrock of a strong relationship, along with honesty and integrity. When Sam cheated it wasn't just the betrayal that broke my heart, it was the lies. I can't lie to Jack. I have to tell the truth.

'Look, Jack—' I begin, but I'm interrupted by a loud crackle on the line.

'Ruby? Are you still there?' But his voice is so faint I can barely hear it.

'Yes, I'm here,' I say loudly, trying to make myself heard over the noisy hissing that's started.

'Hey, I can't hear you, the line's really bad . . .'

'Can you hear me now?'

But there's nothing, just the sound of crackling and buzzing.

'Hello, Jack?' I press the phone to my ear, trying in vain to hear his voice, but nothing.

Abruptly, the line goes dead.

I snatch the phone from my ear and study my screen, but no, the connection has been lost. We barely had a chance to speak and now he's gone again. Feeling a kick of disappointment, I look up and stare out across the Seine, gazing at the banks of the city as it floats by. A huge part of me feels so much better that he didn't abandon me for any old work project, yet I wasn't truthful. I never told him I was here in Paris. I never told him about being at this party, or staying with Harriet, or my lunch with Xavier. I never even told him about Madame Dumont's apartment.

A warm breeze catches the hem of my dress and I shiver,

despite the balmy evening. In the past we've shared everything, but now there are all these secrets. All these things left unsaid. All this miscommunication and misunderstandings. When did it get so messy and complicated?

Troubled, I turn away from the water and make my way back across the deck to find Harriet. I spot her chatting to a group of people and make a sort of waving gesture to avoid the inevitable round of introductions. Spotting me, she quickly excuses herself.

'I was just about to come and find you,' she says, wobbling over, her face flushed. 'I tried calling, but my battery died.' She waves her phone at me, tipsily.

'Too much texting?'

Her face flushes even deeper. 'So are you enjoying yourself?' she asks, swiftly changing the subject.

'It's a great party,' I say, deflecting the question, 'but I'm actually pretty tired . . .' As I'm talking, I can see we're heading for the next dock at the Musée d'Orsay, and I realise this is my chance. 'I was thinking I might head back to the apartment, if you don't mind, that is,' I add, hastily.

Harriet's face falls. 'So soon?'

I'm suddenly reminded of how vulnerable she'd sounded when she'd called me from Paris, and during our first night at the apartment, when she'd shared her true feelings over takeaway pizza. I quickly change my mind. 'Actually you're right, I'll stay a bit longer.'

'No, you go,' she says, patting my arm, 'It's all boring work stuff anyway.'

'Are you sure?'

'Absolutely. You've got your keys?'

'Yes Mum.' I grin and feel around in my bag for them, only after a few seconds of fruitless searching it dawns on me that they're not there. 'Damn, I must have left them in the apartment when I dropped off Heathcliff.'

'Never mind, take mine.' She fishes out a jumble of keys

and hands me a set. 'I'll see you at home, I won't be long. I just want to finish up this fascinating conversation about Bauhaus lamps . . .'

She waves from the deck as I disembark and for a few minutes I watch her float away, before glancing at the keys in my hand. There's a tag attached to the key ring and I notice something written in felt-tip.

Madame Dumont.

As I read Harriet's handwriting, a pulse somewhere starts beating. She's given me the wrong keys. These must be the keys for the mystery apartment. And as it registers, something flickers inside. No, that's ridiculous, I can't – *can I?* I stare at them for a moment, uncertain what to do. And yet, Harriet's phone's dead and who knows how long it'll be before she gets home. I can't just wander the streets.

Plus, this is the perfect opportunity to put the letters back, I suddenly realise. I have them with me in my handbag. I can go there now and no one will ever be the wiser. It makes total sense.

But as the idea hits, I feel a stab of disappointment. I haven't finished reading them. I'll never be able to find out what happens to Emmanuelle and Henry. I'll never be able to unravel the mystery of the apartment—

I quickly grab hold of myself. My whole life I've been fascinated by people's stories of love and romance, but this time it doesn't just involve me, it involves Harriet as well. I can't risk getting her into trouble. So what if I never get to discover the ending to this love story or the reasons why an apartment in Paris was kept a secret for over seventy years? What does it matter?

It's all in the past now. Madame Dumont has died and it's likely Henry has too. And with them, so has their love story. It's not important any more.

What's important is that I took these letters and I have to put them back.

17

Just to clarify, it's not breaking and entering if you have the keys, right?

Twenty minutes later, I'm inside Madame Dumont's building. Luckily, I remembered the passcode from when Xavier first passed me the slip of paper a few days ago. Except it wasn't really luck; I had memorised the digits, almost as if I knew I'd be coming back here again. Travelling up in the lift, my heart flutters like a trapped bird. I don't know whether it's nerves or excitement, or both. I try to reassure myself it's going to be just fine. I'll only be a couple of minutes. I'll put the letters back where I found them and then I'll leave. No one will ever be any the wiser.

As the lift reaches my floor, I pull back the metal concertina doors, and step out into the corridor. The whole building is quiet. It's late; the other inhabitants are probably fast asleep. I check to make sure there's no one around, then carefully slip the key into the lock. It's still stiff and I have to jiggle it around a bit, but after a few moments the door releases and creaks quietly open.

My breath catches and I have to steady my nerves. Now I'm here, I can't quite believe it's real. Slowly, I step through the doorway. It feels different this time. Before I was entering the apartment of a stranger, Madame Dumont, an old lady of ninety-five I knew nothing about. In my mind I'd imagined her as this white-haired pensioner in her nineties, a cranky, crooked Miss Havisham from *Great Expectations*.

But now I'm entering the home of Emmanuelle. A flame-haired twenty-one-year-old with a passion for ballet, silk dresses and jazz. A young woman on the brink of a clandestine love affair with a young American writer called Henry. This is where they met in secret during that long, glorious summer before the war, in a city filled with artists, writers and musicians. Rubbing shoulders with such legendary names as Picasso, Henry Miller, Josephine Baker . . . It's the stuff of dreams. Of a magical era long gone by.

And it's this apartment in Paris that connects the past to the present. Together with Emmanuelle's letters it gives us the ability to time-travel, to step through some portal, I decide, with a tingle of anticipation.

It's dark inside but for a shaft of moonlight shining through a gap in the shutters, which have been left slightly ajar, casting everything in a pearlescent glow. Usually I'm a little afraid of the dark – it always feels slightly spooky – but tonight the moonlight makes it feel almost enchanted.

Closing the door behind me, I make my way further inside the main drawing room, retracing the steps Emmanuelle would have taken after her first chance meeting with Henry at the café. My mind flashes back to the letters, how he talks about walking her home. After saying goodnight, maybe she even stood by this window and watched his departing figure, I reflect, glancing out at the street below, at the yellow circles of light being cast from the streetlamps onto the cobbles.

It's quiet, there's no one around, apart from a stray cat that makes its way stealthily in and out of the shadows. I can picture Henry now, hands in his pockets, smile on his face as he walked home on air, bathed in that happy glow you get when you've met someone you're crazy about. And Emmanuelle, intrigued by this writer from Brooklyn, secretly hoping he would contact her, gazing out into the night. Just like I'm doing now, over seventy years later.

I turn away from the window. Here alone, without Harriet and Xavier, it's just me and the ghosts of the past. Slipping off my shoes so I don't make a noise on the parquet floors, I pad quietly through the rooms, careful not to disturb anything. I notice a few things have been moved and Harriet has left a few files, but mostly it's still as it was.

Overhead the chandelier rattles, the crystal droplets making a faint chinking as they swing back and forth, and my heart skips a beat. I glance around me, half expecting to see someone, but there's nothing. It must be just the neighbours upstairs. Or maybe the rumble from a car on the street outside is making the building shake slightly. I feel faintly ridiculous. I'm being silly. There is no such thing as *real* ghosts, right?

Shoving my childish fears down inside me, I walk into the bedroom where I first found the letters. It's just as I remember, with the covers still thrown back and the dressing table filled with her things. Only now they're not an old lady's dusty possessions, they're Emmanuelle's and she used them to get ready to meet Henry at the jazz concert. This is her lipstick case and her mother-of-pearl hairbrush, a needle and thread used to mend a repair, or maybe sew on a button – and look, these are her bottles of perfume.

As the moonlight squeezes through a crack in the shutters, catching the perfume bottles, one catches my eye. Made of delicate blue glass with faint silver stencilling around the neck, it casts coloured prisms against the wall. I gaze at it. I daren't touch and yet . . .

The temptation is too much. Carefully I pick it up, turning the smooth glass over in my hands and feeling the curved edges with my fingertips, before lifting it gingerly to my nostrils. After seventy years the scent is faded, but it's still there. I dab a little on my wrist and as I inhale, I close my eyes, letting the aroma release my imagination.

There's something special about a scent. Something so powerful that it can transport you to another time and place. Seeing a photograph or listening to a song can remind you of the past, but the sense of smell has the ability to make you travel through time.

The sweet scent of pipe smoke that takes you back to sitting on your grandfather's knee as a child; an old suede coat that you discover in an attic, still smelling of youth clubs and sneaky cigarettes and long-spilled cider and suddenly you are fifteen again; the heady mix of the sea and fish and chips that transports you back to that old bus shelter in Cornwall where you had your first kiss.

But it's not just about revisiting your past; a scent can take you somewhere different entirely. It can conjure up a whole new world. Like a key unlocking a door, it can transport you into another place – like the one in which Emmanuelle was a young woman getting ready at her dressing table.

I can picture her now, combing her hair and putting on her perfume, dabbing it on to the insides of her wrists and her neck with the delicate glass stopper. I can feel the anticipation of the evening ahead, imagine her excitement at seeing Henry again, see her in her yellow silk polka dot dress, the way it flares gently as she twirls excitedly from side to side in front of her mirror to gaze at herself—

The loud creak of a floorboard jolts me back to the present.

'Hello?'

I snap open my eyes. Spooked, I glance around me, a shiver running down my spine. But the room's empty. There's no one here, I remind myself again firmly. Honestly, I'm so skittish, I don't know what's wrong with me. Next I'll be thinking this place is haunted! Putting the perfume bottle back on the dressing table, I take a deep breath to calm myself.

OK, I'm here to return the letters, remember?

Reaching into my bag, I pull out the bundle. Then pause. I can't leave without reading just one more. Glancing around the room, my eye is caught by an old leather club chair in the corner. A teddy bear is propped up against a cushion, a smile on his face, as if waiting for me to join him.

Careful not to disturb anything, I gently sit down next to him, curling my dusty feet underneath me. The leather is surprisingly soft against my legs and I feel suddenly weary. I'm tired, it's been a long day and the cocktails are weaving their drowsy path through my veins. I stifle a yawn and rub my eyes, then unfold the next letter.

This is probably the same spot where Emmanuelle originally read this letter from Henry, I realise, goose bumps prickling on my arms as the moonlight catches the handwriting. And feeling an even closer connection, I begin reading:

My darling Manu,

Oh, how I love that we have secret names for each other. To the rest of the world you might be Emmanuelle Renoir, but to me you are my darling Manu and I am your darling H. It's fitting don't you think? If we are to keep our love a secret, then we should create our own special, secret world in your apartment. It can be our world where we laugh and dance freely, where we share our hopes and dreams without fear of reprisal.

Who needs the jazz clubs of Stage B or Club Bobino or the late-night cabarets and bars of Montmartre and Montparnasse, when instead we can dance to jazz records on your gramophone? Who needs to dine in the finest restaurants of L'Ami Louis, Boeuf sur le Toit, or Le Vaudeville, when we can eat fresh moules and drink a fine Chablis at your table? Who needs to walk along the Seine in the bright, yellow

*sunshine when we can curl up on your chaise and watch the
pale moon rise into the clear night sky?*

*The real world outside no longer feels real to me. My reality
is our world inside. A world without boundaries or rules,
without threat of war or family traditions, without fear of
reprisal. What can we call this new world, Manu? It needs a
new name for we have found a new world, like an astronomer
when he has discovered a new planet. We have our own sun
and stars and moon, and yet we are the only inhabitants.*

How lucky are we?

*Well, my darling, for now the other world beckons. I have
lots to do, today I am moving out of my room at the hotel as
they have raised the price to a silly number of francs. I didn't
tell you before, as I knew you would worry. I knew also that
being such a sweet soul you would offer to help, which is
something I could never allow. I am rich in pride, if not in
wealth and your generosity would have caused me great
heartache.*

*Yet, there is nothing to worry about my darling, indeed you
should be excited for me, as I am excited for myself. I have
found new lodgings at Shakespeare & Company, a little
bookstore not far from here on Rue de l'Odéon. Oh, it is such
a wonderful place. Just imagine, I will be following in the
footsteps of such luminaries as Hemingway and Fitzgerald
and Joyce. I will be in the company of giants, Manu.*

*So, from today you must write to me every day at that
address. Several times a day if you would like, for I never tire
of reading about what you are doing. I could read forever about
your daily ballet practice and the shy piano player or your walk
to the boulangerie with its moustachioed owner and his overfed
cat.*

*Oh, how I love your observations. To hear you describe
how you wear my small gift of fragrance daily and breathe the
scent of your wrist whenever you think of me makes me so very*

happy. (I thought the blue bottle was so pretty, it is the same color as your eyes.) As does your confession that you wear my necklace hidden beneath your dress and how you prefer it to any diamonds, which makes me smile as I doubt that very much, but I love you all the more for saying it.

These are just small tokens of my affections my darling, mere trinkets to make you smile when I am not in your presence. I wish we could be together every minute of every day, I miss you when we are apart, and worry about you so, which is why I am sending you a teddy bear with this letter. He is to keep you company in my absence.

Do you like him my love? I have named him Franklin, after my president, and he has a smile as big as mine when I see you. I have found him to be a very good listener. You can tell him anything, for I promise he will keep all our secrets.

Today, I heard a song on the radio. I could not understand all the lyrics as my French is still sadly lacking, but I knew immediately it should be our song. It is called 'J'attendrai'. Have you heard it? I shall buy the gramophone record and we can dance to it together the next time we meet.

Write to me my darling. Write to me and tell me when I can see you.

For you, always, I will wait.
Your beloved
H

Wow, what a beautiful letter. Feeling my eyes prickling with tears, I wipe them away with my fingertips. It's just so romantic, so heartfelt, so—

My thoughts stall as I'm distracted by the faint sound of music. I turn my head, trying to hear. It must be coming from a neighbour's apartment. It sounds like a TV; maybe someone's watching a movie and they've got the soundtrack turned up high. I strain harder. Though, it doesn't sound like a soundtrack. Maybe it's coming from a car radio in the street below . . .

Then I hear it. Much clearer this time. Louder. It's someone singing, a woman, a soprano . . . I listen to the voice as it rises and falls to a melody. I can't quite catch the lyrics but it's the most beautiful thing I've ever heard. And now I can hear violins accompanying her, the tinkling of a piano, and is that a trumpet? The music swells and as it does I'm aware of something else, something much more subtle, a faint crackling, a static, almost like the sound of a needle on an old record. *A record playing on an old gramophone.* And as it registers, I realise she's singing in French.

It's that song. 'J'attendrai.'

Abruptly, I feel the hairs stand up on the back of my neck.

What the—?

My heart skips a beat. That's unbelievable. What a freaky coincidence. But that's all it is, I remind myself quickly. Just a coincidence. I listen harder, totally absorbed by the arrangement of the orchestra, the soaring voice as it swoops and trills, the haunting melody, and as I do it hits me.

It's coming from the next room.

No sooner has the thought struck than a shiver scurries down my spine and goose bumps prickle on my arms. I'm hearing things. It's impossible. It can't be. There's no one else in this apartment—

My mind is scrambling, and yet even though the rational, sensible, *sane* side of me knows there has to be a logical explanation, there's a secret, romantic, quite frankly *terrified* part of me that is thinking the unthinkable.

They're here.

My breath catches inside my chest and I freeze. It's Emmanuelle and Henry. They're dancing to their record, just like Henry wrote in his letter. The spirits of two lovers, bringing their memories alive again . . . and yet I don't feel as if I'm surrounded by the ghosts of the past, I feel as if I'm in the present. *Their* present. As if somehow I've slipped through the cobwebs of time and stepped into their secret world.

For a few moments I sit completely still, listening to the music, then with my heart hammering in my chest, I slowly rise up from the chaise longue. Something is propelling me forwards. Curiosity. Desire. Fascination. This is *insane*, completely and utterly insane.

But it's also exciting, I realise, every nerve ending in my body tingling. I can hear my breath coming out in short, sharp bursts and I try to steady myself.

This cannot be happening. It just can't. I don't believe in ghosts.

But I do believe in Emmanuelle and Henry. I believe in their love for each other. I believe in the power of love that compels us to do the most incredible, wonderful, mind-blowing things, like lifting cars up with our bare hands or paying the rent on a secret apartment in Paris for seventy years. A love so strong that it continues to burn like an eternal flame, long after we are gone. An everlasting energy that in itself is a kind of magic.

I wished that the music would never stop playing and we would forever twirl together around the dance floor. And in my heart we always will.

This is what Henry wrote of in one of his letters, what he wished for . . .

Slowly I push open the door, heady with anticipation. The music is even louder now. I can hear footsteps on the floor-boards, see the flash of yellow silk reflected in the patina of the mirror standing opposite, catch the sounds of laughter. And now I barely dare breathe as I step forward to catch sight of Emmanuelle and Henry, dancing around the room, his arm round her waist, her hand on his shoulder, her silk dress twirling around her as they—

'Ruby?'

A voice jolts into my consciousness.

'Ruby, are you there? Can you hear me?'

Huh? What's happening? I can hear Harriet. Where is she? *Where am I?*

Disorientated, I sit bolt upright, my head spinning, my eyes darting around me. I'm still on the chair in the bedroom. The music's stopped. Or was it ever playing? I feel something hard wedged underneath my thigh and pull out my phone.

'Ruby?'

It's Harriet's voice again, coming out of the speaker. Confused, I stare at it, my thoughts whirling. I must have fallen asleep and been dreaming – the music I thought I heard must have been my ringtone – somehow my phone must have slipped out of my bag and I answered it by accident when I shifted in the chair—

'I can't hear a thing, it's so loud at this party, hang on I'm going to call you back—'

'No!' I blurt hastily, 'I mean yes, it's me, I can hear you.'

'Oh, thank goodness!' Over the top of the *umps-umps* beat in the background, I hear a relieved sigh. 'I've been trying to get hold of you, your phone was ringing for ages and then when you didn't answer . . .'

'Sorry, I was just—' I break off, groggily. I cannot even begin to explain. 'I thought your phone was dead?'

'It is, I borrowed a colleague's when I realised I'd given you the wrong keys. Golly, sorry Ruby, I'm such a klutz! Anyway, don't worry, I won't be long, I'll be home soon!'

'Um yes, OK,' I reply dazedly, hanging up.

I remain motionless for a few seconds, still absorbing the sudden turn of events, then quickly stand up. OK, I need to pull myself together. I need to leave. The letter I was reading is still lying on the chair, and hurriedly I slip it back into the bundle.

I glance towards the bed underneath which I found them. And as I do, I think about everything that's happened. Before I came here tonight I tried to convince myself that their love story wasn't important, that it had happened so long ago, before the war, and that it was all in the past. But I was wrong, I was so very, very wrong. It *is* important. And it's not just in the past. Our bodies might not be eternal, but love is.

Madame Dumont closed the shutters on this apartment over seventy years ago, but she kept it for a reason, just like she kept these letters for a reason. *And I found them for a reason*. Fate, destiny, call it what you want, but I just can't leave them here and walk away.

But what about the repercussions if anyone were to find out I had these letters? What if Harriet got into trouble? I can't risk that. And yet, on the other hand, how *can* anyone find out? No one knows of their existence but me.

I stall, an internal battle raging. I feel completely torn. But still, despite my misgivings, I know I have to do the right thing.

Holding the letters, I reluctantly walk towards the bed. I wonder who will end up finding these? Probably whoever clears out the apartment ahead of the auction. Most likely they'll be read by dozens of strangers, experts, maybe even lawyers, to see if they hold any value or importance, before being passed on to her distant heirs.

My fingers hold tightly on to the faded ribbon, my thumb tracing Henry's handwriting. Maybe they'll keep them, treasure them, as Emmanuelle treasured them, but even as I'm hoping, I know it's unlikely. They're not valuable in a monetary sense. The chances are they'll be tossed away with the rest of her belongings that don't carry a price tag. Gone for ever.

And in that moment I know I can't let that happen. I don't have a plan, I don't know what's going to happen, but whatever happens, I owe it to Emmanuelle and Henry. Like I said, I need to do the right thing – *and I'm doing it.*

Clutching their letters tightly to my chest, I turn away from the bed and walk quickly out of the bedroom. As I do, I pass through the moonlit drawing room where I thought I'd heard music and dancing. I glance across at the gramophone player with its large brass trumpet, lying silent in the corner. Curiosity prickles. Which is crazy. It was just a dream, remember? A bad case of REM. A figment of my overactive imagination.

But still, I can't resist. I step towards it. Though I don't know what I'm expecting to find—

'J'attendrai' by Rina Ketty.

As I see the gramophone record on the turntable, I stiffen. Coincidence. It has to be. Nothing more. And yet . . . I stare at it for a few seconds, my eyes tracing the grooves in the shiny black disc, something else niggling at me, before dismissing it. Enough of this nonsense, I need to hurry up and get home. Quickly turning away, I pull open the heavy panelled door, but it's only as it closes behind me that it finally hits me.

There was no dust on the record.

18

Fast forward to the next morning and I'm in the café on the corner with Harriet, drinking café crème, before she heads off to work.

'He's working for a charity?' she repeats, as I finish filling her in on last night's phone conversation with Jack. 'So he's not been kidnapped by Colombian drug lords?' She looks almost disappointed.

'No, sorry.' I smile and shake my head.

'Oh well, at least that's good news,' she says. 'You must feel much better.'

'Well, yes and no.'

Harriet frowns. 'Hang on, let's recap. The man you're madly in love with called you last night from a far-flung corner of the globe. In the middle of a storm, no less. Furthermore, he's not being chopped up and sent to you for ransom. He has all his bits intact.'

'True.' Well, if she puts it like that.

She stares at me across our wobbly table. Despite various napkins from previous customers being wedged under one of its legs, one misplaced elbow and our morning coffees are liable to end up in our laps. 'So, how can this not be good news?' she demands.

'Because now I feel even more terrible about the row at the airport,' I confess, with a heavy voice. 'He had a good reason for not coming and I totally lost it. I should've trusted him.' I stir my café crème glumly. 'I just didn't understand, and the thing is, I didn't *want* to understand.'

'Since when are men and women supposed to understand each other?' she says dismissively. 'We're from Venus, they're from Mars. We speak a different language.'

I nod in agreement. Harriet isn't known for her sage advice when it comes to relationships, something she admits herself, but for once she's actually talking a lot of sense.

'Women will forever be a mystery to men and vice versa,' she continues wisely. 'For example, why do men send us pictures of their penises?'

I've been listening and nodding, but now I nearly choke on my café crème. 'What did you just say?' I splutter, putting an elbow on the table to steady myself and spilling coffee on myself in the process.

She waves her smartphone at me, and I have to use my saucer to shield myself from the image on her screen. 'Ugh, god Harriet, what *is* that?'

'You can't tell? Hang on, let me see if I can zoom in—'

'No! No! I don't mean that.' I start waving my hands madly and Luc looks over from behind the espresso machine. After last night's run-in at the party, he's kept his distance and has instead been flashing furtive glances across at Harriet. I think he's still sore about her going on a date.

'Is everything OK?' He beetles his eyebrows.

'No – I mean yes,' I say hastily, and flap my hands even harder, 'it's just a fly – buzz . . . go away . . .'

He nods, satisfied, and continues making coffee.

I turn back to Harriet, who's peering at her screen, angling it this way and that.

'I suppose it makes sense if he's six foot seven . . .' she's murmuring.

'That's *WineNot?*' I look at her, aghast. I'm not a prude, I've had Skype sex, remember (though admittedly I was pretty rubbish at it) but even so. 'He sent you that before you've even gone on a date?'

I'd expected Harriet to be shocked – after all this is someone who still uses the phrase 'front bottom' – but instead she seems curiously composed.

'His name's Rupert,' she reminds me calmly, 'and believe me, he's not unusual. Chaps are forever sending photos like those to girls these days. When they're not posting skydiving selfies they're taking pictures of Mr Winky.'

'*They are?*'

Seriously, where have I been? I don't remember it being like that when I was single, but then again, I didn't date. I just sat on the sofa eating crisps and nursing a bottle of wine and a broken heart. By the sounds of it, I had a lucky escape.

She nods matter-of-factly. 'Give a man a camera-phone and . . .' She trails off with a Gallic shrug of her shoulders and takes a sip of her coffee.

'Well, I suppose it's a bit different from the traditional bouquet of flowers,' I concede, stirring extra sugar into my coffee. After that shock, I need it.

'Maybe I should post this to his Facebook page,' she says, tapping on her smartphone.

I shoot her a look. 'You're not serious.'

'No, of course not,' she giggles, 'anyway, he hasn't accepted my friend request yet. I do follow him on Twitter but that's quite dull as it's his company's account. Just lots of tweets about grapes and vintages.' She waves his Twitter page at me.

'Does he know you're stalking him on social media?'

Harriet looks affronted. 'I'm not! I'm just trying to get to know him.'

'What happened to actually meeting someone in real life?' I suggest, 'getting to know them in person, instead of through status updates, and likes and photos on their Instagram?'

'He's not on Instagram,' she points out innocently.

'You know what I mean,' I say, my mind flashing back to the road trip I'd taken with Jack across Rajasthan and how we'd gradually gone from strangers to lovers, through a million, small things. Like a smile after a stupid argument, a shared sunset in the desert, a comfortable silence.

Or dancing around your apartment together to a favourite gramophone record, I reflect, suddenly thinking about Henry and Emmanuelle and feeling goose bumps prickle, despite the morning heat.

'I am going to meet him. It's our first date tonight, remember?'

At the reference to a first date, Luc's head flicks towards us, his ears almost visibly waggling.

'Sorry, yes, you told me,' I apologise quickly. With everything that's going on it had slipped my mind. 'That's great.' Despite my misgivings, I want to be supportive. I know how much this means to her. 'Where are you meeting?'

Lowering her voice so she's out of earshot of Luc, she continues, 'A boutique hotel in the eighth, apparently it has a fabulous new oyster bar—' Abruptly, at the mention of oysters, she suddenly goes very grey.

'Are you all right?' I look at her, concerned.

'Yes, fine, just a tad hungover.' She winces and reaches for the plate of pains au chocolat Luc had insisted on giving us with our cafés crèmes. 'I wouldn't, but I need to settle my stomach,' she says, although it's muffled through a mouthful of flaky pastry.

I nod, understandingly, though quite frankly it's not the idea of oysters that's making my stomach go funny. I've still got the image from her phone seared on my mind, like when you've looked at the sun for too long. Actually, doesn't looking at the sun make you go blind? Which is probably the same effect as that photo has, I reflect, with a shudder.

'Anyway, you were saying, about Jack . . .' she prompts, coming back to me again.

Reminded, I let out a deep sigh. 'I just feel awful. I gave him such a hard time and yet he's there working for a homeless charity in the middle of goodness knows where, and here's me cavorting around Paris.'

'Hardly. Not in those heels you were wearing last night,' she corrects me, pulling a face.

I smile ruefully. 'I've tried calling him back a few times, but it just goes straight to voicemail. I just want to explain. I feel so guilty.'

'Well don't,' she says firmly, fiddling with her smartphone, 'you had every right to be upset and anyway, he doesn't look like he's working too hard.'

I look at her in confusion. 'What are you talking about?'

'Give the World a Home has a Facebook page.'

'So?'

'And Jack's been tagged in a photo.'

'*He has?*' I look at her incredulously. 'Here, let me see.'

'I thought you didn't believe in stalking on social media?' she says archly, not letting me look.

'I'm not stalking, he's my boyfriend!' I dive into my bag and start scrambling for my own phone. Sod data roaming charges, I'm getting online.

'Who's Beth?'

It's like someone just plugged me into the mains. My head jerks up. 'Jack's ex-girlfriend. The one he met at a fundraiser in New York. Why?'

Harriet pauses, in that 'me and my big mouth' kind of way. 'Oh – oh, no real reason . . .' she says trying, and failing, to sound all nonchalant, 'she was just tagged with him, that's all.'

That's all?

Reaching across the table, I grab her phone from her before she can protest. 'I thought she worked for a charity in India.'

'Maybe she got transferred to a different office. Or maybe it's not her.' Realising she's just dropped a bomb, Harriet is quickly trying to engage in damage limitation. 'Beth is a really common name, there must be millions of Beths—' but even as she's saying it I recognise the pretty, dark-haired girl immediately.

Well, c'mon, who doesn't Google their boyfriend's ex-girlfriend?

'No, that's her,' I say, looking at the picture of them together, wearing hard hats on a construction site, and the biggest smiles you've ever seen.

'He didn't mention she was working on the same project?' I shake my head dumbly.

'Well, he probably didn't know until he got there, and anyway, it's not important, they're over, he's with you now . . .'

Harriet is chuntering away in the background, but it's like everything around me has disappeared and all I can concentrate on is the photograph of them together. I pinch the screen with my fingers and zoom in, making their smiles bigger and bigger until they fill the screen. I feel vaguely sick.

'It's just some silly photo, it doesn't mean anything,' she says dismissively.

'Yes, I know.' I nod, handing back her phone. But it's stirred something inside me: the fear of being betrayed, of being let down, that lurks beneath the surface like some kind of monster.

'Golly, is that the time?' Glancing at her watch, Harriet tuts loudly. 'I'd better go.'

'Already?' I feel a beat of disappointment. Usually I'm totally fine with my own company, but today I could do with being around a friendly face. 'You don't have time for another coffee?'

'I wish,' she sighs, 'but work's crazy. The catalogue for Madame Dumont's apartment is back from the printers and

I need to do a final check of it. I've got to head down to Provence tomorrow to present it to her beneficiaries, ahead of the auction.' She stands up to leave.

My stomach twists up at the mention of the auction. 'Provence? But why? Aren't they coming to Paris?'

'No, they're too busy.'

'Busy?' I can't help but feel angry at the thought of Emmanuelle's home being broken up and them not even bothering to show up.

'Apparently.' Harriet shrugs.

'When is the auction?'

'Sunday, but the removal people are going in today to clear out everything so it can be marked up and viewed beforehand.' She pauses. 'It's very exciting, but rather sad to think of it all being sold off after all these years. I wonder why she kept it like that?' She gazes into the middle distance for a moment, then gives a brisk little shrug of her shoulders. 'Still, I suppose we'll never know now.'

'No, I guess not,' I reply, and I feel a sudden sense of futility.

I mean, seriously, what am I doing, thinking I can solve some half-a-century-old mystery? I'm a novelist, not a real-life detective. Being fascinated by love is all very well, but let's face it, I'm never going to find out what happened through a few love letters. It's hopeless. I don't even have a clue who Henry is, let alone anything else. Plus, in a few days the apartment will have been cleared out and everything auctioned off. There won't be a mystery to solve any more, it will be all gone. Like it never even existed.

'What about you?' she asks, turning back to me. 'More sightseeing?'

I snap back. 'Actually, I was thinking of visiting some bookshops, you know how I love them. Paris has such a great literary history, I thought it might give me some inspiration for my new book.'

I say it more to remind myself than Harriet. I need to get a grip. Concentrate on the present, *my* present. I've been so wrapped up in Madame Dumont's apartment and Henry's letters, I haven't given much thought to anything else. But now I need to focus on my own life and forget all that other stuff.

'Well, in that case you must go to Shakespeare & Company,' she suggests.

My stomach flips. 'It still exists? I mean, I thought, what with the war . . .'

'Yes, it's on rue de la Bûcherie. It's not the original bookshop – that closed during the war. This one is at a different address but it's still completely wonderful. You'll love it.'

I feel a surge of excitement, but I try to keep my voice calm. 'Great, thanks, I'll go check it out.'

'OK, well I really must dash,' she says, gathering up her things. 'I'm going straight on my date after work, so I'm not sure what time I'll be home.' She smiles excitedly. 'Don't wait up for me.'

'I won't.' I grin and, saying goodbye to Harriet, I set off across the cobbles. Everything I'd thought has just flown out of the window and I feel a renewed sense of determination. I can't give up now. It's a sign, it has to be.

And with every step I take, I feel one step closer to Henry, and one step closer to solving this mystery.

19

When I say I love bookshops, it's a bit like saying Madonna loves attention. Just a slight understatement. What I really mean is, I *lurve* bookshops. I'm obsessed by them. Even addicted. I can't walk past one without diving inside, only to emerge several hours and pounds later, weighed down with carrier bags.

From the floor-to-ceiling bookshelves filled with a thousand treasure chests waiting to be opened, to the way the spines feel as you run your finger along them, to the sheer intoxicating smell of all those books, I love everything about them.

But most of all I love the quiet contemplation. The hours lost browsing shelves. The chance to switch off. In this fast-paced digital world I love the chance to look away from a screen and, merely by turning a page, be transported to another time and place entirely.

My favourite bookshop in the whole world is a beautiful Edwardian shop in London, boasting oak galleries, parquet floors and a gorgeous stained-glass atrium. Or at least it was until now, I reflect, as I turn a corner on the Left Bank and see a small shop tucked away, its green facade almost hidden behind shelves of books overflowing onto the cobbles. And the sign, *Shakespeare & Company*.

It's love at first sight.

As I step through the doorway, everywhere I look there are rows upon rows of books. Bookcases stretch from floor to ceiling. Every inch of conceivable space is filled with an assortment of titles. It's as if you can feel the stories seeping out of the walls and hear the cacophony of authors' voices, past and present, all around you.

It's busy with customers, many of them tourists flocking around the shelves dedicated to Ernest Hemingway, James Joyce and F. Scott Fitzgerald, the writers that Henry talked about in his letters to Emmanuelle. Making my way past them, I venture into the shadowy recesses. I'm not sure what I hope to discover – after all, this isn't the original bookshop – but still I can't quell a growing sense of anticipation.

At the back of the shop there's a wooden staircase, and I climb upstairs above the shop to find a rabbit warren of reading rooms. Here the books aren't for sale; instead the volumes are stacked several rows deep, spines jostling against spines, oversized hardbacks against well-read paperbacks, leather-bound classics against pulp fiction.

It's much quieter here, away from the crowds, and I wander through the rooms. In a tiny cubby-hole a vintage typewriter sits on a desk. Absently I brush my fingertips over the keys, my imagination working overtime. I wonder if Henry used one like this? Perhaps it could even be the very same model. On the wall above are pasted photographs and scribbled notes left from visitors, torn pages from manuscripts, typewritten excerpts: I read them all for some clue, some hope that I can find a connection.

Because as crazy and implausible and as far-fetched as it sounds, I can't help feeling there's some trace of him here, that some part of him still remains. I just don't know what.

'*Pardon—*'

I nearly jump out of my skin. Snatching my fingers off the keys, I twirl round to see one of those hipster types with a beard and a beanie hat pulled down low over his eyes. He's carrying an armful of books.

'Oh sorry, I thought this was open to the public—' I start backing out.

'No, it's OK, please stay.' He speaks with a heavy French accent. 'Be not inhospitable to strangers lest they be angels in disguise.'

I look at him questioningly and he smiles.

'It's above the doorway downstairs, it was one of the owner's favourite epigrams,' he explains, then smiles. 'Do you need help?'

'No, thank you, I was just looking.' I gesture to the walls. 'It's fascinating.'

'So much history.' He nods.

'What happened to the original shop?'

'It closed down with the outbreak of the Second World War. It was run by Sylvia Beach, an American. Apparently, she was quite a character. She published James Joyce's *Ulysses*.'

'She did? Wow.' So that explains the crowds of tourists queuing up to buy their own copies.

'And so many other writers visited,' he continues, 'Fitzgerald, Miller, Hemingway – it was the meeting place for the lost generation. At night the couches turned into beds where writers slept in exchange for stacking shelves.'

Just like Henry did. He was one of those writers, all those years ago.

'It must have been incredible,' he continues, shaking his head. 'If only there was a window into the past.'

I think about the letters in my bag and for a moment I'm almost tempted to share my secret.

'Are there any records of all the writers who stayed there before the war?' I ask instead.

'I don't know but I doubt it.' He shakes his head. 'It's so long ago.'

It was unlikely, but still, I feel a stab of disappointment.

'Why? Are you looking for someone?'

'Yes, a young American writer called Henry.'

'A relative?'

'No.' I shake my head. 'He's—' I pause. What is Henry to me? He's no longer a stranger, I feel like I know him. 'He's a friend,' I say, finally.

'What's his last name? Maybe I have heard of him?'

Until now it's never occurred to me that Henry might have made it as a writer, that he might have been published, that he might be nestling somewhere among these shelves. But even if he is, I would have no way of knowing – he signed his letters merely H or Henry, and there was never a return address on the envelope.

'I don't know his last name,' I confess, and as I say it I realise how tiny my chances are of ever finding out his identity. It's like a needle in a haystack. Actually, make that about a zillion haystacks.

He casts me an apologetic look. 'In that case, I'm sorry . . .' He trails off, with a shrug of his shoulders. 'Can I help you with anything else?'

'No . . . no, thank you.' I shake my head.

He smiles kindly, then turns back to stacking the shelves.

It was a long shot anyway.

Still, I can't leave a bookshop without buying something and so for the next few hours I lose myself in the heady world of literature, browsing shelves and thumbing pages, before finally stepping back out to the street. It's bright after the dimness of the shop and, just across the water, on the Île de la Cité I can hear the bells of Notre Dame chiming.

Standing on the cobbles I hug my purchases to my chest and pause to listen. I've never felt more like I was in Paris than I do at this moment. Never felt more touched by the magic of the city. I think about Henry. I feel both exhilarated and disappointed. I've reached a dead end, and yet after my visit to the bookshop I feel inexplicably closer to him some-how. Which doesn't make any sense at all, I reflect, as I turn away and start walking. But then none of this makes sense, does it?

It's still only early afternoon and I briefly consider doing some more sightseeing. This is my third day in Paris and I've barely seen anything. My mind flicks back to Xavier and his advice to throw away my guidebook. Maybe he's right, maybe that's not the way to *see* a city, but I still feel like I should. I can't help it; I'm always compelled to do some sightseeing when I'm in a different country, like it's my duty.

But then I guess most people are the same, aren't they? Visit something famous, have your picture taken in front of it, tick it off the list. Done. Strange really, when you think about it.

Anyway, my bags of books is heavy and I've left Heathcliff in the apartment – after the incident at the Louvre I was worried bookshops, too, might not be dog friendly – so instead I decide to head home. I can pick up some food on the way. With Harriet out tonight on her date, it will be just me and Heathcliff.

It's not far to the apartment, and I start weaving my way through the backstreets. I've grown more familiar with the neighbourhood and I'm no longer getting lost every few minutes and having to stand on street corners with my nose buried in a map. Pretty soon I'll be like a local. Feeling rather proud of myself, I turn a corner without a moment's hesita-tion. In fact, I'm feeling so confident, I might even try a bit of a new route home, I decide, overshooting my usual turning and taking a different street.

I stride out along the narrow pavements, my eyes passing the windows of the unfamiliar shops. My gaze flicks over the intricate displays. Shop-window displays in Paris are like pieces of art. Gravity-defying towers of pastel-coloured macarons fill the window of a patisserie, while a shoemaker shows off exquisitely hand-stitched sandals by suspending them on invisible wires so they float, temptingly, in front of your eyes.

Everything is so chic. So stylish. So elegant. So unlike my uninspiring local high street back home, I reflect, my attention caught by the window of a parfumerie. Jewel-coloured bottles glitter en masse and I slow down, mesmerised. Suddenly my attention is caught by a blue one. I feel a beat of recognition.

Hang on, that looks similar to the one Emmanuelle had on her dressing table.

No sooner has the thought fired through my brain than I stop dead in the street. A fellow pedestrian nearly crashes into me and I apologise profusely, before turning my attention back to the window. I peer at it closer, studying its intricate design. Actually no, it's not similar; it's exactly the same bottle.

Curiosity bubbles up inside me and without a moment's hesitation I reach for the ornate brass handle. A faint chime heralds my entrance and, pushing open the heavy door, I step inside. The fragrance hits me as soon I enter – well I say hits, but it's more of an embrace. It enfolds me in the most delicious scent, like breathing in the most wonderful bouquet of flowers.

I cast my eyes around me, marvelling at the interior. It doesn't look like it's changed for over a century. Old oak shelves line the walls, displaying glass vats of essential fragrances, each labelled with an old brass sign, while glass-fronted drawers reveal a dizzying number of bottles of all different shapes and sizes. At the back of the shop is a long leather-topped counter, behind which stands a stooping, white-haired gentleman, wearing wire-rimmed glasses and an apron.

The shop is empty and as I step forward he looks up and says something to me in French and I do my usual embarrassed apologising that I don't speak the language.

Resting his large hands on the countertop, he leans towards me, his eyes shining. 'Scent has its own language,' he says in a low voice, as if sharing a secret.

A look flashes between us and I feel a sudden sense of intrigue.

'It cannot be translated into words,' he continues, reaching for one of the many bottles. Removing the glass stopper, he wafts it underneath my nose. 'It's an emotion.'

As the delicious musky aroma hits my nostrils my brain throws up the taste of spices, memories of India, dreams of sultry evenings and images of exotic landscapes.

'The mystery of scent lies in the deepest forms of memory.' He smiles, a knowing look in his eyes as he sees the expression on my face.

'Yes,' I nod, feeling myself transported out of this little shop in Paris and into another time, another place, another feeling.

Weaving through the shelves, the perfumer deftly chooses another bottle from the hundreds on display.

'A scent is all about layering. Like a person, you have to unravel the layers,' he says, spraying a little on a small strip of paper and passing it to me, but not before he's held out a small bowl of coffee beans. 'It refreshes the palate,' he explains.

I breathe in the bitter scent of espresso, then lift the strip of paper to my nose. I'm met with a delicious burst of sweet floral scent.

'To begin with you have the top notes. These scents evaporate quickly but they are like first impressions. We also call these the headnotes.'

It's like a fragrant mixture of citrus and jasmine, but as the intensity begins to fade, I can pick out something else.

'These are followed by the middle notes, which are also called heart notes. It is the main body of the perfume, and the one you will be able to feel when the top notes have worn off.'

Sure enough, I can detect a spiciness and something that smells a lot like sandalwood.

'And finally you have the base notes, this is the depth of the perfume. But you will have to wait for these to develop for at least thirty minutes,' he adds helpfully.

Absorbed with enthusiastically sniffing the stick of paper for what new smells I can detect, and wondering why I can't, I break off, blushing.

'Oh, I see.' I smile. 'Wow, that was amazing, thank you for explaining everything.'

'My pleasure.' He smiles back. 'If there is anything else I can help you with?'

'Well actually—' Turning, I point to the window, '—I noticed the blue bottle in the window, what scent is that?'

Pushing his spectacles further up his nose, he peers at the display, then nods in comprehension. 'Oh, that is a very old bottle. The window is showing a retrospective of all our perfumes. We are celebrating our one-hundred-year anniversary and this one is from the 1930s.'

I gaze at it, the blue glass sparkling in the light. How funny to think I'm in the very same shop that Henry must have visited all those years ago. It probably looks exactly the same as it did then.

'OK, well thank you,' I say, and am just preparing to leave when he says something that makes me falter.

'We used this bottle for our custom perfumes.'

'Custom?' I repeat curiously.

'Sometimes a customer will want an individual scent that is unique, that no one else has—'

'And you make them here?'

'We have been creating perfume here for three generations,' he says proudly, 'I learned the ancient craft from my father, and he from his father. There is a magical alchemy to producing a fragrance, it's not simply about layering notes and ingredients, it goes much deeper—' he breaks, off and taps the side of his nose, 'and of course you must train your senses to distinguish between the different scents with the most heightened accuracy.'

As he's talking, I suddenly remember I dabbed some on my wrist last night when I was at the apartment. I wonder—

'Would you be able to recognise any scent?' I challenge, holding out my wrist.

The old man looks at me curiously, then a smile spreads on his face. 'The pulse point will warm the perfume and release fragrance continuously . . .' He bends closer, his large nose pressed up against my skin as he inhales. 'It's very faded, the top notes have long disappeared, but there is a musk and an orange blossom—' He breaks off and gazes at me. 'Where did you get this?'

'It was bought from here for someone seventy years ago.'

He looks both impressed and proud. 'Then we are better parfumiers than even I thought, for the scent to have endured for so many years.'

'Yes, it was in the same blue bottle as the one in the window.'

'In that case, we will have a record,' he says confidently.

'You will?' I feel a beat of sudden excitement as he goes to a drawer and pulls out an ancient, leather-bound ledger, which he lays out on the countertop. He opens it to a page filled with tiny handwriting and, peering so closely his nose almost touches the page, he scrolls down with his forefinger. 'Do you know which year exactly?'

'1939 I think. Before the war.' I feel my heartbeat quicken as I speak.

'And what name?'

'It was a gift for an Emmanuelle Renoir.'

I can't believe it, I'm going to find out Henry's identity!

'No, the name of the customer please. A monsieur . . . ?'

Abruptly my excitement disintegrates. 'His first name was Henry, I'm afraid that's all I know,' I say, feeling a wave of disappointment.

He glances up from the ledger and, seeing my expression, smiles kindly.

'Ah, but that is not true, we have the scent, we know there was musk, and orange blossom and . . .' He grabs my wrist again and inhales deeply. 'I can't quite tell, there is something elusive . . . some fragrance—'

We're interrupted by the faint chime of the bell as someone enters and I suddenly realise the shop's got quite busy. In fact there's an assistant serving another customer. Gosh, I hadn't even noticed, I've been so absorbed.

'If you leave me your telephone number I will call you if I discover anything. Don't be disheartened. Remember the mystery of a scent is all about removing the layers.'

Smiling gratefully, I take a pen and scribble down my number on his card.

'Thank you,' I say, passing it to him.

He nods kindly and, slipping it into the pocket of his apron, turns back to the line of customers that has now gathered behind me. Including a very tall man with his back to me who must be at least six foot seven. Wow, he's almost a giant, I think, trying to scoot around him, but he's blocking my path, talking to a sales assistant. I can't help but overhear their conversation as she says something to him in French.

'I'm sorry, do you speak English? I'm afraid my French is a little rusty.'

I smile to myself. At least I'm not the only one. My attention caught, I glance at him as I squeeze past and feel a jolt of recognition. It's *WineNot*. I mean, Rupert. I recognise him from his photograph.

No, not *that* photograph.

Reminded, I give a little shudder. No, I'm talking about his black and white headshot. I peer at him out of the corner of my eye. He's gained a bit of weight since it was taken, and I have a feeling those skydiving photos are more than a couple of years old, but it's definitely him.

I watch him curiously. What's he doing buying perfume?

Loitering in the doorway, I zone in on his conversation.

'Could you wrap it? It's a gift.'

A gift? My ears prick up. Of course! I bet he's buying a gift for Harriet, ahead of their date.

'How wonderful.' The sales assistant beams at him. 'Is it for a special occasion?'

'Do you need a special occasion to buy a beautiful woman perfume?' he asks, smiling.

The assistant smiles, completely charmed, and pulls out a length of ribbon. As she begins tying an elaborate bow, I feel a burst of excitement for Harriet. Maybe I've been wrong and he's not such a bad guy after all. I watch for a moment, then, pushing open the door, step out onto the street.

20

Dearest Manu,

When I woke this morning and saw you still asleep by my side for the very first time, I thought I'd died and gone to heaven. To be able to wake up and see you sleeping next to me has been something I have dreamed of all these months, ever since I first laid eyes on you outside that café. I don't just say this as your lover (I truly am your lover now my darling), for it was never just your nakedness I desired, but your soul. As we lay together last night in each other's arms, lit by the moonlight that shone in through the gap in your shutters, I felt it was not just our bodies, but our souls that were entwined.

Oh my darling, it was so hard to leave your soft, warm body early this morning when the light was still grey and walk back to the bookstore. Even now, after Paris has washed over me, I can still smell your scent on my skin. I can think only of you. I should be writing, but I cannot concentrate, for my mind keeps returning to you.

Last night, when you whispered to me in the darkness that you loved me now and would love me forever, you made me the happiest fellow on this fine earth. Happier even than I was before, and I didn't think that was possible. I'm glad I have Franklin to act as witness, for I fear I might otherwise believe it was all just a dream! Do you know how wonderful it is for me to hear that? To hear it whispered to me in the shadows as we lay together in your bed?

I hope this joy can last, but I also know of your father's wishes for you to accept your cousin's proposal. I know you are trying to protect me by not telling me the extent of your fears, but sometimes when you think I am not looking, I see the worry etched on your face. But darling, do not worry! We will always be together now, don't you see? Nothing can undo this love we have for each other, we have promised ourselves to each other, in body and soul, and whatever happens, nothing can break such a bond.

Oh, I know you think me a romantic fool, and perhaps I am, but I am also a realist. The realities of war look set to be upon us soon and the world is changing fast. No one can stop it. Not even your father or tradition or Paris itself. Everything will soon be turned on its head and who knows what the future will bring.

Let's run away together now, before it is too late. Let's escape this madness. I know that you don't want to leave your family, and I know the love you hold for them, but I also know of your desire for freedom, to love who you choose, and after last night I now know for certain that is forever to be me.

Before I was happy to wait, to see what fate had in store for us, to leave it up to destiny, but that was before I woke this morning in your arms. Now I know I can no longer take a gamble. I want – I must – wake in your arms each and every morning for the rest of my life, I must be able to feel such joy again and again forever. To not have you by my side would be torture.

I know, I am speaking with feverish excitement, and you must be thinking I have gone half crazy, but let me assure you I have never been more sane in my life. Be brave my darling. Hold my hand and let's be together. To start a new life. In a new world.

Please reply to me my darling, and when you do, it must be only one word.

Yes.

J'attendrai,

H

Feeling the golden evening light fading on my face, I look up from the letter to discover it's grown late. Dusk is falling, yet my heart is still racing from Henry's words. I must have been here for hours.

I'm back at Harriet's apartment, sitting on the tiny window seat that's tucked snugly underneath one of the large, arched windows. There's not much room – I'm wedged, knees up to my chest, on a small cushion – but it had looked so inviting when I'd got home, with the sun streaming in across the rooftops, that I'd curled up like a cat with Emmanuelle's letters, basking in the warmth of the evening sun and Henry's love, being transported back in time to a different Paris.

Or is it? I wonder, gazing out at the view that stretches far beyond. For while of course the fashions and music were different back then, and there was the threat of war and feeling of uncertainty for the future, up above the city there's a feeling of timelessness. Did this view look any different through their eyes? I muse, imagining Henry and Emmanuelle staring out across the rooftops of Paris, just as I'm doing now, as the daylight fades into dusk.

It's like a whole other world up here in the sky, among the chimney pots and pigeons and roof terraces. Famous landmarks stretch their heads and shoulders up above the skyline, like tall people in a crowd, while the rest of the city falls away beneath them. Down below on the streets, the city has gone through some real changes, has witnessed so much history, but up here at these still, lofty heights, it feels like a different Paris. A secret Paris. An eternal Paris. A Paris that hasn't changed since Henry wrote these letters.

My mind is still buzzing with the urgency of Henry's words. What happened next? What was Emmanuelle's reply? Left with this cliffhanger, I think about her note to Henry that I first found in her apartment. In it she spoke of her resolve to go against her family's wishes, and her love for

Henry. So what caused her to later change her mind and marry Monsieur Dumont after all? There's more to this story and I'm desperate to know what happens, but at the same time there's a part of me that's afraid.

Slipping the notepaper carefully back into its envelope, I gather up the rest of the letters in my lap and put them away safely with the rest in my bag. It's late. I'm going to wait. Sometimes it's better not to know. Even if it's only for a little while.

Stretching out my stiff limbs, I pad barefoot over to the small fridge. I stopped at a few shops on the way home and bought some cheese, fresh figs, a baguette and a bottle of red wine. Well, when in France and all that.

Locating the corkscrew, I open the bottle of wine and pour myself a large glass. I don't usually drink red wine, not since I downed several glasses at my publishers' Christmas party and spent the evening chatting to lots of Very Important People and trying to impress. It was only later when I went to the loo I discovered my teeth had turned black, along with my tongue, and realised my smile was less winning and more terrifying.

But tonight, with Harriet out on her date, I won't be able to scare her until she gets home – though who knows what time that will be. I feel a twinge of concern as I think about Rupert and all the red flags, but I brush them aside. I'm just being overprotective. He bought perfume, remember? He can't be all bad.

Hungrily, I start unwrapping the round of Camembert I've left out on the counter, then have to stand back for a moment as the pungent smell hits me. The man in the shop gave me strict instructions that I had to keep it out of the fridge. Apparently it's important to let the cheese ripen. Though I'm not sure I'd call that ripened, more like stinks to high heaven.

Taking a knife, I cut through the thick white rind. Its pale yellow insides ooze out, thick and creamy, and, tearing off a hunk of bread, I scoop it up. As soon as it hits my taste buds, the smell is forgotten. Crikey, this is delicious. Now I know why the French are so famous for their *fromage*. OK, so we Brits make a nice Cheddar, but it's like your boring old aunt compared to this big, charismatic Gérard Depardieu of a cheese.

I cut another large wedge and this time I combine it with a bite of plump fig. If the first mouthful was delicious, the second is like a high-definition version of delicious, with surround sound thrown in. I have no idea how French women don't all become the size of houses. This stuff is to die for and about three zillion calories. Just to add to the other three zillion calories I consumed this morning with all those pains au chocolat, I remember, loosening the waistband of my jeans.

Carrying a plate of food and my wine glass, I head back to my little spot by the window. It's grown dark now, and as I take a sip of wine I notice the twinkling of the Eiffel Tower in the distance. It's almost out of my eyeline, but I can just see it, like a giant sparkler lighting up the night sky. I feel a little burst of delight, the way you do when you catch a gorgeous sunset, or a rainbow, or the fin of a dolphin arching over the waves.

Wow, isn't this wonderful? To be here in Paris, looking at this view, on a Thursday night—

Gosh, is it Thursday already? It'll be the weekend soon and my birthday . . .

I'd lost track of the days, but now I'm suddenly reminded. Still, that's fine. So what if it's my birthday soon? I'm going to be spending it in one of the most beautiful cities in the whole world. I mean, seriously, how lucky am I? Some people spend their whole lives dreaming of visiting Paris. In fact, there're probably millions of women out there who would love to trade places with me right now, sitting here with my lovely wine and my delicious cheese and my amazing view and—

Oh for god's sake, shut up Ruby. You're not fooling anyone, and certainly not yourself. Paris is wonderful and you are lucky. But you're also upset and missing the man you're in love with like crazy and no woman in the world would want to trade you for that.

And suddenly, as I admit it to myself, I feel myself start to crumble.

Because I can block it out as much as I like. I can push it down inside of me so hard I can make it seem like it's disappeared. I can jump on the Eurostar and be here for my friend. I can read someone else's love letters from nearly three-quarters of a century ago and lose myself in their romance. I can buy fancy wine and look at gorgeous views and tell myself that everything's all right. That it's more than all right.

But at the end of the day, it's all just a trick. It hasn't really disappeared. Like a magician with his sleight of hand and top hat, all the hurt and fear and insecurities are still there; I've just hidden them somewhere, deep down inside of me, where no one can see them. Not even myself.

On the surface, the row with Jack might have blown over, but the emotions and doubts that were triggered by it haven't gone away. I didn't leave them behind in London when I came to Paris. On the contrary, I brought them with me. And the harder I try to ignore them, the bigger they get.

Falling in love is a scary business. It leaves you vulnerable and it's risky. You're taking a leap of faith and there isn't a safety net. But when I met Jack I didn't have a choice. You don't when you fall in love. Swept up in a whirlwind, you just jump. It didn't matter that we lived thousands of miles apart, or that we hardly knew each other, or that we both had pasts – none of that stuff was important, we just dived straight in at the deep end.

But now the sobering reality of our relationship has set in. We've been apart for three months and the closeness I felt to him is fast growing distant. It's so long since I buried my face in the crook of his neck and inhaled his unique Jack-smell that I can barely remember what it's like any more. So long since he wrapped his arms round me and held me close and I felt like there was no one else in the world but us.

Will that feeling ever come back? Was it ever real in the first place? It felt real, but now everything between us feels as if it's disintegrating. Seeing the photo today of Jack and his ex has only added to my fears. Fears that, ever since I discovered Sam was cheating on me, I've tried to keep buried.

Harriet said it was better to feel the pain of love than to have never been in love, but I'm not so sure. I'm not sure of anything any more.

Least of all, Jack – which is the scariest thing by far—

A faint beep distracts me from my thoughts. It's my phone. I've left it buried in the bottom of my bag to prevent any temptation to check it, but now I get up and dig it out.

> Hey, sorry we got cut off yesterday, it's been crazy here. Finally found a signal. How are you?

It's a WhatsApp message from Jack.

I stare at it, my hearting beating fast. It's so normal and matter-of-fact, as if our row at the airport never happened, and what caused it has all been forgotten.

> Good, just eating dinner.

Using the same tone as him, I ignore the thoughts that have been swirling around in my head.

> How are you?

I don't mention Paris. Funny, but my earlier desire to tell him I'm here has vanished. Right about the time I saw the photograph of him with his ex, I realise, remembering their smiles and then wishing I hadn't.

> Still working on site and pretty exhausted, but not too tired to miss you.

It didn't look like he was missing me that much in the photo, grumbles the monster under the bed, but I refuse to react. I'm just being paranoid. Jack has never done anything to make me not trust him. I can't let the ghosts of my past come between us.

> I miss you too. When can I see you?

I press send and for the first time in our conversation I feel myself letting down the barriers and reaching out to him. There's a pause, and then I see the icon that says he's typing.

> I don't know. There's a bit of a crisis going on here. One of the structures collapsed in the storm and I need to figure out how to fix it before I can jump on a plane.

The message is swiftly followed by another.

> It might be a while yet.

Disappointment stabs, but I don't let myself react.

> Oh well, it can't be helped, just do what you have to do.

He replies straight away.

> I'm not complaining. I'm out here to build housing for people that are a lot less fortunate than me.

See, he's a good guy. How can I even think about doubting a good guy like Jack?

Plus I have a great team helping me.

At the mention of his team, I get a flashback of his ex in a hard hat on the construction site.

That's good.

I pause, then do something that I know I shouldn't, but I can't help it.

Have you met any of them before?

I wait. A few seconds feel like the longest time. I see he's typing. I hold my breath. Then beep, the message pings in.

No, no one.

And suddenly my insecurities don't feel so stupid any more.

21

I must have crashed out on the sofa, because the next thing I know I'm being woken up by the sound of the key being rattled in the lock and the door being flung open.

'Ugh . . . hello?' Blearily, I open my eyes just as the light's switched on, and blink at the sudden brightness.

'It's only me,' yells Harriet, in a voice that tells me she's had a bit too much to drink. Whenever she's had a few, the volume control goes off the scale.

'How did it go?' I ask, sitting up groggily.

'I've fallen head over heels!' she shrieks, lurching into the apartment.

'You have? Wow, I knew you liked him, but—'

'No, literally,' she gasps, collapsing next to me on the sofa. She holds up her ankle and waves at it me. 'I've twisted my ankle on these damned heels.'

'Ouch.' I take a sharp intake of breath. It's already swollen to twice its size and is starting to turn all kinds of garish colours. 'That looks painful.'

'Actually, it's not too horrendous at the minute,' she says, her voice slurring slightly, 'wine's rather a wonderful anaesthetic you know—' She breaks off as she spots my bottle of wine next to the sofa. 'In fact, I could do with a top-up.' She lunges for it, then frowns. 'There's none left.'

I look at the empty bottle in her hands and my mind flashes back. Harriet wasn't the only one in need of an anaesthetic tonight. I'd finished it after reading that message from Jack.

Our conversation had ended soon after. He said his battery was about to die.

I have no idea if he was telling the truth. Just as I have no idea if this sick feeling I've got at the bottom of my stomach is justified. His message doesn't have to mean anything. After all, I haven't been completely truthful, have I? I haven't told Jack I'm in Paris. I told him I was home watching a movie on TV when I was at a party on the Seine.

At least, he assumed I was home watching a movie on TV, and I just played along. Does that make it different? Does that make it less dishonest?

I don't know. I don't know about lots of things any more. The last few days have turned everything upside down and inside out. But what I do know is his ex-girlfriend is with him in Colombia, and he doesn't want me to know about it. He flat out denied it. And rightly, or wrongly, that sure as hell feels a lot like a big deal to me.

'Urgh! What am I going to do?'

I zone back to see Harriet staring at me, her eyes slightly glazed, the bottle dangling dangerously from her fingers.

'Um . . . I think I might have some paracetamol you can have instead,' I suggest, taking the bottle from her before she drops it and we add cuts to sprains.

'No, not about the pain,' she groans, and flops her head back onto the sofa. 'I mean about tomorrow.'

'Why, what's happening tomorrow?'

'I'm catching the train to Avignon in the south of France to meet with Madame Dumont's heirs,' she groans again, only louder this time. 'Well, I *was*, but I can't now. Now I can barely walk.'

'Can't you reschedule?' Getting up off the sofa, I walk over to the tiny fridge and delve into the even tinier freezer compartment. As luck would have it there's an ice-cube tray and it's got ice in it, which, if you knew Harriet, is a miracle.

'Impossible. The auction is Sunday. Tomorrow's the last day I can go as I have to be in the office on Saturday – there are still a hundred and one things to do.'

Popping the ice cubes out, I wrap them up in a tea towel.

'Oh bollocks, what am I going to do? This is a disaster!'

'Here, this should help.' I walk back over to her and wrap the ice round her ankle.

She winces, then lets out a grateful smile. 'Thanks.'

'Is there anything else I can do?' I start plumping up a cushion.

'No, I don't think so . . .' She shakes her head, then seems to sort of stiffen.

I stop plumping to see she's looking at me funny.

Uh-oh.

'Actually, there is something you can do.'

'There is?' Why do I get the feeling this is going to involve more than fetching a couple of painkillers?

'You could go instead.'

Yup. I knew it.

'Go where?' I try to play dumb.

Which of course, doesn't work. 'The south of France!' she says exasperatedly.

I look at her like she's gone mental. 'You want me to go to the south of France instead of you?' I repeat, more for my benefit than hers.

At the prospect, I feel a flash of excitement. But I quickly grab a hold of myself. I can't go gallivanting off to the south of France. I need to focus on my own life, which right now feels on the brink of falling apart.

'Yes.' She nods, her face lighting up with the idea. 'Oh, sweetie, would you mind terribly? You'd be doing me such a huge favour, I've been working so hard on this auction and I don't want to screw it all up now. This would be the perfect solution—'

'Aren't you forgetting something?' I interrupt.

Harriet frowns, deep in thought, then looks triumphant. 'Of course! But don't you worry, I can look after Heathcliff, I'll be home all day. You love your Auntie Harriet, don't you?' She starts making clucking sounds at Heathcliff, who eyes her warily.

'I'm not talking about Heathcliff,' I gasp. 'I'm talking about how I don't know the first thing about antiques.' I mean, honestly, talk about pointing out the obvious.

'Oh, well that's not a problem.' She bats it away dismissively. 'You can say you're my assistant like we did before. All you need to do is deliver the catalogue.'

'In that case, what about FedEx?'

'They want it delivered personally. They're very demanding clients.' She looks at me. 'They've taken over the running of the family estate, where Madame Dumont lived, and it's not far from the station. You can catch a cab. It'll be easy.'

'Harriet, this is crazy—'

She makes a little whining noise like Heathcliff when he's begging for something. 'Please Ruby, this is really important. You know how I've always wanted to be an auctioneer instead of just cataloguing, this is my big break, I might never get another chance . . .'

How can I refuse? Harriet has done a million favours for me in the past, it's the least I can do for her. 'OK, OK.' I say, giving in.

Her face breaks into a huge, drunken smile and she throws her arms round me. 'Thank you darling, oh thank you! You're a lifesaver!'

As she smothers me underneath her bosom, the reality of what I've agreed to hits me. Wow, I can't believe it. I'm going to the south of France. I'm going to see where Emmanuelle fled to at the outbreak of the war. I'm going to meet her heirs—

Oh, please. Of course, I can believe I'm going. The moment Harriet asked me there was never a moment's doubt.

Fast forward to very early the next morning and I'm bumping and *excusez-moi*-ing my way down the central aisle of the TGV, bound for Avignon. Clutching a coffee in one hand and my ticket in the other, I'm looking for my seat. Only I'm being super careful this time. Last time I was on a train, I sat in the wrong seat and we all know what happened there, don't we?

My mind flashes back to India and the moment I locked eyes with an unshaven American in a fedora. Actually I saw his feet first, as I was lying on my berth – well, *his* berth, as it turns out. I remember they were very tanned and wearing a pair of flip-flops. And I remember thinking they were nice feet, until he told me I was in his seat and had to move, and then I realised he had wonky toes and I didn't like them at all.

But most of all I remember his eyes. They were hazel, and the whites looked really white against his deep tan and dark messy hair. And even though he was rude and annoying and a total pain in the ass, he was also absolutely bloody gorgeous.

Jack.

As the memory hits me like a tidal wave, I momentarily lose my balance and nearly fall into a French lady's lap. My coffee spills and there's several moments of me saying *pardon* about a million times and feeling like a clumsy moron and her dabbing her tweed skirt with her tissues and saying something in French that it's probably a good thing I don't understand.

Still, I get the message, no translation necessary, and I set off to make my way down the rest of the carriage until finally I realise the numbers are getting much closer. In fact, that must be my seat right by—

'*Xavier*?' I say in astonishment as I spot his handsome profile sitting by the window, tapping away on his laptop. No, it can't be.

Hearing his name, he looks up from his keyboard and pushes his reading glasses onto his head.

Oh my god, it is him. I feel an unexpected tingle of excitement.

Seeing me, he looks momentarily surprised, then his face breaks into a wide smile. 'Ruby, what are you doing here?'

'I could ask you the same thing,' I say, shaking my head in disbelief as I sit down opposite him. 'What a coincidence that we're on the same—' I break off as the penny drops.

Of course. This isn't a coincidence. Harriet and Xavier must have been due to travel together, though I wonder why she didn't tell— Suddenly I have a distinct suspicion Harriet has used her twisted ankle as an opportunity to try to play matchmaker.

'I have a meeting with Madame Dumont's heirs in Provence,' he replies.

'Me too.' I nod, trying to refocus. I can't believe Harriet. What on earth is she thinking? She knows I have a boyfriend.

Who is currently in Colombia with his ex-girlfriend, a voice in my head reminds me. Like I could have forgotten.

He looks surprised. 'Where is Miss Fortescue-Blake?'

'She hurt her ankle last night, she's had to go to the hospital this morning.'

'Is she OK?' His tanned brow furrows with concern.

OK probably isn't the word I'd use to describe an ankle the size of a balloon and all the colours of the rainbow. Poor Harriet had been very stoical, stiff-upper-lipped and all that, but still, she'd turned green with the pain as I helped her into the cab. 'She just needs an X-ray to check nothing's broken.' I spare him the details.

'I'm sure everything will be fine,' he reassures me.

'Yes, I hope so.' I nod. 'So, anyway, she asked me if I could deliver the catalogue for her. In my role as her assistant, obviously,' I add quickly.

'Obviously.' He nods, his eyes meeting mine, and for a

moment I'm sure I see the corners of his mouth twitch in amusement. Something tells me he hasn't entirely fallen for our assistant/boss story.

'Though I don't know why she couldn't just have asked you,' I add pointedly. I want to make it clear that this wasn't my idea.

'Conflict of interests,' he replies, 'as their lawyer overseeing the sale I cannot be involved in this side of things.'

'Oh I see,' I nod, though I don't really. All that legal stuff goes over my head.

'Besides, now we get to carry on from where we left off.' He smiles, his dark eyes meeting mine.

'Left off?' I try to keep my voice steady, but abruptly the air between us feels charged.

'At the café at the Louvre, I had to get back to the office.'

Reminded, I feel a stab of guilt. And something else. A faint, secret flutter of excitement.

'So tell me, where were we?'

Drinking champagne. *Flirting.*

'I can't remember,' I say quickly, my words stamping firmly on the embers of our previous conversation. Flirting might be an entirely innocent pastime to the French, but it's not to the English. It feels risky, dangerous, like I'm playing with fire.

'Really?'

After last night, the distance between me and Jack feels ever wider. Insecurities are bubbling. Doubts are multiplying.

'Really.' I nod firmly.

'Well in that case, I should get back to my work,' he says and turns to his laptop.

It only needs one spark, and this whole thing could ignite.

22

Travelling on a train through France is a totally different experience from my train journey in India. Modern and super fast, it's much more plush and comfortable and *quiet*, with fellow passengers sitting around me, reading books or working on their laptops. In India it was the total opposite. Loud and chaotic, it was about talking to strangers, feeling the warm breeze on my face and watching the world go by. It was about the journey, not the destination.

But this time it's all about the destination. I'm eager to get to Avignon and, this being the TGV, it's no time before we've left Paris and are hurtling through the countryside. Xavier sits opposite on his laptop while I gaze out of the window, at the blurring scenery speeding by.

I'm tired – I didn't sleep much last night and it was an early start – but adrenalin and nerves are keeping me awake. I'm out of my comfort zone and the reality of the situation is beginning to dawn on me. What am I doing? What am I hoping to find? Reading Emmanuelle's old love letters is one thing, but now I'm actually travelling hundreds of miles to meet her heirs and see where she lived, and where she died. I mean, it's all a bit mental really.

I glance across at Xavier, his designer glasses framing his eyes as he studies some legal document lying on the table beside him. My eyes take in the immaculate cut of his suit, the stitching of his lapels, the crisp white collar of his shirt. I watch him rubbing his chin in concentration, notice the curve of his Adam's apple—

He clears his throat and I quickly look away. I'm on edge. Adventures might sound exciting, but they end up getting you into all kinds of trouble. My family and friends think I'm holed up in the country with Jack, wafting around in his and hers waffle bathrobes and making up for all that distance. Not gallivanting off to the south of France with a seriously handsome French lawyer.

Still, there's no turning back now. I glance out of the window. The train is travelling at two hundred miles an hour. The country is rushing by and we are moving further and further away from Paris, from London, from my life as I knew it. Leading further and further into something new and unknown. Nerves flutter, but underneath I feel a secret rush of exhilaration. And the truth is, I wouldn't want to turn back anyway.

After just a couple of hours, we arrive in Avignon. It's a busy, bustling station and Xavier expertly navigates himself through the terminus to the taxi rank outside where we transfer into a dark Mercedes that's already waiting for us. No standing with all the other hot, sweaty tourists or a crappy minicab for him. He speaks briefly to the driver in French, his voice low yet with the kind of authority of a man who's used to being listened to, then settles back against the plush leather seats.

I watch him, impressed. Everything about Xavier is so seamless and unruffled. So in control. I think about my own life, which seems to be spinning out of orbit, rapidly unravelling, all messy and crumpled. Like myself. I grimace inwardly, looking down at my skirt, which bears a stain from the sandwich I dropped on my lap on the train. Note to self: rubbing it furiously with a napkin and Evian water does not make it better, it makes it much worse.

Xavier, meanwhile, is a picture of smart composure. Despite the stifling heat, he is still looking cool and crisp in his suit and tie and a freshly laundered shirt, and giving off a fresh scent of cologne.

'Would you like me to ask the driver to turn on the air conditioning?'

'Oh, yes please,' I nod, fidgeting uncomfortably. Despite liberal applications of deodorant I feel hot and sticky.

He murmurs something to the driver, then settles back in his seat. Is it just me or does he feel a hair's breadth closer? I cross my legs nervously, then uncross them again. Honestly, what's wrong with me?

'The estate is in a village some kilometres away, but we should be there within the hour.'

'Oh, it's that far?' I say in surprise, then catch myself. Why am I surprised that Harriet's 'jump in a cab' is not quite the whole truth?

'Yes, I'm afraid it's a bit of a drive, but at least you get to see one of the most beautiful parts of the world.'

'Yes.' I nod. 'I'm looking forward to it, I've never been to the south of France.'

'*Non*, this is not possible!'

'I'm afraid so.' I laugh at his shocked expression.

Though obviously I've heard all about it. Who hasn't curled up with *A Year in Provence* and hankered after lavender fields and gorgeous hilltop villages, or seen paparazzi shots of celebrities and their yachts in St Tropez and fantasised about the glitz and the glamour? It's the stuff of dreams.

'Trust me, once you have been you will never want to leave,' he says, smiling.

It's also where Emmanuelle fled to from Paris almost seventy-five years ago. And, feeling a flutter of anticipation, I turn to gaze out of the window as the car purrs quietly into the traffic.

After a short while we turn off the motorway and begin winding our way through the countryside. Despite the heat, I buzz down my window, breathing in the warm scented air as we drive past fields of purple lavender and yellow sunflowers that seem to turn their heads to follow us. Old stone farmhouses and rolling hills, pretty villages and sweeping valleys; everywhere I look is picture postcard perfect. The Provençal landscape makes it hard to believe we just left Paris this morning; it feels like we're a million miles away.

Gone is the fast pace of city life with all its pollution and traffic and stresses, and in its place is a natural landscape. We pass through whitewashed streets ablaze with pink and purple bougainvillea, shaded fountains and squares where locals and tourists gather under the dappled light of the plane trees, and old men in checked shirts and straw hats play boules.

Xavier is right. Already I feel like I never want to leave.

After nearly an hour of driving, we turn off from the road and steer through a pair of impressive iron gates.

'Are we here?' I ask, turning to Xavier. He's been quietly reading the whole journey, engrossed in the contents of his briefcase, which I feel quite relieved about. For a moment there, I thought—

Well, whatever. I brush the thought quickly away before it has a chance to germinate. It doesn't matter.

'Yes.' He nods, looking up from his paperwork as we begin rumbling down a long sweeping driveway that seems to go on for ever.

On either side of us are rows and rows of small bushy trees, as far as the eye can see, and I peer at them curiously until suddenly I notice the clusters of dark purple grapes hanging from each one.

'Is this a vineyard?'

'One of the finest in the area.' He nods.

Of course. How could I not have realised? But then I've never seen one in real life, only in photographs. In my defence, they don't have many vineyards in west London.

'It has been in the Dumont family for many generations, it's where Madame Dumont lived until she died.'

'Yes, now I remember you saying,' I murmur, gazing all around me at the sprawling estate. So this is where Emmanuelle came to, all those years ago, when she fled from the Nazis. I marvel at the endless stretch of lavender blue sky, the row upon row of ancient vines and the grandeur of the huge stone chateau we're approaching. It all feels so vast and impressive and a million miles away from the busy cobble-stoned side streets of Paris. What emotions must she have felt when she first arrived here to start her new life? I wonder if she knew she would never go back.

The car wends its way through seemingly endless acres of vineyards, before sweeping through manicured gardens and a lane of cypress trees that leads up to the chateau. Built out of yellow stone that glows golden in the sunlight, the main building is three storeys high with large arches and a wide terrace, while at one end there appears to be a bell tower and at the other a large turret, covered in ivy.

As we advance up the gravel driveway, the tyres of the Mercedes make a satisfying crunching sound before coming to a halt as we pull up at the impressive entrance. Immediately a man in a uniform appears, opening car doors and ushering us in through the large arched doorway and into the expansive entry hall, lit by a large Murano chandelier and hung with dozens of large portraits. A few words are exchanged between him and Xavier, who quickly translates.

'We are to wait in the main *salle*,' he explains, our footsteps echoing on the polished marble floors, as we are led through to a large vaulted drawing room where we are greeted by a huge fireplace, several antique sofas and lots of strategically placed lamps and expensive-looking ornaments. A grand piano sits in the corner, next to a wall on which is draped something that looks like the Bayeux Tapestry.

Actually, maybe that *is* the Bayeux Tapestry, I wonder, before quickly dismissing the thought. Of course it's not, silly. That's a priceless artefact and in some museum some-where . . . But still. It wouldn't surprise me. This place reeks of wealth. Everything in here looks like some priceless antique. No wonder Madame Dumont's heirs have little interest in coming up to Paris for the auction. They must be absolutely loaded after inheriting this estate. The proceeds of the auction will probably be like loose change for them.

'Please—'

Xavier gestures for me to sit down and I perch gingerly on the edge of one of the sofas. I'm being careful not to knock anything over. Clumsy is my middle name. I feel apprehensive and not just a little bit intimidated. Which is ridiculous. What did Mum always used to tell me whenever I felt nervous? Oh yes, it was to imagine the person in their underpants.

'Welcome.'

I almost jump out of my skin as I turn round to see a large man stride into the room. Extremely tanned, with snow-white hair, he's smoking a cigar and wearing slippers with crests on them, billowy linen trousers and a shirt that's open way too far to reveal his extremely large paunch.

Actually, on second thoughts, forget the underpants thing.

'It is wonderful to meet you,' he booms, blowing out a large cloud of cigar smoke, through which he appears like a singer from an eighties music video. Grabbing our hands, he shakes them vigorously and introduces himself as Felix.

'I hear you are from England?' he says, fixing me with eyes that are too closely set together.

'Yes, London.' I nod.

'Oh, how I love London,' he says, in an accent I can't quite place, 'We lived there for a few years before we moved to Gstaad.'

Of course, it's one of those international accents that super wealthy people always have.

'You live in Switzerland?' I make an attempt at conversation.

'Hell no,' interrupts a loud voice and a woman appears in a bright pink tracksuit, carrying a ball of fluff.

Blonde and terrifyingly thin, at first I think she's my age, but as I focus in I realise she's probably closer to fifty, though it's hard to tell as she's had so much work done and is wearing sunglasses. The kind with rhinestones on the side, though in her case I wouldn't be surprised if they were real diamonds.

'The Swiss are so damn boring I insisted we move to Manhattan. Trust me, once you've seen one cuckoo clock, you've seen 'em all.'

'This is my wife Trixie,' says Felix, looking slightly pained. 'She's American.'

'Texan,' she corrects icily. 'Unlike my husband who's Swiss, in case you hadn't noticed.'

Felix fidgets in his monogrammed slippers and sits down on an armchair, looking suddenly more like the henpecked husband than the wealthy landowner. I watch him sucking on his cigar, like a baby would on a dummy, and suddenly feel rather sorry for him.

Well, trust me, you haven't met Trixie.

'And you must be Xavier,' she purrs loudly, directing her gaze greedily towards him. 'So awesome to put a face to a voice.'

Adjusting the ball of fluff, which I now realise is a small dog, she proffers a spidery hand, dripping in diamond rings, for Xavier to kiss. Which he does with the utmost grace and a murmuring of '*Enchanté*'.

'And you are?' Finally she turns to me, as if only just

noticing I'm here. Her inflated top lip curls slightly as if there's a bad odour.

'Ruby Miller,' I introduce myself, holding out my hand for her to shake.

She ignores it and, turning back to Xavier, instead whispers loudly, '*Who is she?*'

'Miss Miller is here to deliver the catalogue for the auction,' he says, not letting his smile slip.

'Oh, I see.' Her face registering, she turns back to me. 'So where is it?'

'Um, one moment, it's in my bag . . .' Feeling all eyes upon me, I scramble around in my backpack and pull it out.

'Felix, look after Snookies,' she commands, plonking the fur ball on his lap. He winces as it digs its painted nails into his linen crotch. Something tells me that wasn't an accident on Trixie's part.

Taking the catalogue from me, she quickly flicks through, a disappointed look on her face. 'I thought you said she had a Picasso?' she demands, looking up at Felix.

'It was just a rumour,' he says defensively.

'There's some rare china,' I say brightly, remembering Harriet's excitement when we first walked in.

Turning to me, she gives me a withering look.

'My wife's just a little upset,' explains Felix.

'Oh, of course,' I say, realising. I suddenly feel bad for the less than kind thoughts I've been having towards Trixie. She's obviously grieving. 'I'm very sorry to hear about your loss,' I say hurriedly. 'Please accept my condolences.'

'Oh, it's no loss to me,' she tuts disparagingly, 'We weren't related. Monsieur Dumont was my husband's great-uncle, or something like that. I can never remember the boring details.' She bats her hand around dismissively.

'Second cousin once removed,' corrects Felix, barely concealing his annoyance.

'Whatever.' She shrugs. 'I never met the guy, his wife was already a widow when Felix and I got together. It's the third marriage for both of us,' she adds in explanation and glances at her husband with an expression that says it won't be her last.

'She seemed like an interesting lady,' I prompt.

'Crazy you mean,' she scoffs. 'She lost her mind in the end you know. She spent the whole time living in the past, talking nonsense—'

We're interrupted by a young girl in a uniform carrying a tray of drinks.

'Refreshments, anyone?' asks Felix, helping himself to a large glass of rosé.

'Just water for me, thanks,' I say and Xavier says something in French to the girl, who pours us both a glass from the large jug.

'This iced coffee tastes weird,' frowns Trixie, taking a sip from her drink. 'Did you make it with sweetener like I told you?'

The young girl looks at her warily and murmurs something about *sucre*.

Trixie glances at Felix for a translation, then explodes. 'Sugar!' She looks like she's just been poisoned and thrusts the glass back at the girl. 'Just bring me a San Pellegrino with ice.'

As the young girl scurries out of the room, she tuts loudly. 'Honestly, you can't get the staff here like you can back home.'

'We'll be home soon my dear,' soothes Felix, then glances at me. 'There's been so much to sort out, it's been exhausting for my wife.'

I look at her, sprawled out on the sofa, and doubt that very much.

'Well, the auction is all taken care of,' I reply, then add pointedly, 'My boss Harriet has worked around the clock to get everything ready.'

'So all we need to do now is finalise the sale of the chateau,' continues Felix.

I look at him in surprise. 'You're selling it? But I thought it had been in the family for generations?'

'There's no room for sentiment in business,' replies Trixie, looking to Xavier for confirmation, 'isn't that right?'

I glance at him, surprised he's never mentioned this.

'We're just finalising the paperwork,' he says with a nod. 'Mr Nawasaki and his corporation have just a few more questions before the finances are put in place.'

I feel an unexpected sense of loss. God, what a shame. They're selling it to a Japanese corporation. And no doubt for a small fortune. I glance at Trixie and Felix and can't help thinking how nothing seems to have any value to them apart from its monetary one.

'Plus my husband would only drink it dry,' she adds, shooting a contemptuous look at Felix, who's draining the last of his glass. 'Darling, if you need me I'll be with our lawyer going over the particulars,' she says curtly, and getting up from the sofa she plucks the fluffball from his lap and turns to Xavier. 'Shall we?'

Xavier and I exchange glances and then, before I know it, she's linked her arm through his and is leading him swiftly from the room.

23

Leaving me with Felix.

Oh god.

'So, Ruby—' He nods, regarding me from his armchair, his hands clasped round his paunch, which looks more enormous than ever now he's sitting down, '—do you mind if I call you Ruby?'

'No, not at all.' I smile politely.

'Such a pretty name.'

'Thanks.' I fidget uncomfortably under his gaze. Damn, I wonder how long Xavier is going to be?

'They shouldn't be too long,' he says, as if he can read my mind, 'though my wife will want to go over the small print.'

'Yes,' I say, though judging by the way Trixie had looked at Xavier, I don't think it was the small print she was interested in.

'In the meantime, why don't I give you a tour of the estate?'

I'm torn between wanting to sit tight and wait for Xavier and wanting to look round the estate where Emmanuelle lived.

'That would be great, thanks,' I reply, my curiosity winning out.

'It's the largest in the region,' he boasts, hoisting himself up from his armchair with a loud grunt. 'We produce more than a hundred different wines including champagnes.'

'Wow.'

'Though I haven't yet tasted them all, despite what my wife might say,' he adds with a small laugh. 'But then my wife and I take a different approach to things. She takes care of the business side of things, whereas I prefer to be a lot more hands-on.'

'I see,' I say, feeling his hands-on approach round my waist as he ushers me out of the room. Once through the doorway, I quickly step to one side. 'Please, after you,' I say, gesturing for him to lead the way.

He pouts slightly, his large fleshy hand still outstretched, then, seeming to think better of it, drops it by his side and walks dutifully ahead, chewing on his cigar.

'So did you know the Dumonts well?' I ask, trying to sound nonchalant as we pass through the long marbled hallway.

He shakes his head. 'Not at all. I met Monsieur Dumont a couple of times as a young boy. Our families were not close.'

'And Madame Dumont?' I persist.

'Just once at her husband's funeral over twenty years ago. She was old and rather frail even then, hard to believe she was deemed to be quite a beauty in her youth . . .' He pauses by several black and white photographs on the wall, and gestures to one of a couple.

'Is this them?' I gasp, peering at an attractive young woman in a ballgown, standing stiffly next to an older, smartly dressed man.

'Yes, it was taken for *Paris Match*. They were quite the society couple in their day. The magazine even featured their wedding.'

It's the first picture I've seen of Emmanuelle and I gaze at her face staring out from the photograph. It's not how I imagined her to be; she'd sounded so alive in Henry's letters, so happy, and yet here, despite her beauty, she looks empty.

'Rumour has it she'd been a dancer before she was married.'

'Yes.' I nod, then catch myself. 'I mean – really?'

He nods. 'Though no one ever saw her dance. Apparently she would always refuse if asked, even by her husband.'

I think of her dancing with Henry, on their first date at the jazz club in Paris and then later, secretly together in her apartment. His descriptions of what a wonderful dancer she was are so vivid, so full of happiness and joy, it's so sad to think she never danced again. Yet, in a way, I can't help thinking it's because she still loved him. That even after she was married, to dance with anyone else, even her husband, felt like a betrayal.

But in that case, why did she marry Monsieur Dumont? Why did she choose him over Henry? I feel a sense of indignation, quickly followed by resignation. Much has changed in the past seventy years, nothing more so than the sense of duty she must have felt, and which she must have ultimately given in to. And yet, even though I only know Emmanuelle through Henry's letters, somehow I didn't think she would.

You spoke of society and tradition, of rules to be followed and appearances to be maintained. Yet you also spoke of your secret desire for freedom. Of being true to yourself. Of being able to follow your heart wherever it leads you.

'But then by all accounts their marriage wasn't a happy one.'

'It wasn't?' I turn to him expectantly. 'Why?'

'Monsieur Dumont could be quite a bully. I was rather scared of him as a boy.'

My eyes flick back to the wall of photographs. There are various ones of them at different society events, and then I see a framed page taken from *Paris Match* that must be of their wedding.

It features a photograph of a bride and groom, surrounded by bridesmaids. The setting is lavish. The dress is exquisite. Emmanuelle looks beautiful. But I can't stop staring at the older man with a handlebar moustache who is now her husband. His expression is hard and unflinching. If a picture tells a thousand words, then none of those is love.

I glance at the date in the corner: *19 July, 1945*. I feel a beat of surprise. So she didn't marry him until after the war. Five years after she fled Paris.

'Please, this way.' Felix gestures towards a door and reluctantly I turn away, my mind still full of questions, and follow him down a small staircase, which leads into a series of dimly lit rooms with arched ceilings. 'These are the wine cellars,' he says.

'Wow,' I murmur, my eyes adjusting to take in the hundreds of large oak-aged barrels piled high, row upon row of them.

'I call it the church as it's quite a religious experience,' he continues, spreading wide his arms like a preacher in a pulpit. 'Here we have over fifty thousand bottles stored in oak kegs – Merlot, Cabernet, Pinot, Côte de Provence . . .'

'It's quite impressive.' I nod.

And a little unsettling, niggles an internal voice, as I realise we're down here alone.

'Everything is climate controlled . . .'

I make more favourable noises.

'. . . all the bottles are aged a minimum of three years . . .' He leads me further into the shadowy depths, '. . . and three times a day we turn them—'

'You know, maybe we should be getting back upstairs,' I suggest, hanging back slightly. Call me paranoid, but I don't trust Felix's hands-on approach.

'Oh they will be ages,' he says dismissively, 'we have plenty of time, plus we're just getting to know each other . . .'

Uh-oh. He gives me the kind of look that you see in wildlife documentaries where the poor little baby gazelle is being eyed up by the hungry lion. You know, that look just before the lion pounces.

'Though I already know we both share a love of the finer things in life,' he continues, moving closer.

'We do?' I step backwards. It's like we're doing some kind of dance.

'Wine and antiques,' he says.

'Oh, right, yes, of course.' I nod. Seriously, I am so going to kill Harriet. A favour is one thing, but what part of 'delivering a catalogue' includes fighting off a lecherous old soak?

Frantically I try to remember what I'd learned in those tae kwon do classes I signed up for a couple of years ago.

'And I'm sure we'll discover we have a lot more in common . . .' Out of the gloom, his white linen bulk continues to slowly advance towards me, like a cruise liner.

But my mind's a blank. Oh, I know, wear comfy clothes, yes that was it. Well, I only went to the first one, the classes clashed with *Downton*.

'Oh, I wouldn't think so,' I laugh, trying to make light of the situation. I swear, any minute now and he's going to be saying his wife doesn't understand him.

'You know, my wife doesn't understand me.'

Argh. This cannot be happening. It just can't.

Only it is, and as I edge backwards I realise I'm now trapped between one of the barrels and his chest. I take a deep breath. Right that's it, this is ridiculous. I need to be firm but polite.

'Felix—' I say sharply, drawing myself up to my full height.

'Claude—'

Huh, what? I twirl round to see a tall, older gentleman in a beret, holding a clipboard.

'Claude is the *maître de chai*, the cellar master, one of the estate's most trusted employees,' says Felix, trading a few hurried words with him in French. 'There is nothing that this man does not know about wine.'

'Claude, hi!' I say, manoeuvring my way out of my tight spot and clinging on to his hand with relief. 'I'm Ruby, so nice to meet you.'

Claude looks rather taken aback by my exuberant intro-
duction, but shakes my hand nonetheless.

'I was just showing our guest around the cellars,' interrupts Felix, 'explaining the wine-making process – in case my
wife should ask,' he adds pointedly.

'But of course,' says Claude and a look flashes between
them that tells me this isn't the first time Felix has
been caught giving a guest a private tour of his wine
cellars.

'Would you care to taste some of the wines?' he asks
solemnly, turning to me.

'Yes, that would be lovely,' I say eagerly. Anything not to be
alone with Felix.

'Monsieur?'

He pretends to think about it for a moment, then gives a
little fake shrug of defeat. 'Well, I suppose it would be rude
not to accompany my guest,' he concedes, and without
further need for encouragement swiftly takes two glasses
from Claude and passes me one.

'The first thing you have to look at is the colour,' instructs
Claude, ceremoniously uncorking a bottle of red wine and
skilfully pouring out two large glugs.

Oh dear. This is probably where I should confess that I
know absolutely nothing about wine and that I buy whatever is
on special at Tesco Metro on the corner. However, I'm standing in one of the most prestigious wine cellars in Provence, if
not the world, in front of what is probably one of the leading
experts on wine-making.

'This is very important,' he continues gravely, his expression serious.

Somehow I don't think now is the right time to share my
story of 'the night I got hammered on Merlot' or start explaining about Tesco Clubcard points.

'What do you see?'

I stare nervously at my glass. Call me a Neanderthal, but it looks red.

'Look for the transparency of the grape, the tones of red and yellow—'

'—and pink and green.' Automatically I finish off the rhyme and then feel my cheeks flame as I suddenly realise what I've said. Oh god.

Felix frowns slightly. 'Green?' he repeats, swirling his glass and peering at it intently.

'Well . . . um – more purple,' I say vaguely and glance at Claude, imploring him to move on. Which he does, thankfully.

'Next are the legs,' he continues, 'which is an indication of the alcohol.'

'Oh, yes, I know all about that!' I interject. Maybe it *is* OK for me to tell my wine story, if we're talking about what wine does to your walking ability. 'You should have seen me the night I drank a bottle of Merlot,' I exclaim. Rolling my eyes, I do an impression of me wobbling all over. 'Honestly, I could barely stand up! I was legless!'

Claude stares at me blankly. As does Felix, who I notice has downed most of his glass already.

'You know, legs, legless,' I repeat, only this time in my best French accent. It mustn't translate well, that's why they're not laughing.

'"Legs" are what we call the streaks of wine that appear on the side of the glass, like so,' intones Claude sternly. Expertly he swirls the wine and holds it to the light.

'Oh, you mean . . .'

Oh bloody hell. How embarrassing.

'Next, we smell the wine,' he says, sticking his nose deep into the glass. Personally I wish I could stick my entire face in the glass, I'm so mortified, but I breathe in while he talks about scents of melon and peaches and freshly cut grass.

'Now we taste a sip—'

Finally, I take a grateful gulp.

'—Allowing the air to be drawn over it—' Claude makes a gurgling sound.

Fuck. I've already swallowed mine. Hastily I take another sip before anyone notices. Somewhere deep in my memory I seem to remember something about spitting out the wine when you're tasting, but after my earlier faux pas I'm not about to start spitting. I glance sideways at Felix and briefly consider whether I should ask him if I should spit or swallow, then, as he smiles lecherously from the shadows, I hastily think better of it.

'How was that?' I turn back to see Claude looking at me expectantly. His glass appears to be empty as well.

'Mmm, yes delicious.' I nod, and glug the rest of it back. Well, I don't want to look rude.

In fact I don't want to look rude for the several more wines that we taste and so I spend the next thirty or so minutes swirling and sniffing and swallowing. It's only when we've reached the last bottle that I notice a bucket in the shadows behind Claude.

Hang on a minute. I point at it. 'Is that—?'

'For the wine, yes,' he finishes my sentence, before turning away and reappearing with an empty glass.

I stare at him open-mouthed. How did I not notice that before? But then it is quite dark in here and I've been mostly keeping my eye on Felix, who's been surreptitiously refilling his glass between tastings.

'Thank you Claude, that was most educational,' he slurs, thumping him on the back.

'Yes, thank you.' I smile gratefully, inadvertently distracting him while Felix swipes the rest of the bottle.

'I think I should double-check the legs on this Pinot,' he says, realising he's been caught red-handed, 'quality control and all that.' Pouring himself a large glass he, swirls it enthusiastically and pretends to inspect it in the light.

I see my chance to escape. 'If you'll excuse me, I need the ladies' room,' I say hastily and, before Felix can protest, I quickly dash out of the wine cellar and leg it back up the stairs.

Back in the bright safety of the hallway, I breathe a sigh of relief. Actually, I feel quite tipsy. Steadying myself against the wall, I head back towards the main *salle*, but it's still empty. There's no sign of Xavier whatsoever. Disappointed, I turn to walk back out of the room.

'There you are!'

And bump straight into Felix.

'Oh, yes, here I am,' I say, forcing a smile and noting the wine stains down his linen shirt and the Cabernet fumes that are wafting towards me.

'Can I can show you round the rest of the vineyard?' He pins me in the doorway.

'No! I mean, thanks, but I think I've taken up enough of your time,' I say, a little more tactfully, and try to move past him, 'I've troubled you enough—'

'It's no trouble.'

Seriously, he's not budging. He's like a cork, stuck fast in a bottle.

I try again. 'I think I might explore the village, I hear they've got some lovely ceramics—'

'I can drive you, I have the Porsche outside.'

My heart sinks. An old man in a Porsche. Could there be anything worse?

Felix staggers back slightly, giving me just enough room to slip past him. Actually yes, there is: a drunk old man in a Porsche.

'No, it's OK, I could do with the exercise, I'll walk,' I say hastily, striding towards the entrance.

'It's quite far,' he protests, shuffling after me in his monogrammed slippers.

Determined, I step out on to the gravel driveway, then pause. Oh crap, he's right, we're in the middle of nowhere. I glance around me and spot an old yellow Renault reversing out of a space. For a moment I think about trying to hitch a ride, but it's too late; before I've had a chance it's disappeared in a cloud of dust and exhaust fumes.

'It's too far to walk,' Felix calls after me from the entrance. He's right. It is. And yet . . .

As the dust settles I spot a bicycle leaning against the wall where the yellow car has just been parked. It's rusty. I have no idea who it belongs to. And I haven't ridden one in years.

'Ruby!'

Still, you never forget how to ride a bike, right?

24

Wrong.

That's absolute rubbish. In fact, whoever said it should be forced to ride a bike after drinking about eight glasses of wine, in thirty-degree heat, with a semi-flat tyre and a seat that goes right up your—

Ouch.

Wobbling down the gravelly path, I jig up and down on the hard leather saddle. I can't remember it ever being this difficult to keep my balance. Or this painful. I grimace, wishing more than anything that I had chosen not to wear a G-string today. I'd rather have a visible panty line than bits that are being torn to shreds. Imagine a cheese grater and your labia and— actually, no, on second thoughts, too much information.

Wincing, I try standing up on the pedals, then lose my balance and collapse back down again on the razor-sharp seat. Argh! If I didn't know where my pubic bone was before, I certainly do now. It's probably not helping that all that wine's gone right to my head and I feel a bit – well, tipsy would be one word. Rattling down the path, I clutch the handlebars and try to focus. It's really weird, but it's like there are two paths, almost as if I've got double vision. I close one eye. Ah, that's better, now there's just one path.

Another word would be pissed.

Well, no one told me I was supposed to spit, did they? And I didn't want to be rude. Not when I'm here representing

Harriet . . . I sway dangerously as I go round a corner and hang on for dear life.

The path winds upwards and I press down hard on the pedals. I'm not sure at the moment that the person who invented the bicycle really thought it through. I mean, why skimp on wheels and only have two? And why sit so high up? I eye the ground warily from over the top of the handlebars. It's a long way down if you fall off. Not that I'm going to fall off of course, I tell myself firmly, I just need to get the hang of it. After all, half of London is whizzing around on those free bikes, so it can't be that hard. I'm just a bit out of practice.

Huffing and puffing up the hill, I wipe the rivulets of sweat that are dripping down my forehead. God, it's hot. Like a furnace. I wish I'd brought some suntan lotion and a hat. I can feel myself already getting sunburned.

I suddenly have one of those out-of-body experiences that I sometimes have. You know, the ones where you're in the middle of doing something and you look down on yourself and think 'How on earth did I get here?' And not in a good way.

I mean, hello? Whenever I thought about visiting the south of France for the first time, this is not how I imagined it. I imagined wafting around St Tropez looking cool and chic, with one of those straw bags slung casually over my tanned shoulder. Or snapping selfies of myself on a sunlounger while sipping eye-wateringly expensive cocktails and spotting celebs. Or enjoying a romantic candlelit dinner in a quintessential village square with a man who's crazy about me, sipping rosé, nibbling on gastronomic delights, kissing underneath the stars . . .

I did not – repeat not – imagine being a big sweaty lobster-red ball on a bicycle in the middle of god knows where.

Good one, Ruby. As usual, you've scored ten out of ten in life.

For a brief moment I think about turning back, returning to the coolness of the chateau, but then I have a flashback to Felix, and I seem to find from somewhere a renewed strength in my legs.

Plus of course, this way I get to explore the village where Emmanuelle spent the rest of her life as Madame Dumont. It's a chance I can't miss.

Thighs and heat permitting, of course.

Fortunately, there is a God and just when I think I'm going to have to get off and push, the path levels out and I cycle the rest of the way without too much effort. In fact, I actually start to enjoy it. The path turns into a country lane on either side of which are fields of lavender and old stone barns, hedges of wild flowers and butterflies that circle and swoop around me like tropical-coloured confetti.

Gosh, it really is gorgeous here, I muse, gazing at the landscape, which is like something you'd see in a Cézanne painting. Bright blue skies, rusty red rooftops, rich ochre earth. The colours are amazing – and the light. Oh, the light. Even in the height of summer, you never get this kind of light in London. It has a luminosity and a radiance that makes my heart sing. That makes me feel like I've been hibernating my whole life and suddenly bam, I'm alive.

I swear, right at this moment it's all I can do not to log on to Zoopla and start looking at what I can get for the price of my dark little basement flat in Zone 2. Well, I wouldn't be the first writer. If it was good enough for Peter Mayle—

Oh, I'm here already! Turning a corner, I see a small square with a fountain and realise I've arrived in the village. I've been so busy daydreaming I didn't realise how close I was, but now I stop pedalling and slow down.

Café tables – at which are seated locals and a few tourists – spill out onto the cobbles, shaded from the midday sun by the large plane trees. Little winding streets meander up and down.

I hop off my saddle, hop being a euphemism for a groaning-wincing-dismount that leaves me walking wide-legged, like I'm in a Western, and wheel the bicycle to a small shop boasting a huge fridge selling ice-cold drinks. I buy a bottle of water and drink it straight down in one go. To say I needed that is something of an understatement.

After letting myself revive for a few moments, I feel about a million times better, and with renewed enthusiasm I set about exploring the village. Perched on a hilltop with a view of the mountains on one side, and a sweeping valley that leads down to the coast on the other, it has stunning vistas and a sleepy charm. After the frenetic pace of London and Paris, the rhythm here is much slower.

Locals sit fanning themselves in doorways, shopkeepers pass the time of day, children dangle their hands lazily into the fountain. Even the cats, so skittish in cities, roam casually around the narrow streets, stopping only to flop down on a sunny windowsill.

Which is what I'm tempted to do after my mammoth bike ride, but I'm not here to relax, I'm here to see if I can find out anything about Emmanuelle. I mean, there must be something here that will help explain the mystery of her apartment, surely?

I keep walking and after a few minutes I come across a small church. It's as inviting as it is pretty and, propping my bicycle outside, I enter through the old wooden doors.

It's much cooler inside and I relish the drop in temperature after the intensity of the sun. It's also much darker, after the brightness of the day, and it takes a few moments for my eyes to adjust, but when they do I note the rows of small wooden pews, the ancient stained-glass windows casting prisms of coloured light, the carved stone ceilings. Did Emmanuelle come here? I wonder, casting my gaze around me.

I shuffle along one of the pews and sit down, like a thousand others before me. There's no one else here, just me, and in the quiet I take a moment, trying to imagine what it must have been like for her to come here all those years ago, to leave Paris and her life behind. To leave Henry. I feel a beat of sadness. I wonder if she sat here and prayed to see him again. I wonder if her prayers were answered . . .

My imagination turns like a wheel. In my head I picture their reunion, a happy ending to the story, and yet I know there can't be one. I saw the photograph in the chateau. She didn't marry Henry, their romance didn't last – she became Madame Dumont, wife to a wealthy landowner, and lived the rest of her days out here in the south of France. She married well, as they always used to say in those days, and lived to a ripe old age. So why does it sadden me? Why is that not a happy ending?

I gaze at the empty pulpit, at the shaft of light being cast from overhead, and search for an answer. Is it just the hopeless romantic in me? That part of me that believes in soulmates and true love and that magical feeling you have when they walk into a room and everything else disappears? In an invisible, intense, once-in-a-billion bond between two people that can never be broken, not even by death?

And who cannot let go of the conviction that in this mad, crazy, screwed-up world of ours, if you're lucky enough to find that person, you never *ever* let them go?

She never let Henry go.

As the thought whispers in my head, I'm convinced of it. It's not the fact that she kept secretly paying for her apartment, for all those years. It's not the loveless photograph of her and Monsieur Dumont. It's not even that she never danced again. I just know it, deep in my heart. And that's why I can never think of this as a happy ending. In fact, that's why I can't think of this as an ending at all.

Leaving the coolness of the church I walk back outside, into the bright midday sunshine. I pause by the bicycle, partly because I'm reluctant to get back on the instrument of torture but mostly because I'm not sure where to head. There must be more to discover in this village that would give me further information about Emmanuelle.

It's then I notice a small cemetery beyond the church, where several headstones and crosses hug a small grassy patch of hillside. I wonder if that's where she's buried? Curiosity prickles and, leaving my bicycle again, I pass through the small iron gate and follow the narrow path that leads between the gravestones. It's so nice here. So many cemeteries are gloomy and depressing, but this one is dappled in sunlight and offers its sleeping guests the most gorgeous view.

I pick my way between the headstones, shading my eyes to read the inscriptions and looking for any mention of Emmanuelle. All are in French, but still I can read the names. After a few minutes I come upon a large marble tombstone, much bigger and more imposing than all the rest, and I see the name ALEXANDRE DUMONT and the dates 1901–70. This must be Monsieur Dumont, the dates seem right, and yet – why is there no mention of his wife, Emmanuelle? Puzzled, I frown at the inscription. And surely she would be buried next to him? Instead there's just an empty plot—

'*Est-ce que je peux vous aider?*'

A voice behind me makes me jump and I spin round to see a woman. She's wearing a headscarf and carrying a gardening trug.

'I'm sorry,' I begin to apologise, '*Je ne* – um – *parle Francais.*'

Her hooded eyes look me up and down. 'You're English? My father was from Newcastle.'

'Oh – nice.'

'Not really, too many people.' She wrinkles her nose. 'Can I help you? I look after the cemetery.'

'Oh, no, thank you, I was just . . .' I feel as if I've been caught doing something I shouldn't.

'Are you looking for someone?'

I glance back to the tombstone. 'I was looking for Emmanuelle Dumont. Is this her husband's grave?'

'Yes,' she says with a nod, 'but she is not buried here.'

'She's not?' I frown, surprised.

The woman eyes me suspiciously. 'I haven't seen you before. Are you a relative?'

'No, I'm just . . .' I pause. What am I? It's the strangest thing. I never got to meet Emmanuelle in her lifetime, but through Henry's letters, I feel as if I know her. 'I'm a friend of a friend,' I say vaguely.

'Madame Dumont was cremated, her ashes were scattered.'

'Oh, I see.'

'The Dumonts' was a double plot, but it is said she left strict instructions not to be buried there.'

There's a pause, and I feel like the woman wants to tell me more. There's something about villages and the desire to gossip. My parents live in one and there's always someone eager to say something about someone.

'Many people were surprised, but not me.' Pursing her lips, she shakes her head.

'Really, why?'

'Would you want to lie for eternity next to someone who cheated and lied? *Pah!*'

Crikey. I wasn't expecting that outburst.

'Well, I had heard rumours . . .' I trail off, hoping she'll say more.

I'm not disappointed.

'He liked too much of a drink and when he did he was very loose with his affections, you know?' She raises her eyebrows pointedly. 'And his money.'

'He was a gambler?'

'It was said she had to hide family heirlooms from him so he couldn't gamble them away. They would have probably lost everything if he had lived longer. It was lucky for her that he left this mortal coil early.'

As she's talking I suddenly have a memory of Trixie talking about a Picasso. Felix dismissed it as a rumour, but what if it wasn't? What if she did have a priceless painting, and she kept it hidden in her apartment in Paris?

As one thought strikes, another follows. What if, in fact, I've got this completely wrong and the answer to the mystery isn't anything to do with love at all?

I'm distracted by the chimes from the church bell and I look up to the clock tower. Gosh, is that the time already? Xavier should have finished going over the documents with Trixie by now; he's probably wondering where I am. I glance at my phone, but there's no signal. I'd best be getting back to the chateau.

Quickly thanking the woman for her time, I make my way out of the cemetery and, mounting the bike, slowly begin to pedal. The whole village feels like it's gone to sleep as, weaving through the narrow backstreets, I pass houses with their faded shutters pulled tight, shops with their grilles down – even the square with the fountain, which was so busy earlier, is now deserted. I start to slowly climb the hill that leads out of the village, pushing down hard on the pedals and fantasising about my own siesta.

All this exercise and sun has exhausted me. Not to mention the bucket of wine I drank earlier. What I wouldn't do to be on Harriet's sofa bed right now, and trust me, that's saying something.

Daydreaming about feather pillows, I barely notice that the road has flattened out. It's only when I realise I'm not having to pedal any more that I see I'm starting my descent. I feel a rush of relief. And delight. Gosh, I've forgotten how much fun cycling can be. Freewheeling down the other side, I begin picking up speed. The warm breeze rushes up, blowing my hair back from my face and cooling my sticky skin. This is so great!

The countryside whizzes by as I gather speed, and I feel a rush of exhilaration. Feeling braver, I lift one hand off the handlebars, letting my hand surf the stream of air rushing past me. Wow, I haven't done this since I was a kid. In fact, I remember I used to be able to take both hands off my handlebars, which of course was really dangerous, and something I'd never do now—

I feel a prickle of temptation. *Oh my god, don't be insane*, yells the voice in my head, *you're way too old and sensible now, you could kill yourself!*

But giddy on adrenalin and my own speed, I don't feel old and sensible, I feel young and alive. Whizzing down a country lane in the south of France on a bicycle, all my worries blow like cobwebs out of my mind. I'm not thinking about Emmanuelle or Henry or me and Jack. I'm not thinking about the past or the future. I'm totally in this moment. Here. Right now. I feel like a kid again. I *want* to be a kid again. I lift off one hand, then slowly peel back the fingers of the next, four, three, two – until it's just my forefinger left and then—

Look, no hands!

'Woo-hoo!' I cry, throwing back my head and laughing, and in that split second I see a flash of yellow out of the corner of my eye, hear the sound of a car horn, the screech of brakes—

Then everything goes black.

25

I'm floating. Like a balloon. Higher and higher. All around me is silent and dark. And soft. Everything is so soft, it's like being wrapped up in cotton wool. Warm cotton wool. Wow, I've never felt this relaxed. It's so peaceful and calm. I can feel myself drifting further and further away . . .

Except now I can hear something. A faint pattering. Almost like rain on a windowpane, *pat-pat-pat-pat* – only it's not raindrops, it's louder than that. It sounds more like tapping, or a drumming. And now I can feel something on my face, but it's not warm, wet splashes, it's more cold and hard, and actually not very nice. In fact, it kind of hurts, rather like someone's slapping my face—

Hang on, someone *is* slapping my face!

What the—?

Dazed and confused, I open my eyes and make out a blurry shape bent over me, slapping the sides of my cheeks and saying something in a flurry of French. I blink rapidly as everything starts swimming into focus. I see flashes of purple, something glittery, a mouth filled with lots of white pointy teeth that seems to be moving in slow motion.

Ugh. What happened – where am I . . . ?

But it's the weirdest thing. I can't speak, all I can do is lie completely motionless as slowly I become aware that the mouth belongs to a woman who has a purple scarf tied in her hair, a twinkly nose stud and lots of earrings that go all the way round the outside of her ear. And there's something else.

Out of the corner of my eye I can see a large yellow shape, and as the image sharpens I realise it's a car. Hang on, that's the same car that I saw . . . My fuzzy mind grinds to a halt as I try to remember where. It's like grasping at something just a little out of reach. Actually it's all a bit tiring, I might close my eyes again, go back to sleep—

'*Merde!*'

I'm jolted back awake by a string of expletives and a much harder slap.

'Ouch!' I cry loudly, snapping open my eyes. All the warm cotton wool has disappeared and suddenly I feel sore as hell.

More French. And now hand signals. There's lots of gesturing and hands being waved around. Bracelets are jangling. A dragon is bobbing up and down—

A dragon? Oh god, I must be hallucinating.

Everything is swimming before my eyes. I try to sit up on my elbows, but the woman shakes her head and pushes me back down, and says something to me. Crikey, these French can really talk fast, can't they? It's coming out in a torrent.

'*Parlez-vous anglais?*' I finally manage to croak, coughing dust.

'Ah! You're *English!*' she suddenly gasps, hitting her forehead with the palm of her hand.

'Ugh . . . yes – from London,' I splutter, putting my fingers up to my temples. Ouch, it feels really sore. I look at my fingertips and let out a shriek. 'Oh my god, I'm bleeding.' I suddenly feel like I'm going to faint again.

'Don't worry, you're OK.'

OK? I have blood coming out of my head. I might not be a doctor, but I'm pretty sure that blood coming from anywhere is not the definition of OK.

'Don't worry, I did a course in first aid.' Pulling the patterned scarf from her hair, she dabs my head. 'You're in the recovery position, your airways are clear and nothing appears to be broken,' she reassures me.

She sounds so confident, I feel slightly comforted. 'Um, what happened?' I mumble, trying to move, but my legs are in a tangle and my body is doing that thing it did when I drank too much Merlot.

'I'm so sorry, it's all my fault, I didn't see you, I need to get my mirrors fixed—' She gestures to her car, '—but then I had to pay the rent and more bills and . . .' She makes a blow-ing-out noise. 'I'm just glad you are OK, I feel terrible, I was rushing, I wasn't looking where I was going—'

She looks so upset that for a moment I think she's going to burst into tears. 'It's OK, it's not your fault,' I say quickly, 'It's my fault too. I shouldn't have been riding a bicycle with no hands,' while under the influence, I add silently.

'No, no, I should have been paying attention,' she berates herself, shaking her head. 'I take full responsibility.'

I don't have the energy to argue. Instead I tell her I want to sit up and she helps me, holding me underneath the armpits and putting her arms round my waist as I shakily go from sitting to slowly standing. I feel like I've been run over by a truck. Though in my case it's a battered old yellow Renault.

'Let me drive you to my house, I will clean you up, I need to dress that.' She points to a rather nasty gash on my shin.

'What about my bike?'

It's lying in the road, all mangled up. From where I'm standing I can see the front wheel is all bent out of shape, and its tyres both look like they have punctures.

'Don't worry, I will put it in the car,' she reassures me, seeing my expression. 'Stay here, please,' she instructs.

Gingerly I prop myself against a stone wall and watch as she strides over to the bike in her frayed denim shorts and clumpy workman's boots. She's small and slight and for a moment I think of offering to help, even though I'm in no fit state, but instead she picks it up as if it weighs nothing more than a feather. I stare at her rippling biceps in astonishment and it's then I notice the large dragon tattoo running down one arm. So I wasn't hallucinating.

As she chucks it in the back of the car I hear a loud squawking, and notice a crate of chickens in the car. 'Shush,' she says with a frown, putting her fingers to her lips. 'It is the cockerel, he is always complaining,' she says to me, shutting the back door with a slam. 'Men, huh?' she grins.

She opens the passenger door for me. It swings off its hinges and makes a loud squeaking, rusty noise. Striding back to me, she helps me hobble across the road. 'Please.' She motions for me to get in. The seat is covered in tie-dye fabric and what looks like lots of dog hairs and several feathers.

'I'm sorry, Napoleon normally likes to travel in the front with me,' she apologises, and gestures into the back where I spy a black and white mongrel squashed between the chickens and my back. He doesn't look very happy.

'Thanks.' I nod and gingerly climb inside.

Inside the car is like a treasure trove. The dashboard is a little shrine, filled with various crystals and a small carved Buddha, while hanging from the rear-view mirror are long strings of coloured beads.

'Are these from India?' I ask, recognising them as the same as the ones I saw in Rajasthan.

'Yes, aren't they beautiful?' she says, fingering them. 'I would love to go there one day.'

'You must, it's magical.'

'You've been? Oh wow, you are so lucky! One day, when I win the lotto . . .' She smiles. 'But first I need to make money to fix my side mirrors, huh?'

I look out of the window and for the first time I realise there actually aren't any mirrors.

'By the way, I'm Gigi,' she smiles, and sticks out a tanned hand, its fingers filled with lots of silver rings with big stones.

'I'm Ruby.'

She grasps my hand in hers and gives me a firm hand-shake, then turns the ignition. The engine fires up with a loud splutter, then she sticks the car into gear and we lurch away.

After only about ten minutes, we turn off the main road and into a narrow dirt lane that can obviously only accom-modate the width of one car. It's unmade, and as we drive down it we bump up and down on the front seats of the car, the springs of which appear to have gone, almost hitting our heads. Crikey, I've only just been concussed, I don't want it to happen again.

I glance across at Gigi, but she seems unperturbed. Crunching the strange gearstick, she keeps her foot firmly on the accelerator. I hang on to the door handle as the car rocks from side to side. There's a loud noise as a stone is spat from underneath the tyres, and the crunch of the undercarriage on a rock. And I thought driving with Harriet was bad. At least with her I felt the car was going to stay together.

I glance at the glove compartment, which appears to be held together by a piece of string, and have second thoughts about hanging on to the door handle. I release my grip slightly before I risk it coming off in my hand.

After what feels like for ever, we finally pull up in front of a small stone house with faded blue shutters and a large vine from which cascades an abundance of creamy white flowers. It's attached to several tumbledown outbuildings, and what looks like an old barn where chickens run around, pecking at the ground, and a donkey stands chewing lazily from an old wheelbarrow filled with hay.

As we get out of the car, a little sandy-coloured dog with a grey snout runs out to meet us, wagging his tail nineteen to the dozen. Gigi says something to him, stooping down to scratch his ears, then opens the boot so he can be reunited with his obvious companion. I say obvious as no sooner has the door opened an inch than the black and white dog that's been held captive in the back leaps out, and the two dogs begin playfully chasing each other round and round in delight.

'Let me help you into the house. I'll come back for the chickens,' she says, ignoring their squawking chorus as she helps me get out of the car and hobble up to the front door.

'*Maman!*' she calls, flinging it open and leading me into a small flagstoned hallway that in turn leads into a small kitchen on the left. She gestures for me to sit down at the scrubbed pine table, moving a glass jam jar filled with wild flowers and a large patterned fruit bowl to clear a space. Then, pouring me a glass of water, she begins busying herself opening and closing cupboards until, finding what she's looking for, she pulls out a small first aid kit.

'This might sting a little,' she warns, unscrewing a bottle and shaking some of its contents on to a cloth. She goes to wipe my temple.

'Argh, fuck,' I gasp, shooting backwards in my chair as a searing pain shoots through me. 'Sorry, I didn't mean . . .'

'It's OK,' she says with a smile, 'I don't mean to hurt you, it's just I need to use antiseptic, it's important to clean the wound.'

I nod, understanding, and she holds up the cloth. 'I promise I will be as quick as possible.'

I brace myself, then give the go-ahead, and for the next few minutes I wince and grimace and bite my tongue as Gigi carefully wipes and cleans and patches me up. '*Fini*,' she says finally, putting away the spare dressings and snapping the lid closed on the first aid kit.

'Thank you so much,' I say gratefully.

She bats away my thanks with her hand. 'It is the least I can do.'

'Gigi?' a voice calls from another room.

'Finally, she speaks,' she says, rolling her eyes. 'She can hear, she just chooses not to.'

'Is that your mother?'

'Yes,' she says, 'please come and meet her, you can rest where it is more comfortable.' She motions for me to follow her and leads me from the kitchen, instructing me several times to watch my head as we pass underneath low beams, and into a cosy living room with a huge old fireplace. In the corner an elderly lady sits in an armchair, watching a portable TV that looks almost as old as she is.

'*Maman*,' says Gigi, turning down the volume, which is blaring. Kissing her on both cheeks, she says something to her in French.

Her mother turns to me. She has curly, salt and pepper hair pulled back into a bun that looks almost white against her skin, and although her face is deeply lined, she has the most wonderful high cheekbones. Despite her frayed pinafore, she has a certain regality about her. Her gaze sweeps over me. She might be hard of hearing, but there's nothing wrong with her eyesight and her dark eyes observe me before she breaks into a smile.

'*Bonjour Madame*,' I say with a smile, then before I say something with the completely wrong pronoun or verb ending and offend her inadvertently, I switch safely back to English, 'it's lovely to meet you. I'm Ruby.'

Gigi translates, and her mother quickly responds. 'She says please, call her Grace and she is delighted to meet you also and is sorry for the accident—' I attempt an 'oh-it's-nothing' type expression, even though my entire body is fast turning into one big purple bruise, '—and to make yourself comfortable.' Gigi gestures to the worn, slouchy leather sofa, with its brightly coloured cushions and large woollen throw.

I sink down gratefully. The leather is so soft it's like butter, and it's all I can do to stop myself pulling the woollen throw round me and drifting off to sleep. Instead I glance at the TV, on which the news is playing, and what appears to be a procession.

'What's happening?' I ask, curiously.

'It's the celebrations for the D-Day landings,' explains Gigi, 'they are showing a recording of yesterday's big parade down the Champs Élysées in Paris. I think your Queen was there.'

'Oh yes, of course.' I nod, remembering the veterans I'd seen at St Pancras en route to France. I think about the girl with the pink hair and her grandfather, who came to my rescue with Heathcliff. They'll be there.

'*Maman* is very interested in watching all of this as she was born during the war.'

I look back at the TV. Old black and white film is playing, intercut with footage of old soldiers in their heavily decorated uniforms, together with heads of state.

'So many brave men lost their lives, it is terrible,' continues Gigi, shaking her head.

'Yes, they are all heroes,' I say, echoing the words of the girl I'd met at the station with her grandfather.

The old lady turns away from the TV to look at me, then says something to Gigi.

'She is wondering what brings you here to our village,' she translates, 'are you on vacation?'

'No, I'm here to visit the Dumont estate, I've travelled down from Paris.'

'Oh, the estate.' She nods at the mention of it.

'Do you know it?'

'Everyone around here knows the estate, it's been here for ever. It employs many people in the village.'

Worry pricks. I wonder what will happen after it's sold to the Japanese corporation but don't say anything.

'Including myself.'

Of course. Now I remember seeing her little yellow car driving away from the chateau earlier. 'You work there?'

'Yes.' She nods. 'I work on the vineyard, there is a team of us looking after the vines. They need a lot of care, pruning, irrigating, making sure they grow properly so we have a good harvest. My trick is to sing to them—' She breaks off as she sees my expression and laughs. 'I used to be a singer, but that was before my son was born when I had no responsibilities.'

'You have a baby?' I look at her in surprise; she doesn't look much older than me.

'Oh he's not a baby any more, Jean-Paul is eighteen,' she says with a laugh.

At the mention of Jean-Paul's name, Gigi and her mother exchange a few words.

'My *maman* is upset. He recently left to work in Paris and she misses him. Especially after Papa died, Jean-Paul was the man of the house from being just a small boy.'

She doesn't need to translate; the expression on her mother's face says it all. 'Still, he has a job already, that's impressive,' I say. 'At his age I was at college.'

Unfortunately my clumsy attempt to put a positive spin on it completely backfires as Gigi's face falls.

'He wanted to go to college to study to be a journalist, but I could not afford the fees, it was just too much money for me, what with looking after *Maman* as well . . .' She trails off and shrugs her shoulders. 'Have you got children?'

'No.' I shake my head.

'Well make sure you choose a *papa* who's not going to run away,' she says, shaking her head, before unexpectedly breaking into a smile. 'But I am glad he did, otherwise I would have had to run away from him.' She laughs again. 'We played together in a band, he was a terrible musician as well as a terrible father.'

I smile. I like Gigi a lot. Despite her diminutive appearance, she has a strength that shines through.

'Did you know the Dumonts?'

At the mention of the name, her mother says something in rapid French.

'*Maman* grew up in the Var but moved here when she married my father. She says it was well known that Monsieur Dumont was always chasing after skirt in the village.'

'And Madame Dumont?'

'She was very kind. She did a lot of work for local charities, but that was before she fell ill.'

'What happened?'

'Pneumonia I think it was, and old age of course.'

'So she didn't go . . .' I think about how Trixie described her, 'a little crazy?'

Gigi gives a little snort of laughter. 'Who said this?'

Realising I've spoken out of turn, I don't want to say. But I don't have to.

'Don't tell me, it was that silly fool of a woman and her drunk oaf of a husband at the chateau.' Gigi wrinkles up her nose in displeasure. 'As if they would know anything. They never visited Madame when she was alive, not even when she was ill. It was only afterwards they appeared, hungry for their inheritance, like vultures, pah!'

Listening to Gigi, I feel a new dislike for Trixie and Felix. My opinion of them before wasn't good, but now it's even worse.

'Madame Dumont was pretty incredible for her age. Her hearing was bad, she was almost deaf in the end, and her sight wasn't too good either, but her mind was totally sharp. She loved literature and once I told her about my son, and how he loved to read, and after that she would often give me books to bring home to him.' She gestures to the books that line the bookcase. 'These all belonged to her, you know.

When she died the heirs kept only the valuable editions and threw the rest of her collection away. They were going to burn them, can you believe it? Burning books! And she calls Madame Dumont crazy!'

Gigi looks shocked, as well she might.

'Really? I can't believe it, that's sacrilege.' But even as I'm saying it, I can believe it. Words aren't worth anything to Trixie and Felix. After all, you can't spend them.

'Of course I could not allow this, so I rescued them,' she goes on. 'My son got to travel the whole world in his bedroom from these pages. That's probably why he wanted to become a journalist and where he got his love of writing.'

I nod, thinking about Henry. Is that why Madame Dumont loved reading so much, because it reminded her of him?

'May I?' I ask, carefully easing myself up from the sofa and looking closer at the spines that are neatly aligned on the bookcase on the wall. 'Are they all in French?'

'Oh, no, not at all, she used to like to read in English a lot, she said it was important for her to remember . . .' Gigi trails off.

'Remember what?' My ears prick up.

Gigi shakes her head. 'She never explained. I didn't speak to her often, she was the owner of the estate and I was just one of the many workers there, but sometimes I would see her when she didn't think anyone was watching and she always seemed to have a sadness that she carried around with her, like an overcoat you know. She had everything, and yet—'

'She had nothing,' I say out loud before I can stop myself.

Gigi nods and for a moment we exchange a look of understanding. 'I do not think she loved her husband. From everything I hear Monsieur Dumont was not a man to be loved. And without love in your life, you have nothing. Nothing at all.'

But she did have love, I think with a beat of sadness. She had a great love.

'I have never married but I have my Jean-Paul and *Maman*, but who did she have?'

Henry, I reply silently. She had Henry. And once upon a time, for the brief time they were together, she had everything.

'So what did you say you were doing at the estate?'

I snap back to see Gigi surveying me, her head cocked sideways.

'Oh, I was delivering a catalogue for the auction. It's come to light that Madame Dumont rented an apartment in Paris for many years.'

'In Paris?' Gigi looks surprised. 'But I never saw her leave the village, not in all the years I have worked at the estate.'

'I don't think she'd visited in a long time,' I explain, 'but it held several antiques—'

'*Antiques?*' The old lady's head flicks away from the TV and she looks at me with interest. Gigi is not wrong, there's nothing the matter with her mother's hearing.

'Yes,' I nod, and watch as she says something to her daughter, her expression animated, as she pulls out a necklace from underneath her dress. Meanwhile Gigi is frowning and shaking her head. There seems to be quite a heated argument going on between them.

'*Non, Maman!*' she cries.

Oh dear. I feel a beat of alarm. What have I said now? I look at Gigi quizzically and she looks back at me as if not wanting to explain, but her mother is insistent. I watch as she tries to take off her necklace, her fingers struggling with the clasp, until finally her daughter gives in and goes over to help her.

'*Maman* wants to know if this is worth anything,' says Gigi, releasing the piece of jewellery and holding it out for me to see. 'As you are an expert in antiques.'

'Oh – I don't know . . .' I fluster, suddenly feeling like a fraud, 'My friend in Paris is the actual expert, I was just helping her . . .'

This is translated back, but her mother is still resolute.

'Would you take it with you and ask her?' says Gigi, with obvious reluctance.

Her mother looks at me pleadingly.

'Of course I will,' I say, then hesitate, saying to Gigi, 'only, you don't want me to, right?'

Gigi sighs. 'It is the only thing she was given by her real mother. My *maman* was left at the convent when she was born. She never knew her real parents. There is not even a birth certificate, but unfortunately this was very common. It was during the war and everything was chaos.'

'What is she hoping to find out?' I ask, looking at the necklace. It's just a plain gold chain with a loveheart-shaped pendant. Nothing remarkable.

For a moment Gigi looks almost too pained to answer. '*Maman* wants to know if it is of any value because if so, she wants to sell it to pay to send her grandson to college . . . my son,' she adds, looking ashamed. 'I failed as a mother to be able to afford these things, my mother should not be selling her most prized possession.'

Gigi's jaw clenches and I can see her fighting back tears. I've only known her a short while but I have to resist the urge to give her a hug.

'Your mother's most prized possession is her grandson, not her necklace,' I say kindly.

Gigi's eyes meet mine and a look flashes between us.

'Thank you,' she says softly.

'No, thank you.' I smile. 'It's the least I can do after everything you have done for me.' I gesture to my patched-up shin and temple. 'I will give it to my friend in Paris. If you give me your details I will call you afterwards.'

Gigi smiles gratefully and gives me her number, which I'm just punching into my phone when suddenly it starts ringing.

'Hello?' I answer it.

It's Xavier, wondering where I am. I quickly explain what's happened and after a flurry of concerned questions he informs me that he's finished at the house and is coming to pick me up. I pass him to Gigi for directions.

After she's hung up, she passes my phone back to me along with the necklace. 'Don't worry, I'll keep it safe,' I reassure her mother, aware that she's entrusted me with the only thing she has from her real mother.

She smiles and, reaching out her hands, clasps them tightly round mine. And for a moment, I don't know what I want the outcome to be. That her necklace is an antique and worth a lot of money so she can sell it and help her grandson? The family is obviously poor and the money could be life-changing. Or for its value to be only sentimental, and for her to keep it?

Then I say goodbye to Gigi, who gives me a warm embrace and instructs me on when to remove my dressings in the strictest fashion, and in such detail that it's only the sight of Xavier in the Mercedes pulling up outside the window that stops her.

As I go to make my exit, she says, 'Oh, before you leave—'

I turn.

'Do you want something to read for the train?' She gestures to her bookcase and as I look at Emmanuelle's books, I can't help but feel a spark of excitement.

'Do you mind?'

'Not at all,' she says with a smile, 'books are not for keeping, they are meant for reading. Stories are not possessions, they are to be passed from one person to the next.'

She plucks out a book and gives it to me, then as Xavier toots his horn, I say my goodbyes to Gigi and her mother and leave.

26

'You know, you could have been killed.'

An hour later we're on the train speeding back to Paris and Xavier still hasn't dropped the subject of my accident.

'I should sue her sorry ass,' he says, spitting out the American words in his strong French accent. It would be quite comical, if it wasn't quite so alarming.

'What? No!' I protest, 'it wasn't Gigi's fault.'

I'm fast regretting telling Xavier about what happened. After his initial relief that I was OK, he'd proceeded to fire questions at me for the entire journey back to the station. I wasn't on trial exactly, but I'd certainly felt like it and so it had been a relief when we'd finally boarded the train and he'd announced he had to do some work on his laptop.

He hasn't done much work yet, though.

'She was driving dangerously. Did you see her car? It has no mirrors. It shouldn't be on the road, it is illegal.'

He's looking up at me from his screen, his face a mixture of anger and concern. And a protectiveness that makes my stomach flutter.

'I wasn't looking where I was going,' I protest, taking the blame, 'I was in the middle of the road, I was riding with no hands.'

Xavier looks at me like I'm crazy. 'But why would you do such a thing?'

'I don't know.' I shake my head, then smile sheepishly. 'I guess it made me feel like a kid again.'

He stares at me for a few moments, as if not knowing what on earth to make of me, then unexpectedly throws back his head and roars with laughter. 'You are very different from any woman I have ever met, Ruby Miller,' he says, shaking his head.

I smile, not sure whether that's a bad thing or a good thing, but then his face turns more serious.

'Sometimes we all do things that are reckless, we must all take risks,' he says, fixing me with his slate grey eyes, 'because it's that which makes us feel truly alive.'

His gaze is unwavering and the air feels suddenly charged. I know he's not talking about the bike ride any more.

'But what if you risk losing everything?' I challenge.

'What is everything?' He throws it back. 'A life without adventure and thrill is not a life.'

My pulse quickens. 'Do you really think that?'

'But of course.' He nods. 'You don't achieve your dreams by playing safe.'

I hold his gaze, but don't reply.

'What are your dreams, Ruby?'

I feel like we're doing some kind of dance. Just the two of us, here in this train carriage, surrounded by all these people.

'I . . .' I stammer, then stall.

His gaze urges me to go on, but I can't.

'I'm not sure,' I finish. I know it's a cop-out, but I'm not ready to confide in Xavier. It feels too intimate. Like I'm opening a door to something I might not be able to close. Or, more dangerously, want to.

'I don't believe that for a moment,' he says, his face relaxing and a smile playing on his lips. 'But it's a been a long day, you're tired—'

'Exhausted,' I confess, relieved the conversation has taken a turn.

'Me too. Demanding clients.' He raises his eyebrows. He doesn't need to say any more. He glances at his wristwatch.

'It's still a couple of hours to Paris, we should both get some rest.' Closing the screen of his laptop, he takes off his glasses, undoes his collar and loosens his tie.

'Yes,' I agree. I feel the release of pressure that's been building up, escaping like steam from a window.

'About your accident—' he begins again.

But immediately I shut him down. 'Seriously, it was all my fault, I don't want to sue anyone—'

'I wasn't going to say anything more about that.'

'You weren't?'

'No.' He shakes his head. 'I should. But I won't.'

His earlier anger has dissipated and been replaced by his usual composure. I study his face but he's giving nothing away. Sometimes it's so difficult to read him. To know what's going on behind that unwavering lawyer's gaze of his.

'So, what were you going to say?'

'That I'm just happy you're OK,' he says quietly.

A look passes between us, then, closing his eyes, he rests his head against the window. I watch him for a moment, taking in his handsome profile, the darkening of stubble in the cleft of his chin, the small triangle of exposed skin at his throat, then glance away.

Perhaps it's better if some things are left unsaid.

After half an hour I give up. I can't sleep. Sometimes I think you get too tired for your brain to even have enough energy to switch itself off. Sitting up, I unroll the makeshift pillow that I've fashioned out of my cardigan and slip it back over my shoulders. I glance across at Xavier. He's fast asleep.

Turning my attentions back to my bag, I pull out the book that Gigi gave me. It's a paperback copy of Ernest Hemingway's *A Farewell to Arms*. I open it, hoping for an inscription from Madame Dumont or even Henry that would shed more light on things, but the title page is blank. I smile to myself. That would have been too easy.

I turn the book over and read the blurb on the back, but it's more to jog my memory as I've already read it. I didn't want to tell Gigi – it was such a thoughtful gesture, and anyway it was a long time ago that I did my A levels, so I'd actually like to read it again. Yet, there's something else I need to read. Something a lot more pressing. Something I've been putting off since yesterday, for fear of what it might say.

Slipping the book back into my bag, I pull out the bundle of letters.

Henry was such a prolific letter writer. Since their chance encounter outside the café he had kept up his promise to Emmanuelle to write regularly, but not all of his letters are as impassioned and heartfelt as the last one I read. Many are just about normal, everyday things. Random thoughts and observations that he wished to share with her. Often they are just a few lines, a simple protestation of his love and his usual sign off, *J'attendrai, Henry*, but there are others, longer and more detailed, where he pours out his heart and hopes of their future.

Like the one I read yesterday, when he asked her to say yes.

I find the next dated one only to discover I've come to the end of the envelopes. This is Henry's last letter. My chest tightens with trepidation. What is it going to say? I slip out the notepaper inside and unfold it.

It's just one sheet.

Darling Manu,

It's 3am and I can't sleep for thinking about the last time we met. Regret keeps me awake. I regret more than anything that we argued, especially when our time together is so precious. You were angry with me for not understanding. You said I refused to listen and was being selfish. You were right, all your accusations were true and I'm sorry I lost my temper. I couldn't help it. I'm hot-headed like that sometimes, especially when that sometimes involves the woman I'm in love with talking about marrying another man.

For you see even now, despite this regret, I still find it difficult to understand how you can even say those words. How you can even give them your breath and voice. For to do so is to give them life.

I know your fears and concerns for the future, and I know your love for your family. I love them too, despite what you think. It doesn't matter that I have never met them, nor am I likely to, and it matters not that they would disapprove of me. I love them because they created you, and for that I will be forever grateful.

You are right, I don't care about what your father says, and I care even less about tradition. But I do care about you my darling, I care about you more than anything in the world, and I don't ever want you to suffer because of me.

So you see, I am filled with regret, but I am also filled with resolve. I am going to leave Paris for I need to stop being selfish and let you go. I should never have asked you to run away with me, it was wrong to put you in such an impossible situation. I will never believe that the best man won, but neither will I ever want you to suffer any shame, embarrassment or hardship. So go if you must, marry him, bear his children, and live a life of riches that you could never have with me.

I ask only one thing. Just never forget me, Manu.

Please, never forget me.

H

My eyes well up as I read those last lines. It's as I feared. She didn't say yes, despite how much she loved him. But oh, how I had wanted her to! Instead she wrote him a note that he never received. He never knew how she truly felt. *Just never forget me, Manu. Please, never forget me.* As I sit in the darkened carriage, tears silently leak over my cheeks and I brush them away before they fall upon his letter. His last letter. It's over seventy years ago but the emotion is just as raw as if he had written this only yesterday.

With a sense of finality clinging to me, I fold the sheet of notepaper in half. It's over, yet despite seeing the pictures of Emmanuelle's wedding, I didn't want it to end like this. I was hoping for – what? I don't know. Some kind of miracle. Something else. A happy ending somehow.

I slip his letter back in the envelope, but it catches on something. Wait, there's something else inside. I pull it out with my index finger and thumb. It's a photograph; a black and white headshot of a man. I turn it over. On the back in the same familiar handwriting is the simple inscription: *Your beloved H*.

So this must be Henry.

I look at his face. At the dark wavy hair swept off his forehead, almond-shaped eyes, a strong, determined jaw and the kind of wide, American smile that lights up a room. Dressed smartly in a suit and tie, he's gazing into the camera. Finally, after all this time, I see the handsome young African-American who was to fall in love with a beautiful Parisian heiress and write these letters.

And all at once I can see clearly the odds that were stacked against them. Now, more than ever. No wonder they couldn't marry – not only was he a poor writer from America, he was also of a different race. Paris might have offered artistic, racial and emotional freedom to many musicians, artists and writers during the twenties and thirties, but Emmanuelle's family wouldn't have shared the same liberal attitude when it came to a suitor for their daughter.

I peer at him intently. There's something familiar about him. I look straight into his eyes. They stare back at me, unblinking. He reminds me of someone, but I can't think who, and my mind slips back to his last letter. As we hurtle across France, I sit in my darkened carriage gazing at the photograph, and ask myself silently: Oh Manu, did you ever forget him? Did you ever forget your beloved H?

27

'You're a complete star, I don't know what I would have done without you, Ruby.'

The next morning I'm sitting at the café on the corner with Harriet. Thankfully her ankle isn't broken, it's just badly sprained and she's been instructed to wear flat shoes and use crutches. Which she's completely mortified about.

'What if someone sees me?' she'd wailed earlier, as she'd hobbled down the street.

'Don't be silly. There's nothing embarrassing about having to use crutches,' I'd reprimanded her sensibly.

'I'm not talking about the crutches. I'm talking about the flat shoes!' She'd motioned in horror to her feet, which were encased in a pair of huge white men's trainers. They were the only things that would fit. 'They make my feet look even bigger!'

Reaching the entrance of the café, we'd stood aside to let a chic Parisian couple leave. As they passed they'd both glanced down, then cast horrified looks at each other, much to Harriet's mortification.

'Mummy was right, no man is ever going to walk me down the aisle with feet this size.'

Thankfully, a large chocolate croissant and two cups of creamy hot chocolate later – 'Just this once, I need the energy, I've got to go into the office' – she'd perked up and, having dropped the subject of her feet, was now busy thanking me for yesterday's trip to Provence.

'You did me a huge favour, I'm forever indebted,' she gushes, between mouthfuls of pastry.

'Oh, it was nothing.' I feel a bit embarrassed. I didn't actually do anything, apart from snoop around a bit and nearly get myself killed.

'No sweetie, you did, so I want to say thank you by taking you out for dinner—'

'Please, you don't have to do that,' I protest.

'Yes, I do,' she cuts me off, 'plus it's your birthday,' she reminds me, even though I wish she hadn't. I'd been trying to push it to the back of my mind and forget about it. 'And if I need another reason, which I don't, I want to celebrate being asked to fill the role of auctioneer tomorrow . . .'

She trails off and looks at me across the table, trying to keep a solemn face.

'You're not!' I gasp, suddenly registering. 'You're going to be the auctioneer!'

Her face splits into a delighted grin and all she can do for a moment is nod. 'Well, it's not an official promotion or anything,' she says, quickly playing it down. 'Franck, one of our senior auctioneers, is off sick, and seeing as I've done most of the valuing it was probably easier to give me my first opportunity than ask someone else—'

'Stop being so modest!' I cry, and she blushes. 'This is amazing, Harriet.'

'Well, it's a step,' she says, trying to hide her excitement. 'I mean, if I'm terrible at it this will be my first and last auction.'

'You'll be wonderful, I know it.'

Harriet can never accept a compliment, but for once at least she doesn't argue with me. Though, keen to downplay her achievement, she moves swiftly on. 'And on top of all that I'm rather ashamed that we're in Paris, home to some of the finest restaurants in the world,' she continues, 'and yet all I've offered you so far is takeaway pizza . . .'

As she says 'takeaway pizza' she lowers her voice and hisses it across the table as if she's talking about something illegal. Though maybe in Paris it is.

'So I'm taking you out for dinner tonight and that's final,' she announces loudly.

I know when not to argue with Harriet. 'Thanks,' I say with a smile, 'that's really sweet of you.'

'Fabulous!' Her face brightens. 'So where do you fancy going?' She begins to reel off a list of very glamorous-sounding restaurants.

'Um, I don't know, they all sound amazing.'

'Oooh! I know, what about La Djionnaise, that fancy new bistro?' she says excitedly, 'I've always wanted to go there! The food's supposed to be incredible.'

'Great,' I nod, even though I've never heard of it.

'Two ticks, I'll make a reservation.' Grabbing her phone, she quickly dials and gabbles down the phone. There's a pause, and I watch her smile turn to a frown.

'Bugger, all booked,' she says, hanging up and looking disappointed. 'Oh well, never mind, it's probably all hype anyway. I'll try somewhere else.' She makes another phone call. It's the same reaction. 'Buggery bollocks.' She tries again. 'Blasted buggery bollocks!' And again. 'Bloody blasted—'

'Why don't we stay in?' I quickly interrupt, before Harriet runs out of expletives beginning with B. 'Honestly, I really don't mind.' I feel a sense of relief. Thank god for Parisians and their love of gastronomy.

But Harriet is not giving up that easily.

'Nonsense!' she retaliates. 'We're not staying in, not on your birthday! There must be a restaurant in Paris that has a table tonight, there just must—'

'May I make a suggestion?'

We both turn to see Luc, who's appeared beside us. He clears his throat nervously.

'My friend has a restaurant, it's only small, but the food is incredible.' At the mere mention of food his shy demeanour disappears and he begins gesturing passionately with his hands, the tattooed daggers on his forearm waving wildly. 'You will love it, it is truly superb, and I am sure I can get you a table . . .'

I'm expecting Harriet to completely pooh-pooh the idea – she and Luc haven't exactly been on the best terms the last couple of days – but instead she smiles brightly. 'Really? That would be fabulous.'

'But of course.' He nods, beaming with pleasure. 'I shall call him immediately.' He starts to turn away, then pauses. 'How was the soup?'

'Delicious,' she enthuses, 'what was the spice I could taste?'

'Ah, that would be the saffron,' he says knowledgably, 'it brings out the delicate flavour of the chanterelle *champignons*—'

'Mushrooms,' she corrects, and he laughs throatily.

'Ah yes, mush-*roooms*,' he repeats, 'such a peculiar word.'

I look back and forth between them in confusion. 'What soup?' Maybe it's the knock on the head, but I don't remember any soup, with mushrooms or saffron or anything. It's been just coffee and croissants.

'Luc brought me soup yesterday,' explains Harriet, smiling. 'It was really kind of him.'

'I saw her in the taxi when she came back from the hospital,' he jumps in to assist in the explanation, 'and I helped her up to her apartment, all those stairs!' He shakes his head, tutting. 'And I knew she must be very hungry, so I brought her some of my home-made soup, and also some little pastries for dessert.'

Harriet blushes. 'I still have your Thermos, I forgot to bring it back.'

'Ah, no problem, I will collect it later . . . one evening, perhaps – when it is convenient, of course,' he adds, blushing.

'Of course,' she says with a smile, and then there's a pause as they just look at each other, without saying anything.

Er, hang on, what on earth is happening here? If I didn't know better I'd think there was something going on. Harriet has gone soft on Luc.

'So, about the restaurant?' I remind them, for something to say. Well it's either that, or sit here feeling like a big green hairy gooseberry and feeding Heathcliff, who's snuffling under the table for croissant crumbs.

'Ah yes, of course, the restaurant,' says Luc, seeming to snap to. 'I will call now, no problem.' And, shooting Harriet one last smile, he darts off into the back of the café to make a phone call.

Harriet's gaze follows him until he disappears, then she turns back to me.

I raise my eyebrows.

'What?' she demands.

'Don't give me "what",' I retort.

'I don't know what you're talking about.' She makes her eyes innocently wide.

'You and Luc!' I gasp, not buying it at all.

'There is no me and Luc. I was just being friendly. He's been very sweet, bringing me soup, an angel actually. If it wasn't for him, I would have starved yesterday.'

Highly unlikely, Harriet is rather prone to exaggeration, but still.

'You like him,' I tease, smiling.

'I do not!' she snaps. 'I mean, of course I like him, he's a love, who couldn't like him? But not in that way, obviously,' she adds.

'Obviously.' I nod.

She narrows her eyes and glares at me across the table. 'I'm dating Rupes, remember?'

He's 'Rupes' now?

'Did he bring you soup?' I say pointedly.

She glares at me across the table.

'Or perfume?' I prompt, suddenly remembering. I'd meant to ask her the night of her date, but had completely forgotten. She must have forgotten to mention it too, because of everything going on with her ankle. I smile expectantly.

'Perfume?' she repeats, her brow furrowing.

Or she didn't get any, I suddenly realise, because in that instant I know she has no clue what I'm talking about.

'Why perfume?' She looks at me quizzically.

'Um, no reason,' I say, my mind scrambling, 'I was just thinking, with you hurting your ankle, he might have paid a visit to see if you're OK, brought a gift perhaps . . .'

Shit. If the perfume wasn't for Harriet, then who was it for?

'Rupes is away,' she says defensively, 'which he's actually very upset about.' She picks up her phone and to prove it, shows me a message:

SS bout yr ankle. Wish I cud b there bt awy til nxt wk. Let's h%k up thn & I'll mke u feel btr 😉

'Sorry, I don't speak text,' I say, staring at it blankly. It's like some modern form of hieroglyphics.

Harriet translates impatiently, even the smiley face at the end, which is actually animated and keeps winking at me. As she does, I try not to compare it to the letter Henry sent Emmanuelle after their first date – after all times have changed – but it's impossible not to. If the text is anything to go by, it's certainly not changed for the better when it comes to romance, I reflect, looking again at the smiley face and wondering how we went from courtship to an emoticon.

'Anyway, enough about Rupes.' Seeing I'm obviously unimpressed, Harriet changes the subject sniffily. 'Tell me more about yesterday.'

My mind flicks back to Provence. 'Beautiful,' I smile, thinking of the landscape, 'though not without its surprises.'

'Surprises?'

'You didn't mention Xavier was going.'

'Didn't I?' she says, trying to look all wide-eyed and innocent and completely failing. 'Well anyway, it's a very good thing he was there, to come to your rescue after you fell off that bicycle.'

She motions towards my bruised shins. I'd taken the bandages off this morning and the grazes were almost healed already, thanks to Gigi's first aid skills, but the bruising was now coming out in all the colours of the rainbow.

'Tell me what happened? You never said what you were doing exactly.'

'Oh, it was nothing,' I say, not wanting to go into details, 'I decided to get some fresh air and cycled into the village—' I suddenly remember my conversation with the woman in the cemetery. 'Harriet, did you find anything priceless in the apartment?'

'Priceless?' She looks at me, surprised. 'Why do you ask that? I didn't think you were interested in antiques.'

'I'm not,' I protest with a little laugh, before remembering that's probably not the most tactful thing to say to someone for whom they're a lifelong passion. 'I mean, I don't *hate* them, I just don't know enough about them. I'm not an expert like you.'

'Well, I wouldn't say I'm an *expert*.' Harriet blushes at the compliment. 'I've still a lot to learn.'

'Yes, but you'd be able to spot something like a Picasso, wouldn't you?'

Now she's the one to laugh. 'A Picasso? Golly yes, I would hope so!' she snorts, looking completely amused.

'Right yes, I thought so . . .'

Her smile turns to a frown. 'Ruby, what's all this about? Why are we talking about priceless antiques and Picassos all of a sudden?'

I hesitate, then come straight to the point. 'Well, the thing is yesterday, Trixie, Felix's wife, mentioned something about a Picasso. Apparently she'd heard a rumour there was one in Madame Dumont's apartment and it's worth a fortune.'

'I see.' Harriet's expression turns grave. 'That would explain why she's been calling constantly about the cataloguing—' She breaks off, then heaves a sigh. 'Believe me, I would have loved to have been the one to discover a forgotten masterpiece, but I'm afraid in this instance it was indeed just a rumour.'

I smile ruefully. 'Oh well, never mind,' I say, but inside I feel a sense of vindication. I knew Emmanuelle hadn't paid rent on that apartment for all those years just because of some painting. I knew it had to be much more than that.

'But that still doesn't explain how you hurt your leg.'

I snap back to see Harriet still staring at me.

'Oh, it was just a silly accident.' I quickly bat her concerns away. 'Luckily I met a girl who works at the estate who knew first aid—'

Reminded of Gigi and her mother, I unfasten my pocket.

'I nearly forgot, she gave me this.' I pull out the necklace. 'She thought I worked in antiques and wanted to know if it was worth anything.' I hold it out in the palm of my hand. 'Of course I didn't have a clue, but I promised I'd bring it back to Paris and ask my friend, the antiques expert.'

Harriet smiles again at the compliment and takes it from me.

She turns it over carefully in her fingers, her professional eye flicking over it. Almost immediately, she shakes her head. 'It's just a trinket. It's not even real gold; most of it is brass. These lovehearts were very common between sweethearts during the First and Second World Wars. I'd say this was more around the time of the Second.'

It hadn't looked valuable, even to my amateur eyes, but even so I feel a crushing sense of disappointment. So

Jean-Paul won't be going to college after all. And just like that his dreams and those of Gigi and her mother disappear. Their family could really have done with a windfall, and not just for college fees but because it was pretty obvious Gigi was struggling financially to support everyone.

'I'm afraid it doesn't have any value.'

'Perhaps not in monetary terms,' I say. But as the only possession left with a baby from its mother, it's invaluable, I think sadly.

'It's not something we'd ever sell at auction, though I have seen them at flea markets.'

Still, at least this means the grandmother gets to keep it now, I console myself, and yet somehow, it doesn't make me feel much better. I'm going to have to call Gigi and let her know. She'll be pleased that her mother won't have to sell it, though I know despite all her protestations, deep down there was a part of her as a mother that was hoping it might be worth something so she could afford to send her beloved son to college. What a shame. There are people like Felix and Trixie with all this money and then there are people like Gigi and her mum. It just doesn't seem fair.

'Thanks anyway,' I say, holding my hand to take it back from Harriet. 'I'll let her know.'

'Sorry,' she says apologetically, 'but it is very pretty regardless. I mean, look at how fine this chain is, and there's a concealed catch.' Running her thumb along the edge of the loveheart, she carefully presses it . . .

'I didn't realise it opened,' I say, as it releases into two halves.

'Yes, the heart is actually a sort of secret locket.' She eases it slowly open, then frowns. 'That's strange, there are no pictures. It's empty.'

'It is?' I say, but I'm not surprised. After all, Gigi's mum never knew her mother, so it's unlikely there would be any photographs inside. As Harriet peers closely at the inside of the locket, I take a sip of coffee and mull over what I'm going to say to Gigi. I wish I could give her some different news.

'Though there is an inscription.'

'Oh, really,' I say absently.

'Gosh, it's so tiny it's hard to read, and it's in cursive . . .' She frowns, angling it to the light.

'Do you want me to try?' I offer. 'My eyesight's probably better.'

'I'll have you know these are very good contacts,' she replies sharply. 'My eyesight is perfect.'

'OK,' I smile, turning back to my coffee.

'Wait a minute – I've got part of it . . .' she murmurs, squinting hard.

I watch, amused. Harriet will never accept defeat.

'*J'attendrai.*'

I suddenly get goose bumps.

'It means "I will always wait" in French,' she translates helpfully.

'Yes, I know,' I manage, trying to keep my voice casual. 'What does the rest say?'

'Hmm – hang on . . . it's to someone, but I can't quite make out the name.'

My heartbeat quickens.

'Ah yes, got it,' she says triumphantly.

It can't be. It's impossible.

'*Darling Manu,* J'attendrai, *your beloved H*'.

And it's like someone just dropped a tonne weight on my chest.

28

It's a coincidence. It has to be.

Having said goodbye to Harriet, I'm walking down the street in no particular direction, my thoughts whirring. Why would Gigi's mother have Emmanuelle's necklace? It's impossible.

Unless—

The answer thrusts itself at me. Unless of course, Gigi's mother is Emmanuelle's daughter.

It's like flinging open a door. No sooner is the thought out there than a rush of others follow.

Did she have a baby and give her up? Henry wrote about them spending the night together. Did Emmanuelle find herself pregnant afterwards? My mind flicks back to the very first letter I found in her apartment, the only one I've ever found written by Emmanuelle to Henry. Was this her big secret? The one she needed to share with him?

It would make sense, and yet, she never finished the letter, she never got to send it. What happened? Did she get to see Henry again? And if so, why did she give their child away? Did he reject her? Or did she flee Paris without telling him? And if that's what happened, why didn't she look for Henry after the war? Why did she still go on to marry Monsieur Dumont after saying she wouldn't?

There are so many unanswered questions, but there are no answers. The clues are in the letters, but there's more to discover. There has to be. Because one thing is for certain – their story didn't end with Henry's last letter.

Far from it. It only really began.

I think about Gigi and her mother, I need to call them about the locket, I could ask them—

Ask them what, Ruby?

A voice of reason stops me in my tracks.

I have no proof. No hard facts. It's all surmise and conjecture. I can't start throwing around wild stories about Madame Dumont. Revealing her love affair with Henry would be one thing, but telling Gigi's mother, Grace, that she's their child would be quite another. I can't just drop a bombshell like that and play havoc with an entire family's emotions. On the basis of what? A trinket and some old love letters?

After all, who's to say the old lady's story is true? I've read that children who grow up without ever knowing their birth parents often invent stories about them, and over the years they come to believe them to be true. What if, in fact, the locket came into her possession some other way? It could have got lost during the war and turned up at some flea market, for example.

And even if it *is* true, even if Grace *is* Emmanuelle's daughter, it wouldn't change the family's finances. The fact that she was adopted would prevent her from being Emmanuelle's heir. She would still inherit nothing.

I pause by a small park on the corner, set back from the street. I say a park, but it's more a small square of grass, a few shady trees and a wooden bench tucked away behind some iron railings. I step inside and sit down on the bench, relishing the coolness of the shadows and the quietness. Taking a few deep breaths, I try to collect my thoughts. I have to call Gigi, but first I need to be able to think straight.

Or at least, not sound like a totally mad, crazy woman.

Pulling out my phone, I dial her number and after a few seconds she answers.

''*Allo?*''

'Hi, Gigi, it's Ruby – the girl on the bike,' I add for clarification, just in case.

'Ah, Ruby, how are you?' she says warmly.

'Much better, thanks.'

'How are the bruises?'

'Big and purple.'

She laughs. 'I'm glad to hear it, it means you're healing.'

I smile, her relaxed manner instantly putting me at ease, then pause. I'm not sure how to break it to her about the necklace, so I dive straight in. 'I asked my friend about your mother's locket . . .'

'Yes?'

'I'm afraid it's not an antique,' I say simply.

There's a moment's pause, then, '*Bien*,' she says firmly. 'I didn't want *Maman* to sell it.'

'Yes, I know,' I reply, softly.

'It is the only thing her mother gave her when she was born. How can you put a price on this?'

I pause, my mind doing calculations, but they have nothing to do with money. 'When was your mother born, Gigi?' I blurt, finally. Because I have to ask. *I have to be sure.* If Emmanuelle did fall pregnant in that spring of 1940, then the baby would have been born—

'The nuns said it was Christmas time, 1940.'

I feel a shiver of excitement. The timing couldn't be more perfect. I think about Grace's face, those dark eyes, the cheekbones, the regality. She's Emmanuelle and Henry's daughter, she has to be!

'But it's so long ago now, most of the nuns have since died and there is no birth certificate, or record of adoption—'

Wait a minute. 'She was never adopted?' I say in surprise.

'One of the nuns, Sister Edith, had a cousin who was married to the local doctor in Fayence, a small village a couple of hundred kilometres from here, and she was taken in by them, but no, it was never a legal adoption. *Maman* says when she was a child she overheard a nun say her real mother had refused to give her permission.'

'Refused? But why, if she had given her daughter away?'

'I don't know how much of that is true or just hearsay. It is many years ago now and time has a habit of changing the past,' she says, and I can imagine her shrugging her tanned shoulders.

'So your mother was never able to find out anything about her real parents?' My mind has started to race. If Gigi's mother was never legally adopted, and it could be proven that she was Emmanuelle's daughter, she could inherit everything.

Everything.

'She never tried. She didn't want to hurt the feelings of the kind couple who looked after her . . .'

There's a pause.

'And you?' Something tells me Gigi didn't share the same sense of loyalty.

'Apparently the convent kept files of information on all the children they took in during that time. Sister Edith believed in meticulous record-keeping. However my enquiries were met with a wall of silence. It would seem Sister Edith also believed in absolute secrecy . . .' Gigi pauses. 'I did consider taking it further, asking a lawyer perhaps, but lawyers are expensive – and anyway, what does it matter? *Maman* had a happy childhood, that's all that is important.'

'Yes,' I murmur in agreement, but my mind is working overtime. Something tells me it's neither hearsay nor rumour that Gigi's mother wasn't officially adopted, but an important piece of this jigsaw.

'Are you still there?' Gigi's voice snaps me back.

'Yes, I'm here,' I say, flustered.

'My boss is calling me, I am afraid I have to go back to

work, but if I give you my son's telephone number, would you mind calling him?'

'No, of course not.'

'Jean-Paul is working in Paris now, so he can come and collect the necklace from you—'

'If you want, I can drop it off,' I offer, out of both kindness and curiosity. If I'm right about this, Jean-Paul is the great-grandson of Henry and Emmanuelle. My stomach flutters with excitement. I'm dying to meet him.

'Would you? That would be so kind. But can I ask you a favour? Could you say you just had it fixed for *Maman*, I don't want him to know—'

'I understand,' I reassure her quickly.

'Thank you.' There's a sound of relief at the other end of the line. 'He works in a bookshop, it's on the Left Bank, I can't quite remember the name, I think it's Shakespeare and—'

'Company,' I finish, my mind flashing back to the bookstore I visited, only a couple of days ago. What a coincidence.

'Yes that's it,' she says. 'Are you sure you don't mind?'

You can call it coincidence, but you can also call it destiny.

Without further ado, I stand up and, stuffing my phone back in my pocket, set off towards rue de la Bûcherie. My chance encounter with Gigi, finding the inscription in the locket, Jean-Paul working at the same bookshop where Henry lived and worked over seventy years ago – the sensible, rational, level-headed part of me tells me this is all just an incredible string of coincidences.

But the Ruby who sat in the desert in Rajasthan and gazed up at the stars, and who in that glittery darkness experienced something so much bigger than herself, can't help feeling there's some greater power at play. That all these seemingly random things are actually part of some grand design. And like the music she heard playing in Madame Dumont's apartment, this isn't just her imagination.

It sounds crazy and preposterous, the stuff of superstition and magic, but what if it's not? There's a school of thought that believes everything happens for a reason. In which case it wasn't merely chance that I walked into Madame Dumont's apartment that evening and discovered her letters. Or that Harriet twisted her ankle and I travelled to the south of France in her place, to pick up the rest of Emmanuelle's story.

Call it destiny, or Fate, or whatever the hell you want to call it, but it's like it was meant to happen. As if that apartment remained a secret until it could be found by someone like me. Someone who has spent their whole life being fascinated by the mysteries of love and romance and is forever looking for answers. Someone who, the moment they stepped into that apartment and back in time, knew that love was the answer to unravel this mystery.

Someone, I guess, who you'd call a bit of a love detective.

After ten minutes of walking I turn the corner and see the bookshop ahead of me. It's a hot sunny day but I'm shivery with anticipation. Now I'm here I feel slightly giddy, and a little bit nervous. I slow my pace. My mind is churning and I try to wade through my thoughts. I need to figure out what I'm going to say before I enter. I can't just charge inside declaring, 'Hey, guess what? You're the long-lost great-grandson of Madame Dumont!'

OK, on the plus side it's to the point, and cuts out all the waffle, but it's hardly tactful is it? When it comes to stuff like this, you can't just blurt it out, you need to be sensitive. In fact, now I'm actually thinking this through, something like this should probably involve professionals and counselling and people who actually know what they're doing.

Unlike me, who doesn't really have a clue what they're doing.

Shit.

I slow down until I come to a standstill.

Plus, on the very big downside, who's to say it's true? Maybe I've got a bit carried away. Maybe all the adrenalin and excitement has clouded my judgement. Standing outside the entrance, I feel my confidence take a huge wobble. Maybe I just wanted it to be true so much, I've almost convinced myself it is.

Standing at the doorway, I falter. Nevertheless, regardless of whether I'm right or wrong, I can't stand out here all day. I still have to return the locket. Feeling it in my pocket, I wrap my fingers round it tightly. At the very least I'll just give it back and be on my way.

With renewed confidence, I push open the door and walk inside.

Then freeze.

Because there, standing right in front of me, is Henry.

29

'*Ça ne va pas? T'as vu un fantôme?*'

'I'm sorry, I don't understand,' I stammer, taking a sip of water.

'Ah, of course.' He smiles apologetically. 'I asked if you are OK? You look like you've seen a ghost.'

I stare at him from above the rim of my glass.

'Yes, I'm fine – thanks . . .' I fib, 'I think maybe it was just the heat.'

I can't take my eyes off him. Ever since I walked in the shop and saw him standing behind the counter.

Only this isn't Henry. It's Jean-Paul.

We're sitting in a little cubbyhole at the back of the shop. I must have looked as white as a sheet when I walked in, because as soon as he saw me he ushered me into the back and immediately fetched me the water. The resemblance between him and Henry is uncanny.

But there's something else. Now I've been staring at him for the last few minutes it's dawned on me that this is the same assistant I met the last time I was here, only now he looks completely different. Gone is the beanie hat and the beard, and without either he looks so much younger. And so much more like his great-grandfather. They have the same curly dark hair, the same strong jawline, the same almond-shaped eyes.

Now I realise why the photo of Henry looked so familiar. It's because I'd already met his great-grandson. I just didn't know it.

'Your mother asked me to give you this,' I say, passing him the locket.

'You know Gigi?' he asks in surprise.

'We met, briefly, she asked me if I could fix this necklace for her, my friend repairs jewellery . . .'

'It is my grandmother's.' He nods, then frowns. 'I didn't know it was broken.'

'It was just the catch, nothing major,' I add, hoping I sound believable.

I must do, as Jean-Paul takes it from me without question and tucks it carefully in his pocket. 'I have never seen her take it off, she must have trusted you very much,' he says, smiling. 'Thank you.'

'Oh, it was nothing.' I feel a stab of guilt. I hate lying, but I can't tell him the truth.

'Well, if you are OK, I should return to work, the shop is very busy.' He gestures to all the customers waiting to pay.

Or can I?

'Jean-Paul . . .'

He turns back to look at me.

This is my last chance. There's so much I want to say, so much I *need* to say. I can't just say goodbye and get up and leave and say nothing. It's wrong. Jean-Paul and his family are the rightful heirs to Madame Dumont's estate, not Trixie and Felix. And yet even though I know this is true with every bone in my body, I also know there's no real evidence, no evidence that would stand up in court anyway. Without it I may just be raising the family's hopes for nothing, dropping a bombshell that could shatter their lives.

'Yes?' He waits expectantly.

I need more proof than just a locket and some love letters.

'I hear you want to be a journalist?'

I need a birth certificate.

'Yes, very much.' His voice swells with enthusiasm. 'I have

always loved the written word. One day I hope to go to college to study . . .' He suddenly trails off. 'Have we met before?' he asks, furrowing his brow as if trying to place me.

'Yes, a few days ago upstairs, I was looking around at all the old photographs.'

'Ah yes, I thought I recognised you,' he says, remembering, 'you were looking for someone.'

I nod, thinking about Henry.

'So, did you find him?'

He looks at me expectantly, his wide almond eyes gazing at me just as Henry's did from the photograph.

'Yes,' I say quietly. 'In a way I think I did.'

I think about Jean-Paul all the way home. About how much he looked like Henry his great-grandfather, because I have no doubt. Henry is his great-grandfather – I'm more sure of that than of anything. I think about how if it could be proved, the revelation would change everything. Jean-Paul's family would stand to inherit, if not all of Emmanuelle's estate, then a great deal, more than enough to enable him to go to college, and for Gigi not to have to worry or feel guilty any more.

And I think about Gigi's mother, Grace. Because it's not just about the money, that's only a small part of it. It's about a secret that's been kept hidden for over seventy years. It's about knowing who her parents were, about answering the questions she has no doubt asked herself her whole life, it's about bringing her closure.

But would it? I still don't know for certain why Emmanuelle gave up Henry's child. All I know is that in the chaos of the war the course of both their lives was changed for ever. Emmanuelle fled Paris for the south of France, where she married Monsieur Dumont and endured a loveless marriage to a man who, by the sounds of things, wasn't very nice at all.

But what happened to Henry? Where did he go? What became of him?

And most importantly of all, why did she keep the apartment locked up and a secret for all those years?

My mind is churning, the questions swirling round and round, so fast I almost feel dizzy. So many secrets were lost in the war, but so many more were made. And the more I find out, the more I discover is still hidden. Secrets concealed within secrets. It's like those Russian dolls that go down in size. You open one, only to find out that another needs opening, and so it continues . . .

Will I ever get to the whole truth and unravel this mystery? Will Jean-Paul and his family ever inherit what is rightly theirs? I feel a growing sense of anxiety as I climb the stairs to Harriet's apartment. I dearly hope so, but time is fast slipping away. The auction is tomorrow; soon everything Emmanuelle had will be sold to the highest bidder. Gone for ever.

Turning the key in the lock, I push open the door. Heathcliff greets me and I scoop him up, holding his warm body close against mine as I walk over to one of the small arched windows. I gaze out across the Paris skyline. It's out there, whatever the answer is. It's out there somewhere. The city stretches away from me in all its infinite possibilities and, faced with my overwhelming task, I stand there. I stand there for a very long time.

'Have you seen my lipstick?'

It's later that evening and Harriet and I are running around the apartment, getting ready to go out for dinner. Luc came through and we have reservations at his friend's restaurant for 8.30. Well, to be exact, it's me running around for Harriet as she's still on her crutches. Which I know must be really awful for her as she can't do anything for herself, but I have a sneaky feeling she's rather enjoying it. Well, as a Fortescue-Blake, it is in her genes.

'Which one?' Giving my lashes one last coat of mascara, I have to yell above Harriet's iPod that's blasting out a mix of Rihanna and Vivaldi. They seem, weirdly, to go together.

'The red one.'

Like that narrows it down. Harriet has about a dozen lipsticks, all of them red. Mascara wand in hand, I do a quick dash around the tiny apartment. There's only so many places it can be.

'No, I can't see it—' I turn down the volume on the iPod so I can stop yelling. 'Where did you last have it?'

Sitting on the sofa bed with a glass of wine, Harriet frowns as she tries to remember, then gasps triumphantly. 'Ah, I know! It's in the freezer!'

'The freezer? What's it doing in the freezer?' I ask in astonishment, though I should know better. This is Harriet after all, nothing she does should surprise me. Tugging open the fridge door, I look inside the tiny freezer compartment. Sure enough, there it is.

'Celeste told me to put them in there, it keeps them fresh,' she says matter-of-factly, taking the lipstick from me and slicking two bright scarlet streaks on her lips. 'Here, try some.'

She passes it to me and I dutifully put some on. I'm actually getting quite excited about tonight. I wasn't in the mood to go out earlier – celebrating my birthday without Jack was the last thing I wanted to do – but there's something so cathartic about getting ready to go out with a girlfriend. Whatever stresses or worries you have seem to take a back seat as you try on clothes and swap make-up. It's just so much fun.

Even if one of us is on crutches, and the other wearing the exact same outfit she wore for the party just the other night, I muse, checking out my reflection. Well, after witnessing Celeste's horror at my other clothes, I decided it was probably wise.

'So the cab should be here in a few minutes,' says Harriet, hoisting herself up from the sofa bed on her crutches and angling to see her reflection in the mirror.

'That was so kind of Luc to organise this for us,' I say pointedly, as she wobbles dangerously.

'Yes.' She nods, distractedly pulling down the hem of her dress. 'Though I suppose it was only a phone call.'

'It doesn't matter, it's the thought that counts.'

She fiddles with her hem a bit more. 'Yes, he is very sweet like that.'

'I'd say it was more thoughtful than sweet,' I say, reaching for my bag, 'being sweet is easy, but being thoughtful requires a bit more effort, it means you have to care about someone.'

She stops what she's doing and glances up from the mirror. 'Yes, I suppose so,' she says. 'I've never really thought about it like that before.' She pauses for a moment, her expression turning serious as if reflecting on something, and I wonder if she's going to say something about Luc. If she's going to finally see what's been right there in front of her all this time.

But then her phone beeps. 'The taxi's here,' she says, glancing at the screen. And just like that, the moment is gone.

Outside, dusk is falling over a June evening, casting purple streaks across a crimson sky and turning everything golden. It's what photographers call the magic hour, and the drive through the streets of Paris to the restaurant is nothing less than magical. Gazing out of the window of the cab I watch the scenery passing by and, as my eyes blur out the details, I'm transported momentarily back to India and my trip across Rajasthan.

My mind flicks back to Jack. I imagine him sitting next to me in the taxi, just across the armrest. Remembering how close we were, how small our world was, just me and him on the back seat, cocooned together in a small white car as we travelled dusty mile upon dusty mile across a faraway land. But now all that's changed. Both geographically and emotionally, the distance between us couldn't be any wider. He hasn't been in touch, but then neither have I. Things have just been left to drift.

But for how much longer? How much further can you drift apart before it's impossible to find your way back again?

After about twenty minutes we arrive at the restaurant. Tucked discreetly down a side street with a hard-to-find sign, it's one of those places you have to be in the know about. However, pushing open the door, it's immediately evident that there are plenty of people who *are* in the know about it. Stinking deliciously of garlic and red wine and buzzing with chatter and laughter, the place is crammed to the gills.

It's not very big. Two small rooms curl around either side of the bar, into each of which are shoehorned half a dozen or so tables and chairs. At first glance the place appears to be completely full, but after giving her name to a passing waiter, Harriet and I are shown to an empty table in the far corner. No sooner have we sat down than we're greeted by the owner himself, a rambunctious, bearded man with a hoop earring and unlaced Converse who swoops upon the table, flapping his arms around like a giant bird trying to take flight and exclaiming in torrents of French.

'This is the birthday girl,' says Harriet, gesturing towards me.

'*Bon anniversaire!*' he cries, a large welcoming grin splitting across his fleshy face. 'It is such a pleasure!'

'I'm sure it's all mine.' I redden, slightly embarrassed at finding myself the centre of attention. Several diners are looking over, trying to see what all the commotion is about. 'And it's not actually my birthday until tomorrow—' I begin trying to explain, but I have no chance against this tidal wave of energy.

'*Poof*, nonsense!' he says dismissively, waving his hands around as if swatting flies. 'Luc has told me so much about you!'

'He has?' I ask, surprised.

'Yes, you are 'Arriet, no?'

'No, that's me,' says Harriet, 'this is Ruby.'

'Ah, forgive me,' he gasps, clutching at his chest in his horror and shaking his head so his little silver hoop bobs back and forth maniacally. 'Two such beautiful ladies, my mind is confused! But I will make it up to you! Luc has given me strict instructions, I must cook special food tonight for special ladies!'

I can't help smiling. He really is entertaining. He seems to speak entirely in exclamation marks.

'But I say to him, how can I do this without you?'

'Are you the chef?' I look at him in surprise. He's nothing like I imagined a chef to look.

'Ah *non*! I have a chef, a very fine chef, but I want Luc to come and work with me, because he is the finest chef I know!' He kisses his fingers enthusiastically. 'But he will not leave the café,' he finishes, pulling a sad face.

'But why? He's far too talented to be working there,' I say.

'This I know!' The owner makes his eyes even bigger and throws his hands in the air. 'I tell him this every day, but no, he will not leave.'

'Maybe he likes being a waiter,' suggests Harriet, 'no responsibility, no pressure.'

'No! It is not this!' he protests, almost violently. 'It is because he is very loyal to his customers, he doesn't want to leave them, especially one customer *in par-ti-cu-lar*.' He articulates each syllable and makes a big show of staring goggly-eyed at Harriet. 'He says who else will serve them café crème and croissants?'

A blush rises up Harriet's cheeks and she obviously doesn't know where to look. So it's rather a relief when we're interrupted by a waiter bearing a tray with two small glasses filled with amber liquid.

'*Fantastique! Aperitifs!*' booms the owner, looking delighted as he passes one to each of us, before wishing us to 'Enjoy your meal,' and disappearing in the same bird-flapping manner as he appeared.

I glance across at Harriet. There's so much to say I don't know where to start. Only Harriet beats me to it.

'Well, this is simply lovely, isn't it?' she says with that great British reserve, and then before I can say anything about Luc, she chinks her glass against mine. 'Cheers!'

'Cheers,' I say, clinking my glass against hers.

Something tells me it's going to be an interesting evening.

30

Fast forward through several courses of the most delicious food I have ever eaten. Bowls of thick, hearty onion soup topped with a crusty chunk of bread, bubbling with melted cheese. Deep-fried Camembert, oozing with quince jam on a bed of rocket. Black squid-ink risotto, roasted sea bream, fragrant chicken breast. And all washed down with two bottles of red wine that flows as easily as the conversation.

'Seriously Rubes, I'm so pleased you came to Paris,' says Harriet, as we finish laughing about my recent shopping experience, which I've taken to calling 'Scarfgate', and taking another large gulp of wine she adds, 'it's just what I needed.'

'Me too,' I say, topping up our wine glasses. 'I wouldn't have missed it for the world.'

'Really?'

'Of course.' I nod, 'I can't remember the last time you and I had a night out together, just the two of us, oh actually, now I can—' I break off.

'What?' demands Harriet, before suddenly erupting with laughter. 'Oh god, it was that night I got stood up by that actor wasn't it?'

'He was a mime artist,' I correct her, trying not to giggle, 'and he didn't stand you up, his appendix burst.'

'Or so he said . . .'

'You mean texted.'

'Oh golly, yes.' She starts laughing. 'He said he was texting from the stretcher he was being wheeled on into the operating theatre.' She's trying to stifle her laughter.

'As if! He'd be writhing around in agony!'

'So you came to my rescue and took me out for dinner but on the way home we bumped into him in Covent Garden—'

'—and he said it turned out it had only been rumbling so they'd aborted surgery.'

'But he was painted all green and dressed up like the Statue of Liberty!'

We roll around at the table, collapsing into giggles.

Finally Harriet stops laughing and dries her eyes on her napkin. 'I'm going to take a picture,' she announces, reaching into her bag for her phone. As she does I realise this is the first time it hasn't been on the table. Usually she keeps it there so she doesn't miss any texts from Rupert. It briefly crosses my mind to wonder if anything is wrong, but before I can ask we're interrupted by a bottle of wine appearing at the table.

'From Monsieur,' says the waiter, showing us the label before swiftly opening it and topping up our glasses.

'*Monsieur*?' we both repeat, turning round, and we spot Luc leaning against the bar. He smiles, rather sheepishly, and I glance at Harriet. But if I was expecting her to be less than pleased by his appearance, I couldn't be more wrong. Her face visibly lights up and she waves him over to join us.

'I was just passing and I thought I would say 'allo,' he says, pulling up a chair.

It's so obviously a lie but somehow it doesn't matter. 'How is everything?'

'Wonderful,' gushes Harriet, more than a little tipsily.

'Amazing food,' I agree.

Luc looks pleased. 'Did you have the squid-ink risotto? That was my recipe.'

'It was?' Harriet couldn't look more thrilled. 'Wow, that

was delicious. The best food I've ever eaten. You're so talented.'

Luc beams. 'You really think so?'

'Absolutely,' she says, nodding, and for a moment they lock eyes across the table.

I glance back and forth between them. Something is definitely going on between these two. There's a definite shift. I can feel it. But then I have drunk the best part of two bottles of red wine, so maybe my sensory receptors are totally askew. Maybe I'm just wanting it so hard I'm imagining it.

'Will you take a photo of us?'

I snap back to see Harriet brandishing her smartphone at Luc.

'It's Ruby's birthday.'

'It's not my birthday until tomorrow,' I protest for the umpteenth time, but nobody is listening.

'Yes, of course!' Looking delighted to be asked, Luc jumps up from the table and starts angling the smartphone at us as if he's Mario Testino, issuing commands to '*ouistiti!*'

'No, it's "say cheese",' Harriet corrects him, still smiling broadly like a ventriloquist's dummy.

'Say cheese,' he repeats, proud of the new phrase, and we grin like maniacs. The smartphone flashes. And then we do what everyone does, which is immediately grab the phone and inspect ourselves in the photograph.

'Oh my god, I look drunk,' I gasp, looking at my flushed face. 'And I have a bit of risotto in my teeth.'

'Nonsense, you look fabulous,' cries Harriet, pinching the screen with her fingers and zooming in. She lets out a shriek. 'Golly, look at my hair! It was supposed to be a chignon but I look like I have a squirrel on my head.'

I burst into giggles. 'God you're right, it does look like a squirrel!' I guffaw, unable to stop myself. Well, that's what happens when you're on your third bottle of wine.

'Squirrel? What is this squirrel?' asks Luc, looking bewildered, but Harriet is too busy zooming further in on her hairstyle to give him another English vocabulary lesson.

'I mean, goodness, what on earth was I—' abruptly she breaks off and peers at the screen of her phone, her brow furrowed.

'It's not that bad,' I try to reassure her, looking over her shoulder, except she's not looking at a close-up of herself any more. Instead she's focused in on a table in the far corner of the room behind us, and a man sitting alone drinking wine, a man who looks to my slightly blurry self like—

'Rupes!' she cries, twisting round.

As his name rings out across the restaurant, his head pops up like a meerkat's. And as soon as he spots Harriet, he visibly freezes.

So do I. Otherwise I would have attempted to stop her before she grabbed her crutches and swung herself over to his table. It's incredible how agile she is on those things.

'What are you doing here? I thought you'd gone out of town on business,' she demands in a voice loud enough for the whole restaurant to hear. Harriet's never been a quiet speaker, she has a tendency to boom at the best of times, but when she's had a few drinks she's positively foghorn-like.

I look at Rupert. He's like a rabbit in the headlights. Frozen, he can't seem to move. Hand frozen on his wine glass, he just stares at Harriet. For a brief moment I actually feel quite sorry for him.

'Er – um – bit of a change of plan,' he manages to stammer. His eyes are going back and forth like in a haunted house painting. 'I was going to call you but you know what it's like . . .'

Oh god. I get up from my seat, ready to go Harriet's rescue, but she suddenly seems to notice something. A gift, lying unwrapped on the table, its tissue paper and ribbon discarded.

It's a bottle of perfume.

'No, why, what's it like?' she asks, an edge to her voice.

Uh-oh.

Quickly, I excuse my way through a few tables towards them. 'Maybe we should sit down—' I begin, but don't finish – I'm interrupted by the appearance of a thin blonde who emerges from the bathroom and sits down at the table.

I'm suddenly more sober than I've ever been.

The blonde looks quizzically at Harriet as if it to say who's this woman on crutches and what is she doing at our table?

'Aren't you going to introduce me?' asks Harriet, raising her eyebrows at Rupert.

His expression is the same one as he had on his skydiving photo. Absolute terror.

'This is my wife, Susan. Susan, this is Harriet.'

It's like waiting for a car crash to happen. I hold my breath. There's an infinitesimal pause. I can barely dare look at Harriet as I wait for the inevitable.

Only it never comes.

'Pleased to meet you,' she says, smiling politely.

Harriet behaves with perfect grace, nodding pleasantly at the blonde and Rupert as if she's greeting them at church. 'Well, I mustn't take up any more of your time. I'll leave you to enjoy the rest of your meal.' And without giving anything away, she turns and with as much dignity as she can muster, which on crutches is no mean feat, lurches back to our table.

'You tried to tell me, didn't you?' she says a few minutes later as we sit back down. Luc has gone to talk to the owner and is standing over by the bar, seemingly oblivious to what's just occurred.

'I'm sorry, I didn't want to be right,' I say, and I really mean it. For all my feelings about Rupert, I didn't want Harriet to get hurt.

'Don't be,' she says, topping up her glass. 'Eau de Cheating Husband isn't my scent anyway.'

I smile as she takes a large gulp of wine. 'He's lucky he met you, many women would have made a scene.'

'I just feel sorry for his poor wife.'

We both glance over to see Rupert looking ashen, knocking back a bottle of Shiraz while his wife chats animatedly, seemingly none the wiser.

'You were right, all that Internet dating and social media, it's just a facade to hide behind. None of it's real. We create these perfectly edited versions of how we'd like to be, but all that happens is we end up falling in love with people's profiles, not how they really are. Then when you meet them in real life . . .' She pulls a face.

'There's nothing wrong with you in real life,' I say hotly, 'you're gorgeous, and anyway, that's not the point, you're not the one that said you were single when in fact you were married.'

I'm actually feeling quite angry now. Rupert is very lucky he's in a crowded restaurant because I've had a lot of red wine and I'm wearing very sharp stiletto heels that are just aching to be dug into shins right now.

'True,' she says, 'but I wasn't completely honest either. I thought I had to be a certain way to find love, that there was this formula, if I was just thinner, or had smaller feet and didn't wear glasses, or if my hair wasn't frizzy – or my guilty pleasure wasn't Googling old episodes of *Antiques Roadshow* in bed at night—'

'There's nothing wrong with that,' I say loyally. 'I think that's perfectly normal.'

'And trying to beat the experts when they say how much it is, and keeping score in a little notebook on my bedside table.'

'Well OK, perhaps that's not normal,' I admit, 'but it's still not married.'

She smiles appreciatively and squeezes my arm.

'And so I did this whole makeover when I came to Paris,

and worked so hard trying to find love, that I didn't realise I'd already found it without even trying.'

Hang on. Is she saying what I think she's saying?

'I've been such an idiot,' she confesses with a sigh, 'You were right all along, Ruby, and if it wasn't for you I would never have seen it. I would never have opened my eyes, I would have remained closed to it, because it's just nothing like I expected it to be . . . I had this image in my head of what love would look like, what he would look like, but it didn't fit into the box I'd created for it.'

'And what does it look like?'

Harriet's face creases into a sheepish smile as she nurses her glass of red wine. 'It looks like foam hearts in cafés crèmes and a smile that brightens my every morning; like home-made soup being delivered up six flights of stairs without being asked; like someone who sees me for who I really am and still likes me enough to book me a restaurant when everywhere else in town was full—'

She breaks off as Luc reappears at the table. 'So, is this the date?' He gestures stiffly towards Rupert, his dark eyes flashing.

So he wasn't oblivious after all. Far from it.

'*Was*,' corrects Harriet. 'Past participle.'

For a moment there's a pause as it registers, then Luc's face relaxes.

'You know, we really need to work on your grammar,' she adds after a moment's pause.

'Is it really that terrible?'

'Appalling,' she says firmly, 'in fact, you're going to need lots of private lessons.' Her eyes meet his. 'Lots and lots and lots.'

A look passes between them and his mouth twists up into a smile.

'You think so?'

There's a pause, then Harriet's face breaks into a smile. 'Absolutely.'

31

Luc joins us for pudding and the rest of the meal passes in a warm and gooey blur of melted chocolate soufflés, sticky, chewy toffee-topped tarte tatin and Harriet and Luc staring doe-eyed at each other across the table. At one point I think I catch them holding hands underneath their napkins. It's so incredibly sweet and I don't think I've ever seen Harriet look happier, or more relaxed. But then that's what happens when by some miracle you finally find someone who just *gets* you.

It's as if all those years of not fitting in with her sisters, or being accepted by her mum, of fruitlessly searching for love and being constantly disappointed, of trying to be thinner or blonder or something she wasn't were all whipped up into a perfect storm in Paris. But now all of a sudden, it's over and there's this stillness about her.

Something tells me she won't be going to the summer ball alone this year. Or ever again.

And just for the record, Mrs Fortescue-Blake – Luc has enormous feet.

We leave the restaurant full of good food and spirits, and spill out on to the pavement, where we linger for a few moments, chatting and laughing under the streetlamps, until talk turns to heading home.

'I would give you both a ride but I have only a scooter,' says Luc, shrugging apologetically, 'so there is space for only one person.'

'One person and a pair of crutches?' I ask, grinning.

'But of course, I have a roof rack,' he nods, completely straight-faced.

'Seriously?'

'No, I am joking,' he says with a grin, before breaking into his deep baritone laugh.

'Wait a minute, I'm not leaving you, Ruby!' protests a rather drunken Harriet, suddenly twigging. It's as if she's out of sync with the conversation and is a couple of steps behind.

'Yes you are,' I say firmly. 'I can get a taxi.'

'You know this isn't London, you can't just hail one.'

'That's fine, I can walk to one of the taxi ranks. I feel like some fresh air anyway and it's a lovely night.'

'But it's nearly midnight.'

'Midnight in Paris,' I quip, and feel an unexpected thrill. What could be more magical? 'Who knows what might happen?'

'Exactly. Which is why I'm coming with you,' she says stubbornly.

Honestly, for someone who went to Cambridge and graduated with a First, Harriet can be completely thick. How much more obvious do I have to make it that I am giving her and Luc some time alone?

'On crutches?' I remind her and her face falls as she realises she's been foiled.

I can see her weaken. I know she really wants to go with Luc but is being the loyal girlfriend.

'Please, go,' I insist, 'you'll get to ride through the city at night on the back of a scooter. It will be like *Roman Holiday.*'

At the mention of one of her favourite films, Harriet's face lights up.

'If it's good enough for Audrey . . .' I smile, reminding her of her icon.

Harriet crumbles. Throwing her arms round me, she gives

me a hug. 'Sweetie, you're the best friend in the world,' she gushes into my neck, 'I love you so much, I really do . . .'

Oh god, and now she's getting all teary-eyed. Luc and I exchange looks and I make a motion with my eyes for him to peel Harriet from me. Which he does with an amused grin, lassoing her round the waist with one tattooed forearm while unlocking the top-box on his scooter with the other and pulling out his spare helmet.

'. . . I don't know what I'd do without you . . . I just think I'm so lucky to have such a wonderful—'

She's suddenly muffled as Luc slides the helmet over her head.

'And don't wait up for me,' I instruct, as she clambers on to the back of the scooter behind Luc and, with her arms wrapped firmly round his waist, zooms off into the night.

Turning away, I start walking. It's one of those perfect early-summer evenings. Despite being nearly midnight, the air is bathwater warm and there's not a breath of wind. With my silk scarf slung over my arm, I stroll bare-armed through the cobbled streets, past the pavement cafés and bars that are still busy with tourists and locals, drinking wine and smoking cigarettes.

Paris is so different at night. It's as if one part of the city falls asleep and another wakes, shimmering in the darkness. Now I know why it's called the City of Lights: everywhere I look seems to glitter and sparkle, making it seem magical.

I'm not sure of my way to a taxi rank, but I'm in no hurry to get back to the apartment, so I take my time, meandering through the side streets until, turning a corner, I realise I'm lost. Seriously, I don't have a clue where I am and I don't have my guidebook on me.

I look around to see who I can ask for directions. Only the streets are empty. There's no one here but me—

Except – what's that? Out of the corner of my eye I see a flash of colour and turn round to see a girl in a yellow dress disappearing into the shadows.

'Hey! *Excusez-moi*,' I call after her, but she's gone. I hesitate, unsure what to do, but there's no one else around and it's just turned midnight. In the distance I hear a clock striking twelve. She might be my only hope.

I quickly hurry after her and as I turn the corner I glimpse her again. She's just a little way ahead of me. She turns briefly, as if hearing my footsteps behind her, and I'm struck by her long red hair; it covers the side of her face and almost reaches her tiny waist.

'*Excusez-moi*—'

As she passes underneath a streetlamp I notice how the folds of silk swing round her legs, the dainty pattern of white polka dots against the yellow, the vintage silhouette. Quite unexpectedly it strikes a chord of recognition. Wait, I'm sure I've seen that dress before—

All at once my heart starts to race.

It's Emmanuelle's. It was hanging in her apartment. It was the one she was wearing when Henry first saw her at the café.

I can almost feel the hairs stand up on the back of my neck. But that's impossible – it can't be.

I'm suddenly reminded of the gramophone playing in her apartment, the sounds of Emmanuelle and Henry dancing. It was all just a dream, I was asleep, I was imagining things . . . and yet, I'm not asleep now. I'm wide awake. This is happening. This is real.

Is it her? *Can it really be her?*

I swallow hard, my heart thudding hard in my chest, then find my voice. '*Emmanuelle?*'

As I call out, the girl in the yellow dress pauses. For a split second I think she's going to turn to face me. And for that briefest of moments everything stands still in that silent little street, in the depths of Paris, at some magical moment past midnight. But then, blink, and she's gone again and all I'm aware of is the echo of her footsteps catching on the cobblestones.

I stand, frozen, my mind whirling, listening to her hurrying away into the night. It's almost as if she wants me to follow her, as if she wants to lead me somewhere—

No sooner has the thought struck than I hurry round the corner and stumble across a small garden square. I probably never would have noticed it, sitting quietly opposite a church and lit only by the pale glow of the streetlamps, but for the large wall covered with writing that lies beyond the railings that catches my attention.

For a few moments I peer at it, trying to make out what it says. I wonder if she's gone in here? I can't see her further down the street. I try the gate. At first I think it's locked, but when I push at the chain it releases and swings open. I hesitate, feeling suddenly apprehensive. There isn't anyone else around and it *is* very late. But I'm also incredibly curious, and buoyed up by several glasses of Merlot and my keys, which I dig out of my bag and grip in my hand, a home-made knuckleduster for self-defence, I walk inside.

There's no sign of anyone, least of all a girl with red hair and a yellow silk dress, but I needn't have worried. It's empty and quiet, but instead of feeling scared, I'm imbued with a sense of peace and tranquillity as I approach the wall. It's made up of hundreds of dark blue tiles and covered in white writing, hardly any of which I understand, but as I draw closer I make out a phrase in French. Then in Spanish. Then in English. It's the same phrase over and over but in a hundred different languages. And it's then that it dawns on me.

It's a whole wall of I love yous.

Standing motionless, I stare at it transfixed. It wasn't what I was expecting. So often walls divide, but this one brings everyone together in a great big symbol of love. Just as it was with the Taj Mahal, I reflect, feeling again the rush of emotions I'd felt when I was in India faced with that monument to love.

Reaching out my hand, I trace my fingers over the words, marvelling at all these different languages made into one: the language of love. And I think about all the couples from all over the world, all the lovers since time immemorial, all the people who have whispered this to each other. I think about Henry and Emmanuelle. About me and Jack. Because it doesn't matter how many different languages it's written in, or how many ways you can say it – for each person there's only one other in the whole world who you want to hear say those words.

For me that's Jack.

Is that why I was led here? To remind me of what's important? Except, now, in the sobering stillness, such a thought feels faintly ridiculous. I don't believe in ghosts, remember? It must have been a trick of the light. A heady mix of wine and the magic of Paris.

It's then that I notice the fragments of red. Scattered among the words, they're like pieces of a broken heart that the wall is trying to mend and I feel an ache, deep down inside me. It seems like for ever since I heard Jack say I love you.

Out of nowhere a breeze appears, fluttering the leaves above me and carrying a trace of scent. It smells like musk and orange blossom, just like the perfume I found in Emmanuelle's apartment. A shiver runs down my spine.

Will I ever hear him say it again?

32

I don't know how long I've been standing there, staring at the wall, when I'm distracted by the feel of something on my skin. It's a drop of water. I brush my fingers against the wetness. Is it raining? Lifting my face to the sky, I stare up into the darkness. Nothing. I must have been mistaken. I can't see anything—

There. Another drop. This time it lands on my cheek.

It *is* raining.

Reluctantly I turn away from the wall and make my way out of the park. Already the raindrops are falling faster. I feel their warm wetness on my bare arms, hear their faint pattering on the leaves of the trees.

Still, never mind, it's probably only a shower.

Suddenly there's a pistol crack of lightning, followed immediately by a crash of thunder. Then the heavens open.

'Argh!' I let out an involuntary shriek as a deluge of water cascades down from the skies, drenching me within seconds. I shriek again, holding my scarf futilely over my head as I race across the cobbles, which have now become so slippery I can barely keep my balance.

I'm getting completely soaked.

Another loud splinter of lightning and drumroll of thunder. Rain hammers on my face, drenching my scarf and turning my hair into soggy rat's tails that cling to my forehead.

I need to find a taxi rank, and quick.

Dashing into a main street, I try blindly to search for one, but it's impossible through the curtain of water that's pouring from the sky. Instead I spot an awning and dive underneath it, sheltering under the sodden fabric. But it's hopeless. Already it can't take the weight of the water and is leaking at the sides, pouring in rivers on to my feet and down my shoulders.

My teeth start to chatter.

Oh fuck, what am I going to do? I'm totally drenched. I've got no hope of getting a taxi. And it's well after midnight.

'*Ruby?*'

Amid the drumbeat of rain hammering down on the awning, I listen intently. Was that really someone saying my name? I peer out from underneath the awning, scrutinising the blurry figures hurrying past.

Then I see him across the street. A guy in a suit, his white shirt clinging to him as he holds his jacket above his head. His face is obscured, but I would still recognise him anywhere.

Xavier.

He crosses the street, ducks his head underneath the awning and yells above the sound of the rain.

'What are you doing here?'

'I was at a restaurant,' I cry, trying to make myself heard over the drumming of the rain. 'I'm trying to find a cab.'

'You'll never find one here.'

I nod dumbly, shivering as the rain hammers down around us.

'Come! My apartment is just across the street, you can call one from there.'

I watch as he holds up his jacket for me to shelter beneath and, for the briefest of moments, hesitation flickers in me like the lightning in the sky. Then the rumble of thunder explodes above me and I dive underneath it and together we rush across the street, getting sprayed as we dodge cars, their headlights streaking in the rain.

A couple caught in a thunderstorm in Paris, their figures blurring against the backdrop of the city, like an Impressionist painting.

Xavier's apartment is indeed just across the street. We burst in through a grand doorway and our footsteps clatter on the tiles of the small hallway.

'We made it,' he pants, lowering his sopping jacket, which drips heavily all over the floor.

'Yes,' I manage.

Our breathing is loud as we try to catch our breath. We look at each other, both soaked to the skin, the rain still running in rivulets down our faces and dripping from our hair, our chests heaving. It's so textbook erotic it's almost a joke.

'Please—' he motions to where the lift is waiting for us and pulls open the metal door.

Wordlessly I do as he says. Inside, the space is small and we stand, huddled next to each other, as he closes the door behind us. I can feel his damp skin close to mine, the heat from our bodies being generated despite our cold wet clothes, *the intimacy*.

Stop it. I should not be having these thoughts.

I should not be having these thoughts.

I repeat it to myself like a mantra. It's wrong. I have a boyfriend. I love him. I'm not interested in Xavier.

And yet, even while I'm thinking that, I can't deny the adrenalin I can feel coursing through my veins, the quickening of my heartbeat, the sheer physical desire.

As we climb the floors the mirror next to us begins to steam up. I stare steadfastly at my toes, wrinkling them up in my sandals, feeling the wet leather beneath, trying vainly to distract myself.

I'm relieved when we step out of the lift and into his apartment.

It's as I expected. Modern, tasteful, expensive. As he disappears I glance around, taking note of several photographs of Xavier on the mantelpiece, all in expensive, heavy silver frames. Most of them look to be him with members of his family, though there are a few with his arms thrown round various attractive girls. I peer at them closely, feeling a flutter of jealousy. It catches me by surprise.

'Here.' He reappears with large, fluffy white towels and I quickly turn away from the photographs. 'You can dry off.'

'Thanks.' I take one from him and start drying my hair.

He does the same, sweeping his hair back from his temples. It looks even darker when it's wet, a silky black, and his shirt is now transparent. I try not to look but it's impossible not to. The expensive white cotton is sticking in wet folds to his chest, revealing his tanned skin underneath, the smattering of hair on his chest, his muscular back and shoulders—

Oh lord.

It's like Colin Firth when he came out of the lake as Mr Darcy, only about a million times sexier, which until now I didn't think was humanly possible.

I lower my gaze hastily and hope he hasn't noticed me looking.

He's noticed.

'I might just go and change out of these wet clothes . . .'

'Yes, of course.' I nod, reddening and burying my head in my towel. How embarrassing. I'm like a schoolgirl with a crush.

He returns a few minutes later in a grey T-shirt and jeans, his feet bare and tanned. I watch them walk over the wooden floor towards me. 'I've brought you this,' he says. I emerge from my towel to see him holding out a thick waffle bathrobe. 'If you want, I can dry your dress . . . ?'

Alarm flashes through me at the thought of taking off my clothes in Xavier's apartment. 'No! Um – thank you,' I say hastily. 'It's silk, it might shrink in the dryer – or even on a radiator – it's dry-clean only . . .'

I'm babbling. I sound like a complete idiot.

He shrugs. 'OK, I just thought . . .'

His eyes flick away from my face and it dawns on me that his shirt isn't the only thing that the rain has turned see-through. My silk dress is clinging to me, the delicate fabric having gone completely sheer. Even worse, its straps are so delicate I decided not to wear a bra, so now my nipples are on full display.

'But I'll wear it, to keep me warm,' I say, hurriedly slipping my arms into the sleeves of the bathrobe and tying the belt tightly.

He nods and smiles, his eyes flashing with what looks like amusement. Is he laughing at me? I can't tell. I perch awkwardly on the side of an armchair and wish I was more sophisticated.

'So, tell me, what were you doing out alone in the rain at midnight?' he asks, heading into the open-plan kitchen. It's all stainless steel and minimalist with acres of empty counter-tops. It doesn't look like he's ever cooked here, but then Xavier doesn't look like the kind of guy who stays in and cooks.

'I went for dinner with some friends, they were on a scooter,' I say in explanation, and add, 'I wanted to walk for a little while. It was such a beautiful evening.'

'Even more so in the rain,' he says, his slate grey eyes studying my face. Despite myself, I feel my heartbeat quicken.

'I should call a cab.'

If I wasn't clear before, I am now. A bit of flirting is fun, harmless, no one gets hurt, but this is entering dangerous territory.

'Yes of course.' He nods and, tugging out his phone, he reaches for a card in his wallet. He makes a quick phone call and says something in French, then frowns.

'It will be at least an hour,' he translates, pressing the receiver against his jaw.

'An hour?' Panic flickers.

Or is it excitement?

'It's the weather, everyone is wanting a cab,' he explains. 'It is OK for you to wait here, I don't go to bed early.'

I have no choice. I can't wait in the rain. And anyway, I don't want to.

'OK, thanks,' I say, and he fires off some instructions, then puts the phone down.

'Please, make yourself more comfortable.' He gestures to the large sofa that takes up the far corner of his apartment. 'I'll get you something to drink, what would you like?'

I'm about to propose a cup of tea when he suggests, 'A glass of wine? A liqueur?'

'Um . . .' I stall. I've already drunk so much this evening. I really shouldn't drink any more. I'll have the most awful hangover.

Yet it's raining hard outside, I'm inside a handsome man's gorgeous apartment in Paris, it's after midnight—

'A glass of wine, please.'

His face breaks into a small smile. He selects a bottle of wine from several in a rack. 'So, how was dinner, good?'

'Yes, we went to La Petite Bleue Fenêtre, the food was amazing.'

'You got a table?' He looks impressed. 'It's very difficult to get a reservation.'

'Harriet's . . .' I pause, briefly, then – 'her boyfriend knows the owner,' I say confidently. After tonight something tells me that's exactly what Luc will be. 'She wanted to take me somewhere special—' I break off. I was going to say as a thank you for going to Provence, but I don't want to remind him about my accident and him wanting to sue Gigi. 'To celebrate my birthday,' I finish.

'It's your birthday?' Corkscrew in hand, he raises his eyebrows. 'Well, in that case we should have champagne.'

'It's not until tomorrow,' I counter quickly.

'It's already tomorrow,' he fires back without missing a beat.

It's almost like a dare. Our eyes meet across the apartment and for a moment I'm reminded of that game I used to play with my sister, when the first one to blink was out.

'OK, great.' I reply without blinking.

He pulls out a bottle of Veuve Cliquot from his fridge, with the nonchalance of someone for whom having champagne chilling in their fridge is a normal state of affairs, and reaches for two long-stemmed flutes. Popping the cork quietly, he pours out the pale straw-coloured liquid.

'Though you should really never need an excuse to drink champagne.' Holding both glasses, he joins me on the sofa and passes me one.

'Cheers,' he says in a terrible English accent, chinking his glass against mine.

'Cheers.' I smile and take a large gulp.

The ice-cold bubbles burst on my tongue and fizz up my nose, making me want to sneeze and laugh at the same time. It's a delicious tingling. I don't know what it is, but everything about champagne just *feels* special. It crosses my mind to wonder if the people rich enough to drink it every day still find it special, or if for them it's just like drinking a cup of tea.

I glance across at Xavier, sitting next to me on the sofa, drinking champagne. I can't believe this could ever get old.

'So what's your story?' I ask, turning the attention away from myself.

'Mine?' He smiles, as if amused by the question. 'I'm a lawyer, I live in Paris, my favourite colour is blue—'

'Not that kind of story.' Now it's my turn to smile.

'Ah, you mean the romantic kind.'

I feel myself blush.

'I don't have a girlfriend, if that's what you want to know.'

'No, that's not what I meant!'

Which is a complete lie. That's *exactly* what I meant.

'Though of course I enjoy the company of women,' he adds. 'I am a French man after all.' He gives a shrug of his shoulders, as if that explains everything. Which in a way it does.

'In other words you're a playboy,' I challenge, emboldened by the champagne.

'Not by choice.' He looks amused.

'That's what they all say,' I tease.

'If you really want to know, I'm divorced. Love didn't work out for me—' He breaks off and studies my face. 'Not the first time round, anyway.'

He moves closer, just by a hair's breadth, or is that my imagination? I can't tell. It's warm in the apartment and the champagne is going to my head.

'Your boyfriend is a very lucky man.'

'You think so?'

'I know so.' His tone is light but persistent.

I look down into my glass, watching the thousands of tiny bubbles rising up and bursting on the surface. My eyes blur. My mind skims through memories like a pebble skimming on the water, and without any warning I feel suddenly choked up. 'I'm not sure he thinks that,' I murmur, tears springing to my eyes.

Oh god. It's the damn stupid champagne, it always makes me emotional. I can feel Xavier's eyes on me but I won't meet them. I don't want him to see.

He notices immediately.

'Hey – what's wrong?'

'Nothing . . .' I shake my head, forcing a smile as I look up, but it's hopeless. A lone tear escapes and trickles down my cheek. 'Everything,' I confess, my voice barely audible.

He doesn't ask for an explanation. He doesn't say anything. Instead he simply reaches over and, putting his arm round me, draws me close to him. And I don't know whether it's the alcohol, or the warmth, or the sound of the rain outside the window, or the events of the last few days all coming to a head, but everything seems to release and I let go.

'Sshh,' he whispers, as I bury my face against him to try to muffle my sobs, 'it's OK.' He begins stroking my hair and, wrapped in the warmth of his bathrobe, I breathe him in, inhaling the warm citrus of his cologne. 'Sshh . . .' His voice is soothing and I feel myself relaxing, my eyes closing – his fingertips tracing their way across my collarbone.

My body stiffens. I lift my head to look at him and our eyes meet.

And suddenly everything seems to freeze.

33

Ugh, where am I?

I peel open my eyes. I've woken up in a darkened room. My head is clanging. My throat is dry. I feel dreadful. I peer out into the dimness, trying to take in my surroundings. I'm in bed, only it's not Harriet's sofa bed. This one is all soft and warm, with feather pillows you sink into and expensive high thread-count sheets.

And it's absolutely gigantic. Slowly rolling over, I spread out my limbs starfish-wide but they still don't touch the edges. With superhuman effort I pull myself up on my elbows to try to see more.

Which is when I suddenly realise I'm naked.

Oh fuck.

And I'm in Xavier's bed.

Snatching the sheets to my breasts, I go rigid. Oh fuck. Then into a blind panic. *Oh fuck oh fuck oh fuck—*

Fuck, stop saying fuck! That's not a word you want to be saying when you've just woken up naked with a hangover in someone else's bed. Especially when that someone happens to be an obscenely sexy Frenchman you got drunk with last night. Oh fuck.

See! There I go again.

Pieces of the evening start coming back to me like a jumbled-up jigsaw. Blurred flashes, bits of dialogue, snatches of scenes. The thunderstorm and being caught in a downpour . . . seeing Xavier, coming back to his apartment . . . our wet clothes – the champagne . . .

I'm distracted by the sound of a soft click, and I turn to see a shaft of light entering as the door swings open, revealing Xavier standing in the doorway.

'You're awake.'

He's fully dressed and holding a cup of coffee. He looks as good as the coffee smells.

'Yes, just now,' I mumble, arms still crossed firmly across my chest like an Egyptian mummy.

He walks over and holds out the coffee. I juggle the sheet into one hand and reach out for the cup.

His mouth twists into a smile. 'Don't worry, your modesty is intact.'

I redden, both relieved and embarrassed. 'Did you have to put me to bed?' I ask, not really wanting to hear the answer.

'You were a little unsteady—'

'Oh no, did you have to carry me?' More pieces start falling into place. Me being drunk and upset. Crying on his shoulder about Jack. There are even vague memories of me getting out my iPhone and going through my photo library, showing him the pictures of the two of us in India . . .

But there's something else. A flashback. Me saying I felt sick.

Oh god, I didn't.

'I had to carry you from the bathroom.'

Oh god, I did. I threw up in Xavier's toilet.

'I am so sorry,' I say, waves of mortification rushing over me as I have an excruciating image of me on my knees with my head in the bowl.

'Please.' He holds out a hand to quieten me. 'It's OK.'

I look across at Xavier, his other arm raised up above his head, resting on the doorframe. I take in his smattering of stubble, the simple grey T-shirt that's ridden up slightly to expose his muscular stomach, his jeans hung loosely round his hips. He's like something from the pages of *GQ*. The type you'd lust over while you're having your hair done or a manicure. Sexy, brooding and stylish, he's got the holy trinity of male attractiveness. He even smells good.

And yet, I couldn't be happier that nothing happened between us. That nothing *is* going to happen between us.

Because after last night, it's over. It's over before it even started. All that flirtation and sexual tension, the dangerous sense of anticipation, the sense of uncertainty between us – it just evaporated. Last night we crossed a line, and it wasn't just because I threw up in his loo, though if ever there was anything to kill the mood, that was it. It's as if after the last few days of being thrown together, we both reached a point where if something was going to happen between us, it was going to happen then.

And it didn't.

Though I can't help wondering: was it ever for real anyway? Or was it in fact just Paris, the city of love, casting its spell upon me? I mean, nothing really happened. Nothing but a few glasses of champagne, a train ride to the south of France and a thunderstorm. I wasn't seduced by Xavier, I was seduced by Paris. By its beauty, its history, its romance that oozes from every cobbled side street and wrought-iron balcony.

'Do you want anything to eat?'

At the sound of Xavier's voice, I zone back.

'I can make you some eggs,' he offers.

My stomach does something strange and I shake my head, 'No thanks, just coffee is great.'

He can cook too. He *does* cook in that minimalist kitchen. Harriet was right; dating Xavier would be like dating a Ferrari. What woman could go out with someone like—

My mind suddenly springs up an image of Celeste. Actually, that's not a bad idea.

'Before I forget, Miss Fortescue-Blake called your phone last night, wondering where you were . . .'

I snap back from my matchmaking fantasies. 'She did?'

'Yes, and I answered because you were in the bathroom.'

My blush deepens. We might have reached the friends stage, but I don't really want to be reminded.

'I explained about getting caught in the thunderstorm and how you couldn't get a cab. I told her not to worry, that you would stay here for the night.'

I smile. 'Thanks Xavier.'

Forget ten out of ten. This guy is an eleven. He's taken care of everything. Sinking back into the pillows, I sip my coffee. It tastes divine.

'And there was someone else who called you. Early this morning, just as I'd got out of the shower. A guy.'

My body stiffens. 'What was his name?'

'He didn't say,' Xavier says, shaking his head, 'but he sounded American.'

Jack. It has to be. My heart starts pounding.

'What did he say?'

'Nothing much, he said he needed to speak to you, I explained you were still asleep.'

My stomach does an impression of an elevator and drops about thirty floors. It doesn't take an Einstein to realise immediately how this must have sounded.

'Is this the boyfriend?' He raises an eyebrow.

'Yes . . .' I nod, my mind racing, 'yes – I think so.'

I put down my coffee and start to scramble out of bed, still clutching the sheet. 'I'm sorry,' I gabble, grabbing my dress, which is lying over the back of a chair, 'I need to get dressed – I have to go . . .'

I need to call Jack. I need to speak to him. I need to explain.

Xavier watches me, his expression a mixture of surprise

and resignation at my reaction. 'Yes, of course,' he says. 'If you need anything—'

'No, I'm fine, thanks—' I pause in locating my shoes to shoot him a grateful smile, '—thanks for everything.'

He surveys me for a few moments as if about to say something, then, seeming to think better of it, he shrugs and smiles. 'Any time.'

Outside the city is waking up. It's still early. Rubbish trucks rattle through the streets, flower stalls are setting up, the scent of freshly baked bread wafts from the open doors of a boulangerie. Puddles of water nestle in between the cobbles, a reminder of last night's storm. Only, I don't need to be reminded.

Clutching my phone, I find a quiet corner and hastily dial Jack. My heart is thudding.

It rings for a while, and just when I think it's going to click on to his voicemail:

'Hello?'

He answers.

I swallow hard. 'Jack, it's me, Ruby.'

There's an infinitesimal pause, but it's long enough to feel the chilliness.

'Hi,' he says, coolly.

No warmth, no 'hey babe', nothing. I hesitate. I was so desperate to talk to him, to explain, but now I've got him on the phone I don't know where to start. I try to steady my breath. Come on, just tell him.

'Look, about earlier when you called—'

'There's no need to explain,' he says, cutting me off.

'No, but there is,' I protest, 'it's not what you think—'

'Really?' His tone is sarcastic. There's a pause and then, 'So tell me, what should I be thinking when I call up my girlfriend to wish her happy birthday and I discover not only is she in Paris, but she's asleep in another man's bed?'

Put like that it does sound pretty bad.

'Xavier's just a friend, there was a storm, I couldn't get a cab . . .' I sound more defensive than I'd like.

'Like I said, you don't have to explain.'

God, he's not making this easy for me. I try again.

'Jack, please, don't be like this, nothing happened. I mean, for god's sake, he slept on the sofa!' I cry almost desperately.

'Seriously Ruby, I don't want to talk about it.'

He cuts me off dead and I fall silent. Before suddenly feeling angry towards him for being such a hypocrite.

'You're not being fair!' I round on him, my voice shrill. 'What about you? You're with your ex-girlfriend!'

'What are you talking about?' Now he's the one who sounds angry.

'I saw you on Facebook, on the charity's page, she's with you in Colombia! You've got your arms round each other!' My words are tumbling out and it's impossible to stop them. 'And you're trying to make *me* feel guilty! You're being a hypocrite!'

I break off, panting. I know I've just lost it but I don't care. I'm sick of avoiding this. I'm sick of trying to play it cool and pretend like I don't care.

There's a heavy silence on the other end of the line, as if he's just been hit by a left hook he didn't see coming.

'We're working together,' he says finally, as if choosing his words carefully, 'she's working for the same charity, it doesn't mean anything.'

In hindsight perhaps I should have accepted his explanation. Let it drop. Been reasonable. And maybe if I had things would have taken a different turn; emotions would have died down, we'd have patched things up, maybe even laughed about it.

But it's hard to think clearly when you're upset and hungover. Even more so when all your unspoken emotions that have been pent up the last few days have suddenly found a release valve.

Plus there's a reason why hindsight is so wonderful. It's because nine times out of ten, you don't do what you should have done.

And I didn't.

'So why didn't you tell me?' I persist, not letting it go. 'Why didn't you tell me the truth when I asked you if you knew anyone out there?' I hesitate, then say what's been on my mind for days. 'Why did you lie?'

There's a pause.

'Because I was afraid you'd react like this,' he says quietly.

I fall silent.

'I know what Sam did to you and I didn't want you to worry. In my own stupid way I was trying to protect you, protect *us* . . .' His voice trails off and I feel a tugging inside. 'There's already been enough miscommunication between us, we didn't need any more. But now I find out you're in Paris and you didn't even tell me.'

'Well you haven't exactly been the easiest person to get hold of,' I say quietly, in my own defence.

'True, but when were you going to mention it?'

I feel myself stiffen a little. 'OK, look, I'm sorry I didn't tell you,' I apologise, 'but I think that's a little rich coming from you.'

'Meaning?' There's an edge to his voice.

'Well, you didn't tell me you were going to Colombia until I was standing at Heathrow waiting for you and you didn't show up.'

'That's not strictly true. I tried calling and emailing—'

'When? A few hours before? That's hardly a lot of notice.'

'I've told you, that was out of my control.'

'So you've said,' I reply, a little snappily, 'and I know you're working for a charity so that makes you the good guy and me the bad guy for not understanding, but it still doesn't change what happened.'

'So this is some kind of payback?'

'Don't be ridiculous!'

Oh god. Any headway we might have made is fast getting lost and I can feel everything starting to rapidly unravel.

'It is, isn't it?' he accuses. 'You went to Paris to pay me back.'

'No, I went to Paris because a friend needed me,' I fire back.

We both break off, the silence between us widening, neither of us speaking.

'You know what, I can't do this any more.'

As Jack breaks the silence I feel my heart constrict. 'Can't do what?' I manage to keep my voice even, but inside my stomach lurches. I know we were having an argument. I know things haven't been good between us; but I wasn't prepared for this.

'This long-distance relationship stuff – I'm no good at it, never have been.'

And suddenly it's as if the ground has given way beneath me and I'm in freefall. I can hear him speaking but I can't respond. There's so much I need to say but I can't say any of it. I can't do anything but just stand here on this street corner, the phone pressed up against my ear, as everything comes crashing down around me.

In the background I hear the sound of a tannoy making an announcement.

'Look, I've gotta go, I'm at the airport, they're calling my flight . . .'

I nod dumbly, tears leaking down my face.

So this is it.

'OK. Safe flight.' I struggle to keep my voice steady but I can already feel the sense of him leaving, of him disappearing from my life as quickly as he entered it, of how without him it will never be the same again.

I stay on the line, eking out those last few painful silent seconds, then, mumbling our goodbyes, we both hang up.

And, just like that, he's gone.

34

After that it's all a bit of a blur.

I can't remember much about how I got back to Harriet's apartment. I vaguely recall sitting on the Métro, the rattle of the train, the throng of strangers around me. But nothing really registered. Even the sounds of the city seemed muffled. As if there was a filter between me and the rest of the world, like when I was a kid and would swim underwater in the local pool. I used to be able to hold my breath for a whole length and I remember the strange feeling of being detached from real life.

Back then I used to love that sensation, but now the circumstances are very different. Now, I don't feel much of anything.

Which, to be honest, is probably a good thing.

Climbing the stairs to the apartment, I let myself in. Heathcliff greets me like always, his soft warm body pressed against my legs, his wet raspy tongue licking my hands. And as always I scoop him up and give him a hug and make a fuss. But this time everything looks different. Everything *feels* different.

'Hello?' I call out for Harriet, but there's no answer. Everything is quiet. I tiptoe tentatively towards her bedroom, wary of what I might find, but the door is ajar and the room is empty. I say empty. What I mean is there is no Harriet. There are, however, plenty of signs of her getting ready this morning, with stuff chucked all over the bed and the floor, and out into the hallway.

I follow them, like Hansel and Gretel following a trail of crumbs, and find two coffee cups in the sink. So Luc must have stayed.

I smile to myself. Despite the sadness I feel about my own love life, I'm happy for Harriet. If anyone deserves a break when it comes to love, it's her. And Luc is more than a break, he's the real deal. Absently it crosses my mind to text her, to find out what happened after they left the restaurant, to do what girlfriends do. Though to be honest, I'm not much in the mood for texting or talking, especially about affairs of the heart. Well, I made such a bloody rotten mess of it all, didn't I?

But Harriet's a dear friend and I know she'll be dying to share all the details with me. Well, maybe not *all* the details, but she'll want someone to share in her excitement. I'm reaching for my phone to send a text when out of the corner of my eye, I'm distracted by something on the counter. It's a catalogue for the auction.

Of course, it's today. I'd completely forgotten.

Picking it up, I flick through the glossy pages filled with photographs and descriptions of all of Emmanuelle's belongings. It's so strange to see them catalogued. Her gorgeous dressing table with its ornate mirror has been cleared of her perfume bottles, jewellery and make-up. Wiped clean and dusted down, it's described as: '*a fine tulipwood Louis XV style dressing table with a triptych mirror and gilt-bronze banded tabletop . . .*'

The description is quite lengthy, with mentions of '*cabriole legs*', '*floral motifs*' and '*exquisite ormulu mounts and gilt-bronze sabots*', whatever they are, together with the measurements and starting-bid price.

I feel a beat of sadness. To the rest of the world it's just a piece of antique furniture, but I know it's more than that. This was the dressing table that Emmanuelle sat at to get ready for her first date with Henry. That mirror is the one she would have looked into when applying her make-up and combing her hair; upon which she would have been gazing when Henry fastened his locket round her neck.

I read somewhere once that mirrors work by absorbing energy that they bounce back as a reflection, but that not all of it is reflected. Where does the rest go? Energy can't be destroyed, it has to go somewhere. Is Emmanuelle's energy still there, trapped in the silver mercury?

I flick through the pages, my gaze sweeping across the china tea set that was laid out on her dining table, several first editions of novels by French authors, whose names I don't recognise but who are no doubt well-known, gilt-edged paintings that hung on her walls, the faded lavender chaise longue that graced her bedroom . . . I can't bear seeing her home broken up like this.

Oh god, and look! My chest tightens as I see '*Lot 217*'. It's her gramophone player. Photographed starkly against a white background it's just another item to be sold, but in my head I hear the sounds of 'J'attendrai' playing and imagine Emmanuelle and Henry dancing around her apartment . . .

Swallowing hard, I turn the page.

'*An original, 1930s Steiff bear . . .*'

I stare at the photo, at Franklin's smiling face and big black eyes. This was one of Henry's many gifts. My memory spools back through his letters.

> *He is to keep you company in my absence. Do you like him*
> *my love? I have named him Franklin, after my president, and*
> *he has a smile as big as mine when I see you.*

The yellow fur has become grimy with age, but the years haven't affected the width of that smile. Despite myself, I smile back. Henry's piece of America, for her. Their confidant.

I have found him to be a very good listener. You can tell him anything, for I promise he will keep all our secrets.

Secrets.

I turn the word over in my mind, looking at it this way and that like you might a pebble you've picked up on the beach. So many secrets. The apartment, their love affair, the letters, *a child* . . . Has the apartment truly given up all its secrets? I look harder, turning the word back and forth, searching for something I've missed. Or is there still one more to discover?

I'm distracted by a faint noise. A burbling. It takes me a split second to register – my phone! Dropping the catalogue, I bound across the room and dive into my bag. *Please let it be Jack.*

I get to it and snatch it up urgently, just in time. 'Hello?'

'*Allo*?' It's a man's voice, but not one I recognise. 'Mademoiselle Miller?'

I feel more resigned than disappointed. Of course it's not Jack.

'Yes . . . yes, that's me,' I answer, snapping back.

'It's Monsieur Laurent.'

He says it like I should know who he is, but my mind is a total fog.

'From the parfumerie,' he adds, jogging my memory.

Ah yes, of course!

'Oh, hi,' I say warmly, my mind flicking back to a few days ago when I discovered his scent-filled shop in the backstreets of Paris. So much has happened since then, it seems like forever ago.

'I have found him!' he says triumphantly.

'Found who?' I ask, still not fully up to speed.

'Monsieur Baldwin. He purchased one of our custom scents on the twenty-first of February, 1940. It was to be sent to an Emmanuelle Renoir. I have his signature right here in one of our ledgers, a Mr H. Baldwin—'

Oh my god, that's Henry. That's his full name.

I feel a sudden euphoria as one of the missing pieces of the jigsaw finally snaps into place.

'How did you find him?' I ask, incredulous.

'The missing fragrance that I could not recognise. Finally it came to me, it was lemongrass, an unusual combination if not a unique one, and a wonderful one. And then of course, I knew his first name was Henry and also the year. The rest was easy.'

He sounds so proud and pleased and I thank him profusely, staying on the line for several more minutes while he waxes lyrical about fragrances. Never have I met anyone more passionate about what they do, which is wonderful and fascinating and normally I would love to hear all about it, but I can't concentrate. My mind is buzzing with this new piece of news and I can't think of anything else. Only when I've promised to pay another visit to his shop does he finally bid me farewell.

Henry Baldwin.

I put down my phone and gaze dazedly into the middle distance. Finally, after all this time and all this effort, I've got his name. I reach for my laptop, flick it open and quickly type his name into Google. Over 47 million results pop up. It's a long shot, but maybe now I can find out something. I know the identity of Henry, the lover of Emmanuelle, the author of the letters and yet . . .

So what?

Unexpectedly, the euphoria I felt at first is rapidly replaced by a sense of pointlessness. So what if I know Henry's full name? It doesn't change anything. And that, in itself, just makes everything worse. I got so close, and yet, at the end of the day, close just isn't enough.

Defeated, I close my laptop again and slump back against the sofa bed. Someone once told me that the mark of happiness was setting yourself a goal and achieving it, in which case:

1. Fall in love and live happily ever after with Jack. FAIL.
2. Solve the mystery of the apartment. FAIL.
3. Get Gigi and her family the inheritance that's rightfully theirs. FAIL.

Well done Ruby. Three out of three. I'm such a failure.

Kicking off my shoes, I curl my feet up underneath me and flop my head against my bare arm. Then get a whiff of something unpleasant and realise it's coming from me. *Correction*: I'm a *stinking* failure. I need to get in the shower. Unfolding my limbs, I pad into the tiny bathroom, into which is shoehorned an old cast-iron claw-footed bath. Actually, on second thoughts, I'll run a bath. That way I can soak in my own misery.

I pull back the white shower curtain and reach for the taps. They're made of brass and I can't help noticing their large polished spouts and pretty detailing. Usually, I'd never notice a tap. A tap is just a tap, right? But that's the thing I've learned about Paris – it's all in the details. Like the curling swan neck of a lamp post, the delicious rind on a piece of cheese, the act of cracking the hard, caramelised top of a crème brulée with your spoon and letting the filling ooze out. The little things that transform the seemingly ordinary, everyday moments into what Parisians call *petits trésors*, the treasures of life.

I pour in various oils and shower gels I pick out of the higgledy-piggledy assortment on the shelf and attempt to make some bubbles, trying to cheer myself up. Steam rises, making everything soft-focus, and I slip off my clothes. The bath fills quickly. The taps aren't just pretty, they're like fire hoses, fiercely spurting out water, and turning them off, I dip in my toe.

Then pull it out again. Hang on, I need something to read. I can't lie here, poaching myself in bubbles and brooding about Jack and the auction. I need something to at least *try* to distract me.

With a towel wrapped round myself, I head back into the living room in search of reading material. I've read all of Henry's letters, though maybe I've missed something – a tiny flame of hope flickers, but I quickly snuff it out. It's over, remember. Why punish myself by reading them again? I know, what about a magazine? Harriet must have some . . .

I spy a stack next to the coffee table: *Antiques Weekly, Furniture Restoring for Fun, Ming Vases Made Easy*. Hmm, on second thoughts, perhaps not. Then I remember the copy of *A Farewell to Arms* Gigi gave me that belonged to Madame Dumont and dig it out of my bag.

Perfect.

Being careful not to get it wet, I leave it on the side as I submerge my limbs one by one into the perfumed bubbles, then, drying my hands, reach for it. I haven't looked at it since that time on the train, and now I turn back the cover and read the foreword. Then I pause.

I have a bit of a guilty secret when it comes to reading books. As a writer, I know I shouldn't, and I know my readers would be horrified, but you see, I can never start a story without knowing how it ends. I think it's the hopeless romantic in me – I have to know everything turns out OK and there's a happy ending; only then can I happily enjoy the whole thing. If I didn't I'd worry about the characters all the way through.

Though in this instance I know the ending – doesn't everyone? And it doesn't turn out OK. Yet I still have to read the last page first. It's become a sort of ritual.

'So, with no one to see, I turn to the end of the book, flicking backwards over the pages while telling myself that maybe reading one of the classic all-time tear-jerkers will make me feel better about my own doomed love affair—

Hang on, what's this?

A bookmark slips out and I catch it with my fingers before it falls in the bathwater. At least I thought it was a bookmark, but instead it appears to be a ticket.

I stare at it through the steam that rises up from the water. It's a train ticket, but not the digital kind you get these days. This looks distinctly old-fashioned, with the departure and destination printed clearly at the top – AVIGNON–PARIS – and below, on the line that says *Nom*, in large looped handwriting:

Emmanuelle Renoir

As if someone has pressed play on a recording, I hear Xavier's voice in my head: '*Madame Dumont left Paris sometime in 1940 . . . she passed away recently at the age of ninety-five, having never returned to the city again . . .*' at the same time as my eyes flick to the date, rubber-stamped over her signature. The ink isn't evenly distributed, but I can make out the month and the year: *June 1945*.

I frown. Wait a minute – this means she *did* go back. And just a month after the war was officially declared over.

I stare again at the date, the cogs in my mind turning. This proves Emmanuelle returned to Paris after the war. But why? What happened? Why does no one know? Why did she deliberately keep it a secret?

One tiny word. *Why*? But it throws itself at me again and again and again. I start picking over the pieces of the jigsaw: dates, photographs, the page from *Paris Match* that featured her wedding. Her wedding that took place just a month after she bought this ticket, after she went to Paris . . .

The timing is too much of a coincidence. Henry wrote his last letter to her in 1940 after their row and it's been nagging me why would she wait five whole years before she married '*that other man*'. Something must have happened in Paris that made her return to Provence and marry Monsieur Dumont.

My mind turns faster and faster. The answer's there, I know it, I just can't see it yet. Did she go back to Paris to find something? Was it something she discovered?

Or did she go back to Paris to hide *something?*

And just like that, it's like a light being switched on. They don't call it a light bulb moment for nothing. Jumping out of the bath, I begin pulling on my clothes without drying myself.

I have to get to the auction. Now. Before it's too late.

35

What is it about being in a rush that makes everything in the whole world conspire to slow you down? It's like some secret law of the universe. Keys go missing. Your left shoe hides under the sofa. You get stuck on the stairs behind an elderly neighbour who descends one cautious foot, then the other, on each and every step. A mother with a pushchair cuts you up. A gang of children crowds a pavement. *Every single pedestrian crossing is against you.*

And don't get me started on the Métro.

If there's not a queue for the ticket machine there's one for the turnstiles. Trains are delayed. You finally get on one only to get stuck in a tunnel. Then on the platform behind a group of tourists when you finally get off. Frustration is a word that doesn't even begin to touch the sides. And just when you think the coast is clear, the same woman with the pushchair cuts you up again in the tunnel and you end up offering to help her carry it up the stairs, huffing and puffing.

Forget being late, at this rate I'll be lucky to even get there.

Finally, *finally*, after what feels like for ever, I make it to the auction house. I almost collapse in the doorway. I've run the last bit from the station and am so out of breath I have to rest for a few moments to catch it. Hands on my knees, I take a few deep breaths while at the same time trying to corral my thoughts, which are galloping madly around my head like a pack of wild horses.

Am I really going to do this? I mean, really?

Straightening up, I take in the building in front of me, with its imposing entrance, polished brass sign and high, grand windows. As I do, the sobering reality of my situation sinks in.

Do what exactly?

Now I'm here it suddenly dawns on me that I haven't thought this thing through. Not even slightly. I've been so focused on getting here before it was too late that I haven't thought about what happens next. I can't just burst in, all guns blazing like I'm about to pull a bank heist. I've come completely unprepared. I don't even have a pair of tights to put on my head.

Not that I think wearing a pair of tights on my head would be the *best* approach, but even so—

I feel a lurch of panic. Forget best approach, I don't even have *an* approach. It's not like I can stand here, running through the various options as if this is a multiple choice question. There is no A, B and C. Instead there's lots of scary security, a bloody great big auction, tons of valuable antiques and little ol' me.

I glance at my watch. And I'm fast running out of time.

Oh fuck.

Suddenly I'm not sure this is such a good idea after all. I'm not a fly-by-the-seat-of-my-pants type person. *I do not think on my feet. I think on the sofa with my laptop and Google.* But there's no time for Google. No time to research. And anyway, how do you research 'how to rush in and stop an auction'? I'm not sure even Google could throw up any suggestions.

Like a couple of cops, anxiety and regret begin pounding on my resolve, trying to break it down like a door. Perhaps I should have called Xavier, explained the situation, and got some legal advice before I rushed over here like a crazy woman. Or even my friend Rachel in London, she's a lawyer—

But then, that would have taken for ever. Lawyers are always so careful and obsessed with details, and so, *so* incredibly slow. They're not interested in whims, or gut feelings. They're not into taking risks or acting on impulse, or making a scene. If I'd taken their advice I wouldn't have done anything. I'd still be sitting on Harriet's sofa while the chance of unravelling the mystery of the apartment once and for all would be lost for ever.

And with it, Jean-Paul's chance of going to college.

And no sooner has that thought flown through my mind than anxiety and regret stop pounding and all my doubts evaporate into thin air. I don't have a choice. I have to do this. I am *going* to do this. Because it's not about me, it's about a whole family. It's about an old lady who never knew her parents, a daughter who hasn't felt she's fulfilled her role as a mother and a grandson who hasn't been able to achieve his dreams. It's about doing something that could alter the course of destiny and change all of their lives for ever.

Put like that, I can't just stand back and do nothing, now can I?

In which case I'm going to have to do what I haven't done before. *I'm going to have to wing it.*

Taking a deep breath, I push open the door to the building and go inside. There are several officials milling around wearing laminated badges and a few burly men in suits who look like security guards. I think they might even have guns.

Fuck.

I keep walking. Nobody stops me. A red-carpeted hallway opens up and ahead of me is a large staircase. There appear to be several smaller auctions going on downstairs, but a large sign advertising the catalogue for Madame Dumont's directs me upstairs. I take a quick look around me. Nobody's looking.

OK. Go.

I take the stairs two at a time. Despite the adrenalin coursing through my veins I feel strangely calm. I've read this is how people feel when they're about to do something completely mental. Like jump out of a plane, or rob a bank, *or charge into the middle of an auction room yelling—*

Actually, I have no idea what I'll be yelling. Or even if I'll be yelling. First things first – I have to find this auction.

I charge down the corridor. It's much longer than I'd imagined, with lots of rooms leading off it, some holding auctions, others that look like viewing rooms. Damn, where is it? I'm losing valuable time. I'm going to be too late. Several minutes tick by as I go back and forth, peering into various rooms that all turn out to be the wrong one, and thinking, 'This is it, I'm going to get chucked out,' whenever I spot an official.

Until finally, at the far end, I reach two big mahogany and glass doors. Immediately I recognise the catalogue on display. This is it! This is the one! I pause outside. Remember the bit where I said I was strangely calm? Well, not any more. My heart is now racing and I'm pretty sure my knees actually knocked together just then.

I can hear noise inside. See shapes through the frosted glass. The sound of a hammer.

OK. Deep breaths. I reach for the handle.

This is it. I'm going in.

'*Excusez moi—*'

A loud voice in my ear causes me to spin round. A steely-faced woman with short grey hair and a uniform is staring hard at me, her face immovable like cement. Oh fuck, it's one of the security guards. My heart crashes. I've been busted.

'Oh hi . . . I'm here for the auction,' I stammer.

I've got this far. I can't fail now.

'It is already in progress,' she snaps back.

'Yes, I know – *le* Métro.' I roll my eyes and try a Gallic shrug of the shoulders in an attempt to connect with her.

It's like trying to connect with a guard dog.

There's a pause as her eyes sweep back and forth across me, like Checkpoint Charlie spotlights. 'What is your name?' she demands.

Briefly I think about fibbing, pretending I'm someone else, but before I know it I hear myself saying meekly, 'Ruby Miller.'

Honestly. And to think I'm a writer. What happened to my imagination?

From behind her back she whips out a clipboard on which appears to be printed a long list of names. My heart sinks. Well that's it then, I'm doomed. I watch as her pen slides slowly down the list, taking my hopes with it. What's the point of making this any more painful than it is already? She's going to throw me out, so I might as well just leave. I start stepping back from the door.

'Actually, I think I might need the loo,' I begin, gesturing vaguely behind me even though she's still scrutinising her list, 'so I think maybe—'

'*Bien!*' Striking through a name, she looks up and nods.

What? I stare at her in astonishment. *You mean—?*

Twisting my head, I squint at her list and sure enough, there I am. This must be Harriet's doing, she must have put me on the list. And I'm being allowed in!

'Please, this way.'

I snap back to see her handing me something that looks like a wooden lollipop with a number on it, and before I know what's happening, she's opening the doors and I'm being thrust inside.

It's a hive of activity and for a moment I stand there, frozen. I wasn't expecting such a big room or so many people. Quickly, I survey the scene, like I'm casing the joint. Rows of chairs greet me, stretching all the way to the front, while down the side several news cameras have been set up. I feel a jolt of surprise. I hadn't realised the auction had generated quite so much interest.

The auction is in full swing and I can see lots of the wooden lollipops being thrust in the air to the soundtrack of the auctioneer's bidding. I zoom in to the middle of the stage – which is when I realise it's Harriet standing behind the lectern.

Oh god, of course. In all the panic and commotion I'd somehow forgotten all about Harriet being the auctioneer. This is her big break.

As the doors swing closed behind me, she looks up and spots me. Our eyes meet, just for a nanosecond, but it's long enough for me to register her nervous excitement, the achievement of a lifelong dream, the relief of seeing a friendly face.

Bollocks. Now what? I can't ruin this for her. I can't start yelling or making a fuss.

Thrown off balance, I dive into the only spare seat I can find, in the back row. I need time to think. Across the aisle and a few rows ahead of me, I spot Trixie and Felix. Both wearing dark glasses, they look like a middle-aged Barbie and Ken – well, that's if Barbie was addicted to plastic surgery and Ken was an alcoholic. I thought they weren't going to be here; they must have changed their minds when they got the scent of money.

Clutching the ball of fluff that is her dog, Trixie is also clutching the knee of the man sitting next to her. *Xavier.* Someone coughs at the back of the room and he glances over his shoulder. He catches sight of me and looks faintly surprised. Understandably, considering it's not that long ago that I was throwing up in his loo.

Flashing him a quick smile, I try to duck out of view behind the burly shoulder of the stranger sitting next to me. As nice as Xavier was about it all, it's still mortifying. And proof, if any more was needed, that sadly it's going to take a lot more than a few days in Paris and a carefully tied silk scarf to make me *très chic*.

I turn my attention back to Harriet. I was in such a tizz before, but now I feel a huge burst of pride. To be up there, in front of all these people, orchestrating this entire auction! I watch her in action as one lot is sold and bidding on the next begins.

Crikey she's good. She's just so professional; you'd think she'd been doing this for ever. And to think she used to be nervous about public speaking, I muse, as she switches effortlessly between French and the English translation. I listen to her speaking authoritatively about the different lots, oozing confidence and adding just a dash of the theatrical to the proceedings so as to make them entertaining.

And there was me thinking auctions were dull, I reflect, trying to keep up with the pace as she brings down the hammer on the bidding for a glass vase that just went for a fortune.

'And finally this afternoon, we come to our last lot—'

My heart jumps into my mouth. Oh god, this is it.

'A wonderful and rare Steiff bear dating from the 1930s.'

Holding my breath, I watch as the photo of Emmanuelle's teddy bear is projected up on the big screens.

'It has the original trademark button in its left ear and measures almost seventy centimetres when standing. Made from mohair, it has full joint and limb movement, black boot buttons for eyes and felt paws. There is the appearance of some minor repair stitching on the back seam, but overall it is in extremely good condition . . .'

OK, it's now or never. I need to do something.

'Who will start the bidding at one thousand euros? Thank you, to the gentleman at the back . . .'

Except I'm paralysed. I can't move. I listen as the bidding starts like a sprinter off the blocks and increases at an alarming rate. Fuck, it's all happening so quickly. Hands holding these wooden lollipops are shooting up all around me, while

Harriet sounds like she's repeating numbers from a phone book, at speed. My heart is racing. I need to say something before it's too late.

I open my mouth to say something but nothing comes out. I'm speechless.

Literally. So I do the only thing I can do.

I stick my wooden lollipop in the air.

'On the back row, the lady with the—' For a split second Harriet falters as she realises that the hand belongs to me and I see a puzzled, stricken, what-the-fuck-are-you-doing expression flash across her face. Before professionalism takes over.

'Ten thousand euros.'

Sweet Jesus.

I feel a rush of panic at what I've just done. *Ten thousand euros?* I don't have ten thousand euros! I have a crumpled ten-euro note in my purse and some loose change and—

'Eleven thousand.'

I jolt back. *What the . . . ?* It's going even higher! That's how many pounds? I start to do the exchange, then stop as it spirals upwards. The bidding is frantic. I really don't need to know the exact figure. It's a lot. Way more than I can afford.

'Twelve thousand . . . Twelve thousand five hundred . . .'

I don't know what I was even thinking bidding in the first place, I must be out of my mind—

You can tell him anything, for I promise he will keep all our secrets.

My hand shoots up again.

Fuck it, I've got credit cards.

Harriet fires me another panicked look. She's gone green.

'Thirteen thousand euros to the lady at the back.'

And so have I. I feel sick. Forget credit cards, I'll have to try to take out a loan.

'Do I hear any advances on the current bid of thirteen thousand euros? Ladies and gentlemen of the house . . . ?'

Harriet seems desperate for someone else to bid against me but I hold my breath. Please let me be right. Please don't let my hunch be wrong.

'Thirteen thousand euros, going, going . . .'

I've done it! It's mine! I'm almost dizzy with a mixture of fear and relief and the sheer insanity of it all. But it's for love, and love is a form of insanity.

'Fifteen thousand euros to the gentleman on the phone in the corner!'

What? I swivel round in my seat. Where did he come from? I strain forward, trying to see what gentleman she's referring to. Then I spot him. A bespectacled man in a dark suit, he has a lawyerly air about him. A phone is pressed up against his ear and he's relaying information into the mouthpiece. Fuck. He must be bidding for a client.

'Do I hear sixteen thousand euros?'

My heart is hammering in my chest. Thirteen thousand was crazy enough, but sixteen? I have no idea how I can get that kind of money. I'd have to remortgage the flat.

'Going . . . going . . .'

My mind is racing.

Still, I can't lose it. I can't let this chance be gone for ever. I have to do this for Emmanuelle, for her daughter, for Jean-Paul—

'*Gone!*'

The sound of the gavel being hammered down snaps me back. *What?* No! I glance frantically at Harriet, but it's too late. I've been outbid.

And just like that, it's over.

36

Afterwards I go to find Harriet. She's in the room next door, where a lot of the smaller lots from the auction are being held on display. She looks all flushed and exhilarated, like a rock star coming offstage, and there is a large group of people clustered around her.

Among the various faceless officials I recognise her boss, who's congratulating her, and then there's Xavier with Trixie and Felix. They both look like the cat that's got the cream and well they might; the auction has raised a fortune.

Snippets of French and English waft towards me.

'. . . more successful than we could have ever imagined . . . huge revenues . . . highest price ever achieved . . .'

A wave of unfairness rises up inside me but I push it down. Like I said, it's over.

'Ruby!'

I hear Harriet call my name and see her making her excuses and charging towards me. Her ankle appears to have made a full recovery.

'You were great, well done!' I congratulate her before she can say anything. With any luck this might distract her.

Er yeah, right.

'What on earth were you doing in there!' she hisses, her eyes saucer wide.

Her best friend nearly spent ten grand on a stuffed toy. It's going to take more than congratulations.

'I can explain—'

'I thought you'd lost your mind! Then I thought, perhaps she doesn't realise what she's doing, maybe she's got her paddle confused with something else—'

'You mean the wooden lollipop?'

'See!' she gasps, shaking her head. 'I knew you didn't real-ise you were bidding, I should have explained the procedure . . .'

Her incredulity and bewilderment suddenly turns to self-reproach and I feel a stab of regret. Oh god, this should be her moment of glory, I can't spoil it, I can't let her think she's done anything wrong.

'Harriet, I need to tell you something.' I say firmly, cutting her off before she can go any further. I need to tell her about the letters. About Emmanuelle and Henry. About everything. 'I've been wanting to tell you for ages, but I couldn't.'

She doesn't flinch. 'It's OK, I know.'

I'm thrown off course. 'You know? But how?'

'I called you this morning. Xavier answered.'

Caught in a heavy fog of confusion, it takes a moment for it to clear and to realise what she's going on about.

'Oh god, you think me and Xavier—'

But she doesn't let me finish. 'I knew from the begin-ning,' she declares, talking over me. 'I saw the attraction that first day at Madame Dumont's apartment, I knew he liked you, but even though you were so upset over Jack, understandably of course, I thought you would be perfect for each other . . .' It's like a cork has been popped and it's all coming pouring out.

'. . . and then when I twisted my ankle I thought it would be the perfect opportunity for you two to spend some time together in the south of France, and now everything's perfect as I've found Luc too—' She finally draws breath, her face splitting into a huge smile. 'So it's a happy ending for both of us!'

I look into her eyes, shining with the giddiness of a woman who's fallen in love, and feel slightly dazed. And more than a little heartbroken.

'I'm really happy for you, really I am, but it's not a happy ending for me,' I say finally, finding my voice, 'me and Jack are over.'

She looks confused. 'But what about Xavier—?'

'Harriet, there is no Xavier, nothing happened.'

'But . . .' Her face falls. This is not what she wanted to hear. 'But I don't understand . . .'

I feel a sudden weariness. Oh god, when did everything get so complicated?

'I'll explain everything later, I promise, but first there's something else, something really important—'

'*Magnifique!*'

We're suddenly interrupted by a stout man who appears by Harriet's side and, before I can say any more, he reaches for her hand and begins pumping it enthusiastically, uttering a shower of congratulations in French.

Fuck.

I have no idea who he is, but he looks like a very important person, and I watch helplessly as Harriet switches into professional mode and they begin a conversation.

So now what do I do?

Nothing, says a voice in my head. *Go home Ruby. It's over.*

And all at once I'm hit by a wave of resignation. Staying here is pointless. I've done everything I can do. Telling Harriet won't make any difference. She'll only be furious about the letters and as for the rest, is she really going to believe me? Is she going to put her job on the line for a hunch? I wouldn't expect her to. No, I tried my best, and unfortunately my best wasn't good enough. I need to just go home and draw a line under it.

I turn to leave. I won't say goodbye to Harriet – I don't want to disturb her any more than I have already – and start making my way out of the room. It's still quite busy. Hopefully I can escape without having to speak to anyone, I muse, seeing Xavier in the corner with Trixie and Felix and taking a bit of a detour.

'Pardon.'

Not looking, I bump into someone. 'Oops, sorry.'

It's an official and, as I begin apologising, he turns slightly and I notice he's holding something.

A teddy bear.

Oh my god. My stomach lurches. It's Franklin! Emmanuelle's bear. The actual one I was just outbid on. Here in real life! Right next to me!

For a split second I stand frozen, watching as he carefully removes it from the pedestal it's been displayed on, in readiness for being packed and shipped to the new owner. My mind begins whirring.

It's not over yet.

Without warning the official turns away, leaving the toy momentarily unattended, and I suddenly see my opportunity.

I lunge for it.

After that it all happens so fast it's almost a blur. One moment I'm standing there, the next minute I'm snatching the bear up with both hands, a shutter-burst of random thoughts firing through my mind: me sitting next to him on Emmanuelle's chaise . . . snippets from Henry's letter – *'He is to keep you company in my absence. Do you like him my love? I have named him Franklin, after my president, and he has a smile as big as mine when I see you'* . . . the sewing kit on her dressing table with the needle and thread . . . *'I have found him to be a very good listener'* . . .

He's surprisingly heavy and my fingers clutch at his soft, furry ears. What did Emmanuelle tell him? What secrets did she share? I hear Harriet again at the auction: *'There is the appearance of some minor repair stitching on the back seam'* . . . I pull out the nail scissors that I've brought with me, an image of Emmanuelle's return train ticket to Paris flashing up in my mind. She went to Paris to find someone – *and to hide something*.

Adrenalin is pumping so hard through my veins I feel as if I'm going to explode. Only a few seconds have passed. No one has noticed. The official is still turned away, doing something. Everyone else is busy chatting. My heart thudding loudly in my ears, I focus back on the toy. Along part of the seam, the shade of thread that's been used to repair the back is slightly different to the original.

It's all in the details. Remember, Paris is all about the details.

I plunge the blade into the fur and begin trying to snip at the seam. Oh god, *come on, come on*. It's stitched so tightly. This seamstress wanted to make sure it never came accidentally undone. I've been trying to be careful, but now I stab my scissors harder, attacking the neat row of darning. I don't want to damage it, but I have to look inside. I just have to—

There, finally, I've made a hole! I wiggle my fingers in—

'Argh!'

A loud shriek catapults me back into real time. Immediately I spot the official. Having turned back round and caught me seemingly attacking a valuable antique, he's now screaming the place down. Even worse, he's screaming in French and I don't understand what he's saying. Something that, I know later, I'm going to be really grateful for.

'Ruby! Christ almighty, have you gone mad?'

Harriet's voice. A man's hand. Someone is grabbing me, trying to pull the bear away from me. But now my fingers are deep inside the straw filling and it's falling all over the floor. Shit, I can't feel anything, it's not there, I've screwed up, I've screwed up big time.

Determination kicks in. It has to be there, *it has to be* . . .
Emmanuelle's letter to Henry flashes into my mind:

> *I confess I have a secret and it is one I must tell you, share with you.*

It's the only note from Emmanuelle I've ever found. She wanted to tell him that she was having his child, but she didn't get to send it. She didn't get to tell him. Instead she had to leave Paris before the outbreak of the war. Pregnant and unmarried, she had to give birth in secret and give the baby away. But she never officially gave her up for adoption. She never lost hope that one day she would be reunited with Henry.

There's lots more shouting in French, and then in English: 'Madam, security have been called, they will be here any moment, you are to be placed under arrest for criminal damage . . .'

She kept the only proof she had of their daughter, she hid it, she put it somewhere safe in case Henry ever came back, she put it somewhere they could keep their secrets—

'Madam! Release your hand!'

Suddenly, deep inside the bear, my thumb and index finger brush against something. It's a piece of paper. I grasp it.

'Look!' As the bear is finally snatched away from me, the document comes away in my fingers. In all the chaos I feel a wave of relief to see it hasn't torn.

I hear a cacophony of '*Qu'est-ce que c'est?*' above which a loud American voice that I recognise as Trixie's is yelling, 'Arrest that crazy bitch!'

I see Xavier standing just across from me, and I can tell instantly by his expression he doesn't think I'm crazy at all. I unfold it. *Bulletin de Naissance*, it says. It's all in French, but I see the names. It's enough.

I pass it to him just as the security guards make an appearance, and he reads it, his face solemn. So there was something priceless hidden in the apartment, but it's much more valuable than any Picasso.

'It's a birth certificate.' His voice is clear and authoritative, and the room falls suddenly silent. 'It would appear Emmanuelle Renoir had a daughter before she married Monsieur Dumont.'

There are a few audible gasps, and as the security guards reach me, I twirl round to face everyone, relief, triumph and exhaustion all washing over me. And in a trembling voice, I hear myself saying what I've wanted to say ever since I went to Provence:

'Madame Dumont has an heir, and she's still alive.'

37

After that, all hell breaks loose.

It's like dropping a bomb. My revelation sends a shock-wave around the room. Everything is thrown into confusion. There's a babble of voices. Tons of questions. And an outburst from Trixie, who unleashes a tirade of expletives at an ashen-faced Felix and is led off by security, still swearing and clutching her yapping fluffball.

Amid the huge commotion a few of us move into a side room where it's quieter. Xavier, Felix, Harriet and her boss, and a few officials from the auction house. We all look slightly dazed. I glance anxiously at Harriet. I don't know what this means for the auction and I'm fearful of how she'll react, but for now she's preoccupied by examining the Steiff bear, which has been brought in with us.

I walk over to try to explain, which is when I see she's found something else, hidden deep inside.

It's a letter.

My heart skips a beat. Standing across from her, I watch as she carefully dusts off the straw from the envelope. I recognise Emmanuelle's handwriting. It's addressed simply to 'Henry'.

Harriet turns it over slowly in her fingers, then turns and holds it out to me. I stand motionlessly, a look passing between us, then she smiles. 'I think you should read it, Ruby.'

There's lots to explain, but there'll be time for that later. Now, there's something much more important.

'*Tout le monde* . . . Everyone!'

Having got people's attention, Harriet quickly says something in French and everyone turns to look at me. There's a murmuring of surprise and a palpable buzz of excitement as they wait expectantly.

Nervously I look down at the envelope in my hands. It's still sealed. Carefully running my finger along the edge of the flap, I open it and pull out the letter. My breath catches in my throat as I see Emmanuelle's neat handwriting filling the pages.

Here it is. The answer I've been looking for. The end to the mystery.

I swallow hard, trying to steady my voice, and begin to read aloud:

Dearest H,

Finally after such a long and terrible wait, the war is over and I have come back to Paris in the hope that I can find you and we can be reunited.

Oh Henry, so much has happened since we last saw each other. So many lives have been lost. So many terrible things. So much heartache and sadness. Yet amongst all this has been an exquisite joy. We have a child, Henry, a little girl. Please don't be angry with me for not telling you. I discovered I was pregnant after we had rowed and I was so scared and confused. When I received your letter I finally found the courage to write to you, but it was too late, war was upon us and I was forced to flee Paris with my secret.

Do you know how many times I have wished I had finished that letter? How many times I have wished I had posted it before I fled? How many nights I have lain awake and wished I had defied my father and written to you when we finally reached the South? Too many to count my darling. More than the stars in the sky. Yet, if what you said in your last letter to me is true, you had

*already left the city and my letter would never have found you at
the bookshop.*

*I named our daughter Grace after your mother, for when she
was born she looked just like the photograph you once showed me
of her. Oh, she was so beautiful, Henry. She has your eyes. I
gave her the locket you gave me so she will always have a
reminder of her papa.*

*You see, I couldn't keep her, Henry. I had been forced to
conceal my pregnancy and I gave birth in secret. It broke my
heart to give her away, but I left her in the safe care of the
convent in the knowledge that she would be well looked after. My
plan was never for her to be given away for adoption, my hope
was always that after the war we would be able to return to Paris
and for the three of us to be a family.*

*Oh, but who knew the war would last so long? Who knew
there would be so many hardships and so much devastation?
Many years have passed and now she is with a good family who
love her, yet despite all odds the hope has always remained that
one day we will be reunited with our daughter.*

*So I waited, Henry. Despite what you thought, I did not give
in to my family's pressure to wed Monsieur Dumont. How could
I, when it was always you Henry. Always you that I loved.
Always you who I dreamed of a future with, together with our
daughter. I waited for the war to be over so I could come back to
Paris to find you and finally answer your question: Yes. A
thousand times Yes. I have dreamed of smothering your face and
lips in an eternity of yesses.*

*Yet, now I am here and you are not. On my return to this city
I discovered a letter from you. The postmark is smudged so I
cannot tell how long it has been waiting for me, all I know is I
opened it with such joy and excitement. With such hope. If only I
had known the devastation of its contents.*

*It was sent by your fellow soldier in the event of your death. All
this time I have wondered where you are, and if you were safe, all*

this time not knowing if you had joined the other brave men to fight the enemy. Darling Henry, can this be true? Were you killed fighting for our freedom? Can such a force of life, a dazzling smile and heart filled with love cease to exist? Can it be snuffed out, just like that?

I must return now, I must leave Paris and go back to my life in the south. With your letter has come resolution. Now you are gone I know I can no longer delay my marriage to Monsieur Dumont. Despite the rumours I have heard of his character, I must do my father's bidding. My family has lost everything in the war and he is a wealthy man, our union will ensure my family is looked after. I will try to console myself that I may not be marrying for love, but for the love of my family, so I must do what is best and try and be a good wife.

Yet, I cannot leave without writing you one last letter in case by some miracle, there has been a mistake and you are alive. I have no way of contacting you, no forwarding address, no family that I know of. Yet what I do have is this apartment. I have secretly kept up the rent with the small inheritance left to me by my grandfather, and now I am resolved to do so for the rest of my life. Not as a shrine to our love, but because I cannot give up hope.

For if you are alive, Henry, I know you will come and find me. You will return to Paris, and to this apartment, and with your key you will open the door, just like you used to, and everything will be as it was. The gramophone still in the corner, your record on the turntable, our energy and laughter still hanging in the air. There will be our wine glasses on the table, the armchair where you drank your nightcaps, the bed where we made love.

And Franklin. Our confidant. The keeper of our secrets. He will stay here and wait for your return. Who knows for how long. Weeks, months, years, a lifetime . . . It matters not. Love cannot be measured by time, nor can it be withered.

*I have hidden this letter with him for safekeeping, along with
our daughter's birth record, to ensure it will never fall into the
wrong hands. Only you will ever think to look there. Though I
refuse to feel shame for our love and the creation of our daughter,
society takes a different view, and I cannot risk the shame that
this would bring upon my family should our secret be discovered.*

It is our secret Henry, and ours alone.

*So now it is time to say adieu, but never goodbye. I too hope
that we meet again, if not in this lifetime, then in another. Yet, if
by some miracle you are reading this letter, know that however
much time has passed since I wrote these words, and whatever
has happened, I have never stopped loving you and I never will.*

I look for you around every corner.

Emmanuelle

My eyes are so filled with tears I can barely see to finish her
letter. They stream silently down my cheeks as I unfold the
last page – to find enclosed another envelope. Written in
Henry's familiar handwriting, it's addressed to Emmanuelle.
Inside is a scrap of folded paper that appears to have been
torn from a journal. His final letter to her. I can hardly bring
myself to read it.

For a moment I just stare at it. The room is silent. The
story is yet unfinished. And in that moment of not knowing
lies the hair's breadth of a chance that it doesn't end how I
know it ends. That by willing it, and hoping, and wanting it so
badly, I can somehow magically change the course of past
events.

Except, it doesn't work like that, does it?

I open it.

Darling Manu,

*I don't know if you will ever receive this letter. Time has
passed and I no longer know where you are in this world, so I*

addressed this to your apartment in Paris where we spent so many wonderful times in our secret world.

I don't know how to say this, so I will just come out with it. If you are reading this then I am no more. Tomorrow at first light we are to take on the German stronghold. I cannot say where or how, but it is a dangerous maneuver. I am a lucky fellow, but I fear my luck may not last this time so I am writing this to give to a fellow soldier, to send it to you if I don't make it back.

What final parting can I leave? There is so much to say, it seems an impossible task. How does one fit a love this big into just a few lines? You are everything to me, Manu. I think often of those evenings we would dance together, my hand around your waist, your head upon my shoulder and I want you to know that in those moments, everything I wanted in the whole world, was right there in that room. If I have only one regret, it's that I had not been a richer man, so I could have danced with you forever.

Forgive me if I have said too much. You must be married by now so perhaps you do not think of me anymore. I hope you are happy, my darling. Just know, that I never stopped loving you. You are the love of my life and I would have done anything for you. I hope we can meet again in another life.

J'attendrai.

H

38

A few minutes later, I slip quietly out of the building.

My job is done. Xavier and Harriet will take over now. There will need to be some kind of legal procedure to certify that Gigi's mother Grace is in fact Emmanuelle's daughter. No doubt the convent will finally be forced to hand over their records and reveal the secrets they've kept for over seventy years. I gave them Gigi's phone number, so she will be getting a call shortly. I can picture her now, busy in her tiny flag-stoned kitchen, the shutters thrown open and the sunlight streaming in, completely unaware that her life has just completely changed for ever.

Soon she'll hear the burbling of her phone and answer it with a distracted ''*Allo?*' setting off a chain of events, like a line of dominoes. I try to imagine what her reaction will be to the news of their inheritance, imagine her telling her *maman* about the identity of her real parents, her son Jean-Paul that he can to go college . . .

I smile to myself. It's as if a weight has lifted from my shoulders. I feel a huge sense of relief, of things being how they should be, of finally putting right the wrongs that have lasted all these years. Yet it's bitter-sweet. My happiness or satisfaction for Gigi and her family is tinged with a profound sadness when I think of Emmanuelle and Henry. Their final letters to each other were filled with dreams dashed, love lost and a life together as a family that was never lived. The sense of heartbreak is overwhelming.

I walk aimlessly. After the events of the morning, the adrenalin that flooded my body has begun slowly ebbing away, and I feel almost dazed. It seems like for ever since I woke up in Xavier's apartment and had my last phone call with Jack, and it hasn't all sunk in yet. So much has happened since then, I need time to process it all.

There's something meditative about walking and, feeling the sun on my face and the ground beneath my feet, I let my mind drift. I pass cafés filled with tourists, a busy Sunday market, a long line for a crêpe stall. It's strange to see all these people going about their lives, unaware of what's just taken place; to think that they don't know anything about Henry and Emmanuelle, or even that their love story existed. But I guess that's the way it is with so many great love stories. Right now, there are millions of them taking place all over the world – they're all around us, in restaurants, departure lounges, nursing homes and on park benches. An invisible network of love.

Lost in my thoughts, I lose all track of time and direction until I turn down a street and come upon a glass-fronted building with turnstiles. Looking up I realise I'm standing outside the Rodin museum. It was on my tourist to-do list when I first arrived, but now the moment seems to have passed. My enthusiasm has waned. I'm not in the mood, not after the events of today.

Yet, a sign that says 'Free admission today' catches my eyes. Well, I'm here now. And it is supposed to be one of the most beautiful museums in Paris, if not the world. Plus I've hardly done any sightseeing at all. It's actually quite criminal.

Put like that, I can hardly not go in, now can I?

Pushing open the glass door, I walk through the turnstiles, through the bookshop and out into the gravelled courtyard. From the street there had been no hint of what was waiting for me inside, and for a moment I have to catch my breath.

Ahead of me is a pillared mansion, set in the most stunning walled gardens and hidden away from the hubbub of the city. To say it's impressive is an understatement. If ever there was a beautiful place to see art, this is it.

I stand for a few moments, taking it all in, then turn and follow a gravelled path that leads me through a rose garden. The air is heavily scented with the perfume of the flowers, and I've only gone a short distance when I come across a large marble statue of a man deep in thought. *Le Penseur.* The Thinker.

I gaze up at him. Set high on a pedestal against a spotless backdrop of blue sky, he's overlooking the garden. What are you thinking? What thoughts are in your mind? I ask him silently, reminded of my own that are weighing heavy. I haven't yet begun to try and make sense of what happened between me and Jack, it's still all too raw, but I know somehow I have to.

I walk around the gardens for a while, until finally making my way inside the mansion where, according to my guidebook, nearly three hundred of Rodin's works are on view. However, like most people, what I'm really interested in seeing is his most famous sculpture, *The Kiss*. Not because I'm a romance novelist and it's the most romantic sculpture I know of; not because my very first teenage boyfriend sent me a postcard of it for Valentine's Day; not even because it's so extremely famous, its image can be seen on a million cards and posters the world over.

But because these two lovers, entwined in a kiss, are the true embodiment of love.

I climb up the marble staircase and wander through the majestic rooms. Flooded with light from the huge arched windows, they're filled with paintings and drawings and sculptures. There's no doubt Rodin was a genius – the work is incredible – but I'm too impatient to linger and I move quickly past the displays, weaving through the crowds, until finally I reach a large, circular room.

It's crowded and I pause at the entrance. I note the beautiful chandelier hanging from the ceiling. The large arched windows and patina-speckled mirrors lining the walls. And as the swathe of tourists parts, I see them: two naked lovers, bathed in light so they almost seem to be illuminated from inside; their white marble bodies entwined with one another, caught for ever in an embrace.

The Kiss. It has to be one of the most beautiful things I've ever seen.

For a few moments I simply stand there, transfixed, then move to one of the window seats to sit and stare at them. They're mesmerising. Their bodies appear to fold into each other, his hand on her thigh, her arm round his neck, and the passion and love between them is almost palpable.

It's a powerful image and it's almost hard to tear my eyes away, but after a while I turn to the description in my guide-book. As with so many things that are so famous, I know very little about the statue's history or inspiration. I don't even know who the lovers are supposed to be.

The couple turns out to be the adulterous lovers Paolo and Francesca, two characters from Dante's *Inferno*. They fell in love while reading the story of Lancelot and Guinevere together and were slain by Francesca's husband who surprised them during their first kiss, thus condemning the two lovers to wander eternally through hell.

Wow. I had no idea of the tragic story behind this statue. I stare at the words, taken aback. And there was me thinking it was this great embodiment of love. I feel a kick of disappointment, followed by something else – a sudden realisation that it *still is* the embodiment of love; it's just not how I imagined it.

Because looking at this statue makes me understand that love really isn't that simple after all. It's complicated and messy and filled with contradictions. It can fill you with joy yet it can also be the cause of so much pain. It can hurt you and cause you to hurt those around you. It can make you do things you shouldn't and say things you regret. But it's still love.

Love is a mystery, impossible to define and powerful beyond our imagination, but it's not always the answer. It can't guarantee a happy ending. I wish it could, because then Emmanuelle and Henry would have lived the rest of their lives together. And yet, if it did, we wouldn't have the tragic beauty of this last kiss.

The version of love we see on Valentine's cards and wedding days is the love that makes it into our photo albums. It's the love that makes us smile and warms our hearts and makes people all over the world sign up to online dating. It's the simplified version, sugar-coated and wrapped up in a red ribbon.

But it's not the real thing.

This statue is the real thing. Emmanuelle and Henry were the real thing. Jack and I are the real thing. Joy and tears and pain and confusion, that's the real thing. Loss and hope and heartbreak and feeling like your heart will burst open with both happiness and sadness, that's the real thing. Being in a room with one person and knowing you have everything you want in the whole world, right there. That's the real thing.

And slowly, gradually, sitting here in this beautiful room, in this city of love, I feel my eyes opening. Love doesn't always look like you want it to. It doesn't always work out how you want it to. The nuances of love are endless and ever-changing and all you can do is take a deep breath and go with it.

Because it's still love.

Eventually I get up from the window seat and walk outside. It's a beautiful day, the sun is shining and the sky is still a spotless stretch of lavender blue, and I feel different. Lighter somehow. Clearer.

I don't have all the answers; I haven't begun to think about what happened between me and Jack, and I have no idea what happens next, but it doesn't matter. I'll figure it out somehow.

Leaving the museum, I head back into the street. It's time to go home. Not just back to the apartment, but back to London. Paris has proved to be more than anything I could have imagined, and I'm a different person to when I arrived. Who could have ever envisaged the way events would unfold when I caught that Eurostar a few days ago?

But now Emmanuelle's apartment lies empty, the ghosts of the past buried, and there are no more secrets. I'm ready to say goodbye to the city, but I'll be taking it with me. I have a new book to write and Paris has proved more inspiring than I could have ever imagined. It's given me the most wonderful love story, only this time I'm going to tell it the way I wanted it to be, the way it should have been. Because that's the beauty of being a writer – in real life Emmanuelle and Henry may have been torn apart, but within the pages of a book I can bring them back together.

Turning the corner, I see the Métro up ahead, but it'll be hot on the subway and I'm thirsty. First I need to get some water. Spotting a shop, I cross the street. It's one of those with newspapers in racks by the doorway that appears to sell everything, and it's tiny inside, barely big enough to fit two people.

An elderly lady with a shopping trolley is blocking the doorway, chatting to the shopkeeper, and I pause on the pavement for her to pass. But she's in no hurry to leave. I wait, my eyes passing absently over the racks of newspaper headlines, which are all about the celebrations for the D-Day landings that have been taking place over the last few days.

I'm so thirsty, I wish she'd hurry up. I glance at the photos of the Champs Élysées, packed with people and a large procession of war veterans. Oh look, there's the Queen and Obama and is that the French president? Gosh, I feel terrible, I didn't actually know what he looked like. I peer closer. Actually, maybe I should just forget it and brave the Métro. Evian would be nice, but I'll be here all day—

And then I see something that makes the hairs stand up on the back of my neck. A close-up of a couple of Second World War veterans shaking hands with the president. One is in a wheelchair, a row of medals pinned proudly on his chest. I look at his face. Into his eyes. He might be an old man, but I recognise him. I'd recognise him anywhere.

My eyes dart to the caption underneath. It's in French, but the name jumps out at me. *Lieutenant Henry Baldwin.*

It's Henry. He's alive. *And he's in Paris.*

39

Café de Vanguard, rue de la Merchant, 7 p.m.

Tables spill out onto the pavement, filled with patrons drinking carafes of wine and smoking cigarettes. My eyes flick over them. He must be inside.

I try to see through the windows, but my view is blocked, so I walk up to the door and press my hand against the etched glass. My heart is racing. I never thought this moment would happen. I still can't quite believe it.

I pause, trying to steady myself, and stare at my fingers. For a brief moment it strikes me that this man I believed existed only in another lifetime is on the other side of this pane of glass.

Then, taking a deep breath, I push open the door.

There's the muffled sound of a bell as I step inside. It's much quieter in here; most people have chosen to sit outside to enjoy the warmth of the evening. But in the corner sits an old man in a wheelchair. Slightly hunched over, his legs covered with a blanket, he's accompanied by a plump, middle-aged woman who's fanning herself with a menu.

As I approach him he looks up. The robustness of youth is no more. The smooth caramel skin and thick wavy dark hair of the photograph has been replaced by a face etched with the passing of many years. But as his eyes meet mine there is no mistaking him.

Henry.

My heart leaps. Henry, the author of the letters, Emmanuelle's true love and the reason she kept an apartment hidden for nearly three-quarters of a century, is sitting here in the corner of a small, unremarkable cafe in Paris. The moment is so huge and arching, spanning the decades like a giant rainbow, yet to the rest of the world it goes unnoticed. Customers at nearby tables are paying no attention to the elderly man in a wheelchair; they see only old age and their own mortality. They don't see what I see: a young writer from Brooklyn who fell madly in love with a beautiful redhead in Paris before the war, a love so great it triggered a course of events that lasted a lifetime.

But I do. I see it all.

I promised myself I wouldn't cry. I was firm with myself the whole way here; but when he lifts his hand from his lap and reaches for my own, I realise I'm not the only one fighting back tears. We don't say anything for the longest time. I sit down in the chair opposite him as he squeezes my hand, feeling the warmth of his fingers. Those same fingers that wrote all those letters, that held Emmanuelle's waist as they danced to their jazz records, are now holding mine.

'It's so wonderful to meet you,' I say at last.

He nods, his dark eyes glistening. 'Likewise,' he says.

After I'd seen his photograph in the newspaper, I'd thrown myself at my iPhone. Forget roaming charges, I'd Googled the newspaper and spent several minutes being transferred around different departments. It was the weekend. It was a long shot. Plus my French is still awful. But finally I got the mobile number of the journalist who'd written the piece, who in turn had a contact number for Henry's hotel in Paris.

It was his niece who had answered, a rather scary middle-aged woman who had travelled from New York with her 95-year-old uncle. She was here to take care of him and under no circumstances was she going to wake him up from his nap. So in a faltering voice, I'd told her about Emmanuelle, the apartment, the letters . . . for a few moments there'd been silence on the phone, and then she said she'd have to speak to her uncle and call me back.

That was an hour ago.

'I'm so glad you came.'

'How could I not?'

'It must have come as quite a shock.'

'Not at all.' He shakes his head. 'I've been waiting for a phone call like yours my whole life.'

He's still holding my hand as if fearful that if he lets go I'll disappear, taking Emmanuelle with me again. It was a big enough deal for me coming here this evening; I can't even begin to imagine how it is for Henry.

A waiter appears by the table to take our order.

'Do you have any AC?' quips his niece, who's looking uncomfortably hot, then, seeing that the waiter isn't amused, she turns to Henry. 'Do you want anything, Uncle H? Some iced tea, maybe?'

He shakes his head. 'Just a little time alone.'

She looks unsure, then glances over at me as if to ask if that's OK. I nod.

'Well in that case, I'll just be outside. Where it's hopefully a little cooler,' she adds, mopping her brow with a napkin as she gets up.

As she leaves I turn back to Henry. It's just the two of us and for a brief moment I wonder where to start. I said a little on the phone but there's still so much to explain. But before I can say anything, he begins to speak:

'It was never my plan to stay away, I always meant to come back . . .' It's as if he's waited so long to tell his story, he can't wait another minute. 'After Manu and I rowed I wrote to her but she never wrote back. I figured that was it, so I left Paris,

I couldn't bear to stay, everything reminded me of her. For a little while I went to Spain, but it was a different time then, Europe was in chaos. I ended up going back to America to try to pick up my life – only to find I had no life as she was my life . . .'

His voice is deep, belying his physical frailty, and he speaks with a soft drawl.

'When the attack on Pearl Harbor happened, in a strange way I found a reason to live again. I joined up and went to fight. I was sent with my unit to north Africa first, then Italy, but somehow I found my way back to France, only it wasn't the France I remembered—' His voice breaks. 'I landed on the shores of Normandy on the morning of June sixth, 1944. There were thirty men on my boat, only two of us made it onto that beach alive. We lost so many men that day – the sea turned red . . .'

Despite his years, his mind is still sharp and he falls silent, remembering.

'I managed to make it onto the sand before a shell exploded, blowing me apart. I thought I was dead, but by some miracle I survived and was stretchered out of there. I was taken to a field hospital where the doctors stopped me bleeding to death, but they couldn't save my legs.'

As he speaks I suddenly realise that his blanket is not to keep him warm, but to conceal where his limbs used to be.

'Time lost all meaning from then on. I was transported to England, to a military hospital, where I spent the next eighteen months or so having over twenty operations – I don't remember exactly how many, I was on morphine most of the time, you don't remember much when you're on that stuff.'

Despite the pain of his memories, the corners of his mouth turn up into a smile.

'It sure is one way to try and forget a girl you know, but of course it didn't work – you have a lot of time to think when you're lying around in bed all day.'

'You know, Emmanuelle received a letter from you, saying you were dead,' I tell him.

He nods.

'I found out later. In all the chaos they thought I'd been killed. In a way I was glad – I thought it was better that she believed I was dead. I couldn't let her see me again, not like this. We used to dance together, you know.'

I nod, my mind flashing back to the gramophone.

'It was a few months after they declared the war was over that I saw her wedding in a magazine.'

I look at him in surprise. 'You saw the copy of *Paris Match*? How?'

'It belonged to one of the nurses; she was French but she'd married an Englishman. She left it by my bedside one day. If ever I'd had thoughts about trying to contact Manu again, they disappeared the moment I saw that photograph—' He swallows hard. 'She wasn't my girl any more.'

He says it so simply, so matter-of-factly, it breaks my heart.

'Before the war I would have done anything to stop her marrying another man, but the war changed everything.' He looks down at his hands, and I notice for the first time that he isn't wearing a wedding ring. 'Now I was just happy she was alive.'

'You know she never danced again either.'

I can't let him think she just moved on, that her marriage was a happy one.

He looks up at me.

'Her whole life she refused to dance with anyone else,' I say, and our eyes meet. 'She was still your girl Henry, she was always your girl.'

My words are bitter-sweet.

'You know sometimes at night, I dream I am whole again, young again, and we are back in Paris dancing together in her apartment, just like we used to, all those many years ago . . .' He gazes into the middle distance. 'Do I sound crazy?' he asks, turning back to me.

I think of that night in her apartment, hearing the music playing, thinking I heard footsteps. I shake my head. 'No, not at all.'

He nods, seeming satisfied, then:

'Is it true what you said, that she kept the apartment all these years?'

'Yes, just as you had left it.'

There's a long pause.

'She never forgot you, Henry.'

His eyes fill with tears but they refuse to fall. I can't tell if they're tears of happiness or sadness. Maybe they're both.

'I never forgot her either. I never stopped thinking of her. All these years. After I was discharged from hospital I left England and went back to the States. I became a college professor and taught creative writing for over forty years. I never married, never felt the need. You see, I was still lucky in a way. Most people only have one great love, but I had two. Emmanuelle and writing.'

He smiles and I can't help but smile too, and gently removing my hand from his, I reach into my bag.

'These were in the apartment.' I place the bundle of letters in his lap. 'They belong to you.'

I watch as he slowly turns them over, his face registering. His eyesight might be failing, but he knows immediately what they are.

'There's one last letter in there from Emmanuelle, I opened it, I'm sorry, but maybe later someone can read it to you—' I break off from explaining.

Because, of course, there's something else. I haven't told him he has a daughter. I didn't think it was right to come from me. It should come from his family. Which is why earlier I made another phone call.

The sound of the doorbell distracts me and I pause to look across at the doorway. Standing silhouetted in the entrance is a young man in a beanie hat. Jean-Paul.

I turn back to Henry.

'There's someone I'd like you to meet.'

40

'*Cadenas?*'

The street vendor holds out a piece of card filled with padlocks of all different sizes.

I pause, my eyes sweeping over them.

'*Combien?*' I point at a large brass one.

He tears it from the plastic before telling me the price. No doubt to stop tourists shopping around, I muse, glancing at all the other vendors with their blankets and makeshift stalls, filled with padlocks.

I dig out a few euros and he passes me the small lock and a key, along with a marker pen. Slipping them into my pocket, I climb the steps to the bridge.

It's evening. Dusk is falling. After I said goodbye to Henry I called Harriet to tell her where I was, then came here to the banks of the Seine. There's one last thing I need to do.

I remember overhearing the tour guide saying how according to legend you need to be careful where you attach your lock – Pont des Arts is for your committed love, but Pont de l'Archevêché is for your lover. I chose the first bridge.

It's hard to believe I was here just a few days ago; everything feels so different now. I start to walk across the bridge. The tourists have thinned out, but there are still people milling around: couples taking selfies, vendors plying their wares.

And then there are the locks. Thousands of them, arching across the river like a glittering, metal rainbow. I gaze at them. I think again of the predictions that the bridge could collapse under the weight of all this undying love, of a campaign to prevent people from attaching more locks, to be sensible, to take selfies instead.

But if Paris has taught me anything, it's that when it comes to love, being sensible doesn't come into it.

My eyes drift along the railings, looking for a break in this vast ocean of locks, some small space, a tiny part of the bridge to call its own—

Then I see it, a hair's breadth of a gap.

I crouch down and take out my lock and, with my marker pen, carefully write the two names: *Emmanuelle & Henry*. I want to put this lock on the bridge for them. Two lovers, together for an eternity. Theirs is a love that has survived through all the tragedy, the miscommunication, the war, the years – and now here, in some tiny corner of Paris they are reunited again. One last, small symbol of a love that has lasted a lifetime.

Carefully I lock it to the railings, then, holding the key in the palm of my hand, I stand up straight again. I look at all these locks, all with their own love story attached, and I think about my own. Like I said, love doesn't guarantee a happy ending.

Turning away, I lean against the bridge and gaze out across the Seine. The glittering lights of Paris stretch away from me and I think about Jack, about love, about a city that's taught me so much. It's right that it ends here.

I throw the key into the river. As it disappears into the inky blackness, it makes no sound.

'Ruby?'

Behind me, I hear my name. A voice.

It can't be . . .

Slowly I take my hands off the railings and turn round.

Jack.

The breath catches in the back of my throat. He's standing just a few feet away from me in jeans and a T-shirt, a backpack slung over his shoulder. His face is ridiculously tanned and his hair is stuck up all over the place. He looks like he hasn't slept in a week.

'What are you doing here?' I say, finally finding my voice.

'Looking for you. Harriet told me you'd be here.'

'No, *here* here. In Paris.'

'I wanted to wish you a happy birthday.'

Of course. It's my birthday. With everything that's happened today I'd totally forgotten.

He smiles, that wide disarming smile of his that crinkles up his eyes and never fails to win me over.

'Damn you Jack, you can never give me a straight answer.'

But not this time. I feel my eyes welling up. This time he can't just show up and give me one of his smiles and think that will make everything all right.

He stares at me for a moment, as if not knowing what to say, then takes off his backpack and crouches down.

I watch, wondering what he's doing.

He unlocks the small, silver padlock that's securing the zip on his rucksack, then digs out a Sharpie pen from his back pocket and proceeds to write our initials. Standing back up, he holds up the padlock between his finger and thumb, his eyes never leaving my face.

A look passes between us. It's almost a challenge.

'I thought you didn't believe in superstitions?'

'I believe in you and me.'

My heart turns itself inside out.

He steps towards the side of the bridge and my eyes follow him. Neither of us speaks. Sometimes it's not about words. I feel my chest tighten as he crouches down, looking for a space for us between all the padlocks . . . Some may say that this new tradition is a cliché, but it seems to me suddenly so absurdly romantic, I half expect the music to swell and the credits to roll. I watch as Jack reaches to put it on the railing, aware that this is a big romantic moment—

'Holy moly.'

'What?' I gasp, looking down at him.

'It just slipped out of my hands . . .'

'What do you mean?'

He motions to the wooden floorboards of the bridge. 'It just fell through the cracks.'

'You're kidding.' I drop to my knees to look at him. 'If this is one of your jokes—'

'It's not, I swear.' He shakes his head. He looks stricken.

I look at his hands. They're empty. Then at the gaps in the planks.

'I can't believe it!'

'Shit, I am *so* sorry, I don't know how it happened . . .'

We both peer down through the gaps, as if magically expecting the padlock to reappear.

And then suddenly, unexpectedly, I feel a gurgling of laughter rising up inside me and explode into a burst of giggles. It's just the funniest thing. Jack looks at me in astonishment, his expression one of total shock, then throws back his head and roars with laughter.

There we are on the bridge, on our hands and knees, clutching at each other with tears rolling down our cheeks while all around us kissing couples are looking at us like we've gone bonkers. Maybe we have, I don't know, but it's like a valve has been released and we can't stop. We laugh for the longest time, clutching our aching sides, waves of giggles coming at us, over and over, until finally our laughter dies down and, still sitting on the floor, we lean ourselves against the railings.

Neither of us says anything. We just sit there in silence, catching our breath, until eventually Jack speaks.

'Look, I just travelled halfway across the world because I needed to tell you something.'

He turns to me, his face growing serious, and I feel a flutter of uncertainty.

'When I said I couldn't do this, I mean I can't do *this*.'

He gestures between us.

'What are you saying?' I feel a shiver, despite the warmth of the evening.

'This . . . this kind of long-distance relationship. I just can't do it.'

I look at him, not understanding, fearing the worst, but then he leans forward and wraps his arms round me.

'I'm not doing this any more, we're not doing this any more.'

Pulling me close, he gently presses his lips against mine and then leans back.

'I don't want us to ever be apart again, Ruby.'

Warm inside his embrace, I hear his voice saying those words and for the first time in I can't remember how long, there's no misunderstanding or confusion. There's no difference of opinion or miscommunication. No words going unsaid or feelings ignored.

'Me too,' I murmur, my face pressed up against his chest, and in that moment it's as if all the barriers fall away and it's just the two of us again. Nothing else matters. Just me and Jack.

God, it feels good.

'I did a lot of thinking as we built those homes for those people—' He breaks off and I can feel him swallowing hard. 'I want to build a home – with you.'

He dips his chin to look down at me.

'Come to America, Ruby.'

So many questions. So many what-ifs and buts and details to know. So many uncertainties. They all race through my mind as I hurtle into the future, throwing themselves at me, demanding answers. But I don't have any, and I've learned I don't need any. None of that stuff is important.

In my head I hear Henry's words to Emmanuelle:

Please reply to me, my darling, and when you do, it must be only one word.

I look up at him and my face splits into a smile.
'Yes.'

ACKNOWLEDGEMENTS

Huge thanks to my editor, Francesca Best, and the rest of the team at Hodder for working their magic and turning a story that lived only in my imagination into a real-life book. And to Adrian Valencia and Sarah Christie for such a gorgeous cover.

As always, thanks to my agent Stephanie Cabot, who forever encourages me as a writer. Thanks also to the rest of the crew at The Gernert Company; Will, Rebecca, Erika and Ellen, for everything you do.

As the author of eleven novels I've lost count of the number of weddings I've created for my characters, so it was fun when last summer it got to be my turn. However, writing a book and planning a wedding at the same time can be pretty tricky, so I want to say a huge thank you to my mum, Anita, who was a complete superstar and worked miracles so I could get married *and* meet my deadline. The same goes for my wonderful big sister Kelly and my dear friend Dana. If you're not decorating barns, calming me down, brainstorming plot points or giving encouragement, you're always there making me laugh. I'm a lucky girl indeed.

Further thanks to all my friends who encourage me from the side-lines. And to all my fantastic readers who follow me on Facebook, Twitter and Instagram, I'm forever grateful for your support.

Love From Paris is my most romantic novel to date, so it's fitting that it takes place in what is probably the most romantic city in the world. It's also partly set during the Second World War and though I did a fair amount of research, I'm not an historian, so I apologise for any factual or historical mistakes I might have made in the making of this love story.

Finally, to my AC, for an unforgettable day last summer that was nothing short of wonderful, always believing in me and accompanying me to Paris to research this book. It ain't always easy living with a writer, but without you I wouldn't have the last scene of this book. Or my happy ending. Thank you.

Find out where Ruby's story began . . .

THE LOVE DETECTIVE

Alexandra Potter

'In a way, I'm a bit of a love detective. Because what's a greater mystery than love?'

Meet Ruby Miller. A writer who makes happy-ever-afters happen. Until she discovers her fiancé is a lying cheat and loses her faith in love. So when her sister invites her on a beach holiday to Goa to forget about him, Ruby jumps on a plane . . . and into an extraordinary adventure.

Stolen bags, a runaway sister and a handsome American stranger sweep Ruby into a magical mystery tour across India. Amid fortresses and fortune tellers, and a whirlwind of weddings, she uncovers fascinating stories of love, lost and found.

But as the mysteries deepen, secrets are revealed that turn Ruby's life upside down. And what started as a journey to find her sister, becomes a journey to find herself – and love – again.

Out now in paperback and ebook

HODDER

When one book ends, another begins...

Bookends is a vibrant new reading community to help you ensure you're never without a good book.

You'll find monthly reading recommendations, previews of brilliant new books, and exclusive features on and from your favourite authors. We'll also introduce you to exciting debuts and remind you of past classics.

There'll be a regular blog, reading group guides, competitions and much more!

Visit our website to see which great books we're recommending this month.

welcometobookends.co.uk

f /welcometobookends
🐦 @teambookends